CW00350990

YOUNG EMMANUEL

YOUNG EMMANUEL

(Third of the Gollantz Saga)

Naomi Jacob

First published by Hutchinson & Co (Publishers) Ltd in 1932

This new hardback edition published in Great Britain in 1984
by Judy Piatkus (Publishers) Limited of London

ISBN 0 86188 297 0

Printed and bound by Mackays of Chatham Ltd.

To
ELLALINE TERRISS
and
SEYMOUR HICKS
who have never learned to grow older
but have only remembered to grow wiser
and more understanding.
With my love
MICKIE

CHAPTER ONE

ANGELA gave a sigh of relief. As a sigh it was a trifle overdone, just a little theatrical, and it did not disturb Max in the least. He said nothing, smiled and waited.

'Max dear,' she said, 'I like your friends, you know that. I like the Davises and the Bermans and the Salamans. I like all of them, but I do wish that they weren't all so disgustingly rich.'

'Why should it be disgusting to be rich?' Max said.

'I don't suppose it is—really. But the sight of six or seven Rolls standing at the door, in a long and expensive line, rouses some distant Communistic feeling in me. I wish some of them would arrive in battered Fords and Austins for a change.'

Max Gollantz chuckled. 'They may be rich, but none of them are rich enough to do that.'

He came over to where she sat by the fire, with its high steel fender and furniture which gleamed like silver. Max looked down at her, as she lay back in the big chair, covered with wonderful old embroidery that he had found, he remembered, in a little village in Spain. As he watched her, his keen face softened, and he smiled. Max Gollantz had never been a handsome man, but when he smiled his face was very pleasant.

'Talking of cars,' he said, after a long pause, 'Julian has smashed his again. Did he tell you?'

Angela showed no sign of either surprise or anxiety. Julian was her second son, and she adored him. She prided herself upon being a woman of sound common sense, but she admitted to Max and to her father-in-law, old Emmanuel, that this admirable quality deserted her when she thought of Julian.

'He's not hurt,' she said contentedly, 'because he came in

just now and was talking to Reuben Davis. Julian will break cars—and probably other things—all his life. We were too successful in Julian, Max. We managed to combine your charm and my looks, and then add something.' She went on, speaking thoughtfully, 'I sometimes wonder if Julian hasn't got too much of everything—looks, brain, personality. It's not quite fair, is it?'

'He's a wonderful fellow,' Max agreed, 'but he's damned expensive!'

'You can afford it,' she said easily. 'We both have far too much money. Julian, of necessity, must be something of a luxury. Not,' quickly, 'that they are not all wonderful—Emmanuel, the dearest thing in the world. How like our own Emmanuel he is, Max. It's startling sometimes. And Bill—Bill's a dear. I love them all, but to each other we can admit that there is something additional in Julian. He's rare—that's the word—rare. I have met four perfectly charming and delightful men in my life, this is excluding the Founder of the House, they are my three sons and the man I had the good taste to choose as a husband.'

Max said, 'And after that I must pay up for Julian's car and look pleasant, eh?'

'You'd have done that without my paying you compliments.' She stretched out her hands to the crackling wood fire, and smiled up over her shoulder at her husband. Max, looking down at her, thought, as he thought so often, that she was as charming as she had ever been. She remained the ideal woman. They had been married for twenty-five years, each year had seen them drawing closer together, seen them more and more content with each other, and had found their love and their friendship more securely cemented.

Angela often said that if she had not married Max, she would have lost her best friend; and that if she had kept him in her life only as a friend she would have lost the ideal husband.

He stood beside her now, in the great drawing-room at Ordingly, the house which his father had bought twenty-three years before. In those years the house had taken on something of the character of the man to whom it belonged. It was beautiful, dignified, and it had personality.

Max had modelled himself on his father, and had succeeded in attaining the same position, the same respect and the same reputation for taste and integrity. He had never succeeded in being as spectacular as his father, but as Angela said, no family could have two Emmanuel Gollantz in it and survive.

He stood by his wife, very erect, his dark hair turning grey, his face well cut and his smile one of the pleasant things of the world. His smile radiated kindliness and sympathy. His whole nature was clean, and as kind and sympathetic as his smile. When his father had retired from the great business of Gollantz and Son, its reputation had been world wide; and Max had done nothing to diminish that reputation. He had added to the great premises and warehouses, without materially altering their structure. He had bought wisely and with courage, and he had always sold well with profits which were never small, but which had never permitted men to stigmatize him as a profiteer.

Max had not only a specialist's knowledge of beautiful things, but he had a real love for them. Ugly things, which might happen to be in vogue for the moment, he bought under protest, but they remained in his showrooms and were never allowed to have a place in his own home. With all his knowledge, and all his experience, Max never hesitated to ask advice of his father; and when at the age of eighty-eight, old Emmanuel Gollantz had declared his intention of going to the great picture sale of the year, Max had hailed his decision with delight.

It had filled him with pride that he was able to walk into the long room, filled with the best known connoisseurs of the world, accompanied by his father, the great Emmanuel Gollantz. Max never forgot the impression that his father's entrance had made. Tall, and still erect, dressed in the style which he had adopted sixty years before and still retained. His long tight coat, with its collar of astrakhan, his high collar with its black satin stock and the famous 'Anstruther' black pearl, his top hat with its low crown and very curled brim, his ebony cane with its great ivory knob—men turned their eyes and whispered as he passed.

When the bidding had started, Emmanuel had taken out his gold pencil and made notes, as he had done years before. He made no bids, the pictures were not worthy of his consideration. Max bought, and his father was silent. But when the Gainsborough was brought out, and the precious thing was placed on the easel, Max felt his father catch his breath and knew that his muscles stiffened.

He leant over to Max and whispered:

'Please, Max—this is vere I vill speak. You don't mind?'

'I'd rather you did, father. It's going to be a tussle.'

His father had laughed softly. 'Vot is that vord—tussle? There will be no tussling, if you please.'

The room had waited—they had listened to bids of a thousand guineas, two, three, four, five, and still Emmanuel Gollantz had not spoken, had not even stirred. The dealers whispered that old man Gollantz waited until it was worth his while to expend his energy. Someone else waited too, and when the bidding reached fifty thousand and the figure was called in a voice with a distinct nasal accent, Emmanuel moved.

'Fifty-fife,' he said.

The nasal voice returned, 'Fifty-six.'

Emmanuel said, 'Fifty-seffen.'

'Fifty-eight.'

There was a pause, the silence was terrible. Max took out a handkerchief and wiped his forehead. Was his father going to let it go, was he going to allow this lovely thing to cross the Atlantic, was his nerve going to fail him? Max felt that he must make the next bid for the honour of the House of Gollantz.

'Fifty-nine.' Emmanuel had spoken.

Again a silence. Emmanuel turned, lifted his single eye-glass and stared round the room; finding the eyes that he sought, he gave a very small, almost imperceptible bow. The silence continued, it seemed to Max to have lasted for years, in reality it was perhaps six or seven seconds. The hammer fell, and a voice said:

'Mr. Emmanuel Gollantz.'

Emmanuel rose, made his little inclination of the head to the auctioneer, turned and walked out followed by his son.

'I was obliged to hev it,' he said to Max as they drove home. 'It was unthinkable that she—' he often spoke of pictures as 'he' and 'she' according to the subject—'should have gone to America. It was my duty as well as my very great pleasure.'

Max had the same pride in their business; like his father he looked upon it as a kind of trust, that England's beautiful things should be kept for England and the enjoyment of the English people.

If his pride in his business was great, his pride in his family was even greater. His wife, to Max Gollantz, was the most delightful woman in the world. No other woman had ever demanded his love, and he argued that this fact alone proved that Angela was unique. His three sons, Emmanuel John, Julian Edward, and William Hermann, were second only to their mother in his affections. Emmanuel at twenty was in business with Max, Julian had chosen politics as his destiny. William was still at school.

Emmanuel, who might have been a reproduction of his grandfather at the same age, was clever. He had his grandfather's taste, and in addition to his father's knowledge had the same flair for beautiful things that had been of such assistance to old Emmanuel when he first came to England. He was the only one of the younger generation who retained the spectacular methods of his grandfather. Emmanuel, while being a perfectly normal young man, had learnt what suited him, and wore his clothes with an air which took his mother and father back to the time when old Emmanuel Gollantz was the best-dressed man in London.

Young Emmanuel worked hard, and played hard. He kept fit because he disliked men who were flabby, and he wanted to keep his figure. He loved beauty, he adored music, and he rarely missed a first night. Women affected him very little. He liked them, but when their liking began to be tinged with sentiment, Emmanuel fled. His great passion was for his mother. To him, she stood for all that a woman could and should be. All his life he had regarded her as someone removed from ordinary mortals. She was, quite literally, the centre of his world, and all his actions were determined by the thought of what she would feel about this or that. She was his final court of appeal, his authority for everything.

Once, when he was seven, she had been very ill, so ill that Max and his father went about with white strained faces and lived only to hear the latest reports of the doctors. Max remembered how Julian had cried and refused to be comforted, how little Bill, frightened by the strange new atmosphere, had whimpered and asked for his mother perpetually. Emmanuel had said nothing, done nothing but sit silent with a drawn face, and dark eyes which held nothing but misery. His father had found him, sitting on the stairs, listening for the doctor's footsteps. He had lifted the boy in his arms and looked into his face, appalled at its wretchedness. Finally, in despair he had carried him down to old Emmanuel hoping that he might find some way to distract him.

'Why this vite face, if you please?' Emmanuel had said.

The boy caught a sob and strangled it before it left his lips.

'I'm frightened.'

'But vhy frightened? Presently ve shall hev goot news of your mudder.'

The little boy shook his head. 'She might die,' he said, 'that's what frightens me, because I should die too, and I might never find her. The place she went to might be too big.'

He had sat there, on his grandfather's knee, white and rigid. Emmanuel had found nothing to say, and they had sat there like two carved figures. Then the door had opened and Sir Nathan Bernstein had come in. He had looked at them, and smiled. Rather a pale smile for he had not slept for two nights.

'Ith's all right,' he lisped. 'The crithis is over. We have only von battle left to fight—veakness.'

Emmanuel had said: 'Dayenu!'

Bernstein had nodded. 'Indeed, yes! Give me the little boy—he has fainted.'

And with the years this love had grown, until his mother was everything to her eldest son, and he wanted no companion if she could give him her company. Not that he was a sentimental young man, for Emmanuel could drive a bargain, rule his workpeople, get the better of most men in a deal, play a hard game of tennis, ride hard, and swim like a fish.

Emmanuel knew, though he never allowed himself to dwell upon the fact, that his mother gave the greatest share of her love to his brother Julian. It did not distress him in the least—his mother had a right to give her love where she wished, and Emmanuel would have been the first person to admit his brother's fascination. He loved Julian dearly, though young William mattered perhaps more to him. The fact that he realized that his mother was happiest when Julian was at home, when she was going off to some theatre with Julian or talking to him in the garden under one of the huge trees, did not hurt him. Angela gave him a great deal, and whatever Angela did was automatically right.

Julian was, as Angela Gollantz had said to Max, rare. He had too many fairies at his christening. At school, he had carried off prizes and rewards in an endless procession. Now he was secretary to his mother's second cousin, Sir Gilbert Drew, a cabinet minister at forty and noted for his brilliance as well as his caution. Drew stated openly that Julian had a great career before him.

'He mops up facts and figures as a sponge mops up water. He makes deductions which are not only rapid but invariably correct. He holds his audience, and makes dry bones live for them. He can do more work in four hours than the average young man can do in ten.'

Like his brother, Julian played hard as well as worked hard. He refused to believe that success was found by keeping one's nose perpetually to the grindstone. He put his theory into practice. He worked from ten to five, he took an hour for lunch and half an hour for tea. No one had ever known Julian to work over hours, and yet no one had ever been able to reproach him with leaving work undone. After dancing hard until the small hours of the morning, Julian arrived at the office clear-eyed and clear-headed and fell upon his work with undiminished energy.

A woman had once said of the two brothers, that you believed Emmanuel to be the handsomest youngster you had ever met until you saw Julian; that you believed Emmanuel to be the most delightful companion in the world, until Julian came and talked to you.

As a little boy he had been delicate, and when he first went to school, Angela had suffered tortures for fear he might be taken ill, or might be miserable in his new surroundings. He had come home for the holidays, and stated that he adored school, that he had made heaps of friends, and that he looked forward to the next term with delightful anticipation. His mother had been vaguely disappointed. She remembered that Emmanuel, though he had done well at school, had never hesitated to say that he loathed it and only lived for the holidays. Later he had decided that school was 'not so bad', but had never concealed the fact that nothing could ever be as perfect as Ordingly.

Julian spent a great deal of money. Old Emmanuel said: 'Not spent, if you please—vastet!'

Angela remembered the first night Julian had come home for good. How she had come down early and found him standing in the big drawing-room. He had looked so slim, and tall, so really beautiful with the light catching his fair hair. He had stood near her and looked down at her, with a little smile on his lips.

'Why are you staring me out of countenance?' she asked.

'So sorry,' he said. 'I was just thinking that I had never really seen you before, thinking how lovely you are, and how blind I was not to have seen it sooner. Oh, it's heavenly to be home and know that we can get to know each other! You're terribly amusing, aren't you?'

'I don't know.' She had felt almost shy.

'Old Bill Masters says that you are. He said that you were the most effective woman he had ever known.'

'Poof! Bill Masters, bless him, thinks that he has been in love with me for twenty odd years. He isn't to be relied upon as an authority.'

He had settled down to his work, and had taken it for granted that he should be allowed to live his life as he wished. He had rooms in Bury Street, and for days neither Max nor Angela saw him. He never failed to telephone to her once a day, and would spend five minutes talking quite happily to her. No one ever questioned Julian. It was obvious that no young man could look so fit and be leading anything but a perfectly reasonable life. He came and went as he pleased. Angela realized that he paid her far less attention than Emmanuel did, but when he asked her to go to a theatre with him he made elaborate arrangements, ordered a dinner which he knew would appeal to her, and was so dear and attentive that those evenings stood out as evenings spent with anyone else never did.

Bill—William Hermann—who was leaving school and going up to Oxford was the youngest of the brothers. He had none of the Gollantz good looks, none of the Gollantz rather foreign attraction. William was all Heriot. He was reasonably good looking, with broad shoulders, and a figure which inclined to heaviness but not to fat. His hair was fair without having the gold of Julian's, his eyes were blue, and his mentality was excellent without being brilliant. Bill worked hard and Bill succeeded in following in his brother's footsteps. But what Julian had won easily and without very much effort, Bill won through sheer hard work and determination.

In the big dining-room there were four portraits which had been painted at the order of old Emmanuel. Angela, very lovely and a trifle artificial; old Emmanuel, wearing his celebrated cloak and leaning on his famous cane; Max, by Sargent, which Angela said made Max look much more a man of the world than he ever could be; and the three boys painted when Emmanuel, the younger, was fifteen.

Bill looked at it gravely one day when he and his mother were dining alone, then said:

'Pity they dragged me into it.'

'My dearest, why?'

'Emmanuel and Julian are so decorative, they go so well with you and grandfather. I don't fit in. Mind—' quickly —'I don't want in the least to be spectacular, there's nothing I should hate more. I never know how Emmanuel lived up to it at school.'

'Or Julian,' Angela added.

'Oh, Julian revelled in it,' Bill said, 'it amused him.'

They had settled at Ordingly, this family of Austrian Jews, who had come to England and become the most loyal citizens. They were, except old Emmanuel, to all intents and purposes entirely English people. Only young Emmanuel had difficulty with his 'r's' and would double and treble them when he forgot to watch himself carefully. They made no attempt to hide the fact that they were Jews, though even old Emmanuel was declared by his orthodox friends to be deplorably 'link'. They had never attended *shule* in their lives, and the only time Emmanuel had insisted upon any Jewish form or ceremony being introduced into the house was when the boys were circumcised.

True, the name of both Max and his father appeared on the lists of subscribers to Jewish charities, but they appeared on the lists of many Christian charities as well. They were rich, and they loved to spend money, they loved to give money to others; and they felt a sense of shirked responsibility when they heard of poor people to whom they had not offered help in its most practical form.

Angela's family, who were staunch supporters of the Church of England as by Law Established, without knowing very much about it, had feared that Max would try to make her join his faith. Her mother had said as much and warned her to resist any such attempt.

'Max's faith!' Angela had said. 'What is his faith? Decency, charity, clean dealing; faith in the House of Gollantz and—in me. That's his faith, and I'm ready to subscribe to it.'

At first the heaviness of Emmanuel's Jewish friends had worried her a little. She found the older generation so serious, and inclined to be melancholy. Old Reuben Davis, Sir Nathan Bernstein, the Salamans and the foreign contingent of the Gollantz family—Ishmael Hirsch, Ludwig Bruch, and Ferdinand Jaffe who came periodically from Vienna. They sat and talked so gravely, ate with such serious intent faces, played cards with absorbed interest and scarcely ever laughed.

But she had learnt to understand and like them. She had found out how good were their hearts, and how wide was their charity. And when the younger generation had begun to come to Ordingly, people who were of her own generation and Max's, she found them charming. Elizabeth Berman, the daughter of old Reuben Davis, and her daughter Hilda were delightful, so were Julius Davis and his son, Reuben. Her cousin, Walter Heriot, might turn up his highly coloured nose at them, and his son—whom Angela stigmatized as a young decadent—agree with his father. But Lady Heriot, who had been a Gaiety girl and still looked it, liked them and begged Angela never to omit her name from the lists of guests when the 'Tribe of Judah' were invited.

The last time Lady Heriot had come to Ordingly, she had brought her daughter with her, and Angela had liked the girl and felt it a pity that the title must go to Walter—pale, pimply-faced Walter—and not to the girl. Lady Heriot, whose stage name had been Beatrice Grantley, and who had been born Beatrice Grant, had become more 'county' than the county. She had developed into a hunting woman, and her conversation was couched in terms of the stable and the hunting field.

'Wattcher think of my girl, Viva? Nice filly, eh? Well ribbed up. Nice legs, comes out of a good stable. Walter's, not mine! I'm not in the stud book! Might do for one of those boys of yours, Angela! Keep the family together. Think it over—only second cousins—not too near, what?'

Angela sat now, with her chin propped on her hand, staring into the fire thinking it over. Max too sat very still, watching her. Once she lifted her head and looked round her, then turned and smiled at him.

'Pretty solid, Max?'

'What, the house?'

'Not the bricks and mortar. The house—our House of Gollantz.'

'Thanks to you, yes.'

She stretched out her hand and took his. 'Not really. Thanks to our wonderful patriarch upstairs. You and I might have come a dreadful cropper without him. I owe him a debt that I shall never be able to pay him.' She rose and faced him. 'But I will pay it. I'll pay it by making the House of Gollantz just what he wants it to be. It's international in its business side, and it shall be international in its blood. My people—the earth, the soil, old houses, fields and things that go to make up England. Your side—your people—the best that the Jews can produce, and one side shall never forget what it owes to the other.' She stopped and laughed. 'I'm getting sentimental and tub-thumpy—terrible! I'm as proud of it all as Emmanuel is, as you are, as young Emmanuel is. There.' She bent and kissed him lightly. 'I'm going up to talk to Emmanuel before dinner. I like talking to him, he flatters me so beautifully. I adore flattery.'

CHAPTER TWO

WHEN Angela had planned a dance for Christmas, she had asked old Emmanuel what she should do to amuse the young people who were to stay in the house. He pursed his lips for a moment, then said:

'Nothing—exactly nothing. Hev a bend vhich can play jezz, hev a grreat deal to eat, and not too much to drrink, und your duty hes been fulfilled. Young people like to amuse themselves.'

The house had been filled with people, and Angela had

loved every minute of it. Old Emmanuel had been very well, and had come down to dinner on Christmas night and made shameless love to every pretty woman, no matter what her age. They had clustered round him, and made no secret of the fact they they preferred talking to him than to the younger men.

She had given them entire freedom, they had the smaller drawing-room given over to them, and in the early hours of the morning, when the dancing was over, they had gathered there and stayed to talk. Emmanuel, tall and wearing his clothes with an air which made them look different from those of the other men, poured out drinks and carried them round. Viva Heriot watched him and decided that she liked him better than any man she knew. She liked the slight air of eccentricity in his clothes—his very tight cuffs, his black pearl studs, his trousers strapped under his patent boots and his tie which was old-fashioned and yet looked smarter than the butterfly ones which the other men wore. She liked the way he handed you a glass with a little bow, and his voice and his duplicated 'r's'.

Julian made no attempt to look after anyone, he sat on a cushion at her feet and talked to everyone about his new flat. He had moved to Ebury Street, because, he explained, the landlord in Bury Street disliked his suggested scheme for redecoration.

Bill, who sat on a table swinging his long legs, said:

'I didn't know that you'd moved. Does the Guv'nor know?'

'Not yet. I didn't want to tell him until I could announce that the place was finished. There is an old Scottish saying, my son—"Fools and bairns should never see things half done".'

Emmanuel said, quietly: 'The Guv'nor is neither.'

Betty Davis said: 'Tell us about it, Julian.'

Julian twisted round so that he could see her as he talked.

'It's more modern than anything that has ever been done yet,' he said. 'It's luxurious and yet austere; it's slightly decadent, and yet it's terribly pure. Oh, it's a pippin of a place! Three rooms, and the world's best bathroom.'

Walter Heriot blew out his fat pale cheeks, and said with some pomposity: 'Pal of mine has installed an American bar into his place. That's a novelty, if you like.'

'My dear Walter, a novelty!' Julian sighed. 'It was a

novelty the year that I was born. I don't copy, I invent.'

'I shouldn't like to be you,' Henry Drew said, 'to foot the bill.'

'I shan't foot the bill.'

'Why didn't you come to us?' Emmanuel asked.

Julian laughed. 'How could I bear to see my own name hanging on the front of the house every time I went to have a look at it! That neat little imitation of a giant's visiting card would have embarrassed me terribly. No, I went to a friend of Walter—Claude Marton.'

'I hate Walter's pals,' Viva said. 'They're a loathsome crew.'

'Here—I say!' Walter expostulated. 'That's too much.'

'Not a bit too much,' she returned. 'I only met them *en masse* once. It took me weeks to get over it. They've all got such dirty little souls and sins to match. And, poor things, they're so pathetically proud of them!'

'Catch me taking you to a party again!'

'Catch me going to one with you; anyway, it wasn't a party, it was a "four-ale" bar gone crazy.'

Julian said idly: 'Tell us, Viva.'

Viva sat upright on the big divan, and clasped her hands round her knees. She was a pretty child, with something of Angela's charm. Emmanuel, watching her, contrasted her with her brother Walter; and remembering that Walter took after his father, the Fifth Baronet, decided that they had a good deal to thank Miss Beatrice Grantley, late of the Gaiety Theatre, for.

'It was in a large filthy room,' Viva said. 'They called it a studio. I saw no sign of pictures, only bottles. There were millions of bottles. People were dressed or not dressed—in every sense of the word—as they liked. They were also drunk or sober, as they liked. Or washed or unwashed. Or decent or indecent. A girl asked me if I'd dance with her. I did. She said, "My sweet, how divinely you dance."'

'That'ul do, Viva,' Walter said. 'Cut it out.'

Julian, without turning, said: 'Shut up, Walter. Go on, Viva.'

'There wasn't much more,' she said. 'I made my exit after that. Walter expostulated, but I was bored to death. He took me home. But you went back, didn't you, Walter? I heard a pasty-faced horror beg you to. He said, just as we were going, to Walter——'

Emmanuel came forward, cocktail shaker in hand. 'Viva, darling, this is my own special concoction and it's very, very nice. Try it.'

She looked up at his grave face and grinned, a grin which must have been inherited from some ancestor on her mother's side. It was so entirely the grin of an impudent street arab, checked in some mischief.

'All right, Emmanuel,' she said. 'I'll be good.'

Walter Heriot walked over to the table and helped himself to a dark whisky and soda. He drank it in huge gulps, and his pale face became even more pale and less healthy looking.

One by one they drifted off to bed, and the three brothers were left alone. Julian went back to his cushion on the floor, Emmanuel stood by the fireplace and Bill sat down in a big chair from which he could see them both.

'Nasty bit of work, Walter Heriot,' Bill said.

Julian sipped his drink, then said slowly, 'Oh, I don't know.'

'Hate that Chelsea muck,' Bill went on. 'I sampled one of those crushes a month ago. Not for me. I got out.'

'Nice clean little feller,' Julian said.

'Not a bit. I'll try anything once, but I'm damned if I'll go on eating a thing that turns my stomach.'

'You're heading for being a first rate prig,' Julian told him. 'Things exist and there's no sense in pretending that they don't. You can't wipe things away with a wave of your hand. They're in the world, let's try to understand them.'

Emmanuel spoke quietly. 'It's surely possible to understand without having to participate, isn't it? It's all sufficiently easy to understand, and pity, and——'

Bill frowned. 'Pity! What the hell has pity to do with it? I can't see much reason for pity.'

'You don't see much reason for anything outside what can be proved by square root, do you, Bill?' Julian's voice was too pleasant, and Bill flushed. Emmanuel moved to the table and set down his glass.

'I'm for bed,' he announced, 'it's late—or early, and I'm riding to-mor-rrow with Viva.'

'Shop closed tomorrow?' Julian asked. His face was mischievous, he wanted to draw Emmanuel as he had drawn Bill. Emmanuel laughed.

'The shop,' he said, 'is open, but they can do without me for one day. Good night.'

Julian chose the next day at luncheon to make the announcement concerning his new flat. It was typical of Julian that if he had to face anything which might be unpleasant, he liked to do it in the presence of all his family. Not that he wanted support, but it amused him to watch how they reacted. At luncheon, the following day, he dropped his bomb.

'When do you go back, Julian?' Max asked.

'Tomorrow morning early,' then after a slight pause, 'I shan't go to the office, I'm "moving in".'

Angela leant forward. 'Moving in? Where to? You're not leaving Bury Street?'

'I've left it, darling. You must come and dine with me at the new flat. It's charming, I know that you will like it.'

He laid the faintest stress on the 'you'.

He folded his arms on the table and directed his words to Angela. 'Ultra modern. Lots of glass and polished steel. That's the modern idea, rather hard and bright like the younger generation. Not a great deal of colour, but where it is introduced it's very brilliant. I have some of the new steel chairs.' For the first time he turned to Max: 'Have you any of them, father?'

'My dear Julian, I'm not Tottenham Court Road. No, I don't indulge in steel chairs.'

Julian laughed, and said, 'Sorry!'

Max said, very politely, 'Not at all!'

Angela said: 'Well, if I don't like it, I shall refuse to come again. I won't sit in rooms I hate. Your father has educated me too well in the matter of furniture.'

'Please like it,' Julian said, smiling at her as he spoke, 'because if you don't, I shall have to move again, and it's so damnably expensive, this moving business.'

'Expensive for whom?' Max asked.

'Oh, I was thinking entirely of you,' Julian said quickly.

Emmanuel began to talk rapidly, slurring his 'r's' and obviously making conversation. He knew that Max was angry; he was more angry than Emmanuel had ever seen him. His lips were pressed tightly, his eyes were cold. The fact that he said so little, was to Emmanuel an indication of his annoyance. Bill, trying to help Emmanuel, blundered into the conversation, and Max hid his anger and made suitable answers to their questions.

When they rose from the table, he touched Julian on the shoulder and said, 'Could you spare me a minute, Julian?'

In the study, Max sat down at his desk, the same desk where his father had always sat in the room in Regent's Park. He always felt, when he sat there, that some of old Emmanuel's strength and certainty came to him and helped him.

He turned to his son, and pointed to a chair.

'Sit down, Julian.'

Julian's eyes twinkled, his lips parted in a smile. When Julian smiled it was very hard to remain angry with him.

'I'd rather stand,' he said, 'and get my wigging over. I'll sit down afterwards, if I may. Go on, father.'

'This flat——' Max began, but Julian interrupted him.

'I know,' he said, 'I know, it's been unpardonable. I just didn't think. I saw this new stuff, new colours, and steel and everything and I wanted it. There's no excuse at all. It was idiotic and silly. I know that I ought to have come to you, but I was conceited enough to think that it might be fun to do it alone. I wanted to surprise you——'

Max said, 'Oh, you've succeeded there!'

'Let me finish, father. I thought that I could pay for it out of what grandfather and you always give me for Christmas. I intended to do that. I never thought that it would be so damnably expensive.'

'Who did it—with your help?'

'Claude Marton, of South Molton Street.'

'Pah!' Max's face expressed disgust. 'That rubbish! In a year it won't be worth a fiver. Nasty gimcrack stuff. I wonder at you, I do really, Julian.'

'I rather wonder at myself,' Julian agreed.

'What has it cost?'

There was a moment's pause. 'Four seventy-five.'

Max pulled his keys on their long flexible gold chain out of his pocket and unlocked a drawer.

'I'm going to pay it,' he said, 'and you'll please clear this debt at the earliest possible moment. I can't afford to have it said that we owe a firm like Marton's anything. It's grotesque.' He picked up a pen, and wrote, repeating as he did so, 'Four seventy-five', then tore out the slip and handed it to Julian.

'You're frightfully angry, father?'

Max frowned, and paused before he replied. 'Not so angry as annoyed at your lack of good taste. Oh, I admit that I was angry at first. Can't you see, Julian, that these things aren't done. In the first place, surely Gollantz and Son should be good enough for Gollantz. Secondly, it's cheek—cheek to assume that you can incur debts in this fashion. You're becoming damned expensive, Julian. It's not fair to your brothers. If you incur debts of four seventy-five now, what will you be doing in ten years' time?'

Julian came nearer. 'Let me hand over to you what you and grandfather gave me for Christmas. That will help to pay for it anyway.'

Max swung round in his chair. 'You'd like to do that?'

Julian nodded. 'Honestly I would.'

'Very well—I'll take it.'

From a pocket-book, which bore his initials, Julian extracted two cheques and handed them over to his father. Max glanced at them, read the amounts aloud:

'One hundred; one hundred. Thank you.' Then suddenly he turned and laughed. 'There, take your cheques, Julian! I don't want them. You'll be punished enough by having to live among your dreadful furniture and your stainless steel! Only,' and his voice regained its gravity, 'this mustn't happen again.'

'It won't, father.' The boy stammered a little. 'It's terribly good of you, I'm everlastingly grateful. Now, can I tell you something nice—at least I think it's nice. No one, not a soul knows yet. They're going to adopt me as candidate for the next election.'

'No! My dear Julian, that's wonderful. Where for?'

'Harroby.'

Max chuckled. 'They wouldn't approve of your newfangled furniture in Harroby, my lad. They'd distrust you for having such stuff. But, joking apart, it's wonderful. Harroby—it's dead Conservative, and you ought to romp home. They want new blood in the Party, and you should give them some. When do they expect the election?'

'In about six months' time. I shall have to work pretty hard, nursing the place. Make myself popular and so forth.'

Max nodded. 'Yes, but, Julian, do it with personality and sound sense. Don't think that money and cups to the football team and a new billiard table for the Working Man's Club will get you in. I promise that you shall have every chance, but the real battle you'll have to fight yourself.' He laid his hands on Julian's shoulders. 'Go in and win, and we shall be the proudest people in England.'

'Thank you, father. I'll try.'

'Cut along now and tell your mother. She'll never forgive you for having told me first.'

Alone Max Gollantz sat at his big desk and smiled. Julian a candidate for the next election! He might be a member at twenty-one! He had brains as well as charm, he had everything that could help him. He had handed over his cheques without a moment's hesitation. The boy would grow out of his steel furniture and his vivid colourings and come back to decent English oak and soft old velvets in time. Max thought of the furniture that he loved with a feeling that he was evolving a parable. You might like the modern stuff, you might think that it was attractive for a time, but the other things, the gracious things, the proved things, were what you came back to in the end.

He took a cigar and lit it carefully. 'Julian's suffering from a sort of decorating measles, he's got an eruption of modern furniture. How long do measles last? Ten days—a fortnight. In a year he'll come and tell me that he's sold the lot.' He laughed softly. 'I only hope that he has enough sense to let his brother Emmanuel sell it for him!'

Then, because he was proud of his sense of justice, Max sat down and wondered what he could do for Emmanuel and for Bill that would equal in expense Julian's wretched furniture.

Julian, contented, sought out his mother and sat down to tell her his news.

Angela listened, her eyes shining, her cheeks rather flushed.

'Darling, how awful!' she said. 'I shall have to be continually transporting myself from Ordingly to Harroby. Do you think your constituents will approve of me? Oh, you must win! I couldn't bear you to lose. Out of sheer annoyance and revenge I should join the Left Wing of the Labour Party, and get myself adopted for East Ham, or Billingsgate, or somewhere really smelly.'

'If it's humanly possible, I'll get in,' he assured her. 'You see, I have a good deal of knowledge; economics—but not too much of them. I've learnt a great deal from Gilbert Heriot. And,' more slowly, 'I have certain convictions, you know. I'm not doing this only as a means to a career. It's more than that, it is really. I suppose that it's an axiom that the Conservative Party of today isn't the Conservative Party of twenty years ago, it's changed and it's got to go on changing. You know, the Labour men are a good deal nearer to us than some of the Liberals could ever be.'

Angela, who loathed politics in any form, nodded and said:

'I once met Mr. James Maxton. I thought that he was most attractive. Oh, Julian, about this new flat. It's very naughty of you to do things and incur expense without asking either your father or me first. It must have cost a frightful lot of money. I'd better give you an extra Christmas present to pay for it . . .'

'Father paid up like a lamb, bless him! It won't happen again. It wasn't very nice of me, and I'm rather ashamed of myself. I hate feeling ashamed of myself, too. It gives me stomach ache . . .'

He came a little closer to her and laughed. 'But you will come and see my despised steel chairs, won't you? It's nicer than you'd think. If you can discard the carefully cultivated taste of Gollantz, you'll rather like it. I'll give a party and say that you're my sister and watch all the young bloods fall in love with you, shall I?'

'Idiot,' she returned, 'you forget that I'm over forty.'

'If you weren't perfectly certain that you didn't look anything like forty,' he said, 'you wouldn't always be referring to your age. That "over forty" of yours is a form of swank.'

He went back to town the next morning, driving his mother's car because his own was being repaired, loaded with presents, and waving his hand to Angela as he took a most unwarrantably dangerous turn out of the gates. She stood watching the car as long as it was in sight, thinking how much she loved him and how she would miss him. Then turning back she met Bill, and felt disloyal to Bill for loving Julian so much. She hurried towards him, slipped her hand through his arm and walked back to the house, talking as she went. Bill listened, and laughed when she stopped to draw breath.

'Angel,' he said, 'what a funny little soul you are. I don't mind your missing Julian like hell. You don't have to try to hide it—not to me.'

'I don't believe that you and Julian get on awfully well, Bill.'

Bill pursed his lips in a way that reminded her suddenly of Max.

'Oh, I don't know,' he said, 'we're different, that's all. Julian's clever—I'm only hard-working. He's—well, he's all the things that I'm not. We're fond enough of each other, only we don't see eye to eye, and we don't, honestly, speak quite the same language. That's all.'

'You're not jealous of him?'

Bill threw back his head and laughed. 'Jealous? I wouldn't be Julian for all the money in the world. I should hate it. One day when Julian is Prime Minister, I shall be Solicitor-General. One day when someone sells Emmanuel a fake Titian, I shall win his case for him.'

'I doubt,' Angela said, 'if anyone will ever sell Emmanuel a fake Titian. He knows too much about Titians.'

'I dunno,' Bill said doubtfully, 'if they said that they had a dying wife and six starving children, Emmanuel would try to believe that the Titian was real. He'd hate the fellow who sold him the pup, but he'd keep thinking of the wife and kids. Emmanuel is like that.'

'Then he wouldn't make a case of it,' Angela said. 'You're wrong somewhere, my clever William.'

'You're right,' Bill agreed, 'he'd only bring cases against profiteers who had seven grown-up sons all doing well, and a wife who had an income of her own. Anyone else's character you'd like me to sum up for you, darling? No trouble——'

'I'd like to know what you think of Viva, Bill?'

Bill halted and stared at her, his mouth a little open, then he said:

'You don't want to hear me say that I adore Viva, do you?'

'Good Lord, no! You're far too young to think of girls.'

'I'm far too busy,' Bill corrected. 'I've mapped out my work for the next six years, and there aren't any half-hours left for girls.'

'Oh, you can do a lot in less than half an hour.'

'I can't,' he objected. 'I need a full half-hour to get to know what a girl's name is—at least correctly. Whom do you want to be interested in Viva?'

'I thought that Julian was.'

'He may be,' he said, 'but she's interested in Emmanuel.'

'Really?'

Bill nodded gravely. 'I think so. No, I'm sure of it. She watches Emmanuel when he talks, she only glances at Julian. The other night—morning, to be exact, when she was ragging Walter, Emmanuel thought that she was going a little too far. He just gave her a hint, you know how decently Emmanuel can give hints, and she stopped like a lamb.'

'Oh,' Angela sounded thoughtful, 'what was she ragging Walter about?'

Bill shrugged his shoulders. 'I dunno—or if I did, I've forgotten. Nothing much anyway.'

CHAPTER THREE

JULIAN lay in his ultra modern bed and sipped his very hot, very strong coffee. He had got home very late, after an adoption meeting at Harroby, and in half an hour he must get up, bathe—in his beautiful new bathroom which was all pink marble and silver taps—and dressing with suitable care, make his way to the office.

But for half an hour, he might take his ease and smile over his recollections of the meeting. He had driven to Harroby in his mother's car. He had arrived at the Conservative Club, and had been greeted by the Secretary and the Chairman of the Local Party. He entered the big committee-room, and was presented to the local lights of Toryism.

He smiled when he remembered how different had been their greetings. A tall thin man, with an old-fashioned collar and a blue tie with small white dots, had offered him a dry brittle hand and murmured something inarticulate. A stout fellow, with a heavy gold watch-chain which carried several medals of the same metal, had gripped his hand until he flinched with the pain, and said:

''Ope we'll satisfy you, and 'ope you will satisfy us, Mr. Gollantz.'

A thin, worm-eaten little creature with rimless glasses, had bowed and said in a high thin voice:

'I sincerely hope that you will carry our banner to victory. Last time, we were, *Traditus non vicus.*'

Another man had said in a deep voice: 'Ah! That's true.'

They had sat down and the Chairman had made a dry-as-dust but reasonable speech and he had formally asked Julian to speak. Julian had risen feeling that he knew nothing about politics, and that his one impulse was to tell them a new and highly improper limerick which began:

'There was a young girl of Japan——'

He had mastered this impulse and had begun to speak. The words had come easily, he knew that his thoughts had crystallized and that he was voicing them clearly and with effect. He watched the faces of his hearers, and knew that he had caught and held them. They nodded in agreement, they pursed their lips, they smiled and once they chuckled. He spoke for thirty minutes, and sat down feeling as fresh as when he started. A round of applause had followed.

The Chairman had asked if any of the Committee wished to ask questions, there was a long pause, while various members hunted out scraps of paper and studied them diligently. Then the questions had come, two men had got to their feet at once. They had deferred to each other, bobbing up and down like corks in a pail of water. Finally one of them had turned to Julian and put his question.

For the next three-quarters of an hour he had answered questions on every conceivable topic, and made mental notes that on this reply and that he might count himself the richer by so many votes when polling day came.

'Mr. Gollantz, I venture to put this question to you on be'alf of the Licensed Vict'lers of this district——'

'Might I ask the candidate—er, the prospective candidate—what are his sentiments with regard to Birth Control?'

'Could Mr. Gollantz give us, briefly, his feelings and beliefs with regard to the adoption of tariffs?'

'It would be interesting to know what are your views, Mr. Gollantz, with regard to religious teaching in the council schools?'

More and more questions; questions regarding theatres

and their bars, regarding playing football on Sundays, regarding early closing. 'Dora', dog-racing and a dozen other things. Was he in favour of easier divorce, was he in favour of the reformed prayer book, was he—and he would pardon the speaker—a Jew by religion or only by birth? Julian listened, waited, and answered, and with each answer noted the ripple of satisfaction or disappointment that ran round the table. He fancied that there were considerably more waves of approval than of dissent. It was over. The committee begged him to retire into the smoking-room for a few moments. He knew that their decision had, to all intents and purposes, been made when he came to Harroby. Gilbert Heriot had said so.

'They've virtually adopted you, Julian. This is only a formality. They know that I shouldn't back anyone who wasn't sound.'

But sitting there in the big smoking-room, looking at the walls, where hung depressing portraits of former mayors of Harroby in their robes of office, Julian felt nervous. Suppose they refused to accept him? Suppose that instead of being formally adopted for Harroby, this 'safe seat', he was sent back to London as 'unwanted'. Marked 'not up to sample'. A particularly unpleasant face, that of His Worship Alderman Berresford, who had been Harroby's chief citizen for twelve months (1897–8), looked down at him with marked dislike. He felt that he was less than the dust in the sight of Alderman Berresford's painted eyes. He hated the man, was thankful that he had not been a citizen of Harroby during that year of office (1897–8). On the other hand His Worship Alderman Thos. Watney, who had worn those hideous robes of office from 1901–1902 and again five years later, looked at him pleasantly enough. He knew the face—knew that massive watch-chain to which the artist had done full justice. Of course, it was the fat old chap who had hoped that he might satisfy them. Julian felt his heart warm towards Alderman Thos. Watney, and hoped that he might be mayor again.

The door opened, and Watney himself entered, his broad face wreathed in smiles.

'Well, Mr. Gollantz—an' by the way, is it Goll-anz or Goll-antz—accent at t' start or finish, which? Oh, finish, eh? Well, they have finished pow-wowing. They like you, and they 'ope you'll like them. I'm sure as I do. Joost a word in your ear, before you go back and 'ear t' sentence. Keep right wi' Nonconformists—and Kill-Joys. Publicans is with you—I'm one—but "Kill-Joy" lot were a bit upset with your answer to the Birth Control question, and the easier divorce. See? No names, no pack drill, as the girl said to the sergeant. You know what I mean—like walking on eggs ter please everyone. Come on, and get it ovver.'

Julian went back. The slight air of strain had lifted, and these men round the table seemed less important, less like hanging judges, less formidable. He allowed himself to smile, and look round the table eagerly as if searching for the verdict. One or two men nodded encouragingly. The Chairman spoke, the Vice-Chairman spoke, and Mr. Thos. Watney spoke 'on be'alf of the Publicans of this City'. Julian replied, said suitable and modest things, hoped that he would do justice to their city and the great Party to which they were all proud to belong. It was over. He went back to dine with the Chairman, who gave him an excellent dinner and some remarkably fine old whisky.

He had driven back to town, arriving at half-past two in the morning, and here he was as fresh as paint, drinking his excellent coffee at eight o'clock. After six and a half hours' sleep, after having driven three hundred and some odd miles, he was not even faintly tired. He finished his coffee, lit a cigarette and knew that the world was a good place in which to live, in which to be twenty-one years of age.

He reached to the table at his bedside and picked up his engagement book.

Luncheon with Bill Masters at the Savoy. Dinner with the Heriots—Walter, Viva, Old Walter—who was certain to get a bit tight—and Lady Heriot. Family affair. Quite pleasant, because Viva amused him. Viva and Walter, another man and he were going on to dance, and after they had taken Viva home, Walter and he were going to the new club—what was it called? The Bluebottle! Walter was an original member and very proud of the fact. Said it was amusing.

'Another place for Bill to disapprove of,' Julian thought.

He bathed and lay in the faintly-scented water, thinking hard. Julian found a hot bath an admirable place in which to think. He wondered how soon he must begin to spend week-ends at Harroby, how often he would have to speak there, and what they would want him to speak about? He wondered if the present Government would finish in six months, and if they managed to hang on—for how long? Wondered what Sir Walter Heriot would say to his adoption, and what Viva would think of it? Viva—he found that he wondered a good deal about Viva. She was terribly pretty, clever too. Make an ideal wife for a rising young man—like himself. Julian had no doubt that he was going to rise, any more than Bill had. They were both perfectly aware of their gifts and their ability, and saw no reason why they should pretend to have doubts. It was not conceit, it was that queer Jewish trait which is called *chutzpah,* which is that quality of having the courage of one's opinions about oneself. It is not impudence or conceit, but a sort of firm belief in his own ability. Julian did not know the word, though it is possible that he had heard his grandfather use it among his own people; but he possessed the quality to a very large degree.

That evening as he dressed for dinner at the Heriots, the thought of Viva came back to him again. She had grown remarkably pretty in the last few years, he thought; she had poise and certainty. He liked her quick accurate movements; Julian detested people who fumbled. His own fingers were never clumsy, he never had struggles with his collar studs, never ruined his white ties by muffing the bow as he tied it. He liked her voice, clear without being sharp. Women whose voices sharpened as they spoke were terrible. She had knowledge, and let you know it without making a parade of it. Let you know, in such a way, that you felt safe in embarking on any subject without a slight feeling of apprehension that she might stare at you blankly. No, Viva was eminently satisfactory, and as he brushed his hair with the heavy ivory-backed brushes that his mother had given him a year ago, Julian wondered if he was not a little in love with her? It would be distinctly pleasant to fall—mildly—in love with Viva. Nothing devastating, nothing that would affect his work or upset his plans, but a nice warm affection which would have its moments of passion—in their right place.

He liked women, and had some experience of them. They were part of life; and life, to Julian, was a thing to know, not only to theorize about. There had been a platonic love affair with a woman who knew everything there was to know about economics, housing and factory conditions. It had lasted for three months, until she discovered that Julian had learnt all that she could teach him, and found that his interest in her waned.

There had been a girl with peroxide blonde hair who was in the touring company of *Hats Off*. She had been amusing for a fortnight, he had laughed at her stories and found her criticisms of life in general intriguing. A fortnight had seen the end of it, for both of them. She had begun to bore him, and she had said that he was too serious for her. It had been quite amicable, and friendly. No rows, no recriminations—just, as she had said: 'The curtain can bloody well come down on this act, old thing, I'm through.'

Others—nothing very serious, but enough to have given him some knowledge of women. 'No degree,' Julian said to Walter Heriot, 'only a very good course of lectures and some very useful notes as a result.'

But now, with Harroby looming on the horizon, with the possibility of a Parliamentary career, he must walk warily. Side-stepping was dangerous. He wasn't really afraid that he would 'side-step'. He was cautious, and he would not allow anything to come between himself and his objective. He leant forward and stared at his face in the glass. Cautious—yes, he was cautious, he considered and planned; but once in a way, he knew that he betrayed himself and his own creed of making everything safe in order to obtain his objective. Not often, but Julian, who knew himself because he had studied himself with care, knew that there had been occasions upon which he had thrown everything to the winds, and lived only for the moment.

That business of the new flat had been one of them. He had been a fool. He might have angered his father so that forgiveness and regained trust might have been a protracted affair. He looked back and felt irritated with himself. He ought to have waited, he ought to have been wiser. He ought never to have allowed Claude Marton to rush him into this scheme of decoration. If he had wanted it, he could have had it and with his father's consent instead of without it. To act as he had done, on impulse, argued that he had neglected to use the knowledge which he possessed of his father's and his mother's liberality, generosity and their wish to give their children everything that they might ask for. He felt that he had thrown away an opportunity, that he had handicapped himself in his father's eyes, and made next time—whatever next time happened to be—additionally difficult.

Once before at school, when he was sixteen—Julian caught up his coat and put it on, tugging impatiently here and there to make it sit as he wished. What was the use of going back over things that were better forgotten? Impulses were dangerous, the thing was to consider one's actions and then make them appear to be impulses.

That evening at dinner, he sat next to Viva at the round table in the Heriots' dining-room, and listened to her and laughed and decided that he was right—he felt a little sentimental about her, she certainly was charming.

Lady Heriot watched them and thought what a handsome couple they would make. She still thought of couples as 'handsome', which helped to date her entry into the circles in which she now moved. She liked Julian, liked his fair skin and his yellow hair.

'Funny,' she said, suddenly, 'that you're so fair, Ju.' No one else called him 'Ju', or called Emmanuel 'Manny', or Bill—to his horror and disgust, 'Billee'.

'Why, darling?'

'Well, you're a Jew—they usually turn out dark. But I remember a man I used to know—Paston. Remember Paston, Walter?'

Sir Walter Heriot nodded, he was more than half asleep, and the half that wasn't asleep was pleasantly under the influence of his wine. 'Old Charlie Paston,' he said, 'knew him, what is it? thirty years ago. He won the Three Thousand with a horse called "Cleophas". They said that he trained it himself in Hyde Park—lies probably.'

His wife nodded. 'That's the man. He used to read a lot as well as train horses in Hyde Park. He told me sheenies, when they were fair, were nearly always successful. I remember he said that the Lord Himself was a fair Jew. I thought that was a queer thing to say——'

Viva said: 'Is that old Sir Charles Paston? He's the great authority on racial development. That's what he got knighted for.'

Her mother looked slightly shocked, as if Viva had raked up some scandalous rumour about old Paston, which she must in duty bound suppress.

'I never heard that said about him,' she said. 'He's sixty, if he is a day, and I don't know any man who funks his fences less than old Charlie.'

Julian listened and thought what an old dear Aunt Beatrice was, and how little she attempted to understand anything, and wondered if she wasn't really rather wise.

'Then you think, taking Sir Charles as an authority,' he said, 'that I may be successful?'

'I shouldn't wonder a bit. Not a bit.'

'It never seems to strike any of you,' Viva said, 'that he's fairly successful already.'

Walter, the younger, laughed. 'I should say so. Being able to stand old Gilbert Drew would argue that! He's a dry-as-dust old stick.'

'In the old days,' Sir Walter said, slowly and with painful care, 'old Gilly Drew used to be one'er—one'er the lads. I could tell you of times we've 'ad togerrer——'

His wife said: 'Not at my table you won't, Walter. Save those tales for your pals, and the smoke-room.'

Later, when Julian was dancing with Viva, he said:

'I always enjoy dining at your place, Viva. Your mother's a sheer delight.'

Viva glanced at him. 'Thanks,' she said. 'I don't need you to say that. I loathe that half-patronizing attitude, Julian. There's only one person who understands my mother, and that's yours! Personally I hate our house, lock, stock, and barrel. I loathe father getting tight, I loathe Walter's pasty face and his beastly friends, and I loathe—most of all, the people who come and find mother amusing.'

'Then get out of your home, and find another,' Julian said.

'How?'

'Get married.' He laughed. 'It should be sufficiently simple.'

'Who to? You, Emmanuel, Bill?'

With smiling gravity, he said: 'Listen, Viva, I'm not going to ask questions, or try to extract promises. I don't know that I really know my own feelings at the moment. I think I do, I'm almost certain that I do. If this business at Harroby goes through all right; if I am elected, will you let me come and talk to you, seriously?'

'I'd let you talk, Julian, but I can't promise what my answer would be.'

'I haven't stated what my questions would be,' he said, 'they're not even formulated yet, Viva.'

'Then let it wait. I hate anticipating things.'

Later when he drove her home, and said 'Good-bye' to her on the wide steps of Walter Heriot's town house, he held her hand rather longer than was necessary, and bent down to say 'Good night'. He knew that at the moment he was feeling decidedly sentimental about Viva, and that if he allowed his sudden impulse to rule him, he would say, then and there:

'Don't let's wait until after the election. Let's get it over now. I want you to marry me, Viva.'

But he hesitated, distrusted the impulse and said:

'Good night, angel. You do dance so divinely, bless you.'

Walter, fidgeting in the car, said: 'Thank God, that's over. Now let's get along to the old Bluebottle.'

'I don't know that I want to go to the Bluebottle,' Julian said, slowly. 'I don't know that it's wise, Walter. I've got to watch my step.'

'You're not going to funk it, are you? Good Lord, you're as bad as young Bill. There's nothing to be afraid of. Every precaution's taken. Come on—let's get a move on.'

He found that the Bluebottle was really rather fun. Lots of drink, lots of people rather the worse for it, but quite amusing all the same. Cards, a roulette wheel, baccarat, and poker. They played high, and the thought of losing more than he could afford or possibly winning more than he expected intrigued Julian. He played, and he won, and he went on winning. He sat there, absorbed, scarcely hearing the noise, the high voices, the sudden quarrels that went on round him. This gambling was amusing—he was lucky at cards. He was lucky at everything.

It must have been about half-past two when he rose and went to find Walter and a drink. Walter was sitting between a painted girl and a still more painted boy. He was undeniably tight, and his fat white face looked ghastly.

'Wanner drink, Jurrien?'

'I do. Can I have one?'

The boy said: 'I'll get one for you! What is it? Benedictine, *crème-de-menthe,* or what?' He lowered his voice and said: 'I can get absinthe!'

'Can you get a whisky and soda?'

'Oh, what a brutal drink! But I'll get it for you.'

He minced off. Julian watched him and thought what queer people you met, and wondered if it was quite as amusing as he had thought at first. A few minutes later, the boy came back, white-faced and without the drink. He rushed up to Julian and caught his hand.

'Get out,' he said, 'get out quickly—the police are here. They're on the stairs now.'

Julian felt suddenly very cold, chilled. Julian Gollantz, the candidate for Harroby, caught here, in this more than dubious club, with a pack of gamblers and decadents. He said, very quietly:

'Is there another way out?'

'No, only the one way. They're on the stairs.'

They were, as a matter of fact, in the long hot room. Three burly constables and an Inspector, and with them two men who might have been successful prizefighters, but who were, in reality, plain clothes detectives. They loomed large and menacing in the doorway, then entered slowly and ominously. They were taking names, and the Inspector said:

'No use trying to make off, ladies and gentlemen. I've a couple of men on the door. Just give your names please, and let's save further trouble, if you don't mind.'

Julian stood where he was, and wondered what he could do. Nothing, apparently. Next day, a summons, newspaper paragraphs, his name in the paper, the news carried to Harroby—and the 'Kill-Joys' would turn down their thumbs!

'Your name, sir?'

'Gollantz—J. E.'

'G-o-double h'ell-an-ts——'

Julian said: 'Z not S.'

'Right, and did you say J. E. or E. J.?'

Julian did not speak for a second, then he said, firmly: 'E. J.; and I shall be at my office in New Bond Street—Gollantz and Son, at eleven tomorrow morning, not before. Is that all right? Can I go?'

'Tomorrer at eleven. Right. What's the Bond Street number?'

'Sixty-seven. It's in the telephone book, verify it now if you like. I shan't try to get out of it, only I do want to get home.'

His smile was so pleasant, so frank, and he looked so obviously out of place that the Inspector softened a little. After all, boys would be boys!

'That's all right, sir. Know this gentleman here?'

'Walter Heriot—my cousin. His address——'

Walter looked up and said: 'My address is one forry-four Grosvenor Square and bloody well minn'er own business——'

Out in the cool morning air, Walter sobered suddenly. He cursed thc law with great fluency and ability, and then turned to Julian.

'Sorry about you, Jurrien. Nasty mess for you.'

Julian said: 'I know, I daren't risk it. I daren't, it would finish me at Harroby. I gave Emmanuel's name. It won't harm him. I shall see him in the morning. Only, Walter, not a word. It's between Emmanuel and me. Swear that you won't say anything!'

'Gosh, that was smart,' Walter was full of admiration. 'Trust me, it's none of my business—I shan't open my mouth.'

CHAPTER FOUR

JULIAN drove home, let himself in very quietly, and once in his bedroom, divested himself of his light coat and hat and put them away in his eminently satisfactory wardrobe. He was rather proud of his wardrobe; it was let into the wall, and he had designed its fittings himself. He stopped for a moment to run his eyes over the neat compartments—the rack for ties, the long rods upon which his boots and shoes rested, the admirable hanging room—he turned away, content—it was eminently satisfactory.

From the table by his bedside he took his engagement book—bound in dark blue leather. He ran his fingers with appreciation over the smooth grain, and opening it, flicked the pages over until he found the date that he sought.

January 8th. Old Harburian dinner—Savoy—8.30.

Last night—for it was now past three on the morning of January 9th—had been the old Harburian dinner. He had refused to attend. He hated these reunion dinners, had very few friends left among the boys who had been at school with him, and had known that it would be boring and dull.

Emmanuel had asked him to go. He was going, and Bill would have been going only that he was in Scotland with the Musgroves.

'Why should I go?' Julian had said. 'There's not likely to be anyone there that I want to see . . .'

'There might be several people who would be glad to see you,' his brother had said.

'I can't consider them!' Julian had laughed and chipped Emmanuel about 'love for the old school' and 'playing the game'. Emmanuel never lost his temper or got rattled as Bill did. He only laughed and said that he would represent Harbury's best and brightest products—the Gollantz brothers.

Julian closed the book and laid it down with a sigh of satisfaction. Emmanuel had almost certainly stayed the night in town, and not returned to Ordingly. Julian knew those Harburian dinners—men got into tight little groups and talked about 'Do you remember—' and 'Look at the time when Garthorne—' kicked something or scored something—and so they went on for hours. Emmanuel would have stayed late, and probably have gone on to some place where they could go on drinking coffee and 'fighting battles over again' and living through a dozen football matches before he went back to the hotel where he always stayed when he was in town. Julian did not approve of Emmanuel's choice of hotels, and had told him so.

Emmanuel's defence had been: 'We've stayed there for years. The Guv'nor always stays there when he's in town.'

'Not when Angela is with him.'

'No, that's different, naturally. It wouldn't do for her.'

'It wouldn't do for me either. It's cold and clean and chaste. I don't know how you stand it. The waiters are all drawing the old-age pension, and the chambermaids are all over fifty. I bet they still call you—Master Emmanuel!'

'They used to,' his brother admitted, 'but I gave them a hint about a year ago. Now they call me—Mister Emmanuel.'

Funny fellow, Emmanuel! Julian undressed slowly, got

into his heavy silk pyjamas and got into bed, sleeping peacefully until eight the next morning.

'Ring up the office,' he said to Gray, his man, 'and tell them that business will prevent my being there early. Ask them to tell Sir Gilbert when he gets in. Get on to Black's Hotel and ask if my brother is there . . .'

'Mr. William, sir?'

'No, Mr. Emmanuel. If he hasn't breakfasted ask him to come round here and breakfast with me. If that isn't possible, say that I'll go round in three-quarters of an hour and see him.'

Emmanuel said that he would come round, and within half an hour he was shown into Julian's sitting-room, and for ten minutes wandered about, his teeth on edge, wondering how on earth anyone could live with such furniture.

The white walls—he admitted that the paintwork was fairly good, though he doubted the lasting qualities of the enamel. The orange carpet he eyed doubtfully. Not woven in one piece, only joined strips, 'stair carpet' he called it. The furniture was only painted whitewood, and the shapes hideous, all angles and no symmetry about it. The famous steel chairs—untarnishable—stainless, and all the rest of it, with orange seats, stretched tightly from bar to bar. 'More stair carpeting!' Not a bit of decent stuff anywhere. He wouldn't give a tenner for the lot.

Julian came in, cool, exquisite, smelling faintly of some elusive scent—bath salts probably. His fair hair looked as if it had been newly burnished, his skin was clear, and his eyes shone with health. Emmanuel felt a thrill of pride, what a handsome chap he was!

'Hello, Emmanuel, hungry?'

'Fairly, though Heaven knows I ate enough last night.'

'Ah, the old Harburians, I remember. I wish that I'd gone with you, Emmanuel. I was a fool not to.'

His tone was suddenly grave, and Emmanuel glanced up quickly.

'Where did you go instead? Only to dine with Walter Heriot, didn't you?'

'On to dance with Viva and Walter, and then afterwards to a new and very dashing night club of Walter's.'

Emmanuel grimaced slightly. 'I know Walter's night clubs, all dirt and disorder. Beastly places. I once went to one called the Cradle Snatcher, if you please! Never again . . .'

Julian sat down and began to pour out coffee. 'No,' he agreed, 'that is exactly what I am saying this morning.'

'Why particularly?'

Julian sipped his coffee, wiped his lips carefully with the little coloured napkin, and then leant back in his chair and looked his brother in the eyes.

'Because there was a raid,' he said, 'and I—was caught, that's why.'

'Whe-ew! That's bad luck! I'm terribly sorry. What did they raid the place for?'

'Gambling I fancy. Might have been—other things. There were some curious people there.'

'My God! That's nasty. Anything I can do to help, Julian?'

Julian pushed away his coffee cup and lit a cigarette which he took from a box of polished copper.

'Yes, frankly, a good deal, if you will.'

'You know—I will. You don't need to ask. Go ahead.'

'The police came, and, honestly, I saw Harroby and all the rest of it receding into the distance. They're frightfully Nonconformist conscience in Harroby. I've been warned about it. The police took names—and I gave mine—as E. J. Gollantz, and my address as sixty-seven New Bond Street. There! That's off my chest. No, don't say anything, for a minute. I know that I've no defence, or very little. I knew that it meant a list of names in the paper, they'll serve warrants this morning. The press are bound to spot my name, and remember that I'm candidate for Harroby. What a snip for the Liberals and the Labour people! What a hope for me in Harroby afterwards! I shouldn't have minded so much, for myself. I could live it down. I'm young enough, and people forget anything if you give them time. But Angela's so set on this Parliamentary business, it would almost break her heart. Candidly, Emmanuel, I didn't funk for myself, I funked for her. I'm not in too high favour with the Guv'nor at the moment, and this would have taken a long time to get right. It was Angela and the Guv'nor who settled things last night, when the Robert stood with a note-book and asked for my initials.'

Emmanuel watched him, looked at the clear eyes which met his, and heard the pleasant voice; saw Julian catch his lower lip in his teeth as he had always done since he was a little boy, when he was worried or upset. His anger began to evaporate. Julian was right, it would have hurt their mother terribly. Emmanuel knew how much she counted on Julian's success, how proud she was of him and his brilliance. After all, the fact that he—Emmanuel—had been caught at a disreputable night club, wouldn't hurt him much. The Nonconformist conscience didn't enter much into the showrooms of Gollantz and Son. It was better that he, and not Julian, should have to appear, or at least pay a fine and have the fact recorded in the daily papers, than that Julian, prospective candidate for Harroby, should be so advertised.

He nodded. 'That's all right. I'll be ready for the police when they come. As a matter of fact, it all fits in rather well. I stayed talking with some men until very late, and then we went on to Lyons Corner House—did you know they stay open all night? We had coffee there, and were just leaving when old Billington—you remember him, big chap who played footer?—came in, very, very tight. That was about two. I took him home; he lives at Richmond, and didn't get back until after three. Old Billington took a bit of putting to bed, I can tell you. Now, that's all square. Julian, I was at the—what's the name of the place? The "Bluebottle"—until after three.'

'It's damned good of you, Emmanuel. I'm frightfully grateful.'

'That's all right. I don't suppose that the Guv'nor will mind so very much or—' rather wistfully—'Angela either. Only,' he paused and hoped that what he was trying to say wouldn't sound abominably 'pi', 'only, Julian, remember that your initials are "J.E." and not "E.J.", in future, won't you?'

'My dear chap, you don't need to say that, surely!' Julian's tone was hurt more than offended.

'I know, I know. By the way, what about Walter Heriot?'

'Walter?' Julian dismissed him easily. 'He was too tight to know what happened. He'll never bother, and he won't split on me, because he hopes that I shan't drag the "Bluebottle" into the conversation next time I dine with his people. No, Walter's all right.'

Something in the glibness of his brother's arrangements jarred on Emmanuel, for the first time his voice was cold, his face lost its look of kindliness. It looked suddenly like the face of old Emmanuel when he found that someone had tried to sell him a fake.

'It has all turned out very well, then,' he said, 'it's obvious that Fate is entirely on your side, Julian.'

Julian smiled, held out his hand to his brother and said warmly:

'Not Fate, but a damned decent brother. Emmanuel, I *am* grateful. I shan't ever forget this. I wouldn't have asked you to do it, but it's come at such a critical moment.'

Emmanuel, still a little grim, said: 'I might just point out, that you *didn't* ask me, Julian.'

Again that brilliant smile, and that voice which was so sincere and so filled with gratitude.

'Dare I say that I knew that I could act as I did without asking, and without having even a moment's doubt that you'd see me through? Bless you, Emmanuel, I knew that if there was one chap who would do anything he could to help me, it was my own brother. Why it was almost the first thing you said, when you heard about this—beastly mess, wasn't it?'

'Of course it was.' Emmanuel felt that he had been mean, that he had offered help with one hand and taken it back with the other. 'I meant it too, Julian. That's all right. Forget it all, and leave it to me. I must be off. I have a man coming to see me who says that he has a Quare clock to sell. He's coming at half-past nine.'

Julian glanced up from his second cup of coffee. 'A queer clock? How is it queer?'

'Quare,' Emmanuel repeated, 'not queer. Good-bye, Julian, thanks for that excellent coffee.'

His brother sprang to his feet. 'Good-bye, Emmanuel, and thank you for everything.'

When Max Gollantz arrived at sixty-seven New Bond Street that morning he found a note from Emmanuel on his desk.

> 'Dear Father, I have gone down to Bow Street. Got caught last night in a low haunt! Nothing serious. I have bought a Quare clock, or at least paid a retaining fee. The chap wants a hundred and fifty, but think he will come down a little. E. J. G.'

Emmanuel returned, and Max spoke first about the clock. It was his rule that in 'Sixty-seven' business must come first, while at Ordingly, business must give way to every other topic of conversation.

'What about this clock, Emmanuel? Where is it?'

'In my office at the moment.'

Max rose. 'Let's see it.'

He examined the clock, Emmanuel watched his fine fingers touching it here and there, rapping it slightly, and yet with certainty; saw him take out his magnifying glass and examine the brass mounted dial and the hands. He turned, smiled and nodded.

'That's all right,' he said. 'I'll make out the remainder of the price. What did you give him as a retaining fee?'

'Fifty.'

'I'll send a cheque for a hundred. No, it's worth it. I don't want to haggle over a fiver. It's good, Emmanuel. My compliments on recognizing it. You're coming on.'

Back in his own room, the smile faded, and he sat back in his big chair, and asked for an explanation of what he called 'The Bow Street Incident'. Emmanuel suddenly nervous, not because he feared what his father might say or do, but because he was afraid that he might make some slip and betray Julian, rolled his 'r's' and stood obviously ill at ease. Max was puzzled. After all, to have been caught in some third rate night club wasn't a criminal offence. Boys did these stupid things and forgot them.

'What did the police raid the place for?'

'Dr-rinking, gambling——' he hesitated.

'Yes?'

'I don't know for certain—some rather cur-rious people there.'

Max screwed his face into a grimace of disgust. 'Unpleasant! You're not a member, are you?'

'Good Lord, no! I was taken there.'

'Oh,' shortly. 'Naturally I shan't ask—whom by. We'll leave it at that. Only, Emmanuel, I don't like cheap places, or cheap people; I don't like the cheap press who will announce that you've been in this business. Keep away from people who do like these things, and who like to mix with—curious people. That's all.'

'Thank you, father.'

'Any fine to pay?' Max's hand went to his pocket and his lips parted in a smile.

'Nothing that I couldn't meet, thanks awfully.'

'There wasn't,' Max hesitated for a moment, 'there wasn't any more to it than you've told me?'

He watched Emmanuel's pale face turn suddenly scarlet, knew that the eyes which met his faltered for a second before his son said:

'On my word, not a thing. Honestly, nothing at all. Just an ordinary r-raid for ordinary r-reasons.'

'Very well. That's over.'

But all day Max worried over that flush, over those eyes which had failed to meet his with absolute steadiness, and wondered if his own eyes had played him false. It was so unlike Emmanuel to falter, so unlike him to be anything but perfectly frank. The thing was over and done with, but somewhere at the back of Max's mind that little sense of disappointment remained, half-forgotten, and yet never entirely eradicated.

Julian saw his chief reading the *Evening Special* late that afternoon. Gilbert Drew looked up and smiled:

'What's this about Emmanuel? Not like him to shake a loose leg.'

Julian said: 'Yes, he told me about it this morning. Came round and had breakfast with me. That was what made me a little late. It's nothing. Might have happened to anyone. Just bad luck.'

Julian felt a wave of indignation sweep over him that Sir Gilbert should even infer a criticism of Emmanuel.

'Know the place?'

Julian shook his head. 'No. Not much in my line.'

'A damn good thing too. If this had been you, and not your brother, you'd have had all Harroby by the ears. Tell your brother from me, to watch his step. The town's getting too full of these damn fool places. Now they've got Montgomery at the Yard, they'll have to look out. Not only clubs either, but a few private places. I lunched with him the other day. He told me his scheme, briefly.'

Julian shrugged his shoulders. 'Emmanuel isn't likely to make a habit of going to places like the "Bluebottle". Last night was the old Harburian dinner, probably some chap took him along.'

Sir Gilbert went back to his paper and nodded. 'No, quite,' he said.

Julian, after Emmanuel had left, had taken out his pocket-book and found to his surprise and amusement that he had won seventeen pounds ten shillings at the wretched 'Blue-bottle'. It seemed to him to be astonishingly humorous. He twisted the dirty notes between his fingers, and decided that in common justice Emmanuel ought to get something out of it. As he made his way to the office, he walked down Piccadilly, and turned into Crinks, the jewellers. They knew him, for he loved to give presents, and was generous in the extreme. They regarded him as a young man of taste. It was a pleasure to serve Mr. Julian Gollantz, even though he might not spend enormous sums, his pleasantness was an agreeable thing to remember.

He leant against the counter, and suggested rather vaguely what he wanted.

'Something about a tenner—links, perhaps. Not modern. Something just a little—out of the ordinary. Old paste, perhaps. You know the sort of thing I want.'

They did know, they brought out a tray of old paste, links, brooches, rings—and Julian picked them over daintily.

'Ah!' he gave a little cry of delight, 'these are the very things. Links—and paste and rather—er,' he smiled, 'out of the ordinary.'

'They're not for yourself, Mr. Gollantz.'

Julian looked a little hurt. Crinks ought to know him better.

'Can you imagine me wearing them?' he asked. 'No, of course you can't. But they're just what I wanted. How much?'

'Seventeen guineas.'

Julian pursed his lips, then nodded. 'Excellent. Give me a card, will you, and send them on for me.' On the card he wrote: 'Thank you again, please wear these and please like them very much.'

Emmanuel showed the links to Angela two days later. 'From Julian.' The card he had destroyed the moment he had read it.

'How adorable! Just a little bit flamboyant, but you can wear them, though Julian and Bill never could. How dear of him.' She laughed. 'I suppose he thought that you, poor darling, had got a frightful wigging from us all for that silly night club business and that he'd—if not "gild"—at least "paste" the bitter pills that you'd had to swallow.'

'You weren't frightfully upset,' Emmanuel said. 'I mean—son of Max Gollantz, etc.—didn't shock you terribly?'

'My dear, no! Why should it? I believe I know how it all happened. As a matter of fact I saw Julian last night, he took me to see *That's the Way*! What awful rubbish too! He was talking about it. He said, and I'm certain that he was right——' she laughed, 'perhaps you told him? That it was the old Harburian dinner and that some lad—Julian said, "probably a little bottled", took you round there, and he said, "Poor old Emmanuel was just unlucky." He said that it was nothing at all, and that to make a fuss was only making a mountain out of a molehill. Just the same,' her face lost its smile, and her voice some of its lightness, 'I'm thankful that Julian wasn't with you. It might have gone terribly against him at Harroby.'

Emmanuel said, 'I'm glad, too, awfully glad.'

So the incident was over and everyone except Max forgot it. Max remembered Emmanuel's sudden, painful flush; remembered, too, that for the first time in his life, his son's eyes had not met his quite steadily. He tried to dismiss it, tried to believe that Emmanuel had been tired after a late night, worried to have been dragged into such a position, tried to believe a dozen things—and failed.

CHAPTER FIVE

THERE was nothing that amused old Emmanuel so much as to gather people round him. He said that all his life his business had dictated to him that 'things' must be his primary interest, and that only in his old age was it possible for him to enjoy 'people'.

His old friends, people who had been part of his life for the last fifty years, were necessary to him; but the company he enjoyed most of all was the generation which had grown up since he established himself at Ordingly. He delighted to gather Viva, his grandsons, Hilda Berman and Betty Reubens round him in his own room, listen to them talking, throwing in a word here and there himself.

Betty Reubens, who was studying for the law—a thing which seemed in itself to Emmanuel 'fentestic and impossible to be believed'—said that it was like walking into another world when you entered the old man's rooms.

'To begin with,' she said, to her father, in her clear and rather cold voice, 'the room is immense, and it's filled with nothing but the most marvellous things. You feel that if he has ever been ruthless over anything, Emmanuel Gollantz has been ruthless over his furniture and his pictures and his books. He must have thrown out everything that failed to satisfy him.'

Her father, Julius, nodded. 'Sent them off to the sale-rooms, I shouldn't wonder. He is intolerant about furniture and pictures.'

She nodded. 'I know. And then to find him in the middle of that huge, wonderful room, the most wonderful, beautiful thing in it. Velasquez might have painted him—Ingres could have painted him—Whistler ought to have painted him.'

Julius said: 'Pooh—Vistler! Say what you like—he's thin!'

'He could have painted Emmanuel Gollantz,' she persisted.

'Yes? And made a mess of him as he did of Henry Irving! No, leave it with Velasquez and Ingres, if you please. Go on, Betty——'

She laughed. 'The first time I was asked to go up to his room, I went with Emmanuel—young Emmanuel. His grandfather was sitting in a big carved chair, carved with roses and thistles and——'

'Charles II,' her father interpolated, 'cost two hundred guineas.'

'He sat very erect, his hands folded over the top of a stick with an ivory knob, his hair like silver snow—if there could be such a thing—his clothes were,' she paused and smiled again, 'unbelievable. He ought to have looked like something ready to go to a fancy dress ball, instead he looked like a patriarch. Frills, and a high stock, jewelled pins, and a huge bunch of seals at the end of a fob. Scented just a little more than was quite necessary, perhaps . . .'

'In Emmanuel's day,' Julius said, 'gentlemen didn't entertain ladies smelling of tobacco smoke, or the stables, or the last whisky and soda they had drunk.'

'I know, I know,' eagerly. 'I admit that the whole effect was admirable, wonderful. He made me feel that he had been waiting for me for eighty years, and that he might sing a—what is it?—*Nunc dimittis,* any moment.'

Julius sniffed. '*Nunc dimittis,* indeed! He's a Jew—and always will be.'

'It was a Jew who sang the first *Nunc dimittis,*' his daughter reminded him.

It was at one of these parties which he gave, that old Emmanuel noticed that Julian followed Viva Heriot about the whole evening. He watched them with a certain amount of pleasure. He had always been a sentimentalist, and the idea that they might love each other delighted him. True, he had never become used to the methods which the younger generation used in making love, he regarded them as crude, and often unpleasant. He disliked the free and easiness of it all; and he sighed for the days when young men in love behaved as if they only lived to alternate between anguish and ecstasy. He listened to them talking, and wondered why they sprinkled their conversation with terms of endearment as they did. Julian called Viva—darling, but he called Betty—sweetheart, and Hilda—angel. It was ridiculous, what words would be left when they really wanted to make love?

Julian and Viva came and stood by his chair, he glanced at them and decided that they made a beautiful pair. Julian was the most attractive young man he had ever seen. He wished that his hair hadn't been so fair. Fair hair, in a man, always reminded him faintly of Algernon. He wished that Viva's mouth wasn't quite so red—such a hard red too.

'Fifa,' he said, 'I am going to be rude, now. Vhy do you hev to paint your mouth so red?'

She touched her lips with the tips of her fingers, then examined them carefully.

'It's terribly good stuff,' she said, 'never comes off.'

'It's not a pleasant red,' Emmanuel objected, 'it's hard, ugly.'

'It's the new shade.'

'That's no excuse, though it might be a reason, for it being very ugly, my dear.'

Julian looked at her mouth, his head on one side, his eyes narrowed.

'It's—it's intriguing, grandfather.'

'Intriguing,' the old man repeated, 'thet is another of the qveer words you use. What does it mean—to intrigue? To kerry on a secret plot, to hev a secret love affair. Hev all the vords been put to new uses in these days?'

Julian said, 'A good many of them, I fancy.'

'Then, when you get into Parliament, we shell hear that you made an intriguing speech and proposed a delicious piece of legislature? Poof, what rubbish it all is! Read Burke—read Pitt—read Benjamin Disraeli, and you vill learn what words mean, and how to use them.'

'I have been trying most of the evening,' Julian said, 'to make Viva understand what certain words mean, but she's very slow.'

Viva shot a glance at him, and laughed. Emmanuel looked at her, thought how charming she looked, and laughed with her from a sense of sheer delight at her loveliness.

'Only t'ree words metter,' Emmanuel said, 'none of them very long. Don't be elaborate, Julian. Be simple, and then no one can misunderstand you.'

'It's not done that way now, darling,' Viva said, 'no self-respecting young man says "I love you" and "Will you marry me?". He waits until you're in the middle of the latest and most intricate step, and then offers you something that sounds like a cheap epigram and a crossword puzzle. You have to make what you can out of it.'

'Then you *did* understand?' Julian said.

Emmanuel said: 'Please go avay. You embarrass me terribly. In von moment I shall hear her promise to marry you, and it will be most disconcerting. Take her away, Julian—or Viva, take him avay. I won't hev it!'

Much later she came back to him, alone. The others had gone down to dance, and Emmanuel was alone. Viva drew up a chair and sat down close to him.

'You're not really any relation to me, are you, Emmanuel?'

His eyes twinkled. 'Or, I might say that you are—really—no relation to me? No. Grendfather by merriage might do, or grend-uncle by marriage, or somet'ing of the sort. Vhy, if you please?'

'I don't know. I wanted to know if I'd any claim, I suppose, on you and your time, that's all.'

He inclined his head towards her. 'All my life,' he said, 'it hes been my pleasure and my privilege to put my time at the disposal of any beautiful lady who esked for it. Now!'

'I'm worried.'

'About the new paint for your mouth?'

'Don't be absurd! No, Julian wants me to marry him, and —wait a minute—I believe that Emmanuel wants to ask me to marry *him*.'

'Ah!' He leant back in his chair, laid the tips of his fingers together and prepared to give the matter his whole attention.

'I like Julian terribly.'

'It is not possible to like anything or anyone—terribly. You might hate terribly, perhaps.'

'You must let me talk in my own way,' she said, 'or I shall never finish before the others come back. Please don't give me grammar lessons, darling. I do like Julian—awfully. There, is that better! But I do like Emmanuel—very, very much.'

'You don't by any chance—love—either of them?'

'That's what I've been trying to say,' Viva said impatiently, 'that I love them both, that's why it's so difficult.'

'You love both of them. You mean that you love neither of them.'

'I don't. I mean what I say. I'm not pretending that it's a grand passion—I don't believe that people have grand passions in these days. I've tried doing "Two on a Tower" and even that didn't really help.'

' "Two on a Tower",' Emmanuel repeated, 'Thomas Hardy? A dull book—what has that to do with this, please?'

'Not a thing, angel. You imagine that there are two people on a tower and that you must—really must—push one of them off. Then you know—if you play it quite honestly—which one you love best.'

'The better,' Emmanuel corrected.

'Very well, the better. I tried it.'

'And who was pushed off the tower?'

'Neither of them, because I knew that if I pushed Emmanuel off he'd look so terribly disappointed in me, and I should see his eyes as he went falling, falling down. I knew that Julian—well, Julian wouldn't be pushed off at all.'

'Then Julian—wins?'

To his surprise and dismay she began to cry. He had never imagined that Viva could cry. He had always felt that under all her charm, there was a hard little streak that would never soften. Now she had tears in her eyes, tears which did not stay there either, but which rolled down her cheeks, slowly and pathetically.

'It's Emmanuel's fault,' she said, 'he ought to have come and asked me to marry him. He is a fool! Then Julian came, and he is so amusing, and he's so ambitious, and he has a great future. Even old Dry-as-Dust Gilbert Drew says that—and I'm ambitious too. Oh, it's such a muddle. Julian's wonderful. You don't know how adorable Julian can be, Emmanuel. How he takes care of you, and considers all the little things that any other man would forget. And yet——'

'So you're going to marry Julian?'

She dried her eyes and looked at him almost defiantly. 'Yes. I think I am,' she said. 'Talking to you has crystallized things. I shall marry Julian.'

'I am very gled to be the first person to wish you every heppiness, and I do vish it most sincerely. Only,' he took her hand in his brittle old ones and held it very gently, 'only, Viva—for your sake, for everyone's sake, he qvite certain that—you vould, if necessary, throw Emmanuel off that tower or vatever it vas. Don't make any mistakes—they are too dangerous.'

'I know, that was what made me feel so miserable.'

'Von might—vait a little?' he suggested.

'I might, I might wait until after the election.'

'I should.'

'I will, Emmanuel. I promise that I will. But if, before the election I feel quite, quite certain, then I'll come and tell you.'

As she left him, he watched her go, and when she turned at the door and blew him a kiss he was ready to respond gallantly. When the door closed he leant back in his chair and sighed.

'She'll merry Julian at twenty-one, and at thirty, she'll wonder why she didn't merry Emmanuel,' he said softly.

He lay back and closed his eyes. He was tired, he had talked a good deal, and the room had been filled with young people. He had enjoyed it all, but now that it was over he remembered that he was eighty-nine, and that eighty-nine was a great age. How he detested this feeling of weariness. Sometimes he wished that it might all end, and that he might be done with this worn out body that was washed and scented and dressed with such care every day; shaved and powdered and barbered and manicured! Ridiculous to go on day after day—and yet, he shivered at the thought of old Reuben Davis who had died ten years ago. At eighty-four he had been a revolting sight to Emmanuel Gollantz. Like some neglected corpse, unshaved, untrimmed, and damned unpleasant. Never would he allow himself to look as Reuben Davis had done! Better suffer the boredom and the strain of dressing and shaving and all the rest of the ceremonial. He would get to bed and sleep and forget how old he really was. In his dreams he was never old, in his dreams he was still young Emmanuel Gollantz, able to do anything and go anywhere.

The door opened softly, and someone said in a whisper, 'Emmanuel!'

'Enchela, my dear—this is pleasant.'

His weariness had gone, he sat upright and hoped that his hair wasn't untidy, hoped that his shirt front wasn't creased. Mechanically he smoothed the folds of his great satin stock.

'I thought I'd just slip up for a last cigarette with you.'

He made an effort to rise. 'Let me get them for you. Your own special kind. I keep them in the table drawer when those children are here. They smoke anything, things they call "Virgins", but they're quite capable of smoking yours and never tasting the flavour!'

'I'll get them,' she said, 'then I'll come and sit down.'

He watched her, his eyes full of affection. She was the woman he loved best in the world. They were so much alike, he knew that. They had the same intolerance of stupidity, of cheapness and second-rateness. They had the same pride—a pride which had almost brought disaster to them both during their lives. They both loved Max, and Max's children, they loved Ordingly, and entertainments, and the upper seats at feasts and everything that stood for real success in the world. Not cheap gimcrack success, but the success which was solid and lasting and reflected credit upon their House, themselves and their children. In addition, they both had standards from which neither of them would deviate an inch.

Emmanuel had said so often—so often that Angela had come to know what the words meant:

'For the *shlemihl*, I have sympathy. The best plens of men may go wrong, no metter how carefully they are laid. But for the *schnorrer* who believes that he does me a favour by taking my money—Pah! It is my duty and my privilege to giff to the poor, but that giffs no man the right to treat my duties and my privileges as if he conferred favours on me.'

Neither of them discredited those people who failed, though they both felt that it was a pity that they should have done so; but they were as pitiless towards the man who had never made an effort, as they were towards the man who had succeeded by means which they despised.

'We're an intolerant couple, Emmanuel,' Angela had said once. To which he had replied: 'My dear Enchela, not intolerant of anything except low standards and leck of taste.'

Now, she lit her cigarette carefully, for they were a brand which Emmanuel had especially imported for her. His great-nephew, Menasseh Jaffe, who was a successful merchant in Egypt, dispatched them at regular intervals.

'Two pieces of news for you,' she said when the cigarette was burning to her satisfaction; 'the first, that I have heard from a lady for whom you had a great affection—Juliet Forbes. She sends you a great many nice messages which you can read tomorrow.'

'Ah, so! Juliet For-rbes—in America, vasn't she? She does well? Good. I am more than gled. And the rest of your news?'

'I believe that Julian is going to marry Viva.'

'That, my dear Enchela, is old news. I hev already heard this thing. You vould like him to merry her, or her to merry him?'

'I think so,' she said slowly. 'Though they puzzle me, these young people. They're so hard, so certain of themselves, so utterly lacking in sentiment. Did we puzzle you when we were Viva's age?'

He considered gravely for a moment, then said: 'I think that you did. I think that I used to say to myself that you lecked sentiment, that there was something hard in you, and thet you, too, were very certain of yourselves. I think thet every cheneration thinks those things of the one which follows it.'

She laughed. 'Probably it's what Adam thought of Cain

after that little unpleasantness in the field with Abel. I certainly can forgive Isaac for thinking it of Jacob in his dealings with his brother.'

'Has Julian told you thet they are betrothed?'

'Engaged, darling—not betrothed. Not definitely, but he hinted at it, and Julian usually is sufficiently cautious not to give hints without having some good grounds behind them. I'm very, very glad. A pretty wife, who was intelligent—and Viva is both—might be a great help to him when he gets launched on this Parliamentary career.'

Down in the big hall, Emmanuel was talking to Viva Heriot. He had watched her most of the evening from a distance, and now, at last, he was able to get a word with her. Julian was arguing with Betty, and Viva seemed glad enough to let him talk to her.

He sat beside her, with one slim leg thrown over the other, his fine hands clasping his ankle, his head thrown back a little, and his dark eyes very content. With Emmanuel, Viva was less sophisticated. She might discuss anything with Julian, but there were certain subjects which she knew that she could never mention when Emmanuel was her companion. Not that he was straight-backed, or 'pi'—no one loved fun better, no one was less censorious, but like his mother and his grandfather, there were certain things that offended his taste.

As she sat there, she wondered if she had not been quite wrong about her feeling for Julian. He was brilliant, he was amusing, he was going to have a great career, but when she was with Emmanuel, she knew that she was utterly and entirely content. She knew that with him she had a sense of safety. Emmanuel might be less obviously attractive, but he had enough good looks for any reasonable young man, or any reasonable young woman to wish for. She looked at him now and smiled.

'Nice to talk to you again, Emmanuel. You're always surrounded by so many people. People like you tremendously, don't they?'

'I don't know. Do they? Do you, Viva?'

She nodded. 'Awfully. I always have done. I expect that I always shall. But somehow—I always find myself with Julian and never with you. I wonder why? I believe that I like you better than I like him.'

His grave face lighted, his eyes looked back at her and seemed to smile.

'That's nice, awfully nice. I wonder if you couldn't do more than just—like me awfully.'

She nodded. 'I'm sure that I could.' She was certain at that moment, she knew that she loved this dark-haired man as she could never love his fair brother. She knew that there was something about Emmanuel that was—hers, and for her; knew that there was something in her that only Emmanuel could foster and force to grow. She went on, talking very softly. 'If you gave me a chance to know you, and didn't get absorbed in Betty and Hilda and half a dozen other young women who aren't nearly as attractive as I am.'

'What rubbish,' he said. 'Of course no one is as attractive as you are! As for "knowing each other"—we've done that since we were babies.'

'Oh, the people you knew as babies,' she said, 'aren't a bit the people when they grow up. The "you" that I knew when you were eighteen, isn't a bit the same "you" that I want to know now.' She added very gravely: 'Please—let me get to know you very well, Emmanuel.'

'Viva,' he sat forward, so that his hands almost touched hers, his whole face lit with happiness. 'Viva, will you marry me, will you promise to marry me here and now? You shall get to know me while we're engaged. Viva, I love you so much.'

She did not speak, but sat there as if she wanted to capture and hold the minute, as if she could not bear to make his declaration a thing which was over, as if she wanted to hear it still ringing in her ears even after his voice had ceased. Their eyes met, and Emmanuel knew that at that moment she loved him—loved him as much as he loved her.

Then quite suddenly someone laughed in the big hall, and Viva turned and caught sight of Julian, the light catching his fair hair, his lips parted and his whole beautiful figure making a picture which was arresting and—to her—disturbing. He turned and caught her eyes, and the laughter died from his own. He turned and came towards them.

Emmanuel said, 'Viva—quick before anyone comes—Viva.'

'I can't answer you now, Emmanuel,' she said, 'it's too

much like being rushed. Give me time——' she laughed, 'to get to know you.'

Julian reached them. He held out his hand.

'You mustn't sit here,' he said, 'you're wasting the last precious dance. Come along——'

Emmanuel got up and walked to the other end of the hall where his mother was standing. She fancied that his face looked white, and wondered if he wasn't working too hard. She would speak to Max. He was too young to have a great deal of responsibility thrown on to his shoulders.

'Tired, Emmanuel?'

'A little, I think. Not too tired to dance with you if you'll let me.'

As they danced, Emmanuel felt that his sudden feeling of resentment against his brother flickered and died. What a fool he was! Julian didn't know that he had interrupted—he didn't know that he had checked something on which Emmanuel felt his very life depended. How could he have known? He had only seen Viva sitting out, and had come and asked her to dance. It was ridiculous to feel angry or hurt.

'Let me get to know you very well, Emmanuel.'

That was enough surely. He had no need to feel apprehensive. She should get to know him, he would see to that! Next week, he mentally went through the hours that his business would force him to spend away from her. She had said that he mustn't 'rush her'. She was right, he wouldn't. He'd just see that there were plenty of opportunities in which they could get to know each other. It was going to be all right.

Angela caught sight of his happy face. 'Not so tired?'

'No—not tired at all. Dancing with you has driven the tiredness away. You're a wonderful woman, darling.'

CHAPTER SIX

ANGELA GOLLANTZ sighed. 'I knew how it would be, Max. Last year you wouldn't go to Aix, you wouldn't go anywhere except to that wretched and damned America! No cure, and here we are with you laid up. My darling, it's not a cold at all, it's liver, pure and simple. At least, not pure enough, that's the trouble. You forget that though you may be abstemious enough, you have generations behind you who ate Viennese food until they nearly died. I shall send for Bernstein.'

'But I'm all right. It's nothing, nothing at all, I tell you. I can't possibly lie up now. There's far too much to do.'

She came over to the bed where he lay, and with her forefinger delicately pulled down his lower lid.

'Guinea gold is a poor pale thing compared with your eyes, my lying angel,' she said. 'No, it's Bernstein and Aix, and you know it.'

Max sat up in bed and picked up the pile of letters that lay on the table beside him. He turned them over, and laughed scornfully.

Angela said: 'Don't laugh like that, Max—it sounds like some melodramatic and unpleasant animal at the Zoo. What are the *billets doux*?'

'The Mannington sale on Wednesday, then this stuff that Lord Lavington wants to sell by private treaty—that means a trip to the North and back—there's old Alfred P. Slater arriving by the *Berengaria* on Saturday. I must see him. You know what he means in solid cash. My dear, give me another fortnight and I'll go anywhere you like!'

'Give you another fortnight,' she said, 'and you'll be not only a very sick man, but unbearably bad-tempered. No, it's Bernstein or nothing.' She sat down on the edge of the bed and took his hand in hers. 'I couldn't bear to find after all these years, that you had developed a chronic liver—which always means a chronic bad temper. Be reasonable, Max.'

Max Gollantz, who felt that the whole range of his vision was thickly covered with black spots, sighed heavily.

'Very well, send for Bernstein. Only, if we lose thousands

while I'm away, you'll have to face poverty with me, remember that.'

'Better a dish of herbs with a non-liverish husband,' she returned, 'than the stalled ox of the Berkeley with one who shivers at the sight of mayonnaise!'

Bernstein came, and lisped that Max ought to have gone to Aix, as usual, months ago. He added that the sooner he was away, the sooner he might reasonably expect to return; and spreading his hands wide, with the gesture of an Eastern carpet seller, he smiled and went his luxurious and highly expensive way.

So it happened that for the next month, the time during which young Emmanuel had promised himself that he would see a great deal of Viva Heriot, he was forced to hold the reins of Gollantz and Son in his hands, and scarcely have a moment to call his own.

It seemed as if the devil took a hand in the business, Emmanuel thought. He had to go North, to see the Lavington collection, which contained a number of hideous things and three or four of real beauty. The morning before he left, Viva telephoned and asked if he would go with her to the first night of Henry Dudley's new play, and dance afterwards? Emmanuel said:

'I wish that I could, but I have to go North to Lavington's wretched place in Durham.'

'You promised to come to Dudley's new play weeks ago.'

'I know. The Guv'nor wasn't ill then.'

'I think that it's perfectly sickening, Emmanuel.'

'I think that's putting it very mildly indeed. I could use a good many words that fitted the case better, Viva.'

'Use them then!'

'And have the telephone cut off for bad language. I daren't.'

Then when he got back, Mr. Slater arrived; Alfred P. Slater who was courted by every dealer in Europe. He was the grandson of that G. P. Hewett who had given old Emmanuel his great chance many years ago. Slater, who looked as if he had just been dried and ironed by some patent process, whose face was decorated by the largest horn-rimmed glasses Emmanuel had ever seen, appeared to regard young Gollantz as his personal property. He spent hours in the showrooms and galleries, and then turning to his notes—of which he made thousands—would say:

'Would it be possible, Mr. Gollantz, for you to dine with me and then we might discuss this—er—matter at length, tonight?'

Emmanuel, who knew that however good business might be for his father's firm, they could not afford to let Alfred P. Slater slip, would agree. He would spend a long dull evening, during which his host talked of everything under the sun, but the matter on hand. He was thankful to see the last of Mr. Slater and his packing cases, when he bid him 'Good-bye' at Southampton, and returned to bank a huge cheque in London.

Once or twice he asked advice of his grandfather, and it was a relief to know that here was an authority to whom he could turn when his own judgement seemed at fault.

'A Bellini,' Emmanuel said. 'Who says thet it is?'

'The man who has it. He says that his grandfather served in the French army, under Napoleon, and that he looted it.'

'Who, if you please, looted it—this man or his grend-father?'

'You're pulling my leg, sir.'

Emmanuel chuckled. 'So is he, I fancy. I should tell him the story of the famous Rubens, and the man who cleaned it and found a portrait of Victor Emmanuel underneath it. However, rather than hev any mistake I vill come down and see it myself.' His eyes shone. 'Ve can't afford to let Bellinis slip as if they were—vere epples in autumn!'

He went down to Bond Street. It was like the visit of some old king, Emmanuel thought. Reuben Davis almost begged to be allowed to 'inform one or two old friends—in the antique trade' of the visit.

'No, no,' Emmanuel said, 'I can't have him tired.'

Davis said eagerly: 'It won't tire him, Emmanuel. Believe me, it won't. Let's have Arbuthnot, and Lane, and old Sir Augustus drop in while he's here, and he'll love it. Old Gus is seventy-eight, but he'll be here like a shot.'

Emmanuel came, the supposed Bellini was set up for his inspection and its owner stood by alternately smirking and biting his lips.

Emmanuel leant back and stared at the picture through his single eyeglass, then he rose and examined it through his magnifying glass. He frowned, he smiled, he nodded, and then pursed his lips.

'You hev aut'ority for saying thet it is a Bellini?'

'Documentary evidence, Mr. Gollantz, documentary evidence.'

'Ah! A letter from Bellini himself, I shouldn't vonder!'

'You will have your little joke——'

'This,' Emmanuel reseated himself, and leaning back, laid his finger-tips together, as if he were about to deliver a lecture at his ease, 'this is very pretty—delightfully pretty. But to say thet it is a Bellini, is foolish and almost—impertinent. Emmanuel, please attend. If you vere in doubt as to the painter of this picture, ellow me to explain vhy it might hev been—this or thet—but vhy it could neffer, neffer hev been painted by Giovanni Bellini. Now, this gr-reat painter liffed from 1430 until . . .' and so the lecture went on, giving particulars of the painter's life and methods, his chief works and where they might be seen; then passing on to pigments, use of colour, brush work and arrangement. Gradually building up a huge mass of evidence under which the unfortunate picture seemed to crumble and fall to ashes. 'This very pretty picture,' Emmanuel ended, 'is the vork of one—Carlo Verrocia, a pupil—not by any means the best pupil of the master, Bellini. I shall be pleased to offer you t'irty guineas for it.'

The face of the would-be seller fell. Emmanuel added hastily:

'And vateffer it hes cost for you to bring it here, plus your own out of pocket expenses.'

A few minutes later Marcus Arbuthnot—who had been born Abrahams—entered the offices and asked if Emmanuel Gollantz was really there? Then, assisted by his elder son, Sir Augustus Morris came, and after him fat, old Jacob Lane, who puffed and blew like the proverbial grampus and was very blue about the lips. Emmanuel greeted them all. Reuben had been right, the meeting did not tire him in the least. He smiled on them, had cigars set out, and ordered Reuben to bring in a bottle of Cliquot and another of the '54 brandy.

Jacob Lane looked at the champagne and turned to the brandy.

'Branty for me, Emmanuel,' he said, 'it's der ontly t'ing dot keeps me going.'

Arbuthnot smoothed his heavy white face with heavy white fingers and shook his head.

'Neither, thanks, ole man!' Emmanuel knew that he had learnt that expression from some actors in the 'nineties, when he was trying to acquire the method of speaking English like an Englishman. 'Hev you a drop of soda wat-ah? And—possibly a dry biscuit? Thenks, awf'ly.'

Emmanuel thought: 'Damn it, his accent is as out-of-date as his showrooms! Twenty-five years or more behind the times!'

Sir Augustus said: 'The Widow, for me, Emmanuel. No one calls it "The Widow" now, do they? No, well, it's good enough for me. Not any good for this damned gout, but I like it, and if it kills me I'll have it.' He lifted his glass. 'Glad to see you here again! Like to see you come oftener; we all should.'

When they had gone, Emmanuel lit his second cigar and chuckled contentedly.

'Nice to see them again,' he said; 'worth coming down for, even if I wasted time over the picture. By the way, that is an example of the foolishness of people. It's not a Bellini—it's true that it's a Carlo Verrocia—it's true also that Verrocia wasn't his best pupil. If it comes to thet, Titian and Giorgione were. But Verrocia is very goot, very pretty, very sympathetic. Only dese damn fool people only know about ten names of Italian painters, and his isn't one of them! T'irty guineas plus the man's railway fare! He neffer came in a train! Reuben Davis told me he came in a car, private car, und a chauffeur! Serve him r-right.'

Later, as he poured out the remainder of the Cliquot into his glass, he smiled again.

'They don't vear so vell, do they?' he said reflectively to his grandson. 'Lane's got a heart—only a physical von, and thet giffs him trouble. He never had any "mental" heart! Poor old Arbuthnot, with his silly accent and his liver! And dear old Morris—the best of them all—he's got gout and he doesn't give a damn. Emmanuel Gollantz is worth more—to an Insurance Office—than any of them!'

He flicked a speck of dust off the lapel of his coat, and settled his stock.

'Ring up Fifa and esk her if she vill lunch with me at one. Get me a table at the Berkeley, if you please, and tell one of the office boys to run out and buy me a white carnation for my buttonhole.'

Emmanuel reflected that all the 'office boys' were exquisite young men in beautiful coats, and sent the sergeant instead. On the telephone, Viva said gaily that she was lunching with Julian, but that she would put him off in order to lunch with Emmanuel the Elder.

'Tell her,' Emmanuel the Elder said, 'that she will hev *luncheon* with me—not lunch. Lunch is a thing you eat out of a paper pecket!'

As he was leaving, as the sergeant was putting a final and quite unnecessary polish to his curly-brimmed top hat, Emmanuel said to his grandson:

'Come in and hev coffee with us efterwards, if you like. At—shall we say—a quarter to two?'

He went and found them laughing together at a little table in a corner. Emmanuel detested tables which were in the centre of the room. Angela said that he knew he could see more from a corner, and that more people could see him. Viva looked up and waved to Emmanuel, and he came and sat down with them.

'Coffee, Emmanuel?'

'Please, sir.'

'Liqueur?'

'No, thank you. I have to go and see old Harrison this afternoon. I daren't do anything to muddle my brains.'

Viva said: 'Why do you all slave this poor child? For the last fortnight he's had his nose to the grindstone and not once have I been able to persuade him to lift it! It's disgraceful!'

Emmanuel looked at his grandson, and decided that he was looking tired; 'washed out' is the expression he applied to him mentally. Aloud he said: 'He's doing very well. To-night I shell write and tell his father so. This morning he dottet—no, vat is the vord?—spottet, a Carlo Verrocia, a very pretty one. I vas very pleased about it.'

'I never heard of the gentleman,' Viva said. 'Who was he? Some old college chum of Titian's or a playmate of Rubens?'

'Rubbish!' Emmanuel hated people to talk lightly about the great masters, 'vot silly talk is thet, if you don't mind? Vell, t'ere is no need that Emmanuel puts his nose always on the grinding stone. He hes a r-right to hev time for himself. He is his own master.'

But Emmanuel was an obstinate young man, and not a particularly far-sighted one. This was the first time that Max had left him in charge of the business, and Emmanuel, who was sensitive as well as obstinate, knew that his father had done so with a certain amount of apprehension. He knew, too, that ever since that episode of the 'Bluebottle' there had been a lack of something—he could never put a name to it—in his father's attitude towards him. It was as if some of the stability of his father's faith in him had been shaken. Shaken ever so slightly, but sufficient for Emmanuel, who knew his father so well and admired him very much, to be conscious of it.

He remembered the morning that Max had left. He had handed over his keys, and virtually appointed Emmanuel Regent in his absence.

'Thanks, father. I'll do my best with everything.'

Max had said, readily enough: 'Yes—yes, I'm certain that you will.' But the reply had not carried quite the conviction that Emmanuel had hoped for, and the little frown on his father's face had remained. His mother had said: 'Darling, of course, we both know that you'll do wonders. Probably make a fortune while we're away.'

As he had watched the train steam out of Victoria, he had turned away and felt a sense of acute depression sweep over him. Julian had promised to be at the station, and Julian had telephoned at the last minute to say that he was detained at the office. It seemed to Emmanuel that his mother was almost unreasonably disappointed, despite her assurance that 'it didn't matter a bit' and her repeated statement that 'after all' they were only going for a month. Emmanuel, for a moment, had it in his heart to hate Julian—not only because Angela cared so much, but because he had disappointed her. And Max—Max had said twice:

'Well, Emmanuel, do your best, won't you? Go steadily, and don't lose your head over anything.'

Now, at the end of a fortnight, he had never given a moment's time to anything except work. He had worked at the antique side during the day, and in the evening he had taken home masses of papers relating to the decorating side of the business. He had pored over them, and checked figures and estimates until his head had ached. He had been down at the workshops early every morning, interviewing old Mason, the master carpenter, and Steele, the old fellow who was said to know more about buying seasoned wood than any man in the trade.

In his heart, he had said: 'I'll show them. I'll show them both. I'll make father admit that he can trust me, and I'll show Angela that, in my own line, I'm just as brainy as Julian.'

It was not a particularly pleasant state of mind for a young man of twenty-two, and at times he hated himself for feeling as he did. It was entirely foreign to him to feel resentful, or to imagine slights or believe that people distrusted him. But he stuck doggedly to the line which he had mapped out for himself, and when Viva asked again if he wouldn't come and dance that night at the Embassy, he remembered that Mason had asked him to give his decision about a set of chairs which they were making for the Hon. Marjorie Bowman.

'She's one of the people, Mr. Emmanuel,' Mason said, 'who believe that modern craft's as good as anything that Sheraton or Chippendale ever did. Mind, I don't say that she isn't right. She's got out these here designs, and wants us to make them for her. They're half done, and now she says that she could have bought a set of Chippendale for the same money. I said to Mr. Davis: "Well, Mr. Davis, by her own telling modern stuff's as good, if not better—so why should she expect to get them such a lot cheaper?" Not but what they *are* cheaper, and by a very long chalk, Mr. Emmanuel. However, if you'll cast an eye over the time sheets and the cost sheets, you might be able to answer the lady to her satisfaction and ours.'

Those sheets must be checked by tomorrow, and Emmanuel, still with that sense of doggedly proving his worth to his father, said:

'I'm terribly sorry, Viva. I can't manage it. There's work that must be done tonight, I daren't leave it.'

Viva said, 'Oh, very well, Emmanuel, don't worry.'

All the way back to Bond Street, Emmanuel silently repeated those words, and the tone of them.

'Oh, very well, Emmanuel, don't worry.'

He wanted terribly to dance with Viva, he wanted terribly

to talk to her, and finish that conversation which Julian had interrupted. He knew that when he wasn't actually working hard, interviewing some dealer or discussing business with some client, that his thoughts turned automatically to Viva Heriot. Still—he squared his shoulders and settled down to work again, and decided that his father would be home in a fortnight, and that if Viva cared for him at all, she would understand and make allowances for him. She might even like him better for having stuck to his job.

For the next week he was fiendishly busy. Work seemed to pour into the firm, and everyone was working at top pressure. Max was returning the following Saturday, and Emmanuel glanced with satisfaction at his own private notes, and decided that on the whole the 'Regency' had been a success. On Monday, Lady Heriot telephoned to him and said:

'Manny, dear, are we never to catch sight of you again? It's dreadful! I used to look on you as one of my own special young men, and you've deserted me. What's the matter? Have you got a chorus girl in tow—or what?'

'Just busy, Aunt Beatrice, that's all. Father's away and I'm in charge.'

'Well, the shop closes at six, doesn't it?' Lady Heriot always referred to Gollantz and Son's luxurious galleries and offices as 'the shop'. 'Now, come along here and dine early. Half-past seven. We're all going on to the revival of *The Girl in the Row*. I was in the original show—second row of the chorus, Manny dear! There'll be some pretty fillies, some decent music, and the whole thing ought to go with a bang! Come along . . .'

'I'd love to, thanks awfully.' He thought: 'Viva will be there, and we can get away somewhere and talk, if the music of '98 proves too tinkly.'

'Right—half-past seven—here.'

At five o'clock he was putting his papers together; he had ordered his car to drive him back to Ordingly to change. The telephone rang. Reuben Davis said:

'Lord Matchingly here, Emmanuel. Long distance call. Shall I put him through?'

Emmanuel, who was feeling very cheerful, said cordially: 'Oh, damn Lord Matchingly! Put him through to me.'

Lord Matchingly had been born William Trent, and had

spent his life collecting everything and anything which had a value. His house in Lincolnshire was filled with what Max described as 'fifty per cent. junk, fifty per cent. priceless.' From time to time he saw something he wanted, and like Ahab, was unable to eat or sleep until he got it. At these times he would go through his collection and decide to sell some article of which he had tired, and with the money buy the new thing that had taken his fancy. He said that he believed in keeping his collection fluid. Old Emmanuel had always prophesied that one day someone would get something worth having out of old William Trent.

Emmanuel heard his voice over the telephone, dry and clipped.

'Ah—er—Matchingly here. Mr. Gollantz. Oh, not Mr. Gollantz. His son. Ah, his son. I have a—er—few articles here which I desire to sell—er. Not by auction, no. Sell privately. Silver, yes. George I cream pitcher, George III milk pourers—cows, y'know—cows. A pair of candlesticks—Anne. I want to sell them at once, at once. There is also a writing-desk. It's a well-known piece. I acquired it ten years ago. It's been photographed more frequently than any popular film star! I was in town yesterday and saw Arbuthnot. He wants to come down tomorrow and see these—er—articles. Then I remembered that your grandfather—yes, grandfather—did very well by me over a set of Chamberlain Worcester. I thought I'd give you the first chance—er—first chance. Can you come down tonight? I can put you up here for the night if you can't get back . . .'

Young Emmanuel set his lips firmly. Matchingly—his silver and his desk could go to the devil. He'd promised to go to this show with Viva, and he was damn well going. He was sick of Gollantz and Son, sick of living every hour of his day in the service of the firm. Tonight was his—and he was going to make the most of it. To hell with milk pourers, and desks, and candlesticks!

'You couldn't let it stand over until tomorrow, sir?'

'Arbuthnot's coming down tomorrow,' Matchingly chuckled, 'if he comes I can't let him go away empty-handed, can I?'

'One moment, please.'

He lifted his inter-house telephone and spoke to Reuben

Davis. Davis listened and made little noises of comprehension.

'The silver,' he said, 'it will be all right. I've seen his silver. About £22 the ounce. But the desk! It's that one that he bought from the Marquis of Raddington, y'know. Don't let it slip, Emmanuel. It's worth every penny of six hundred. It's been advertised like a face cream; it's had articles written about it, and Heaven alone knows what! Get it! It's a feather in your cap if you do. Old Arbuthnot will be as mad as the devil! Good old Matchingly!'

A feather in his cap—a really famous bit of furniture. Something that was worth going after. Max would be pleased, and would feel that he had been right to trust his son. If he didn't go, if he sent young Marchmont, Marchmont might get 'cold feet', might let it slip. Anyway, when Matchingly had given them the first chance it was only decently civil to send one of the firm. Viva would understand. Viva must understand. Only five more days and his father would be home, and he could spend as much time as he liked with her. Five days wasn't long. A 'feather in his cap!' He'd go. He spoke to Matchingly:

'Very well, sir. I'll start at once. I'll drive down. I ought to be with you by nine o'clock. No, thanks, I must get back again at once. Dinner? That's very good of you, many thanks.'

He rang up his aunt's house. Lady Heriot had gone out, but Miss Heriot would speak to him.

'Viva——'

'Emmanuel——'

'I can't manage this evening. I'm terribly sorry, but I've got to rush off to Lincolnshire. It's old Matchingly . . .'

'Like your friend Mr. Verrocia, I've never heard of him. You're not coming with us, then?'

'I can't, Viva. I want to terribly, you know that, don't you?'

Her voice was very light and rather hard. 'If you say so I must believe you.' There was a little pause, then, 'Julian's coming.'

'Julian's a lucky fellow. Tell him so from me! Only another five days, Viva, and my father will be home, then I can have more time to myself. You do understand, don't you?'

'Oh, yes. I'll tell mother that you're visiting the aristocracy in Lincolnshire. Good-bye, Emmanuel.'

CHAPTER SEVEN

HE HAD bought the desk, though personally he hated it, and thought it quite the most cumbersome and useless thing that he had ever seen. But it had a pedigree like a racehorse, and its credentials were unassailable. The silver was good. Emmanuel liked silver, and had bought the two George III milk pourers—in the shape of overfed-looking cows—for himself.

He sat in his father's office the next morning, and wished that he didn't feel quite so tired. The drive back had been cold and very long, and all the time he had imagined that he could hear the pleasant tinkling tunes of *The Girl in the Row.* That morning he had glanced at the morning paper, and had seen that the production had been a huge success. He wondered if Viva had enjoyed it, wondered if she had missed him, and wondered if she had danced all night with Julian?

Then letters came, and with them his father's efficient typist, Miss Rosenfelt, and he had dictated to her; and from time to time had answered the telephone and spoken to Reuben Davis about a dozen things. Hannah Rosenfelt had just gone, bearing with her a sheaf of letters, when Marchmont rang through to ask if he could see Mr. Julian.

'Why, yes, of course. Ask him to come up.'

Julian came. He looked very well, and very handsome. His clothes were beautiful, and his whole air was that of a man with whom life is dealing very kindly.

'Hello, Julian. No work today?'

Julian deposited his hat, stick and gloves on a chair, sat down in another and smiled.

'Not today. I have leave for thirty-six hours. Going down to Harroby to talk to——' he grinned, 'my constituents. The Government is going to come a crash very soon, next week probably, though they might hang on for a month. Old Barrington's a beggar for hanging on.'

'Have a good time last night?'

Julian nodded. 'Rattling good time,' he said, 'the old show was quite amusing—George Graves always is. Aunt Beatrice almost cried because he was in the original show, when she was a chorus girl. She said: "Look at him, not a day older—and in those days I daren't have spoken to him to save my life. He was lunching with Walter the other day, and believe me, I found myself saying, 'Yes, Mr. Graves' and 'No, Mr. Graves,' as if I was twenty again and earning three quid a week".'

Emmanuel felt that at the moment he didn't want to hear either his aunt's recollections or facts concerning Mr. George Graves. He wanted to hear about Viva.

'Good time afterwards?'

'Awfully good time. Lots of people there, too many really, Viva gave me your message, by the way.'

'Message?'

'That I was a lucky fellow. I agree, Emmanuel, I am, damned lucky.'

Emmanuel picked up a pencil and began to trace lines on his blotting pad. He felt suddenly very cold, felt as he used to feel at school when he was waiting for the starting pistol, or when he went in to bat and knew that things were going badly for his side. He knew that his hands felt numb, and that the lines which he drew were weak and uncertain.

'Oh,' he said, 'that's good. Yes, I suppose you are.'

Julian laughed. 'Go on,' he urged. 'Can't you guess why?'

Emmanuel laid down the pencil; it seemed of the most vital importance that it should be laid in an exact straight line with the top of the pale pink blotting paper. Then he raised his eyes and met his brother's steadily.

'I suppose I can,' he said. 'Something to do with Viva?'

'Everything to do with Viva!'

'You're engaged?'

Julian hesitated. 'Not quite,' he said, 'because she doesn't want it to be announced until the election is over. Says that if it was she'd be expected to come up and have a semi-official position. But, it's all right. Congratulate me, Emmanuel.'

'I do, very sincerely. I hope that you'll be very happy.'

It sounded stilted and cold, as if he were speaking to a stranger, but if his life had depended upon it, he couldn't have said any more.

'We settled it last night,' Julian said, 'only I promised that we'd keep it dark for the next month at least. If you tell one person, you might as well tell everyone. These things always leak out, y'know. I stipulated that I should tell you though.'

'Viva didn't mind?'

'Good Lord, no! She said that she'd known you all her life. Said that she felt that you were far more her brother than old Walter was. But then, she doesn't like Walter much. She does like you.'

'I'm very glad.'

Julian rose, he came and laid his hand on Emmanuel's shoulder, and when he spoke his voice was very gentle.

'Look, Emmanuel,' he said. 'I don't know if you were—half in love with Viva, yourself. I sometimes fancied that you were. If so, I'm sorry. It's—the fortune of war, eh?'

His brother looked suddenly very like old Emmanuel, even his voice was the same as he answered.

'My dear Julian, what r-rubbish. Half in love with Viva! Please don't ever allow Viva to hear you say such a thing. It would make her uncomfortable whenever we met. I tell you that I hope that you will be ver-ry happy.'

'And you won't mention this until we announce it publicly?'

'Of course not! Why should I?'

Alone, he went back to his big desk, and the huge chair which had been old Emmanuel's in the old days, and had been moved from Campden Hill to Bond Street. He sat there, his face in his hands, and wondered if anything was worth while? He had tried to make a success of his silly little 'Regency'—and where had it led him? He remembered that Viva had listened when he told her that he loved her, remembered that she had said:

'Let me get to know you very well, please, Emmanuel.'

He had done nothing because he believed that his duty was to his father and his father's interests. He had never thrown everything to the winds, and forgotten about time-sheets and price-sheets, and important sales and all the rest of it. He had thought that Viva would understand—and Viva was going to marry Julian. That was what came of sticking to your job and trying to make a success of it all. You lost everything. He rose and walked over to the great cupboard where his hat and coat were hung every morning. Max disliked coats which hung on 'pegs and unpleasant contraptions'. He would get out, drive back to Ordingly and walk in the woods and forget all about Bond Street and pedigree furniture and silver with a history! He swung open the door, and reached for his hat and coat. As he did so the door of his room opened and Miss Rosenfelt entered:

'The letters, Mr. Emmanuel, and Mr. Davis says that you won't forget that the sale at Bingham's starts at two, not half-past, will you?'

Emmanuel closed the cupboard door and came back to his chair.

'No,' he said, as he picked up a pen and began to sign 'Emmanuel J. Gollantz', 'no, I won't forget. Ask him to come here to me and we'll discuss the lots that we're interested in.'

Miss Rosenfelt took the letters and blotted the signature. She was a handsome girl of a pronounced Jewish type, clever, and loyal. Julian said that she was 'too friendly', but Emmanuel liked her manner, he liked people to be friendly.

'Nice signature, Mr. Emmanuel,' she said, 'but then you all have good signatures, haven't you? You all sign full names too. I like that. It's the personal touch. I always think that it's a pity that Mr. Davis signs—R. S. Davis.'

'He likes to remain impersonal,' Emmanuel said. 'I've never signed my letters with initials.' He smiled. 'Perhaps I'm a little conceited over being Emmanuel the Second.'

She smiled back. 'I should think so, and "John" isn't—well, it isn't exactly one of—our names, is it?'

'Our names?' For a moment Emmanuel was puzzled. 'Oh, you mean that it's not Jewish! I forget sometimes that we are Jews, y'know.'

Her heavy face sobered. 'Oh, I shouldn't ever do that, if I were you, Mr. Emmanuel. It's—well, I think that it's a pity to forget it.'

He nodded. 'Perhaps you're right. I'm sure that my grandfather would agree with you.'

So Emmanuel stayed, and went to the sale at Bingham's, and bought wisely, but without much interest. That night he went back to Ordingly and sat in his own room, and tried to read, and wondered if he wasn't a fool to work so hard? He wondered if his father would commend what he had done, and if that little sense of coldness between them would vanish? He wondered how soon Julian would tell Angela, and if Angela would be pleased?

He rose and laid his arms on the edge of the mantelpiece, and stared at the only two photographs of women that were in his room—his mother and Viva. The two women he loved best in all the world. The sight of Viva's face hurt him, her eyes, her mouth, the poise of her head. They were too vivid. These modern photographs were too real. Viva—and Julian. He turned to his mother's picture. Viva had gone, but she remained. Not quite all that he wished, for in his heart there was still that small wistful feeling that he loved her so much better than Julian had ever done, and that she gave him so much less—. But still, she was there, in his life, and that was something for which to be thankful.

He went back to his chair, and sitting there wondered how long he would continue to love Viva Heriot as he did now. Would he still love her when this engagement was announced, or would the first sharp pain have become dulled? What if it lasted when she had married Julian and they came to Ordingly? He shivered—Emmanuel was no heroic young man; he knew exactly what love meant, and what demands it made and where it led. He had no illusions that his love for Viva was a thing which lived on ideals, and sentiment alone. He knew that unless he could change his feelings for her, that the future might be not only very difficult, but even hideous. He loved her, loved her decently, and completely; with his mind, his soul, and his body. He saw no reason that he should be ashamed of his love. No one sentiment outweighed another, the whole thing was clean and natural. Facing this, as he sat alone at Ordingly, he knew that things must be very hard for him; that either he must drive out Viva's image by force; or realize that the future must inevitably hold hours of great difficulty, great distress, and with them, the almost unavoidable result that he would grow to hate his brother, Julian.

He thought of some of his grandfather's proverbs, English proverbs which he invariably got wrong, retaining the sense and losing the exact words. One of his favourites was:

'One nail will make a hole for another.'

That was where his salvation would lie. He must find something which would drive out Viva Heriot by sheer force, he must fill his hours, his days, so that there was no room left for her, and when that was accomplished then—and only then—could he feel safe.

Max and Angela returned to find Emmanuel willing to talk of nothing but business, full of new plans, and new ideas; or ideas which, as old Emmanuel said, were so old that they seemed new. Max, glad to be home, was still more glad to find that his son had attended so well to his business. Not alone for the profit and the advantages which he had brought to the firm, but because it re-established Emmanuel in his opinion, and swept away that last unpleasant taste which lingered after the affair of the 'Bluebottle'.

Viva did not come often to Ordingly, and if she came it was with her mother. Emmanuel imagined that she saw Julian in London, and that the fact that their engagement was not yet made public, made her dislike the idea of coming much to Ordingly and, as it were, meeting his mother under false colours. Of Julian he saw very little. The Government hung on, although everyone declared that they were on their last legs. Julian was busy nursing Harroby. Angela said that he was making a good impression, and that his chances were very good. Old Emmanuel asked who was her informant?

'His agent,' she said; 'a nice, rather common young man called Mainwaring. I met him last week when I was up there.'

Emmanuel snorted. 'It's his atchent's job to say that his chence is good. Don't rely too much on it. If he was fifty he'd have a better chence in Harroby. They distrust anyone under forty.'

Angela saw him, dined with him, and at intervals he rushed down to Ordingly for a night, but he pleaded Harroby as an excuse for not staying for week-ends. Both his father and mother agreed that he must neglect nothing that might go to ensure his victory.

Emmanuel had not seen him for weeks, until he walked into the office one Saturday morning in March. Miss Rosenfelt said, as she gave him his mail:

'Have you seen Mr. Julian?'

'Julian!' Emmanuel looked up from the letter that he was reading.

'Here at ten in the morning! No, where is he?'

'Talking to Mr. Gregson in the big office.'

Emmanuel laid down his letters. 'I'll go and catch him,' he said, 'he may be in a hurry. Giving Gregson some message for me.'

He found Julian leaning over Gregson's desk, his head bent, and he was talking earnestly. Emmanuel came up behind them, and as he came nearer caught the words:

'. . . marked "Private" or "Immediate". Can't mistake them . . .'

He said: 'Hello, Julian, this is nice. Haven't seen you for months.'

Julian turned, held out his hand and said: 'Scarcely months, weeks perhaps. I never have a moment these days, it's frightful.'

'Did you want to see me, or the Guv'nor?'

For a moment Julian's face was blank, then he said quickly:

'Oh, I wanted you to tell Angela, if you will, that I've managed to get the seats for next Friday, and that I'll telephone her tomorrow morning.'

'I see. Right, I'll tell her. Going? Not going to wait to see the Guv'nor? He'll be here in a minute.'

Julian picked up his hat and gloves. 'Can't wait. I have an appointment at ten and it's after that now. Good-bye, Emmanuel.'

Emmanuel walked back to his own office, and wondered why on earth Julian should have taken the trouble to come down in order to give a message which might have been telephoned by his man? He wondered, too, why he was talking to Gregson, and what the words that had reached him meant. Then he told himself that he was a suspicious fool, and that he was allowing his jealousy of Julian to run away with him. He turned again to his letters, and concentrated on them, so that he might drive other thoughts from his mind.

Hannah Rosenfelt said, 'Did you catch him?'

'Yes, he was talking to Gregson, thanks.'

Without any preamble, she said bluntly, 'I don't like Mr. Gregson.'

Emmanuel said, 'Why?'

'I don't know. Perhaps because he's—new, and gives himself too many airs. Anyway, I don't like him, Mr. Emmanuel.'

Emmanuel laughed, he didn't really care much for Gregson himself. 'Poor old Gregson,' he said, 'that's put paid to his bill.'

Then his suspicions grew again, and again he wondered what Julian had wanted with Gregson, and what they had been discussing so earnestly when he entered the office? He wondered sometimes if he disliked his brother, and if that subconscious dislike coloured everything? Then, thinking the matter over calmly, he knew that he didn't dislike Julian, on the contrary he liked him immensely and admired him tremendously. There was, perhaps, just a little feeling of jealousy—that was natural enough—foolish but quite natural. Julian had so much—and Julian was going to have more. He was going to have Viva Heriot——

Emmanuel pulled a catalogue towards him and made a determined effort to forget all about Julian, to drive everything away except work and business. He'd no right to be jealous. Not the least in the world. He had chosen to stick to his work, what he had been rather proud to call 'his job', and he had wanted the credit, and—he grinned—let the 'cash' go. Well, there it was! If he'd made a mistake, at least he had made it, no one had forced him into making it. Viva couldn't really have loved him, or she wouldn't have promised to marry Julian within a month of making that request down at Ordingly.

'Let me get to know you very well, please, Emmanuel.'

It had been just a fancy; a fancy that had come, and passed very quickly. The trouble was that it had only passed with Viva; and had remained with him. He couldn't forget so quickly. He couldn't find another girl who would appeal to him as Viva did—quickly he changed his mental phrase and amended it too—as Viva had done.

Then, with a certain doggedness, young Emmanuel pulled his little pile of catalogues towards him, and set to work.

Three days later he met Viva herself. He had been lunching with Reuben Davis at the Savoy. Reuben liked the Savoy, because his father had liked it, and he devoutly hoped that if he ever had a son, that his son would like it too. Half-way through luncheon, he said to Emmanuel:

'There's Miss Heriot over there with Mr. Wilmot.'

Emmanuel looked over and saw them. Charles Wilmot—who was a sort of second cousin—a K.C. and who managed to look like one. His hair had silvered early, and his clean-cut, keen face made people who didn't know him say:

'That man looks like a K.C. but probably he's a soldier or a sailor. People are never what they ought to be according to their looks.'

Viva was sitting with her arms folded on the table, smoking and talking very fast. Emmanuel felt that queer little ache at his heart that came so often when he thought of her, or looked at her picture. Reuben Davis watched him, and thought that the girl was a fool if she didn't take Emmanuel. He caught the waiter's eye, and even when he had paid the bill, Emmanuel was still watching Viva Heriot. Reuben moved, and Emmanuel turned and said:

'Not going, Reuben, are you?'

'Must,' Reuben said, and sought about for a fictitious engagement. He was a rank sentimentalist, like so many Jews, and he wanted to help Emmanuel if he could. Good fellow, Emmanuel! 'Must,' he said again with fervour. 'Have to go down to Charing Cross Road after a book that some friend of your father wants us to get for him. Sent Radstock this morning, but that fellow's no damn good at anything. Don't hurry, Emmanuel, see you later.'

When Reuben reached the door he turned back, and saw that Emmanuel was already half-way across the room. He went his way, smiling and feeling that he had 'helped things on'.

Charles Wilmot saw him first, looked up and said:

'Hell-o! Young Brummell, by all that's holy!'

Viva turned and met his eyes, and gave him back no answering smile. She only said, 'Oh, Emmanuel, what are you doing here?'

Charles said: 'Have some coffee—sit down—that's better. Hate people who stand round a table. I'm going, stay and talk to Viva.'

'I'm going myself,' Viva said. 'I've got to go to South Audley Street and I'm late already.'

Charles Wilmot leant forward and glanced at her coffee cup and smiled. 'Only half empty. South Audley Street! Rubbish, stay and finish your luncheon. He can drive you wherever you want to go. What are young men for? Good-bye, Emmanuel, my love to Angela. Good-bye, Viva. Thanks for lunching with me, I'm grateful.'

They sat facing each other, without speaking for a few seconds. Then, Emmanuel, trying to keep his voice very even, said:

'It was nice of you not to mind my knowing. I hope you'll be awfully happy, Viva dear.'

She looked up and frowned, then said:

'Mind you knowing? What do you mean by that?'

'About Julian and you. He came and told me the night after you all went to that show—what's its name?—*The Girl in the Row*. I haven't seen you since to offer my congratulations. I do now, very sincerely.'

She pushed away her coffee cup and took out a fresh cigarette from her case. Emmanuel leant forward and held out a match. His fingers brushed hers, and he knew that his face flushed suddenly.

'You're all very anxious to make me marry Julian,' she said, 'it's a sort of family arrangement apparently. You all seem to know much more about it than I do. You're all dreadfully ready to think and believe and imagine. The trouble is that none of you ever take the trouble to come to me! Did Julian say that we were actually engaged?'

Emmanuel hesitated. 'No, not exactly. He said that after the election you would be. He said that you didn't want to be dragged up to Harroby in a sort of semi-official position.'

She nodded. 'I see. It didn't strike you, oh, wise young man, that all this wasn't very irrevocable, did it? You never tried to carry your mind back to something that I had said to you about a month before, did you?' Her face flushed, and Emmanuel saw that she had clenched the hand which lay on the table; when she spoke her voice was sharper, colder. 'Of course, it's just possible that you didn't want to remember. You certainly managed to keep away from me after that night. I never saw you. I telephoned and asked you to dine, to dance, to come to a theatre. You were always too busy—always—always. People don't snub me twice, my dear Emmanuel.' Her voice softened. 'Girls do silly things, when they get hurt, don't you know that? But perhaps they never do such silly things that they can't—still leave the way clear that they want to follow. However, you were too busy, probably are still. I'm fairly busy too. Let's forget it and never think of it again. It's over.'

'But, Viva,' Emmanuel said, helplessly, 'Viva—are you engaged to Julian or not? Tell me. Don't get hard and angry. Tell me in so many words. I want to know, I must know.'

'Why?'

'Because it's the most important thing in the world to me.'

'Emmanuel,' very softly, 'I've been rather a fool. I've been trying to be rather too clever. Look, I'm going to cut this engagement of mine—the one in South Audley Street, I mean. Have you got your car here? Then cut your engagements and drive me out to Richmond and let me talk to you. It's the only way to get things straight. Telephone to the office that you're going down to buy the old Palace, say any damned thing you like.'

CHAPTER EIGHT

THEY neither of them talked much as they drove out to Richmond. Only once, in the Kew Road, Viva turned suddenly and said:

'There's Julian's car! What's it doing at Kew?'

'Can't be Julian's, he'll be at work.'

'But it was,' she persisted. 'I know it so well. That long raking bonnet, and the bright blue and black. I don't make mistakes about cars, Emmanuel.'

'Only about—other things . . .'

In the Park he stopped and they sat looking over the country and saw the river like a silver ribbon in the distance. Then quite suddenly, Viva began to speak.

'Listen, Emmanuel,' she said. 'I've made a frightful muddle, almost as big a one as you have made. You've been a frightful fool, my dear. You stuck to your stupid old work, when it would have been much wiser to cut some of it. After that night at Ordingly, I went home terribly happy, ridiculously happy. I felt that at last I'd made certain. You see, before, I never had been quite certain. I liked you both—only the trouble was that I liked you all the time, and I only really liked Julian when I was with him. I'm not sure that I mean—like, either. I think that I mean—love.'

'Then you do love Julian?'

'I always love Julian when he's there. When he isn't there, I just don't think about him. When he's there he carries me off my feet. He talks well, he makes me laugh, and he always seems to be taking pains to do and say and get everything that I want most. Then, after that night, you never came, you never telephoned, you did nothing—— As a piece of masterly inactivity it was superb, as the behaviour of a lover —it was absurd. Then Julian did all the things that you ought to have done. He called, he took me about, he telephoned, he was the ideal young man with hopes! That night, the night we went to that revival, I was furious. With you, Emmanuel, my dear. I loathed you, and I detested myself for caring what you did or didn't do! Julian asked me to marry him. I hedged. I've learnt how to hedge from my father. I do it rather well, or I thought that I did. I half-promised to be engaged to Julian after the election; and I—*not Julian*—said: "Please go and tell Emmanuel that tomorrow." You see, I thought that you'd have just enough sense left to telephone or come round or something. Not a bit of it. You say nice things to Julian, and leave it at that. Emmanuel, you really are the world's prize fool!'

'Then,' he said slowly, 'you don't consider yourself engaged to Julian?'

'I don't consider myself engaged to Julian, for the simple reason that I'm not!'

'It wasn't very helpful,' Emmanuel said, 'to hear that you regarded me as your brother—more of a brother than you did Walter, was it?'

'It wouldn't have been,' she said, 'if I'd ever said it. I never did. I may have said—once, years ago—six months ago, that I felt that you three would be much nicer to have as brothers than Walter. I don't like Walter, you know that. Listen, Emmanuel, out here, with no one to listen, I'm going to tell you something. Julian's tricky. Julian twists what one says to suit himself. Julian uses everyone. Julian only cares for one person—and that's Julian. If you could repeat every word that Julian said to you that morning, with the right intonations and facial expressions, I should be able to pull it to bits. It might have all sounded like one thing, and actually those things may have been said, but the truth was missing. And Julian meant it to be. I should like,' she said reflectively, 'to hear Julian in the witness-box with Charles Wilmot cross-examining him!'

'But I thought that you said you loved him?'

Viva lifted her hands. 'God give me patience!' she said. 'Emmanuel, my child, are you a half-wit? Apparently. I told you that Julian fascinates me—when he is there!'

Emmanuel turned and caught her hands in his.

'Look, Viva,' he said, 'half-wit and everything else, but it is just dawning on me that you tried to make me jealous, and that you were playing a hand on your own.'

'Certainly, on my own!' she admitted. 'You never tried to cut into the game, did you?'

'It's hard on Julian——'

'My dear, hard on nothing! Julian wants to be engaged. I'm very suitable indeed. Certain amount of money, certain amount of looks, certain amount of intelligence—very suitable for the wife of a rising young politician! Julian doesn't care two damns for me, except in that way. I'd be useful, suitable—I'd fill the bill. How often do you think that I see Julian? Never unless we're going out somewhere. Julian likes to be seen with me. At the theatre, at really good night clubs, the kind that have the very best reputations, of course—at private dances, that's what Julian likes. I've seen Julian once this week, when we went to the Marrats.'

'I think you're wrong about him,' Emmanuel said. 'I don't believe that's the real Julian. Not—the real man.'

She shrugged her shoulders. 'Oh, well, I don't care very much one way or the other. I'm rather bored with Julian.'

'What are you going to do?'

'I am going to allow this storm in a teacup to simmer down. I am going to tell Julian that I don't want to marry him. I never said anything except that I'd think it over and tell him after the election. All the definite engagement rubbish that he told you, is just another example of Master Julian's trickiness, Emmanuel.'

'And then——'

'And then,' she laughed, 'and then, when I've brought you out to Richmond a few times and talked to you and educated you, you may learn to ask me to marry you. It's going to take time, because you're very slow and frightfully stupid, but you'll learn, if I don't make it too difficult.'

Emmanuel suddenly realized that he had been holding her hands in his for a long time, he looked down at them and then lifted them to his lips.

'Viva, it's been such a hell of a time.'

'You ought to have trusted me, after what I said at Ordingly.'

'You meant that? You still mean it? You do want to get to know me—very well.'

'Please,' she corrected. 'I said "Please".'

'Do you?'

'Yes, please, Emmanuel.'

'Can I go back and tell them that we're engaged?'

'You most certainly cannot,' she said quickly. 'I'm not having Julian making capital out of this. I can hear him, telling Angela that I'd thrown him over, recalling a hundred things that I've said and making it sound so real that the family would cut me for ever. He'd rake up the old story of my saying that you'd make a much nicer brother than Walter, and give the whole affair a tinge of incest! No, my dear, in addition, I want to know you. I want to see that I can be taken trouble over. I want theatres, and dances and drives and dinners with you. You may have some hidden vice of which I know nothing. You may like parsnips—I loathe them—or sweet champagne, or a hundred things. Oh, work—I want you to work, but you don't work from eight in the morning until three the following morning!'

'But you do love me? Say you do, Viva. I've been so damnably unhappy.'

She slipped her arm round his shoulder and pulled his head down so that it rested against her cheek.

'Poor Emmanuel—and I thought that I was being so clever! I'm dreadfully sorry, I will make up for it all. I do love you—really, truly. I thought that I loved Julian, and when he went away I never thought of him again. But you—you stuck in my head, and you seemed to come in the middle of the night and say that you'd been so busy and I hated you for it, but I couldn't get you out of my head—never.'

He lifted his head, looked at her gravely, then bent forward and kissed her.

'My dearest,' he said, 'I swear that I'll be terribly good to you. I swear it.'

'Oh, I know that,' she smiled.

'And,' very seriously, 'I don't think that you're quite fair to Julian, you know.'

'No,' she returned, 'I didn't think that you would. All your family have a sort of Julian complex. He's the perfect person. They'll get a shock when I tell them—as I shall one day—that there is only one perfect member of the Gollantz family, and that is the man I am going to marry. Let's leave Julian, he's given us quite enough trouble for one day.'

They drove home in the half-light of the late afternoon, both of them content and happy; only to Emmanuel there came at intervals a faint sense of apprehension concerning his brother. He hated to think that Viva was right, and yet in his heart he knew that Julian had willingly made more of Viva's promise than she had intended. He knew that Julian had wanted to deceive him, and that he had succeeded. Viva had given a half-serious, half-laughing promise that—she would see after the election. Emmanuel knew, now, that it had been said so that Julian might repeat it to him, so that he might be roused to go and see Viva and demand an explanation from her. Julian had added here, and subtracted there, until the whole thing had assumed huge proportions and grave dimensions.

'We settled it last night', and 'I stipulated that I should tell you'. Viva had ordered him to tell. 'Said that she felt you were far more her brother than Walter was', and 'You won't mention it until we announce it publicly'. It didn't ring quite true, it left a nasty taste in his mouth. None of it quite lies, and yet none of it absolute truth. Even after that interview, how often had he hinted to his brother that he was going to see Viva that night?

'Going out, Julian?'

Julian had nodded. 'Yes, dancing. Must have exercise—besides——'

Emmanuel had asked his mother once or twice where Julian was going.

'He rang me up this afternoon,' Angela had said. 'He's dining and going on to a theatre. No, darling, I didn't ask who was going with him. I thought from the way he said it—that I could conclude that I knew.' Max had said to him several times:

'Julian blew in this afternoon. Great hurry as usual. I don't know how he does it. Dining, dancing and all the rest of it. Still, I suppose that he must make hay while the sun shines. If he doesn't some other fellow will.'

And now it appeared that he hadn't been with Viva, that he hadn't been making hay while the sun shone, at all events not the sun that shone out of Viva Heriot's eyes. Oh, well, Emmanuel mentally shrugged his shoulders, what did it matter! Things were straight again, he wished that Viva hadn't used Julian as her stalking horse, but evidently she didn't matter to Julian as much as they had all believed that she did.

'Julian didn't behave too nicely,' he decided, 'and for the matter of that, neither did I. I thought that she'd forgotten, that she hadn't meant what she said at Ordingly, and so we're all quits. It's over—and it can be shoved away and forgotten.'

He got home that night to find Angela worried and Max telephoning to London. Old Emmanuel was ill.

'Not,' Angela assured him with great insistence, 'very ill. Only a cold, but you never know, it might turn to this beastly influenza, and then it would be serious. However,' with great assurance, 'it won't, and we mustn't fuss.'

But when Bernstein came he was grave, and telephoned for nurses and the next morning among the 'Distinguished Invalids' was the name of Emmanuel Gollantz, and the statement that he was suffering from influenza.

Max, white-faced and worried, said to Emmanuel:

'I believe that my father will be all right. I'm afraid for Angela. She's never out of the room. If she catches it we shall have a nice time! My God, it's amazing to me that doctors spend millions trying to find a cure for cancer, and yet can't stop to discover a cure for—a minor illness such as 'flu.'

A few minutes later, he repeated as if the phrase brought him some comfort: 'A minor illness—that's what it is—minor.'

Max refused to leave Ordingly, and once again Emmanuel had to shoulder the business and carry on alone. Every morning Viva telephoned to him, and twice he was able to lunch with her. She was a great help, and she gave him some of her courage. He was miserably anxious about his grandfather, and hated to leave Ordingly behind him each morning. In addition, he had to sack Gregson. Reuben Davis came to him and said that he thought that Gregson must go.

'Thank God that he's a new importation, we're not used to this sort of business here. Everyone gets a fair wage—a decent wage—and when I find petty cash and the stamp book and a dozen other things going wrong, I feel that it's time the chap went.'

'Gregson, eh?' Emmanuel said. 'I never liked the chap. Too smart altogether. Too many new clothes. What is it, horses?'

'God knows! Dogs——' Davis chuckled, 'going to them in more ways than one! Will you see him?'

'D'you want me to? I don't feel much like it this morning.'

Davis nodded. 'No, of course you don't. I'll see to it. Want him to work the week out?'

'No, no. Pay him and let him go, we can't afford to keep men like that on the place. I'm sure my father would agree. We don't prosecute, of course.'

'No, that's never been either your father's or your grandfather's way, Emmanuel. The axe, quick and sharp, but no court business. All right, leave it to me.'

Later he heard Reuben's voice in the next room, firm and rather heavy, and then suddenly raised in anger.

'That will do, Gregson. I know your type. Lies and insinuations won't help you. Go along with you. Get out.'

Then the sound of a door banging and that was the end of Gregson. That night Emmanuel was worse, and his grandson watching his father's anxious face knew that things were going badly. Bernstein had been there all day, he remained all night. In the morning, as Emmanuel sat at breakfast, Max came into the room and said:

'Send for Julian, Emmanuel, will you? And can you telephone to Bill? They must come at once—at once. You'll not go up to town this morning, stay here.'

'He's worse, father?'

Max, his face deathly white, his mouth and nostrils looking pinched, said, very slowly:

'He's dying, my boy.'

All that morning the house seemed hushed, as if it waited for the entrance of some grim stranger, whose coming each one dreaded and yet expected. Emmanuel was thankful that he had something to do, was almost relieved at the difficulty of getting a trunk call through to Oxford. Julian came, and sat huddled in a chair, as if he were frightened of the thought of being in the same house with death. Once Angela came down, and Emmanuel was startled to see how ill she looked. Her youth seemed to have vanished, and for the first time he saw her as a woman who was not reaching, but had actually reached, middle-age.

She glanced round the room, saw them both and said:

'Bill isn't here yet?'

'No, darling. He ought to be here in under an hour.'

'He'll be too late then. Come with me, both of you.'

Julian sat upright in his chair, his eyes wide, his face twitching.

'Is he dying?' He shivered as Angela nodded. 'I don't want to come. I'll stay here. I can't bear the idea of death. Leave me here.'

Angela's voice was very quiet, very gentle. 'There isn't anything to be afraid of, Julian. He's quite conscious—he wants to see you.'

'Conscious! That makes it all the more horrible. I can't come——'

For the first time in his life, Emmanuel heard a note of coldness in her voice as she spoke to Julian.

'Very well, Julian. Come, Emmanuel,' then as they turned to leave the room, she said over her shoulder, almost as if she had been speaking to a stranger:

'If Bill should come, tell him to come up at once, please.'

The big bedroom was printed on Emmanuel's mind as if it had been photographed there. The long windows, the huge carved bed with its brocade cover, and its gorgeous curtains. The heavy carpet into which his feet sank as he walked towards the bed. His grandfather, propped up against the big square pillows. Emmanuel remembered that he had always said that the little English pillows could only have been invented by a nation of heroes.

He looked, as he had always looked—regal. His face was pale, but it had always looked like carved ivory ever since Emmanuel could remember. His dark eyes shone very brightly, and his beautiful hands were lying on the wide expanse of linen sheet. Only occasionally did they twitch at it, as if the old man had lost control of his fingers. To Emmanuel it seemed impossible that he could be dying—but then it had always seemed fantastic to imagine that old Emmanuel could ever die.

His mother went forward with him, holding his hand. Her fingers pressed his so tightly as to be almost painful. Max stood by the head of the bed. Emmanuel thought that he looked far more like death than his father. He stood perfectly still, his head a little bent as if he listened to every breath with fear in his heart.

'Ah, Enchela, you've come beck!'

The voice was weak but quite clear, Emmanuel went closer. Was this how men died then, speaking clearly and distinctly, looking as if they were merely holding a kind of family court?

'Vell, Emmanuel, hev you found annudder Bellini, please?'

'Not today, grandfather.'

Emmanuel nodded and smiled. 'But—maybe—tomorrow, yes! If not tomorrow—von day at least.' He turned his head towards where Max stood, 'Very clever, very clever—like you, Max, a good boy.'

He made a little movement with his hand, and Angela went forward and held it in hers. It seemed to young Emmanuel that she met his eyes and held them, and that in his grandfather's was an expression as if he was at once puzzled and at the same time almost unbearably tender.

'Dear Enchela,' he said, 'my two good children—Max and you.'

'Emmanuel,' she said suddenly, 'Emmanuel, don't go, you mustn't go. We can't live without you. Stay with us—Please stay.'

'My dear, it is difficult for me to deny you anyt'ing, but my time—' the words came very slowly, 'is not my own. My love—to you both—dear Enchela.' Then the white hand was lifted, and Emmanuel saw a nurse dart forward, and heard his father say:

'No, no—it's all right.'

'Hear, O Israel, the Lord is our God, the——'

The voice trailed away into silence, Emmanuel saw his father catch Angela in his arms, and the door opened and Bill came in. He stood for a second looking at them all, then turned and went out closing the door behind him very softly.

Bernstein touched Emmanuel on the arm. 'Help your father to take your mudder avay, pleth.'

Julian lifted a haggard face as Emmanuel went into the room.

'It's over?'

'Yes.'

'Bill got here. I sent him up.'

'Just too late.'

'I'm afraid that Angela was hurt with me. Where is she?'

'In her own room. Father and Bernstein are with her.'

'She's not ill, is she?'

Emmanuel sat down, and rested his head in his hands. He tried to shut out the recollection of his mother's face, white, rigid, and lifeless. The remembrance hurt him unbearably. If she were to be ill—if she were to die—and Julian should refuse to go to her when she asked for him— The thought was horrible, dreadful——

'She's not ill, is she?' Julian repeated.

A sob caught Emmanuel's voice, for a moment he sounded like the little boy who had sat white-faced and silent when his mother was ill.

'Oh, God,' he said, 'let me alone, can't you? I don't know —I don't know. She fainted when Emmanuel died. It's awful——'

He heard Julian get up, heard the door close behind him; he did not move, only sat there with his head in his hands. Then the door opened again, and someone walked across the room, and laid a hand on his shoulder. Bill's voice, calm and kind, said:

'Emmanuel, old chap, she's come round. Don't worry. Father wants us to go into town and bring Reuben Davis back, and some other jobs. I've got a list here.'

Once, as they drove into London, Bill turned and smiled at his brother. Emmanuel thought what a nice smile old Bill had.

'Don't worry,' he said again, 'she'll be all right. I feel that she will. Don't let's panic.'

CHAPTER NINE

EMMANUEL stood on the terrace, and looked over the wide fields towards London. Everything seemed very still, so still that the lack of movement, the absence of noise frightened him. He felt that Ordingly, and its trees and its fields, were waiting for news, waiting to hear news of the woman who loved it all. There was not a sound, the trees stood motionless. Early in the morning there had been a little wind, but it had died. Emmanuel shivered, and mentally changed the word to—dropped. The sky hung low over everything, heavy and leaden. No sun anywhere. Everything dull and grey.

Yesterday they had taken Emmanuel away. It had been like a royal procession. For the first time it had been brought home to young Emmanuel how closely his family were tied up with the Jews. It had made him realize once again that he, his brothers and his father were Jews, however little they might remember the fact. When big things—like death—came, they ceased to be Englishmen and went back to being Jews.

He had watched the cars arrive, one after the other, great monsters of mechanism, polished and shining. Each had carried its cargo of men, and most of those men had borne the marks of their race upon them. He had watched them enter, walking softly and carefully, because they knew that death still hung over the house. Death had taken old Emmanuel, and apparently remained unsatisfied. He was still fighting to take another of the House of Gollantz. So they walked softly, and spoke in whispers, as if they were afraid that Death might hear them, and turn and rend them in anger.

Old Morris, Arbuthnot, and Jacob Lane. Emmanuel remembered that less than a month ago, his grandfather had sat in the office at Bond Street, smoking a second cigar, and sipping his third glass of Cliquot, and had said:

'They don't vear so vell, do they? Emmanuel Gollantz is vorth more—to an Insurance Office—than any of them.' And here they were, waiting to escort Emmanuel Gollantz to his last appointment! There were the Davises and the Bermans, Leons and Salamons, Bernsteins and Cohens. There were the foreign contingent, who had rushed half over Europe to be present—Ludwig Bruch, Ferdinand Jaffe, and Ishmael Hirsch, whom old Emmanuel had forgiven and taken back into the family years ago because they had had the same grandmother. Moise, the great French dealer, was there, and with him a slim youth, extravagantly dressed, whose name was Louis Lara, and who was some relation of old Emmanuel's wife. Then there were the Englishmen, Heriots,

Drews, Wilmots, Wentworths, and Harrises, men who carried more colour in their cheeks than the pale-faced Jews, and who removed their hats when they stood in the house waiting for the procession to start. They had brought women with them, and the Jews had stared and wondered if the women would come to Golders Green or not. Bill Masters had brought a woman with him, and Emmanuel had stared at her and wondered where he had seen her before? Bill Masters had sat in a big chair, because his leg gave him trouble, and she had stood beside him and talked to him very softly.

Max had come into the room, white-faced and anxious, but master of himself. He had stopped here and there and shaken hands with his father's old friends. Old Isaac Berman and Augustus Morris had taken Max's face between their hands and kissed him, and Jaffe had done the same. Emmanuel had watched his father, and all the time had been conscious of the tall woman who stood by Bill Masters. Then Max had come forward and shaken hands with Bill, and said:

'Juliet, my dear, how very kind of you to come. This would have delighted my father. Thank you.'

That was who she was! Juliet Forbes, the singer. He had met her years ago, when she was married to a painter. Emmanuel couldn't remember his name, he only remembered that he disliked him intensely.

There had been a stir, and some of the men had trooped out, and had returned and whispered together in little groups, until a strange man had appeared and said something to Max. They had gone out and climbed into their big cars, and old Emmanuel had gone first, by himself, as a King should. It was all unreal and very strange. Emmanuel sat with Max, and Julian and Bill. They didn't talk. Max was too worried to talk, and Emmanuel wished that he could take away the iron band that seemed to have been clamped round his heart. All the time there was the dreadful feeling that they had left Angela alone, and that she might not be there when they came back.

Max said, once: 'Bernstein didn't come. He went back to her.'

Bill said, 'She's bound to be all right with him.'

Julian didn't speak at all, he sat staring out of the window, and bit his nails. Emmanuel couldn't remember that he had ever seen Julian do that before in his life.

It didn't take very long, and they were driving back. As Max got into the car, Emmanuel heard him say to Gibson, the chauffeur:

'Drive as hard as you can. I want to get back. There was no message?'

'No, sir. I never left the telephone, not for a minute.'

'Right. Get along as fast as you can.'

Back at Ordingly there were very few of them. Most of them had gone back to London. Max disappeared, and Emmanuel followed him and waited outside his mother's door until a nurse came out and told him that she was holding her own, and that he mustn't worry, but get some food.

They had sat in the library after luncheon, and Herbert Wolff, who was the senior partner of the firm of Davis and Wolff, read the will.

'Very short,' he said, 'so far as the general public are concerned. I have added instructions for the principal legatees, but they are embodied in letters, not in the Will itself. It is, perhaps, one of the shortest Wills ever made by a very wealthy man.'

Max was drumming his fingers on the arm of his chair, Bill stood by the long window and stared out at the misty gardens, Julian huddled in an armchair, and Emmanuel sat and watched them, thinking how queer they all looked in black clothes and black ties.

'Everything of which . . . unconditionally . . . to my two beloved children, Max and Angela Gollantz.'

It was over. Emmanuel Gollantz had given his last order, and retired from the firm he had founded.

That was yesterday, and today Emmanuel felt that it all happened months ago. This morning Angela was still holding her own. Julian had gone back to London, and said that he could be back in half an hour if they wanted him. He had seemed relieved to go, and Emmanuel, who had walked to the gate with him, had thought that his face looked less pinched now that he knew he was actually driving away from it all.

Bill was in the house, writing letters and dictating letters to Hannah Rosenfelt, and Max was where he had been whenever it had been possible for the last three days, at the door of Angela's room.

So Emmanuel stood there, on the terrace, looking over the land which old Emmanuel had bought, and wished that something might happen that would stop him thinking for a moment. His thoughts kept going back to the room where his mother lay; he wondered, speculated, and felt that his nerve was going. He longed to be a little boy again, to find his father holding his hand, and leading him down to old Emmanuel. He remembered the sense of security that had come to him as he had sat on his grandfather's knee. He wanted security now——

A little car had turned in at the big gates and was coming up the drive. Emmanuel watched it, and gradually his face softened. Some of the anxiety left it, and he looked young again.

The car stopped some distance from the house, and a girl got out and walked slowly towards him. He ran down the low steps to meet her.

'Viva, darling, how wonderful of you to come!'

'I wanted to come yesterday,' she said, 'but father and Walter both vetoed the idea. So I came today. Emmanuel, my dearest, you look dreadfully tired. Tell me—how is she?'

'Holding her own,' he said, 'that's all Bernstein will say. But it's touch and go—— My God, it's this horrible waiting!'

She held his hands in hers, and he felt the warmth and strength of them, and in a vague way they brought him comfort.

'It's going to be all right. I know it,' she said. 'Perhaps they'll have good news when you go back. Perhaps I have come just as the tide turned.'

'It's good to have you here.'

'Where's Julian?'

'He went back to London this morning.'

'He would!'

'Viva darling, don't be unkind. He is terribly busy.'

'Very well——'

They were back at the hall door, and Emmanuel hesitated for a second before he entered. Viva saw his sudden pause, she caught his arm and said very gently:

'Go on, go in and hear what they say. Don't be afraid. It's this fear that makes dreadful things possible. The only thing is—not to bring fear into the house with you. Be certain, be certain, Emmanuel.'

Max Gollantz was coming down the stairs. He looked very tall and rather gaunt in his black clothes, his face was very white, but his eyes shone and his lips smiled. He lifted his finger as if he feared that either of them might break the quietness, then came to them.

'Bernstein is satisfied,' he said. 'She's sleeping. She's slept for nearly three hours.'

A voice that Viva Heriot did not know as Emmanuel's said:

'Then she'll get better—she'll be well again?'

Max nodded. 'Bernstein thinks so, and Bernstein never says that he "thinks" unless he is certain.'

The tall figure of Emmanuel seemed to crumple, he sank down on the wide oak bench, covered his face in his hands and began to cry. Viva held up her hand when Max would have laid his hand on his shoulder, and whispered:

'Let him cry, it will do him good. Poor Emmanuel.'

It was two days later that Max came in with a face which was wreathed in smiles and said:

'Get on to Julian. His mother asked for him just now.'

Emmanuel said, slowly, 'Asked for Julian?'

Max clicked his tongue impatiently. 'Well, virtually. She said,' his smile became more assured, 'she said: "Have I missed the election? Is Julian in? It's months since I saw him." So get on to him, and tell him to come here at once. Never mind what he's doing——' Max exploded suddenly, 'I don't give a damn if the whole House of Commons has fallen into ruins. Tell him that he's got to come at once!'

Emmanuel did as he was told, and wondered all the time he was talking to operators and clerks and finally to Julian himself, how long it would be before his mother wanted to see him—or Bill?

Julian came. He flung himself out of the car and said that he had never dropped below fifty. Bill said:

'Even along Piccadilly? Marvel you are!'

Julian snapped: 'No, once I got out of London. Don't be a fool. Wait a second, there are some flowers in the back. I'll get them, I'll get them.'

Bill said to Emmanuel as they watched his figure disappear into the house:

'Fancy waiting to buy flowers for her! The damned greenhouses are bursting with them already. That's Julian all over!'

'She won't think of that,' Emmanuel said. 'Julian always knows instinctively what will please her, even when she's as ill as she is now.'

He was allowed to see her himself, the next day. The first thing that he noticed was how weak her voice sounded, the second thing that some flowers, which he felt certain were Julian's, stood on the little table close to the bed.

'Max says that you've been such a help, darling,' Angela said.

'Bill's been far more of a help than I have. Bill's a real tower of strength.'

'That's what your father says of you.' She smiled and he caught some of the old Angela that he had known all his life. 'Darling, tell Bill and Julian and Max—give them all hints, that I hate these black clothes. You all look like undertakers. Emmanuel would hate it. Yes, even yours, my angel, which are better than the others, because they look less—ordinary. Please come tomorrow wearing—your own clothes.'

He laughed. 'Don't remind me that I owe my tailor money.'

'Well, don't pay for those—make him wait.'

He sat and held her hand, and watched her while she dozed, and until she woke again; and as he sat there all his jealousy of Julian melted, and he knew that all he cared was that she should be better, and come back to them. Once again he argued that if she loved Julian best, it was her own business, and probably Julian was really nicer than the rest of them. Anyway, what did it matter? She wasn't going to die, and the world which held Angela Gollantz and Viva Heriot was for young Emmanuel a good place in which to live.

Gradually things slipped back into their old routine. Julian came down two or three times a week, Emmanuel went to Bond Street every day and took up his work again, and young Bill went back to Oxford. It was as if Old Emmanuel had disappeared into the night, and left nothing but his memory to them all. It had all been so swift, and over so quickly. To Emmanuel, it seemed sometimes as if he must return to Ordingly, and hear Max say:

'Your grandfather's back, go up and see him.'

Only Max never did say it, and Emmanuel knew that he never would, and that the tall figure, with its white hair and handsome pale face, had left Ordingly for ever. It pleased him to think that his name was Emmanuel, and that he was part of the great business. He was not a sentimental young man, but he took his work seriously. He believed in the firm, and was determined that he would never make any bargain, never enter into any business deal of which old Emmanuel might have been ashamed.

'If a men is either very rich or very greedy,' he had said, 'then pay him a little less then he esks, or a little less then the real velue of the article. Then you vill be able to pay der poor person just a little more. You are not a philanthropist, Emmanuel, but you may make odder men so, even if it's against their vill or vit'out their knowledge. In eddition,' Emmanuel remembered how his eyes had twinkled, 'it hes alvays been a popular t'ing to rob the rich to giff to der poor! A men vonce called me a "Highvayman". I said: "So! Then please Richard Turpin, a highvaymen, but a popular chentle-men".'

When Angelà was stronger, she talked of him to her son. He thought that never, not even when she spoke of Julian, had her voice been so tender.

'He liked a great many people,' she said, 'and loved very few. I thought that I loved Max until Emmanuel showed me that I hadn't even begun to understand what love meant. He not only loved, but he knew how to love. But when he loved you, that love carried with it great responsibilities. He expected you to live up to his standards, and his standards were terribly high, terribly exacting. If you loved, or told him that you loved anyone, then pride had to go, self had to go, everything had to go except your love for them—or he counted that you had failed.

'He was the proudest man I ever met. My mother always says that my grandfather was the proudest man she ever knew, until she met Emmanuel. She says that she had heard old Walter Heriot—your great-grandfather—say that one of the proudest moments of his life, was when some man repeated to him something Emmanuel had said of him. He said: "Men like Walter Heriot——" only of course, he said "Valter"— "are the salt of the Earth".'

She turned and looked at her son closely, then nodded. 'Yes, you're like him. Bill's like my people—fair and pink. Bill will get a little florid when he's older, as William has done. But you're like Emmanuel, my dear. Oh, Emmanuel the Second, do go on being like him! It would be so nice to have belonged, in a way, to you both.'

He said, very gravely, 'I belong to you, darling.'

'We belong to each other,' she said, 'that was one of Emmanuel's theories. He said that God made men and women, but they—men and women—made husbands and wives and mothers and children, and made them either good or bad.'

'Who is Julian like?' Emmanuel said suddenly.

His mother hesitated for a moment as if she considered the question.

'Julian is like——' she said and paused again, paused for so long that Emmanuel said:

'You're tired. You mustn't talk any more. Lie down and I'll come back when you've had a rest.'

She caught his hand and held it. 'No,' she said, 'no. I want to tell you. No one has ever asked me before—no one who —mattered. People have asked and I have said that he was like his grandmother's people—the Laras.'

'I remember—a lad called Louis Lara came here the day— the day you were so ill. French, and not terribly nice, I thought.'

'She married her cousin—Leone Lara. Her first husband. Algernon—I mean Julian—is like her.'

'Algernon?' Emmanuel said, 'why did you say that? It's not one of our names, is it?'

He heard her catch her breath sharply before she spoke, and felt her fingers close more tightly round his.

'It was,' she said, 'it was the name of Max's elder brother. Julian is like him, only much more handsome.'

'I never heard of him.'

'No,' very slowly. 'I don't think that any of us have mentioned him for years. He was drowned. Max tried to save him, and failed. Don't ever speak of him, darling. It would only hurt Max—and me.'

He left her, and carried away with him the feeling that she had drawn back a curtain which hid something very personal. Drawn it back, and then paused and decided not to uncover the picture after all. It made him wonder who and what this dead uncle had been. Made him long to ask questions, and hear the answers. Yet, somewhere, he felt that he had forced his mother to speak of something that she had wished to forget.

Two days later she mentioned it again. She was sitting up for the first time, and Emmanuel felt a sense of delight that her colour was returning, and she was losing the haggard look which had frightened him.

'Emmanuel,' she said, and laughed, 'it's uncanny. I feel as if you had the mantle of our Emmanuel on your shoulders. He was the only person to whom I could ever talk easily. Oh, I talk a great deal—Max says too much—but only about things that don't matter. I could talk to him about things that did matter, and I can talk to you in the same way. I want to tell you about Algernon. He was older than Max. He was very clever, brilliant—a musician, but he had places in him that were—weak. Emmanuel said that he was too hard on him. I don't know—but I know that he believed that if he had given him more love and less justice, that—things might have been different. Algernon left him, he went to Germany, and changed his name. I met him. I didn't know that he was Max's brother—and I fell in love with him. I was only eighteen then. He—he didn't want to marry me; but he wanted my love, and I ran away. I ran where I have always run to when I was frightened or unhappy—back to Max and Emmanuel. Then I married Max and we were wonderfully happy.

'Years afterwards Max met his brother—through some business. Met him in Switzerland. Algernon tried to blackmail Max and used some letters of mine as a lever. It was unthinkable, and still more unthinkable that Max—being Max—would care for any letters that were written before we were married. Max can't think on petty lines. There was a quarrel. Algernon slipped into the lake, and Max—who was lame then, as he is now, remember, jumped in and tried to save him. He didn't—and the letters came back to England to me. Emmanuel told me to burn them—and I did.

'That's the story, Emmanuel. I've never told it to anyone else except you. Even now I haven't told you quite all. The rest was when my pride began to come between Max and me. But—don't think that I love Julian because he's like the man I once—imagined—that I loved. No, that's not the reason. I love Julian because he is Julian. Like Algernon, he has so much—looks, talent, ability. I want him to wipe out all that Algernon did to lower Emmanuel's pride in the House that he founded. The type wasn't lost with Algernon. It's come again with Julian. Julian will put right what his uncle did that—was wrong. He's the vindication of one of Emmanuel's sons—or he will be.'

'You mean that Julian's future means a great deal to you?'

She smiled. 'All your futures mean a great deal to me,' she said. 'I'm your mother and I adore my sons. But Julian's future is tangled up in this House that I'm so proud of. Very few people know this story that I have told you, and those who do know it only know half of it. I feel that Julian—he's so different from the rest of you in looks, in temperament and tastes—is going to be able to make people forget. It's all rather muddled, Emmanuel dear—that's because I'm still stupid and muzzy, but if anyone can understand, you can.

'Then, Emmanuel comes into it. This is terribly private, darling. I never felt that he loved Julian as he loved you and Bill—and I knew why. I resented it. Julian was my son, and though we never spoke of it I always felt it. It was shown in such tiny things that no one could have noticed them except me. Emmanuel and I were too much in tune! It's not only the world—I want Julian to show what he can do—it's his grandfather—whom I loved and love so much. Say that you understand!'

He nodded. 'Yes, I think that I do. If I can ever help—I will.'

'I believe that I'm more a Gollantz than any of you,' she said, 'but you run a very close second.' Then her smile broke out again: 'I do like the Gollantz men, they are so nice, and so terribly good-looking. Good night, darling.'

CHAPTER TEN

'THE election's certain to come almost immediately. They'll only give us three weeks,' Julian said, his voice filled with excitement. 'Three weeks to do everything.'

'Or nothing,' Viva amended.

'It's not very long,' Julian continued, disregarding her interruption; 'in fact, it's not long enough.'

Charles Wilmot stretched his long length in a still longer wicker chair, and said: 'I have heard candidates say that before every election as long as I can remember. How long do you want?'

Viva laughed. 'Depends on how many novel lies you have in your bag, and how long it takes you to stuff them into the electors.'

'To hear you people talk,' Angela said, 'one would suppose, first, that you had done nothing but fight elections all your lives, and secondly, that there was no honesty in politics.'

'Is there?' Charles asked. 'My touching innocent, is there?'

They sat in the garden at Ordingly. Emmanuel had got home early and was lying on the short turf wondering if there had ever been such a perfect summer. Angela was better, Viva was staying for the week-end, the turf had never looked so green and the big trees had never seemed to give such delicious shade. He sighed with content.

Julian sat near him, smoking innumerable cigarettes. Julian was nervous these days, Emmanuel decided, and no wonder! Awful to have to face electors and to know that a wrong word here or there might cost you a dozen votes. Julian had asked Bill to stay at home and help him at Harroby. Bill had grinned in reply.

'Can't, thanks ever so much. I'm off to the South of France to read and bathe.'

Julian said that Bill was a selfish devil, and Viva retorted that Julian was just as selfish to want him to go and grill at Harroby.

Angela looked down at the long length of Emmanuel and smiled. She found that Emmanuel had grown very close to her lately. He had not taken Julian's place, no one would ever demand the same love from her that he did; but she had come to depend on Emmanuel more and more. During her illness he had been so tender, so thoughtful. In many ways he had shown more actual devotion than Julian. Of course, Julian was terribly busy, his mind was full of this coming election, and he had scarcely a minute to call his own.

She glanced towards Viva Heriot and wondered what Viva was going to do? At one time she had felt certain that Viva was going to marry Julian. They had always been together, they had danced and dined and gone to theatres. Now, the girl scarcely looked at him, and curiously enough Julian didn't seem to care. She decided that young people were beyond her understanding—and anyway, so long as neither Julian nor Emmanuel was unhappy—what did it matter?

Emmanuel raised himself on his elbow, and looked towards the house.

'There's the Guv'nor,' he said, 'wants something!'

He scrambled to his feet, and Angela called to him to tell the servants to bring tea.

'And drinks—and ice, Emmanuel,' she added. 'Sir Nathan never touches tea.'

Max stood at one of the long open windows, and called to Emmanuel to come in to him.

'Emmanuel, I want the key of that little chest of drawers. Where is it?'

'In the long drawer of the desk, father. I'll get it.'

'Wait,' Max said. 'I want that long gold snuff box. I want Nathan to have it. God knows, he deserves a crown set with diamonds for all he's done, but the snuff box will have to do instead.'

Emmanuel found it, and brought it to where his father stood with the little stout Jew, who was also a great physician.

'There you are, Nathan. It's quite pretty—not nearly good enough for you, but the best we can do.'

'My dear Maxth, how very kind.'

'And,' Max caught him by the lapel of his immaculate coat, 'let me tell you this, Nathan. I like you, we all like you, we're glad to see you here any time—but in future—without any of those nasty little professional bags of yours, please.'

'Pleath God,' Bernstein said gravely.

'But mother is all right again, isn't she?' Emmanuel asked.

Bernstein nodded. 'Very much all right, my dear fellow.

But—leth's fathe it! She had a bad time, a very bad time—touch and go! I never wath more frightened in all my life. Nothing organically wrong, and thath's a great deal to thay. But it's left her heart—not ditheathed, but weak—apt to play tricks on her. Maxth, old man, no shocks. Not that I think you go in for shocks here, but if anything of that nature comths along—lie, dethieve, do what you like but don't let it reach Mrs. Gollanth. And if she dothesn't theem well, no matter how much she proteth, thend for me!'

'Terrifying person you are, Nathan!' Max said.

'No, no, no,' he objected, with the old familiar gesture of his white hands, 'nothing of the kind. But careful, and very very fond off you all.' He turned to Emmanuel. 'Your grandfather gave your mother into my hands years ago. I refuthe to ever let her go. I brought all three of you into the world—oh, yeth, your father got panicky and thent for Lord Millward—old ath—kind, but an old ath—but I did the work,' he laughed and showed two rows of unbelievably white teeth, 'and he got the guineaths.'

Later, when he had driven off to London in his huge and hermetically sealed car, when Julian had disappeared into the house with Charles Wilmot, and Viva and Emmanuel had gone off to walk in the kitchen garden, where the strawberries were ripe, Max drew his chair very near to his wife.

She looked at him, raising her eyebrows a little.

'Yes?'

'Thank God, Nathan's finished coming here in an official capacity.'

'Poor little man! What an angel he's been, Max!'

Max nodded. 'Good fellow, stout man. I've a lot to thank him for.'

'Three very pleasant sons for example.'

'Oh, hang it,' Max objected. 'I'm not going to give him all the credit for the boys! You and I did have a hand in that!'

She looked at him curiously, then said, leaning forward and touching his temple with her fingers:

'You're older, Max dear. Older than you have any right to be.'

'I've lived through several concentrated hells during the last few months, Angela.'

'You'd have cared so much——?'

'So much,' he said very gravely, 'that I could never have

gone on without you. That's how much I cared. You're everything, my dear, just everything.'

Viva, standing at the entrance to the kitchen garden, caught Emmanuel's arm.

'Look!' she said. 'Your father watches Angela as if she were the most precious thing in the world. I wonder if you'll look at me so, when we've been married—what is it?—twenty-odd years?'

'I think it's very likely that I shall.'

'You're making promises a long time ahead,' she said, 'not the usual cautious young fellow from Bond Street, today? Do you love me?'

'I adore you, and you know it. Viva, when are we going to tell them all? Soon, darling. I don't want to wait for ever.'

'You shan't. Let's see Master Julian either in or out of the next Parliament, and then we'll break the news. If he's in, they'll all be so thrilled and delighted that they won't really listen to anything we say; and if he's out, they'll be in such a slough of despond that the thought that he can be best man and have his photograph in the *Sketch* and the *Tatler* will cheer them up. I think of others so much more than you do, darling!' She paused and went on. 'You know it might not be a bad idea to tell Julian the moment after the poll is declared. If he's in he can say, "—and what makes this occasion all the more delightful is that I have just heard that my brother, etc." and if he's not in he can say, "What perhaps gilds this bitter pill is the news that my brother, etc." Save the cost of announcements in *The Times* and the *Post*. Father is perpetually grumbling about hard times. And Walter, I gather, is applying for the dole on Monday next.'

'How is Walter? Haven't seen him for ages.'

Viva wrinkled her nose. 'As unpleasant as ever. I actually dislike that man,' she said. 'He gives me creeps. There's something desperately unhealthy about that brother of mine.'

Then, as if she pushed the thought of him away from her, she said:

'Don't let's think about him. Let's talk about ourselves and how nice we are, and how happy we're going to be. This time next year—oh, Emmanuel, where shall we live? Not in London. Just far enough out for you to get back quickly in the evening and not to have to leave too early in the morning. I'm glad that I'm going to marry a Jew—you are really a Jew, aren't you?—they're domestic people, and the husbands stay at home a lot. I read that somewhere, I forget where.'

'Jewish propaganda,' Emmanuel said, 'and anyway, I'm only half a Jew. The stay-out-at-night half might come to the top.'

She considered him gravely. 'No,' she said, 'I don't think so. You see, you're a man of taste, and you'll have married a most attractive young woman. Oh, what rot we are talking—and the strawberry beds waiting too! Come on, let's make pigs of ourselves before dinner.'

That night as Emmanuel undressed, he stood at his window and looked out on to the garden. The whole place was bathed in moonlight, the shadows stood out as if they had been painted on the grass. The tall trees stood motionless, like sentinels on guard. The air was warm and very still, and somewhere in the distance came the sudden call of a bird, wakened from its sleep. Emmanuel leant his arms on the wide sill of his window, and sighed contentedly.

What a night! Glorious and wonderful! He decided that he was fully and consciously happy. Decided that he could stand there and say:

'For this reason, and that and the other—I, Emmanuel Gollantz, am perfectly happy.'

Less than an hour ago he and Viva had gone out and stood there in the shadow of the big cedar. He had caught her in his arms, and she had lifted her face to his and whispered:

'Emmanuel—kiss me—I love you.'

They had stood there, and she had lain in his arms still, and utterly happy. He had known that under all her flippancy, under all her mockery of everything serious, her love for him was as real, and as deep as his for her. They belonged to each other—as Max and Angela belonged to each other. Years would not change them, and they might both face the future with assurance.

'You're mine, and I am yours,' he had whispered to her.

She sighed. 'I know—I'm so glad. Let's take great care of each other. Say good night here, Emmanuel—not in the house. This is all ours, the house belongs to other people.'

He remembered, and his heart beat faster at the remembrance. He was very glad that they should have made their declaration here at Ordingly, under the big cedar tree. It made them both seem to belong to the old house, the old trees and the old gardens with their yew hedges. This was where they belonged, this was where they would live and work and—die, handing it on to their children and their children's children.

He drove Viva up to London on Monday, and still the conscious happiness persisted. He didn't talk very much, but knew that he liked to know that Viva sat next to him, and that she, too, was sufficiently in tune with him to make words unnecessary. He dropped her at the corner of Grosvenor Square.

'Good-bye, Emmanuel—what a lovely week-end!'

'It has been nice, hasn't it? Good-bye, my dearest.'

'Busy week in front of you?'

He nodded. 'Fairly busy. Not so busy that I shan't be able to see you a lot, I hope.'

Viva laughed. 'Times have changed,' she said. 'I don't have to beg and pray on the telephone and then get—turned down for some silly old sale! Can it be that you're beginning to appreciate me?'

'It might be possible,' he said. 'I'm growing older and wiser.'

Hannah Rosenfelt was waiting for him when he arrived.

'I might have time to finish your letters before Mr. Gollantz gets here, if we're quick. There isn't a great deal.' She pushed his letters over to him, then glanced at the pad she carried. 'There's a Mr. Crowther waiting to see you—could you run through the letters first?'

'Crowther? Do I know him? He's not the fellow from Southampton, is he?'

'He says that he hasn't an appointment, but that he has something that he thinks will interest you.'

Emmanuel nodded. 'Let's get the letters done,' he said, 'before my father comes; then send him in.'

A few minutes later he handed the last letter back to her. 'There! Just in time, for there's my father coming in now, and that's the last! Send in this Crowther chap, will you?'

A moment later Mr. Crowther was shown in.

He was a tall, spare man, with a shabby overcoat and a manner to match. He had a face like a horse and not a particularly well-bred one at that. He wore a black tie, and a wide black band on his coat sleeve. Emmanuel thought:

'His old aunt's died and left him a dozen silver teaspoons and he thinks that they're worth the Earth—or perhaps an old print, badly foxed. I know this type.'

Aloud he said:

'Mr. Crowther—what can we do for you?'

Crowther took off his black bowler and laid it on the desk. It was one of Emmanuel's foibles that he hated people to put hats on his desk, especially people that he didn't know. He leant forward, picked up the hat, and said:

'Allow me——' and put it on a chair.

'You are Mr. Emmanuel Gollantz—Mr. E. J. Gollantz?'

'Yes.'

'You're of age?'

'Thinks that if I'm not, I can't offer him a price for his spoons,' Emmanuel thought, and admitted that he was of age.

The man opposite him stared at him, and for the first time Emmanuel was conscious that he hated his eyes. They were too small, set too close together, and they seemed to be trying to outstare him. They were faintly rimmed with red, and a little bloodshot. He decided that the fellow either drank or had some mania—religion, perhaps.

Crowther licked his lips before he spoke, and when he did speak his voice was pitched in a lower key, and the words came very quickly.

'My son died just over a month ago, Mr. Gollantz.'

Emmanuel bowed. 'I see that you are in mourning. I'm sorry.'

'He didn't use my name, he chose to change it, when he left home two years ago.'

'Really?' The man was a lunatic. Emmanuel wondered how much longer he would want to talk?

'He called himself—Wilfred Glaston.'

'Oh, yes——'

Crowther leant forward suddenly, the movement was almost epileptic in its violence, he bent forward so that his face was within a few inches of Emmanuel's.

'That name conveys nothing to you?'

'Nothing, I'm afraid.'

'And yet my son—may Heaven forgive him!—was your closest friend?'

Emmanuel stared at him. 'My closest friend?' he repeated.

'I'm afraid that there's some mistake. I never heard of your son, I certainly never met him in my life. Perhaps he was a client of ours?'

Crowther's hand went to his pocket, and he drew out a letter which he held out to Emmanuel. Emmanuel put out his hand to take it, but Crowther drew it back.

'No, no. Look at it, but you can keep your hands off it. I'm just as clever as you are, Mr. Gollantz. Because we're in a different walk of life, you mustn't assume that you can come it over me. Look at it. My son left this, when he died, in his writing-case. He hadn't posted it. Look at the envelope —marked "Private and Confidential"—addressed to E. J. Gollantz, 67, New Bond Street.' He drew the letter from its envelope, and held it towards Emmanuel. 'Read it!'

Emmanuel half-rose, and resting his hands on the edge of the desk bent forward so that he might decipher the small, fine handwriting.

> 'E. J. darling—won't you come and see me? I know that you're terribly busy, but I have this beastly cold. I must have caught it last week-end at Birchington. You ought to have closed the car as I asked you. You don't take enough care of me.'

Emmanuel sat down in his big leather chair, his hands on the arms, his face white, his eyes staring at the letter which Crowther still held out to him. The small, rather mean, but very affected writing seemed to dance before his eyes. For a moment he wondered if he was mad, or if Crowther was mad —wondered if the whole thing wasn't some ghastly nightmare, from which he must wake——

'Well,' Crowther said, 'that's written to you, isn't it?'

'No,' Emmanuel said, 'it's not written to me.'

'And the letters I have signed by you, written on the note-paper of this firm, they're not written by you either, I suppose?'

'No, I never wrote to your son in my life. I never knew him.'

'Then what do you advise me to do with the packet of letters, signed by you, many of them evidently written by you, that I have with me?'

'How many letters?'

'Roughly, about thirty. Some of them notes—some of them long and very affectionate letters. Some typed, but many written by hand.'

'Show me one of them!'

Again the horrible ritual of a letter being held just beyond his reach, again he half-rose and read the sentences, the ridiculous phrases of endearment; then sank down into his chair and covered his face with his hands. The writing was Julian's.

'Well, Mr. Gollantz, what are they worth to you?'

'Nothing—not a penny.'

'Was that tall gentleman who came through the outer office while I was waiting your father? I thought so. I wonder if I could see him, as the business doesn't interest you?'

For the first time Emmanuel lost his self-control. He lifted his ghastly grey face and stared at the man opposite to him.

'No, my God, you can't see my father—it's impossible!'

Crowther was turning over the letters, licking his finger and flicking over the pages; his eyes seemed to be searching for some sentence.

'Ah,' he said, 'here it is. Another name mentioned—disgusting! abominable! Walter. Now who would "Walter" be, Mr. Gollantz?'

'I don't know—I know no one of that name.'

'Reelly? Yet you say here,' he glanced again at the letter, '"I have always thought old Walter a bit of a fool, and I've known him for twenty-odd years—but this last——"'

Emmanuel said: 'I don't want to hear.' Then, 'What do you want for them?'

'Ah!' He leant back again and it seemed to Emmanuel that he prepared to enjoy himself. 'Let me make it clear, firstly, that I am not a common blackmailer. I am doing this because I feel that through such men as you—rich men—my poor, misguided son was brought to his grave. A dishonoured grave, you might say. I may look nothing much to you, but I am a man who is interested in a new religion—the New Translationists. I won't go into the details. To you, they would mean nothing. I require money to build a suitable meeting-house—a tabernacle. It seems to me to be common justice——'

'That I should pay for it,' Emmanuel said. 'How much do you want?'

'I demand—six thousand pounds.'

'Impossible.'

Mr. Crowther rose and picked up his hat, dusting it tenderly; he put the letters away in the pocket of his shabby overcoat.

'Very well. I must try to see your father. I believe that both he and your mother benefited to an astonishing and—ungodly—amount by the death of your grandfather.'

'You can't see my father. Wait!' Half-unconsciously he said: 'Six thousand pounds—six thousand——'

'Not an impossible amount, is it?'

'How long can you give me?'

'Twenty-four hours, Mr. Gollantz.'

'How shall I know that you'll hand over all the letters? How shall I know whether I can trust you?'

'I'm no common blackmailer, Mr. Gollantz. You shall have them all. I give you my word—take my oath. I'm a religious man—I know the full meaning and obligation of an oath.'

'I will see you tomorrow. No, not here. Yes, here. Come here at ten o'clock tomorrow. Ask for me.'

'Very good, Mr. Gollantz. Good morning.'

Emmanuel stared at him, his dark eyes were blank, his face expressionless, only his lips moved:

'Get out,' he said. 'Get out quickly.'

The door closed, he let his head fall on to his folded arms, and sat there trying to think. Julian—Harroby—six thousand pounds—E. J. G.—Private and Confidential. He remembered that he had heard Julian use those words that morning when he found him talking to Gregson. Julian had learnt the trick of using his name in the 'Bluebottle' episode. He hadn't forgotten it. Julian—and Walter. Viva's brother, whom she detested, but who was still her brother. Angela—a lisping voice saying: 'Lie—dethieve—only no shocks'. Six thousand pounds! He had perhaps two thousand of his own. Max made him a generous allowance, he had his salary—but he had paid a big tailor's bill, had bought a new car—two thousand at the most was all he had in the world.

He stretched out his hand and lifted the telephone towards him.

'Sloane eight seven six four.'

A man's voice: 'Yessir—Mr. Julian Gollantz—just leaving the house, sir. One moment, I'll catch him.'

Then Julian's voice: 'Hell-o! Emmanuel, yes, what is it? Me—you want to see me. My dear lad, I can't stop now. Just rushing off. I'm late as it is. Who? Who? Oh!—Come round here, will you? Very well—yes, I'll wait.' Then with something like entreaty, 'Emmanuel, for God's sake be quick.'

A few moments later Emmanuel walked through the office and nodded to Miss Rosenfelt.

'Tell my father that I've had to go out, will you? I may not be very long—I'll try to get back quickly.'

She rose and came over to him, her inevitable pad in her hand. Emmanuel felt a spasm of crazy amusement; if the place were burning down Hannah Rosenfelt would still pick up her pad. She kept her eyes on it as she spoke to him:

'Mr. Emmanuel, you're not well. What is it? Can't I help you?'

'I'm quite well—nothing wrong——'

Still with her eyes on the pad, and her pencil making foolish little marks as if she were taking notes from him, she said:

'That man—that Crowther. I don't know—— I wondered if there was anything I could do——'

'Nothing at all, thanks very much.' Then after a little pause, he added: 'I'm very grateful, Miss Rosenfelt. Tell my father that I've gone out, please. Good-bye.'

CHAPTER ELEVEN

JULIAN was pacing the room as he entered. He turned round, sharply, and snapped to his man:

'Shut that door, and don't disturb me. I can't answer the telephone, can't see anyone.'

'Very good, sir.'

The door closed, the two brothers were left alone in the room which Julian had decorated, furnished and designed to his own taste; the room which Emmanuel had always hated. He hated it now. He felt that he hated it, and its owner. Hated Julian's good looks, his fair crisp hair, his slim figure. He hated him.

'Well?' Julian said. 'Well? Tell me—don't stand there staring.'

Emmanuel said: 'Thirty letters of yours. He wants six thousand for them. Oh, you fool!'

'That dirty little bastard!' Julian almost spat the words from his mouth. 'That blasted half-wit! He always promised to burn them. Little underbred beast!'

'He's dead,' his brother said coldly, 'we'll leave him out of it.'

'Walter's to blame, he never let me alone until I'd taken—this Wilfred Glaston down to that cottage of his. Walter began all this——'

'And you went on with it?'

'Christ, don't moralize! What are we going to do?'

'We?'

Julian's expression changed, he looked blankly at his brother.

'You'll help me, won't you?'

'Why should I? You've done me sufficient harm already. How dared you use my name? How dared you carry on a filthy intrigue—the most abominable, degraded business—and hide under my name? It's unthinkable. It's—it's beyond belief.'

And as he spoke he knew that he was only marking time. He knew that in the end, he would stand by Julian, help Julian and do all that was possible to keep this from his father—and from Angela. He was talking—using words, words, words that meant nothing; he was saying things that were not true, things which he could never allow to become facts. It wasn't only Julian—Julian didn't count—it was his father, his father's pride, the House which old Emmanuel had founded, Angela, and that dead brother of his father, whom Julian resembled, and whose reputation Julian was chosen to wipe out by his own success.

Julian watched him, and Emmanuel wondered if he could read the thoughts which were in his mind. His face lost its look of desperation; if Emmanuel had been asked at that moment to describe his brother's expression, he would have said that it expressed extreme annoyance, nothing more.

'How much does this man want?'

'Six thousand pounds by tomorrow.'

'Have you got it?'

'No. Have you?'

'Not a quarter of it—about five hundred. Oh, I know that I'm extravagant! Can you go to the Guv'nor?'

'And ask for it for you? Why the devil can't you go yourself?'

Julian turned and walked up and down the room without speaking. Then he came back and faced his brother.

'Emmanuel,' he said, 'I'll admit that this business is damnable. God knows why I ever went into it. It's not my real line of country. Probably—curiosity! Frankly, I'm intensely curious about lots of things.'

'Sewers might stimulate your curiosity. They're pretty beastly, I believe.'

'Don't waste time being sarcastic,' Julian said. 'Listen to me. I'm faced with this election. I'm going to get in; I'm going, in all probability, to have an Under-Secretaryship in the next Government. I've got everything in front of me. I shall want money, money that my father will find, and find gladly, for such a purpose. He's proud of me, he wants to see me climb, and climb I shall. If these letters aren't bought, and bought quickly, it might strike this damned old blackmailer to hand some of them over—for a huge sum, to people who might be very glad to keep me out.'

'Out?' Emmanuel said. 'Out of where?'

'Harroby—Harroby.'

'I see—well, ask the Guv'nor to hand over the six thousand.'

Julian came nearer, and laid his hand on Emmanuel's arm. Emmanuel looked at the long, beautifully kept fingers, and wondered how in a few moments, every scrap of affection he had ever felt for his brother could have been swept away. He felt nothing, except a faint hint of annoyance that anyone whom he disliked should touch him.

'If I do that,' Julian said slowly, 'he'll want to know what I want it for. He'll suspect that I've got into some bother with the election, he'll imagine that I want to bribe someone up there. It would be impossible to explain. The Guv'nor is full of scruples, he still cherishes ideals about Government and Members of Parliament, about elections in general. I'm busy, I'm nervous, and I could never carry it through without giving myself away. At any other time, I might—not at the moment. I've not had an easy time lately. I suspected that—Wilfred hadn't burnt my letters. I knew that he was ill—then Walter told me that he was dead. It's been horrible—I can't bear the thought of death, you know that.'

'Yes, I remember.'

'Can't you go to the Guv'nor and tell him that you've got into some mess with a woman? Say what you like. Somehow, men don't think too badly of a chap who gets into a mess with a woman. Say that her husband threatens divorce, can't you?'

'I don't know,' Emmanuel said, slowly. 'I'm not a very convincing liar, you know.'

'My God, you're damned pi, damned self-satisfied, aren't you? You're the smuggest thing I've ever met! The biggest self-righteous monstrosity that ever walked! My precious brother, Emmanuel Gollantz!'

'That won't help you, Julian. I don't care, you see; that stuff doesn't touch me.'

'You weren't content until you got Viva away from me, were you?'

'Viva never belonged to you, and you know it. Anyway, let's keep Viva's name out of it!'

Then Julian Gollantz played his last card. Whatever was feminine in his nature came to the top, and he let it have full rein over him. He stared at his brother, saw the stern, pale face, which looked at his so steadily. He saw the hard line of his brother's jaw, and the cold eyes that met his with no hint of pity, with no emotion except dislike and loathing.

Julian sat down, put his face in his hands and shivered.

'You're right,' he said, 'of course, you're right. Why should you help me? I've not played particularly straight with you. I know that. I'll go to the Guv'nor—or perhaps to Angela. I'll make a clean breast of it, tell everything. I'll give up the idea of politics, and clear out. I shall have to do that. There won't be any room for me after the fiasco they'll believe I made of Harroby. Someone is certain to guess the truth. Men don't nurse a place for months, and then back out at the last lap, unless there's some scandal at the back of it. Either the Guv'nor or Angela will raise the money for me, and I'll pay this brute tomorrow.' He lifted his face and looked at his brother. 'God, it will kill her——' He caught his breath in a sob. 'I shall kill my mother! I know that I'm not worth it, but she does love me, Emmanuel. She's counted so much on this election. The first thing she said, d'you remember? "Have I missed the election? Is Julian in?" Only yesterday the Guv'nor told me about Nathan. He said: "So no more ditching your car and coming in covered with blood and mud. Not even if it's only from bramble scratches." Now, oh, my God—I can't bear it! What an end to it all!'

Emmanuel watched him and thought:

'It's come, the moment that I was waiting for. It's here and I've got to face it. Whatever I did, she wouldn't care so much. It's not only that she loves Julian—it's what Julian stands for. She told me—Algernon and his story. I promised that I'd do anything I could. She knew that I meant I'd stand by Julian if ever he needed it. It won't hurt me so much. I'm not going to be a public man. I'm only in the firm. No one will know. With Julian it might leak out and finish him. She needn't know. My father need never tell her. Anyway, she won't be so hurt, whatever happens, as she would be if it were Julian.'

Aloud, he said: 'Very well, Julian. Leave it to me. I'll try to lie for my own sake.'

'You mean that?'

'Yes—only remember that I'm doing nothing for you. Nothing! I never want to see you again, or hear from you. I loathe you. This isn't the first time that you've dragged me into a mess of yours. You lied then, you lied over Viva, and you've lied all through this filthy little intrigue with this wretched dead man! You're ready to sneer at Walter—whatever he is, and I suspect pretty well what that is—you're no better. Damn you—damn your soul, Julian. After this you can rot in hell for all I care. It's not being done for you. It's being done for two women—one's my mother, and the other —I—was—going to marry.'

He watched Julian's nostrils whiten, watched his mouth harden, and his hands clench. He waited for him to speak.

'I see,' Julian said. 'I see. It doesn't strike you that as the letters are all addressed to me—or the ones that Crowther has—are addressed to me as "E. J. Gollantz" and sent to "67" —that all mine are signed "E.J."—that it might be just a little difficult to make the Guv'nor believe that the culprit wasn't you? Crowther never set eyes on either of us until this morning, Wilfred's dead, and you don't know—the other fellows, do you? Oh, you needn't look knowing and think Walter would tell, because Walter wouldn't say a damned thing. Walter's in it up to his neck, and he won't talk. No, Emmanuel, it's all right, but it wouldn't be so easy to push it all on to me, after all, would it? Even my writing isn't so unlike yours, is it? And, I never used, quite, my ordinary hand when I wrote injudicious letters.'

Emmanuel licked his lips: 'You swine!'

'Perhaps—well, we won't go on. You'll manage it, not for my sake but for the sake of—what was your expression—two women? Just a hint of melodrama about you, isn't there?'

'Julian,' Emmanuel spoke coldly, but his eyes filled Julian with a sudden fear. At the moment he looked like his grandfather, tall and very dignified: 'You're not in a sufficiently strong position to use words carelessly. I might decide that—after all it wasn't worth it. I might decide that it was not my duty to interfere with justice. Admitted that it might not be easy to prove that I did not write those letters, it's still not quite impossible. Be careful, Julian.'

The answer came at once. Julian's whole aspect changed, his face lost its look of imperious disdain; he was a worried, anxious young man again.

'Forgive me—I had no right to speak as I did. Emmanuel, don't you think that I realize how good you're being to me? Do you think that, but for Angela, I'd allow you to do this for me? You know that I shouldn't! It's terrible that I should be forced to let you make such a sacrifice for me, and no one except me will ever know what a sacrifice it is. You're quite literally saving my life——'

'I'm not sure that it's worth saving,' Emmanuel said. 'It's not your life that concerns me, believe that. Whatever I'm going to be, I don't want you to be under any misapprehension on that point. After today, I'll never willingly speak to you again.'

Julian bowed his head. 'Very well. I'm sorry, because I'm very fond of you, Emmanuel.'

'Yes? You've certainly proved it—up to the hilt.'

'You give with one hand and take away with the other, don't you?'

'I'm giving you nothing—nothing. I'm not even giving you what is called another chance. I don't care what you do after this. You're nothing to me, I tell you. I'm doing this for my own satisfaction, not for yours. If only you were concerned—— My God! you could manage the whole business alone! Don't flatter yourself that I'm doing this because you're my brother, or from motives of affection. I've told you—I don't care a damn for you, or what becomes of you. That's all!'

He turned to go, but Julian rushed forward and flung himself in front of the bright scarlet door, his arms spread wide.

'Emmanuel, wait! What are you going to say, what are you going to do? You must tell me. I must know . . .'

'I am going to let them assume that I am the "E. J. G." who wrote those letters. That's all that concerns you. Let me pass——'

'I'll do anything that I can——'

'You can do—nothing. Let me pass, Julian.'

Julian stood to one side and Emmanuel, without another word, without looking at him again, passed out of the room and let himself out. He hailed a taxi, ordered the man to drive to Old Bond Street, then leant back and tried to think. His hands shook as he lit a cigarette; he knew that he felt shaken and weak, and that his brain seemed scarcely to grasp what lay before him. He must see his father—he would try to conceal the real facts—he might do as Julian suggested and try to pretend that a woman was the cause of his needing the money. He doubted if he could make it sound convincing. He had said that he wasn't a good liar, and he meant it. It was difficult to lie to his father. Max Gollantz boasted that men never told him lies, because he never believed that they either could or would lie to him. Emmanuel knew how keen his father's eyes were, how they looked you directly in the face, and how under all their keenness was a great kindliness and gentleness. It was going to be terribly difficult.

He got out and walked through the big office feeling like a man who walks to the scaffold. Things were never going to be the same again. He was going to shatter his father's faith in him, and his father's trust had meant a great deal to Emmanuel.

He felt no feeling of nobility, no wish to protect his brother. He felt that the whole thing was degrading and disgusting, knew that he hated Julian, and that he shared Viva's dislike of Walter Heriot. To Emmanuel, those two men had become monsters, degenerate things which were outside the pale of decent men and women. Julian had talked of—curiosity. Curiosity! The very cold-bloodedness of it made Emmanuel feel sick! He knew that if Julian had even spoken of love and affection he could have felt more kindly towards him. Even a love which was outside his understanding, would have made him feel less revulsion than that cold declaration that his actions had been prompted by curiosity.

He knocked on the door which bore Max's name, and heard his father call in reply:

'Come in.'

He was alone, busy with some long letter which he was reading. Emmanuel noticed that he always wore glasses now when he read, noticed too how grey his hair had turned in the last two months, and how much deeper the lines at the corners of his mouth had grown. He felt a great sense of pity for his father. He was going to hurt him intolerably, and—he had suffered enough already.

'Can you spare me a few minutes, father?'

Max laid down the letter. 'Why, yes, with pleasure. This is a dull letter from a stupid fellow who thinks that he has found something which is as stupid as himself—some first edition of Shakespeare, written before Shakespeare was ever heard of! There are a lot of fools in the world, I could forgive them if they didn't want to bore me with their folly. Yes, Emmanuel, sit down and make me forget this idiot!'

'I don't know that what I have got to say will please you very much, father. I've come to ask for some money.'

Max smiled: 'Tailors or motor manufacturers, which? I don't suppose it's a hanging job, is it? How much?'

'It's a good deal,' Emmanuel said, and when his father smiled at him with his eyebrows lifted in half-quizzical surprise, he felt that he wanted to sit down and tell him the truth and beg for Julian. He couldn't bear to hurt this man whom he loved so much, and respected so tremendously. 'It's—six thousand pounds.'

'My dear boy, you're joking!'

'I wish that I were, father. That's the amount.'

The smile vanished, Max pointed to a chair, and said:

'Sit down. Now, let's have the truth about this. Don't

be afraid to tell me. It's perhaps something that we can straighten out. But six thousand is a lot of money, and the Death Duties have hit me fairly hard. Now, tell me. Is it a woman?'

Emmanuel clutched at the straw that his father offered.

'Yes.'

'Married?'

'Yes, father.'

'I don't like that very much. Can't you tell me more about it. Is the husband threatening divorce? He is. Don't you love her? I mean—you don't want to marry her? No? This isn't pretty, Emmanuel. I don't like it. I don't want a woman dragged through the divorce courts because of you, and then you don't want to marry her. Come along, let's have the whole story.'

'I want to buy back some letters.' Emmanuel knew that his voice did not sound convincing, and felt that the uncertainty reached his father. Max glanced at him sharply.

'Six thousand pounds for some letters. Rubbish! They're trying to frighten you, my boy. I'll send for Wolff and he can deal with them. That's the best thing to do. Get on to him now. Then make a clean breast of the whole business and let's be done with it.'

Emmanuel looked at his father in silence, his face had a stricken look, the look of some dumb animal who knows that a fate is waiting for it which it cannot escape. Max decided that whatever the boy had done, he was having a bad time, he was punished sufficiently. Probably the whole thing was nothing very terrible. Nothing that Wolff wouldn't be able to straighten out quite easily. Six thousand pounds for a few letters!

'Don't send for Wolff, father. He can't really help much——'

'Why on earth shouldn't we send for him? Come. Emmanuel, don't behave like a fool!' The tone was kindly, almost coaxing.

'Won't you give me the money and let me settle it, father?'

'No, I certainly will not,' Max smiled, 'you're not asking for ninepence, you know. Six thousand pounds is a devil of a lot of money. Be sensible. You can trust me, can't you?'

'Yes—I mean—I don't know—— Father, for the last time, let me have the money and settle this myself, I beg you. I know what I'm saying. I'll pay you back every penny, I'll work like a slave, I'll do anything, only don't ask questions—Let me settle it in my own way.'

For the first time some of the old faint distrust came back to Max Gollantz. He remembered the incident of the night club, he remembered stories that had reached him later concerning that particular club, and others of a like kind. His face lost its look of gentleness, the mouth became a little grim, the eyes suddenly cold.

'We have wasted quite enough time,' he said crisply. 'Now, let's have the whole story and be done with it. Now, Emmanuel, the truth, if you please.'

The young man's face twitched, its pallor almost frightened Max. He was stammering out words, obviously distressed and half-crazy with misery.

'Letters—signed—only with initials—E. J. G.—written on the firm's notepaper—about thirty of them—and at least one that was written to me—and never posted——'

'Why not?'

'He died——'

'Who—this woman's husband? Then what on earth——'

Emmanuel made a sudden movement, and caught his father's hand in his; he bent his head so that he stared into Max's face, and Max recoiled at the despair and utter anguish that he saw written on his son's face.

'Father—swear that if I go on—you'll never tell—Angela. Promise me that—don't ever tell Angela—swear it!'

Max caught his son's shoulders, and knew that his fingers were pressing deep into the cloth, so that he could feel the muscles which lay beneath. His own face was as white as Emmanuel's, his breath was coming quickly, he knew that for the first time he was desperately afraid.

'Go on,' he said. 'I promise.'

'Swear,' Emmanuel said, 'swear it. Say—"The God of my Fathers do so to me and more also if I ever tell her"; say it!'

Slowly Max repeated the words, then added: 'Now—tell me. Who is dead?'

'The man to whom the letters were written.'

'My God!' Then quickly, almost hopefully: 'You're not lying?'

'No, father.'

'Don't call me that——' He recovered himself. 'And who is —blackmailing you?'

'His father.'

'Go and sit down—over there. Now, have I got it clear? This man has letters signed by you—with your initials—he wants six thousand to hand them over. Is that correct?'

'Yes.'

'When will you see him?'

'Tomorrow morning at ten o'clock.'

'You can go. No, not back to your office, and not back to Ordingly. Stay the night in town, I'll see you tomorrow—here—when this man comes. What's his name?'

'Crowther.'

Emmanuel went out and Max sat there at the big desk that had once belonged to a great statesman, in the chair that had been old Emmanuel Gollantz'. He sat quite still, his face like a mask, only his hands moved restlessly. The clock on the high mantelpiece ticked away the seconds, outside Max could hear the hum of the traffic, the hoot of the taxicabs. Outside were people hurrying about their work, their play, their thousand and one affairs. The world was going on just the same. Men died—as his father had died—and the world went on; women fought with death—as Angela had fought—and it still went on; sons proved themselves—admitted themselves to be—Max moved his head restlessly as if to rid himself of some pain. He daren't think—he daren't admit even here, alone, what had happened.

Emmanuel his firstborn—his eldest son. This was as if the Angel of Death had passed over the house and smitten the firstborn as he passed. His son was dead—the man he had believed his son to be had never lived. Always, somewhere, there must have been that strain which had led him to this end. It was over, Emmanuel should go, should be wiped out from their life at Ordingly as if he had never lived. The money should be paid, and that should be the end of Emmanuel the Second.

He rang the bell on his desk, and asked the clerk who answered it to send Reuben Davis to him. Reuben came, smiling and rubbing his hands.

'Yes, Mr. Gollantz—have you heard that Westerhams are going to sell the Constables?'

'No,' Max said. 'I hadn't. Reuben, go to the Bank for

me.' He took out a cheque-book and filled in a cheque. 'It's made out to me. I want six thousand. They won't be able to let you have it at once—I don't think so—do your best. If they can't, they must send it round here before three.'

Reuben took the cheque and looked at it through his strong horn-rimmed spectacles.

'Six thousand——!'

'Get it as soon as you can. Lock it in the safe. I shall want it early tomorrow. That's all, I'm going off now, Reuben.'

As Max glanced round his empty office, his eyes rested for a moment on the picture of his father that hung there. He looked at it intently, then said, softly:

'Thank God, this didn't happen two months ago.'

CHAPTER TWELVE

EMMANUEL walked into his father's room the following morning feeling that he was walking in his sleep. His whole body felt numb, he had not slept, and all night had laid awake cursing himself for a fool. If, for a moment, during the day he had felt that he was doing anything fine or splen did, that feeling had left him during the night. He knew that he was behaving in a way which was so quixotic as to be ridiculous. He was throwing away his whole life, all he cared for, for the sake of a sentiment. Why should he shoulder burdens and responsibilities which were Julian's—and which had been assumed for a mere curiosity, for the sake of a passing sensation? Julian might have a brilliant future, he might be destined for a great place in the world of politics, but he—Emmanuel—too, had a future. A future which was bound up with the firm which his grandfather had founded, a name which was worth as much to him as ever Julian's could be. In addition, he was losing Viva——

That was where he rolled over, buried his face in the pillow and wondered if he could bear to see this thing through? Viva—who had told him that she loved him, Viva, who under all her gaiety had a real, grave side to her nature, who was going to suffer through him and because of him. To have let Julian bear his own burdens, would have saved Viva at least from this pain which he was going to cause her.

Then, once again, came Nathan Bernstein's whispering, lisping voice, and again he heard his injunction that they must guard Angela very carefully—that they must lie, deceive, if it were necessary. Then came that long talk with his mother, when she had told him of that uncle whom he had never seen.

'Julian will put right what his uncle did that was—wrong.'

'Julian's future is tangled up in this House that I'm so proud of.'

'Julian—is going to make people forget——' 'It's not only to the world that I want Julian to show what he can do—it's to his grandfather—whom I loved, and love so much.'

And his own answer: 'If I can ever help, I will.'

His love for his mother swept over him like a great wave. Emmanuel was neither a hero, nor one of those unfortunate young men who believe that they suffer from a 'mother complex.' He was a very ordinary fellow, with a strong sense of the romantic, an almost overwhelming sense of duty, and an affection for his mother which had grown to be as much part of him as his hands and his feet.

When the day broke, and he rose and began to dress, his mind was still going back to all that Angela had told him. He remembered it so vividly. The long room where she sat, with its two windows looking out over the gardens, and the wide park lands. He could see her face, still thin and white after her illness, hear her voice, not yet quite strong, but crisp and decisive as it had always been. He remembered that his grandfather had once said that Angela was all definite colours, that there were no half-tones in her. She reminded him of a lovely Van Eyck that he had seen in Dresden—a picture that he looked back upon as one of the loveliest things that he had ever seen. Vaguely, when he had seen it, his mother had come to his mind. Clear colours, vivid yet never harsh; clear outlines which still remained tender and gentle. That was—Angela as her son saw her. It hadn't been easy for her to tell that story about his uncle—it couldn't have been. She had said that she had imagined that she loved him. Perhaps now it seemed like imagination, perhaps then it had been very real. Perhaps, even though her actual love for him was over, the knowledge that he had died, died alone in a foreign country, had hurt her.

Emmanuel recalled how he had died—drowned in some Swiss lake; his father had tried to save him. They had quarrelled—Angela had said so—quarrelled about her and some letters—and still his father had tried to save Algernon Gollantz. Had leapt into the water, not caring that he was lame, and risked his life.

Emmanuel, standing before the looking-glass, tied his elaborate, rather old-fashioned stock very carefully, arranging it so that exactly the right amount of white collar showed above it. He fixed his pearl pin with exactitude, and then examined the result with intent interest. He was dressing for his execution, and he would dress with additional care. He ran his fingers over his cheeks and chin, to assure himself that he had shaved with as much attention as usual. He glanced at his finger-nails, and going to a drawer congratulated himself that he had always kept a store of linen, collars, handkerchiefs at the old-fashioned hotel—which Julian despised. He chose a handkerchief with care, shook over it a few drops of the old-fashioned Eau de Cologne that his grandfather had always said was the only scent permissible to a man. He surveyed himself in the long glass, twitched his coat into place, ran his hands over his smooth dark hair, gathered up his match-box, his cigarette case and keys, and—almost smiled at his reflection.

His father had tried to save Algernon Gollantz, his brother. His son, Emmanuel, would not only try to save Julian—but he would succeed. It was not only quixotic romanticism, it was a queer dogged quality which had existed in them all—in old Emmanuel, in Max, and was repeated again in Max's son. Julian, himself, did not count, he was only a rather disreputable pawn in the game. The real players were Max Gollantz and his son, Emmanuel.

As Emmanuel passed out of the hotel, he turned and spoke to the reception clerk whom he had known for so long. She was a gaunt woman of uncertain age, and not particularly prepossessing; but she always had a smile ready for Emmanuel.

'What a fine young fellow!' she said to old Barker, the waiter. 'He's what I call a real chip off the old block.'

Barker nodded. 'Gentleman, that's what he is—a gentleman, and there's not too many of them about since the war. That chap in twenty-two wants his bill. That's a nasty bit of work, if ever I saw one, Miss. Not our style at all. You might give him a hint—next time—that we're full up!'

Emmanuel, walking towards Bond Street, shivered. The morning was cold and unfriendly. He wondered if his father had shivered before he took that plunge into the lake? A feeling that the whole thing was unreal still persisted. He kept noticing things in the shop windows with great care, as if he was trying to impress them upon his memory. He noticed that the buses had changed their stopping place, they stopped half-way up the little incline, they used to stop almost at the end, by Piccadilly. That fact seemed terribly important. He glanced at Foulsham and Banfield's showcase, and decided that he didn't like the new photograph of the Prince very much. He crossed the road and realized that he was almost there! His walk was over, there must have been a great many things that he'd missed, things that he might have noted more carefully. It was too late now—the executioner was waiting. He glanced at his watch—five minutes to ten. In half an hour it would all be over. 'Death was instantaneous'—he had read that often in the daily papers. Bill had told him that it wasn't quite true, that death wasn't instantaneous, and that it must be damned painful—to be slowly strangled. Emmanuel took out his handkerchief, and wiped his forehead.

'Oh, God, let me get it over quickly!'

He nodded to Marchmont, and Alan and young Berman. He smiled at Hannah Rosenfelt, and said:

'Is my father in yet?'

'Just come, Mr. Emmanuel. He wants you to go to him. He's got that Mr. Crowther with him in his office.'

He thought how clever Hannah Rosenfelt was, never forgot a name. She might only hear it once, but after that it stuck. Max always managed to get decent people round him. Gregson had been one of the very few mistakes. Gregson had gone —and he was going to follow Gregson!

Max looked up and nodded, but didn't speak.

Crowther was seated some distance from the desk, and Emmanuel felt that his father had indicated the chair and said:

'Sit there, if you please.'

Crowther bowed to him, and mumbled something inaudible.

Max laid down the letter he was reading.

'Now, Mr. Crowther. You want six thousand pounds, I believe?'

'That's right—that's the sum required for the building——'

'I don't want to hear what it's for, thank you. You will hand over the letters—the lot of them—and you will sign a statement to the effect that you have no others. Should you, at any time, reopen this matter, or try to produce other letters, or papers of any kind relating to this affair, you will be handed over and the law will deal with you. This agreement is ready for you.' He reached over and rang the bell on his desk, and when Marchmont came, said:

'Is Mr. Wolff there? He is. Then ask him to come to me.'

Emmanuel scarcely knew his voice, it came harshly and with a metallic ring in it. His face was like the face of a dead man, grey and pinched. He looked old, almost lifeless. His very movements were cramped. His hands looked cold and brittle. He never once looked towards his son.

Wolff entered. He nodded to Max, and gave Emmanuel something which might have been a greeting or nothing at all. He laid a paper on the desk before Max, and stood back watching him as he read it.

'That covers it, I think,' he said.

Max nodded. 'Quite. You'd better speak to this man.'

Wolff puffed out his cheeks, stuck his thumbs into the lower pockets of his waistcoat. Emmanuel had always known him as a kind little man, and his sudden change of tone when he spoke to Crowther almost shocked him. It was arrogant, bullying and coldly offensive.

'Now, my man, I want you to read this, and when you've read it you'll sign it. Here you are.' He picked up the paper and held it at arm's length towards Crowther.

Crowther rose and took it, with his eyes on Wolff's face.

'I refuse to be bullied,' he said. 'I've got right on my side and I won't be bullied into signing any papers of which I don't approve.'

Wolff removed one thumb and pointed it towards him.

'Now, look here,' he said, 'we want none of that nonsense. That's bluff and you know it. I want this business over and finished within five minutes. If it's not, Mr. Gollantz will telephone for a couple of men from Vine Street. The letters—to my mind—are worth about fourpence. I've told Mr. Gollantz so already. They prove nothing. Your son's dead, so he can't tell us anything! Firm's paper—I can get reams of it if I want! Typed—I can type letters any day of the week!'

'Several of them are not typed, let me inform you of that.'

Wolff sniffed offensively. 'I might suggest to you that it's not difficult for a reasonably clever thirty bob a week clerk to forge a very presentable imitation of another man's writing. However, Mr. Gollantz is a busy man, and a man who dislikes any kind of publicity, so get on with it. Just read that and sign it. You can read, I suppose? Here you are.'

Crowther took the paper, read it with the aid of a pair of eyeglasses which tilted sideways on his nose, and handed it back.

'That covers everything,' Wolff said. 'Sign here—have you a pen? Ah, carry your own? That's interesting—I never knew a man of your particularly unpleasant type who didn't. There—that's right.'

Max sighed suddenly, as if a strain had been removed.

'Now—the letters. Wolff.'

Crowther produced a packet and laid them on the table before Max.

'There, Mr. Gollantz, if you'll examine them, please.' With a glance at Wolff, he added: 'I prefer to deal with principals, not underlings.'

Emmanuel held his breath for a second. Suppose that even now, his father looked at the letters. Julian had said that they were not in his usual hand, had said that after all, his hand and Emmanuel's were not unlike. Even now it wasn't too late! A reprieve! The scaffold built for nothing—the executioner not wanted——

Max scarcely glanced at the packet.

'Hand them to my son,' he said, 'they've nothing to do with me. I wouldn't touch them!'

Emmanuel took them, knew that his hands were numb with cold. He barely opened the packet, glanced at the first letter and then nodded.

'Yes—yes—they're—what he said they were.'

'How many of them, Crowther?' Wolff snapped.

'Twenty-nine.'

'That right, Emmanuel? Is it?'

With a great effort Emmanuel said: 'There is one other letter. A letter which is addressed to me and which was never posted. I should like that, please.'

Wolff snapped his fingers. 'Now then, my man. Come over with it. We don't want any nonsense, it won't pay you. Where is it? Give it to Mr. Emmanuel. That right, Emmanuel?'

'Yes, thank you.'

'Here you are. Notes. Count them. Sign this receipt. You've been very clever, my man, but you've been just a little bit too clever. With or without Mr. Gollantz' permission, your dossier goes down to the C.I.D. this morning from my office. Watch your step, Crowther; watch it very carefully. Good morning.'

The three men were left alone. Wolff looked at young Emmanuel and decided that the fellow had guts. He stood there, straight as a ramrod, well groomed, and apparently unmoved. His face was pale, but it was perfectly controlled. The lad had come a mucker, they must hope that he'd run straight after this. He hoped that Max wouldn't be too hard on him. Teach him a lesson, and believe that he'd run straight in the future. He didn't look like a dirty fellow, didn't look the sort of nasty little tyke who was generally mixed up in these scandals. All rather puzzling and decidedly a pity. Max would feel it, he shouldn't wonder if he took it damned hard.

'Well, that's over,' he said, cheerfully, trying to instil some life into the two men who never moved. 'Let's hope that things will go all right after this. Well, good morning, Max.'

'Good morning, Herbert, and many thanks.'

' 'Morning, Emmanuel.'

'Good morning.'

They heard his voice repeating 'Good morning' as he went through the outer office; when it had died away, Max turned to his son.

'Now,' he said, 'you'd better go back to Ordingly and pack. I forbid you to try to see your brother, Bill. I won't have him—contaminated. I can't forbid you to see your mother, but I forbid you to tell her why you are going away. You can hint that we don't get on in the business very well. I've paved the way for you. Say that you're going to go abroad and look round for a bit. See if you can't open a branch in Paris. You mustn't upset her, you know that, don't you?'

'Yes,' rather bitterly. 'I know that.'

'How much money have you?'

'About two thousand pounds.'

'I'll give you another five——'

'Thank you, I don't want it. I wouldn't touch it.'

'It will be paid into your bank, all the same.'

'You want me to go at once?'

'The earliest possible moment. I won't have you spend another night at Ordingly.'

Emmanuel laughed suddenly, laughed because it seemed so utterly ridiculous that his father should be turning him out of his own home, seemed so fantastic that Emmanuel the Second should have to leave the home of his grandfather.

'Where am I to go?'

'Wherever you wish. It's no concern of mine.'

Max watched him, and knew that he wanted to tell him to sit down and explain everything to him, knew that he wanted passionately that his son should find some excuse for what he had done—anything, he scarcely cared what. This fellow was dead, surely he might blame him, anything would do that might give him a loophole to say:

'It's over. It won't ever happen again. Let's forget it.'

But Emmanuel never moved, only stood watching him with those dark eyes, an almost imperceptible smile on his lips, as if he mocked his father, mocked himself for what he had done and laughed at the whole world for caring!

In his heart, Max was saying: 'He's my son and hers. It's not possible. If only he would speak, ask for forgiveness—say something—anything. If only he wouldn't look so scornful, so arrogant. God, he looks like my father. I believe that he despises me for being weak enough to pay the money for him!'

Emmanuel, looking at his father, thought: 'How ready he is to believe it all. He's never asked me to offer an explanation, to make a single excuse. He sits there judging me, finding something that's terrible, disgusting. How hard. I never knew that he could be so hard, especially to his own son. That's the Jew in him, that is the old "eye for an eye". Well, I can play his game, and, by God, I will.'

'Understand, Emmanuel, this is the last time that I shall help you.'

'It will be the last time that I shall ask you to. I shan't be such a fool again.'

'I hope not.'

'Good-bye, and thank you for what you've done.'

'Good-bye.'

His hand was on the handle of the door. Max was leaning forward, his eyes suddenly filled with tears. He wanted to go after the boy, force him to come back, and explain. Emmanuel did not turn, he was going; in a moment it would be too late.

'Emmanuel——'

Emmanuel turned, his face was like a grey mask, his eyes very cold.

'Yes——?'

'Nothing. You may go.'

At Ordingly, they told him that he was to go to his mother at once. He went into her sitting-room, smiling, and ready to play the part that Max had given him. She was sewing, and looked up, taking off her big glasses as she did so.

'Emmanuel, darling, I'm so glad you've come. Sit down. Now, listen, my angel, what is this nonsense about you and Max not—getting on? No, don't answer me, let me finish first. It's ridiculous. Like two schoolboys quarrelling over a—a—top or something.'

He said: 'My sweet, no respectable schoolboy ever plays with a top.'

'Well, whatever they do play with. I won't have it, Emmanuel. I'm very angry with Max, and I'm very cross with you. I never heard of this until last night, when Max admitted it.'

'It's a pity,' Emmanuel said, 'we're very good friends out of business, but in it—we just don't hit it off.' He prided himself that he spoke light, as if the matter was really of little consequence to him.

'Don't you realize what a delightful man Max is?' she went on. 'I have known him for so long, and I know him so well. It's idiotic to think that anyone can't—get on with Max. It's equally ridiculous to think that anyone can't—get on with you. What is the upshot of this—conference—that's one of the silly words Max learnt in America, by the way—this morning?'

He did not meet her eyes as he answered. He felt once again that he couldn't go on with it, it was proving so much more disastrous than he had believed possible. He was to be bereft of everything, of his mother as well as his father. His home, everything was to be taken from him.

'I'm going away,' he said. 'Leaving tonight.'

'Simply because you don't get on with your father in business? I don't believe it. Either one of you, or both of you, are lying to me.'

'Angela—my dear!'

'You behave as though I was a half-wit,' she flashed back at him; 'this story, it's impossible. I simply don't believe it. Now, what is it? If you don't tell me, then Max shall. I am one of the partners of the business. If you and Max think that I'm some fat fool of a Jewess who is content to sit still and accept all that she's told, you're both mistaken. Now, Emmanuel, let me have the truth, please, and at once!'

He sighed. 'Darling, you've had it. We don't see eye to eye—and I'm going away for a little. That's the story.'

'Why have I heard nothing of it until now?'

'Because you were ill, and though we may not get on, we both love you very dearly, and we didn't want to worry you.'

She leant back, and said slowly: 'Yes, I see——' and relapsed into silence. Emmanuel watched her, and noticed that she knit her brows suddenly, and then said:

'Emmanuel, will you swear that what you have said is true?'

'It's true,' he said, speaking slowly, so that he should neither lie to her, not betray himself, 'that my father doesn't understand me, and perhaps I don't understand him. In effect, it would be quite impossible for us to work together any longer, at all events for a time. I don't say—always—but at the moment.'

'You swear that is true?'

'You're like a cross-examining counsel,' he said. 'Why, yes, I'll swear it, certainly.'

Angela Gollantz nodded. 'Yes,' she said, 'yes. All very smooth, very suave, very Hebraic, but you don't convince me. Have you done anything wrong, Emmanuel?'

He lifted his eyes and met hers very steadily. 'No,' he

said, 'and I'll swear that on the most precious thing in the world to me—on your life.'

'And yet you're going away from me,' she asked softly. 'Oh, my dear—can't you be frank and tell me everything, can't you let me try to straighten out whatever this is for you?'

'There is nothing to straighten out,' he said. 'Nothing, nothing.'

She sighed, and her body relaxed as if the effort she had made had exhausted her.

'Very well. You won't tell me, and I must find out for myself. I shall, Emmanuel, I shall. I won't be robbed of my son for nothing. You must go if you want to. You're not a child, though both you and Max might be, you're both so stupid. Where are you going?'

'I thought of Paris, then perhaps Florence, or Naples.'

Angela frowned again. 'To work at your business? Darling, how nasty and touristy!'

'Just the people I shall want.'

'Oh, if you're going to keep a junk shop, of course!'

If anyone could have heard her talking, have heard her laughing and criticizing his plans—plans which he made on the spur of the moment to satisfy her only—they might have thought that Angela Gollantz cared very little that her son was leaving her. Very few people knew her sufficiently well to understand that she possessed a brain which worked, as it were, with two halves, independent of each other. While she talked and laughed, while she encouraged Emmanuel and strove to drive that grey pinched look from his face, she was watching every gesture, every expression, noting each tone of his voice. She was cataloguing them all, putting them away in a kind of mental card index for future reference.

'He's hiding something,' she thought. 'I've not had the whole truth from either Emmanuel or Max. I must be wise and wait until I can come upon it myself. But I shall come upon it, and then I shall bring him back again. My poor Emmanuel, my poor Max. There's a dreadful muddle somewhere. But perhaps after all, it won't hurt him to go out and fight alone for a year. I shan't let him stay longer than that!'

As he was going, she said: 'You'll write to me very often?'

'Very often, darling.'

'Don't tell me about cathedrals and Botticellis. I've seen

them all. I want to know about you, what you're doing, how often you have your hair cut, if you have a comfortable bed —silly things.'

He bent and kissed her. 'My letters,' he said, 'shall all be quite unbelievably silly. I promise you.'

CHAPTER THIRTEEN

EMMANUEL slept that night in town, and early the next morning telephoned to Viva Heriot to ask if she would see him. His train left at two o'clock and he wanted her to know that he could only stay with her a very short time. He knew that his determination would be tried to its utmost at the sight of her, the conviction that he had burnt his boats, and could never marry her.

He had no feeling of satisfaction in what he had done, it had ceased to seem anything admirable or even useful; he only felt that he had acted on impulse and that he was reaping a whirlwind which was unprofitable and worthless. One thing only consoled him, and that was the fact that Angela had been saved the knowledge of the truth about his brother. For the rest, everything was on the wrong side, the balance was badly out, and he had lost everything.

For his father, he felt nothing but the same affection which he had always had. He knew that in Max's place he would have acted as Max had done. He knew that his mother believed that he lied, but she had given no indication that her faith in him, or her love for him, was shaken. Even funny, fat little Herbert Wolff had said nothing at which he might feel even annoyance. Everyone had been very decent, Emmanuel admitted, everyone had made it as easy and as dignified for him as possible. Only one person had left him with a sense of selfishness, and that was his brother Julian. He wouldn't allow himself to think of Julian. He had always heard old Emmanuel declare that hate was a foolish thing, that it reacted upon the person who indulged in it:

'It's stupid, it's useless—it gets you no place at all. It is vasteful, for it demends a great amount of energy, and—for vhat? For not'ing at all. The greatest result thet hate could hev vould be murder—and if you can show me a more foolish t'ing than murder—I shell be gled to know vhat it is.'

He walked round to Sir Walter Heriot's house in a state of mind which was more hopeless than anything else. He had so little to which he might look forward, he had cut himself off from his home, his people and the woman he loved; and had not even the consolation that they knew the reason for his actions. If he could have confided in one person, he reflected that it might have been easier. Not in order that he might be praised and lauded as a hero, but simply that he might know that in all the world, one person understood. It would have taken away something of that awful sense of loneliness.

Viva came into the room, smiling, and holding out her hands towards him.

'Emmanuel, how nice. So early in the morning, too. You're learning how nice young men really behave when they're in love, after all. My tuition has been very good, evidently.'

'Don't rag, Viva,' he said. 'Sit down. I've got to talk to you.'

'Something wrong, darling?'

'Everything,' he said briefly, and wondered how he could tell her. He was getting so tired of acting, and acting a part which he loathed and hated. He had never realized how far this promise to Julian would carry him.

'Viva, I'm going away today.'

'For how long?'

He made a little gesture with his hands, the same gesture that his grandfather had always used when words failed him.

'I don't know—a year—two—perhaps more.'

'My dear, what utter nonsense. I can't possibly get ready and be married just—like that!' she snapped her fingers.

'There isn't any question of marriage, Viva. I can't marry you—or anyone.'

Her face changed, her eyes looked suddenly anxious and startled.

'Darling—you're not ill? It's not some horrible illness, is it? Some old doctor's been frightening you! Dearest

Emmanuel, I don't believe it. They're always making mistakes.'

'No,' he said, 'it's not illness. It's just—that I can't marry you.' He looked at her and again that little smile that Max had seen touched his lips, as if he mocked at himself and the whole world. 'I am leaving my country, for what I believe is called "my country's good". That's all.'

Viva Heriot was a young woman who knew her world pretty thoroughly. She had very few illusions, she hated ignorance, and her general knowledge of men and women and the younger set of London might have shocked even Angela, had she known it. She sat back, in her corner of the big sofa, and looked at Emmanuel gravely. Her face expressed neither surprise nor disgust. To Emmanuel, it seemed like a very lovely mask, which betrayed nothing.

'You've not been forging cheques, of course,' she said, 'you mean—something else. The kind of things that are kept out of the police courts unless some wretched bobby is over zealous? My dear, go and tell that lie to someone else! I simply don't believe it!'

The smile died from his lips, he caught her hands in his, for the moment she had caught him off his guard.

'You don't, Viva, you mean that?' His voice was shaking with eagerness.

'Of course I don't. I rather wonder that you come to me with such a story. It's not very pretty of you, is it?'

His face was grave again. It was as if he had pulled down his visor once more, as if a sheet of steel had been dropped between them.

'Nevertheless,' he said, 'that is why I am leaving England today. That is why I can't marry you.'

Viva shook her head. She was the cool young woman of the world again.

'My dear, I tell you that you're lying. Tell me this—don't you love me? Just say "Yes" or "No". I don't want either explanations or protestations.'

'I do love you, yes.'

'Now tell me—again plainly—you're all too fond of elaborate sentences, you Gollantz people—you swamp one with words. Tell me plainly, that you have been caught in some intrigue—it's a useful word—with some—well, some of the people my delightful brother knows.'

'I don't know who Walter knows,' Emmanuel said.

'Ah! I wasn't quite clever enough, that time, was I? Shall I put it more plainly, Emmanuel? You're making it pretty nasty for me, aren't you? You won't like the words when I use them—I warn you.'

He rose and walked away towards the window. For a moment he stood looking out on to the Square that he knew so well. How often had he come there, walked into houses under a striped awning, over a strip of red carpet! How often he had driven there and sat outside waiting for Viva. He wanted desperately to go back, to kneel beside her and tell her the truth, wanted her to know that he was the same person who had said that he loved her, had held her in his arms only a week ago at Ordingly. He turned and looked at her. She was sitting waiting for his answer. He daren't tell her the truth. He knew Viva, knew how intolerant she was of injustice, how impetuous she could be. Once told, nothing would stop her from going to Max, to Angela, and making them listen to her.

'I am going,' he said, speaking like a mechanical thing, 'because some letters—signed with my name—written on the firm's paper—were found. The man to whom they were written is dead, and his father discovered them. My father paid six thousand for them yesterday. That's the story, Viva.'

'Is that all?'

'There was one letter, written to me, and never posted. The man who died—had left it in his writing-case.'

Quick as a flash, she asked, 'What was his name?'

'I can't tell you. It's not material.'

'It would be,' she returned, 'if I could get it from you! So you're going away? So you won't marry me? Go away, my dear, and I'll bring you back. I'll make you marry me—God knows that you want to badly enough. You're telling lies, you're making people believe lies. All except me. You astute Jews have got together and talked and made damned fools of yourselves. One Jew is clever; a crowd of them are the most stupid things on the earth. It's easy to see that you are the Chosen People—God scattered you for your own advancement!'

He held out his hand. 'Good-bye, Viva. Please, promise me that you won't repeat what I have told you to anyone?'

'I shan't go about London chattering that my young man's

declared that he can't marry me because he's a——'

Emmanuel said, 'Viva, don't, darling, please!'

She shrugged her shoulders. 'I don't see why not. You're behaving very badly, Emmanuel. You're coming here, telling me lies, you're giving me half-truths, and expecting me to fold my hands and say: "Thank you very much for telling me". It's ridiculous. You can't expect me to be pleased and gratified, can you? Are you going to write to me?'

'No, I can't do that. I couldn't bear it.'

'I see. Very well. How can I get hold of you when I want you to come back? Because you are coming back, when I've found out the truth! I suppose your father's lawyers will know—or perhaps Angela?'

'Angela won't have my real address. I shall write to her through some third person. Listen—Viva—just one thing. I ought not to say this—you'll despise me for it, but I can't help it. I don't want you to think that you're bound to me. You must marry whom you please if you love them—only don't marry—my brother.'

'Bill?'

'You know that I didn't mean Bill,' he said, 'don't hurt me more than you can help. Don't make things harder for me.'

'You're making them sufficiently hard for me, Emmanuel.'

'Not willingly—you know that. Viva, promise me that you won't marry Julian.'

'Why not? I almost promised to marry him once, you know.'

As she looked up at his face, she was shocked at the sudden change in it. The man she knew had gone, and in his place stood someone whose face was demoniacal in its hate, fiendish in its anger. His dark eyes were hard, his lips parted in a snarl, his face looked so white that she wondered if he could be ill. When he answered his voice was changed, as was his face. It came biting and metallic.

'Because I hate him. I hate him; and if I heard that he wanted to marry you, I'd come back and kill him! I'd murder him with my two hands. I'd choke the last breath out of——' He stopped suddenly, and stared at her as if he had been wakened suddenly from a dream. 'I don't know what I'm saying,' he said. 'I'm tired—haven't slept for the last two nights. Forgive me, please forget what I said.'

'Then,' she spoke slowly, because she knew that she was torturing him and she hated to think that she, of all people in the world, could hurt Emmanuel Gollantz, 'then—if I find that I love him, I may marry Julian.'

'If you do,' he spoke very evenly now, 'I swear that I will come home to kill him. Good-bye, Viva.'

She put up her hands and laid them on his shoulders, lifting her face to his.

'*Au revoir,* my dearest,' she said, 'thank God, we're young, both of us. I can wait for a year or two, and still have a long time left to spend with you. You're a fool—and you and I know it—but you shall be "a dear fool for an hour"—after that you must come home and be sane again. Kiss me, Emmanuel, and say that you love me.'

He bent his smooth dark head, laid his lips on hers and kissed her with all the pent-up passion that was in him.

'I love you,' he said. 'I've always loved you.'

'And always—*remembered*—that you loved me?'

'Always—always—always.'

'A-ah! You've answered me, Emmanuel. Now you can go. I love you too. Go on loving me, please.'

Without another word he turned and left her. She stood listening, until she heard the front door close behind him, then she sat down and frowned, twisting her fingers as if she derived some satisfaction from the physical discomfort that it gave her.

Emmanuel walked through the Square, seeing nothing, and no one. He walked back to his hotel, collected his luggage, bade the old waiter and the reception clerk 'Good-bye' in a perfectly normal voice, and drove away to Victoria. He stood by the door of his carriage, and thought how queer it was that he should be going away for a year, and that no one should be there to say, Good-bye and God speed. The old sense of loneliness came over him again, and he felt a dreadful desire to telephone to his father, and declare that he was coming back to explain everything. Then, coming towards him he saw a figure that he knew. It was his father's secretary, Hannah Rosenfelt. She walked without hurrying, her large dark eyes searching for him. Her stout figure pushing its way past whoever prevented her from seeing what she wished. She caught sight of him and quickened her pace a little.

'Mr. Emmanuel——' He had never noticed before how thick her voice was, the real 'Ghetto' voice, old Emmanuel used to call it.

'Miss Rosenfelt—did my father send you?'

'No one sent me,' she said. 'I'm supposed to be at the dentist's—half-frantic with toothache. I'm not, I'm here. I've come to see you off. I knew something was wrong, yesterday. Oh, please don't think that I want to ask questions, Mr. Emmanuel, I don't. Then today, your father told me, in confidence, that you weren't coming back. I guessed that something was up. I telephoned the hotel, said it was Mr. Wolff speaking. You'd just left for Victoria. Here I am. That's the story.'

'It's very kind of you,' he said, 'it's kinder than you know.'

'Pardon me, have you enough money?'

He smiled. 'Yes, thank you.'

'If not I can let you have some. I don't spend half that your father pays me. I'm saving up to buy a house at Northwood. You can have it, if you want it.'

'My dear Miss Rosenfelt, how terribly kind. But I don't need it.'

'If you did need any—write to me.' She paused and her rather thick lips quivered. 'I'd—do anything in the world for you, Mr. Emmanuel. I—I believe in you, whatever anyone says. No, don't say anything. It's ridiculous, I know. There, you're going. Remember—anything! And Mr. Emmanuel, watch Carlo Dolci's, they're coming in again, and Vlaminck's, and French flower pieces. I heard old Lane say so to Arbuthnot, don't forget. Good-bye—and the God of Our Fathers bless you and keep you. Good-bye, Salom!'

Emmanuel leant out of the window, and watched her waving her handkerchief as long as she could see him. She had helped him, this queer, rather stout Jewess whom he had hitherto regarded as a sort of efficient machine. She had courage and generosity. 'I believe in you,' and Viva, too, she believed in him. Two women—one whom he loved and who loved him, the daughter of Sir Walter Heriot, Tenth Baronet; and the other Hannah Rosenfelt, daughter of some *schnider* from the Ghetto, perhaps. He had never thought of Miss Rosenfelt as having either father or mother. He only knew that he felt warmer, happier, more established, and not quite such an outcast.

Paris seemed unfriendly. He knew very few people there, and those were only business acquaintances. He played with the idea of opening a shop in Paris, antiques for the Americans. Then, decided that it was too near to London, and that he was bound to meet people who knew him and who knew his father. No, Paris wouldn't do. For three days he was terribly lonely, trying to decide where to go, trying to avoid the places where he was likely to meet people who would recognize him. He had been in Paris so often with Max, had dined and lunched and drunk cocktails with them all in the right places. Now, he must avoid the 'right places' for fear someone should clap him on the shoulder and say:

'Hello, young Gollantz, what are you doing here?'

On the fourth day he was lunching in a little restaurant not far from the Opera. It was clean but unostentatious, the food was admirable and Emmanuel decided that it was safe, no rich English Jews would lunch there. As he ate his meal he watched the people come and go; stout middle class men who enjoyed their food to such an extent that Emmanuel wondered how on earth they could do any work after it. Women, obviously business women, who ate quickly with one eye on a paper or a novel; young men who chattered together and who talked to the elderly waitress as if they knew her very well. He wished that he could talk to someone, even the waitress.

A voice at his elbow said, 'Pardon me, I think that we know each other.'

Emmanuel turned, and at the first sight of the man who addressed him, prepared to make a stiff denial. He was tall, and very slim. He was dressed entirely in black, and his shirt was tucked, with narrow black cord at the edge of each tuck. His tie was too wide, his cuffs too long, and decorated with links which were much too ornate. Though Emmanuel himself dressed in a style which was a faint imitation of his grandfather, nothing would have annoyed him more than to believe that he was conspicuous. One glance at this young man assured him that to be conspicuous was his dearest wish.

Then, looking more closely, he remembered that they had met before; that his father's second cousin, Ferdinand Jaffe, had introduced them. On the morning of old Emmanuel's funeral, this youth was one of the 'foreign contingent', he was Louis Lara.

Emmanuel rose and said, with a hint of coldness, 'How are you?'

'I am very well, thank you. And you?'

'Quite well——'

'Would you permit me to sit down here at your table?'

After all, it was a relief to have someone with whom he might exchange a few words. Emmanuel was a friendly person, and he had been abominably lonely. Louis Lara sat down, carefully hitching his trousers up at the knees, and placing his very smart Homburg on the vacant chair next to him. He turned again to Emmanuel and the series of conventional inquiries continued.

'I hope that your father is well?'

'Very well, thanks.'

'And that your charming mother has entirely recovered her health?'

'Thank you, yes.'

Emmanuel longed to say: 'And the rest of the family are well, so save yourself further trouble, please,' but the questions ceased and the youth in the dreadful tucked shirt broke fresh ground.

'I am so happy to meet you in Paris,' he went on. 'When I saw you in London—at Or-ding-lee, I felt that I wished very much that I might know you all better, but at such a time it was impossible to press one's own wishes. I felt that I was at a disadvantage, and,' he gave a sudden and very charming smile, 'I dislike intensely to appear at a disadvantage.'

Emmanuel said: 'I think that we all do. I know that I do.'

'Ah!' The tone was such that Emmanuel felt that he had given voice to some great truth. 'But now, I am in Paris, as your English poet says, "My feet are on my native he'th." Are you here on business, Cousin Emmanuel Gollantz?'

Here it was! He must tell the old lies again to this strange young man who called him cousin. He told his carefully prepared story as convincingly as possible, and Louis Lara listened and interpolated shrugs and nods at intervals. When he finished, his companion burst out again.

'How sad, and yet—perhaps what a good thing! It is alvays good for a young man to learn to stend alone. I have found it so. You do not quite, perheps, Cousin Emmanuel, know what is my place in this big family of Lara. You may be a little confused, you may say to yourself: "Who is this young men, and why does he talk to me?" Let me explain. Count Leone Lara married his cousin—your grendmother. Very beautiful. Her portrait hengs in my own study, it is a great joy. He hed two brothers—Louis and Isidore. I am the son of Louis—Louis the son of Louis. I should never wish you to confuse me with Isidore's son. We do not speak of Isidore, if you please.'

Emmanuel wondered what had been the crime of Isidore, and felt that it might be wiser to ask no questions. He said:

'Then you are really a generation before me, aren't you?'

'Thet is true. My dear father—Louis Lara—merried very late. He was nearly sixty when I was born. He is dead.'

'I'm sorry.' That was the reason of this wealth of black, which evinced itself on the tucks of his shirt!

'Naturally, I am not in mourning for him. My father died ten years ago. He was seventy-five. I am in mourning for your venerated grendfather, whose funeral I attended at Or-ding-lee.'

Then, having cleared the ground, Louis Lara pushed away the plate that was before him, folded his arms on the table and began to tell Emmanuel the story of his life. It was crowded with incident. As incidents they really seemed insignificant enough, but as Louis Lara related them they assumed enormous proportions. To Emmanuel, it sounded like a fairy story, for apparently Lara had fallen in love ever since he was thirteen with a succession of beautiful creatures who had never returned the love which he gave them. They swam across Emmanuel's mental vision, like a procession of the world's beauties. Louis Lara followed them, a cross between a troubadour and a weary man of the world. The last affair had, he assured Emmanuel, almost killed him.

'Part of me is undoubtedly dead,' he said, touching the place where he believed his heart to be situated, 'dead and in its grave. She was a goddess—an angel—wonderful—superb! I was the most envied young man in Paris, now I am the most pitied! I was overthrown, that is what you say in England, I think?—for an American, with the hideous name of Elfred P. Slatter.' He said it as if it had been all one word. 'Of hideous aspect and old enough to be her father.'

Emmanuel said: 'Old Slater—it's not Slatter, by the way—I know him. Terrible old fellow. An old bore.'

Louis grasped his hand warmly. 'My dear cousin! How splendid it is to hear you say so. Tell me, could a woman love such a man as this?'

'Not easily, I imagine. He's terribly wealthy, y'know.'

'A-ah!' Again Emmanuel felt that he had done the whole world a service by the enunciation of a truth. 'Ah! So now we find the contents of the cocoanut. I learnt that expression from an Englishwoman, Cousin Emmanuel! It was through the mercy of Heaven that I came in here this morning, and met you! Not love then, but money! Her heart may still belong to—to the person to whom it once belonged. That hes made me very happy, I assure you.' Emmanuel decided that the lad was easily content after all. 'I could never bear to feel that my wonderful, superb Olympia—that was her name—she was a dancer at the Casino—had left me for any reason but that of ambition. She was filled with ambition, insatiable! Now, Broadwalk in America will be open to her.'

'Broadway,' Emmanuel said. 'I don't know. Old Alfred's a bit of a tight-wad—bit mean.'

Louis laughed. 'I will trust Olympia to remedy thet. From Bienvenida Bialloblotsky alone she had a fortune; many say five millions of francs.'

'A man with a name like that deserved to lose five million francs, I should think,' Emmanuel said.

Louis smiled. 'That is true; as a name it always offended me, but it's owner offended me much more. But now, Cousin Emmanuel, tell me are you staying in Paris for a long time?'

'No,' Emmanuel said, slowly. 'Paris isn't much use to me, I'm afraid. I have very little capital, and things will be too expensive here. I want to buy antiques and sell them again. I want small profits, but I want them quickly. No great stock, but to buy what people need, on commission. I don't aspire to old masters—not yet . . .'

Lara considered gravely, he took out a gold box, opened it and offered it to Emmanuel. 'Please smoke,' he said, 'it helps the mind, I discovered after my recent affliction over Olympia. Allow me to think for a moment. This may be the Hend of Fate—*Voilà justement comme on écrit l'histoire* . . . I hev great need of distraction. I hev some money—not a great deal—only the vulgar are immensely rich in these days . . . But enough, thanks to my good father, who was more mean than any man in the whole world. I hev taste, I neither drink nor gamble. Women—are as a closed book to me for the future—since my beloved Olympia went to Broadway with this Slatter. Do you know Merano, Bozen, and these places? Little places round about in the mountains? They are gold mines! You speak Italian perhaps—and German? This is planned for us! Let us join armies. No, do not answer me at once, if you please. Take time, a long time. Think well. It is now two o'clock. At four, will you come to my *appartement*,' he took out a card the size of an invitation to a Lord Mayor's Banquet, heavily edged with black, and handed it to Emmanuel, 'and discuss this metter. You must make inquiries, only do not let them confuse me with the son of Isidore Lara, if you please.' He rose, picked up his hat, and smiled again. 'This is the Hend of Heaven! I must go and buy many cakes for the tea. I know that Englishmen like cakes. You will excuse me? *Au revoir.*'

CHAPTER FOURTEEN

EMMANUEL sometimes wondered what his father, Bill, or Henry Drew would have thought of Louis. He could imagine Bill eyeing him up and down, and saying—afterwards:

'Does he have to dress like that?'

He could imagine Henry twitching his eyebrows, and being devastatingly polite, and announcing that Emmanuel had caught a queer fish, but perhaps the fellow had—qualities. That word 'qualities' was a favourite among the Heriot clan, they liked it, it was all-embracing and yet non-committal. He fancied Charles Wilmot, screwing in his rimless eyeglass, and staring out of his rather protuberant blue eyes, summing up and deciding that 'the feller isn't without intelligence. Sees life as a sort of perpetual *crime passionnel* —but would always stop short of actually making it one.'

Emmanuel, himself, had grown to like Louis. His clothes were against him, and his whole manner wouldn't have gone down too well at Ordingly, but after all, they weren't at Ordingly, and weren't likely to be. They were in Paris, and Louis was very kind, hospitable, and more astute than Emmanuel would have believed at their first meeting. They had arranged to join forces, and go south to Italy. Emmanuel had knowledge, spoke Italian incorrectly but fluently, and his German was faultless. Louis spoke German with a pronounced French accent, and his Italian was perfect.

To Emmanuel he had come as a veritable gift from Heaven. He had appeared—as it were, out of the blue—he had talked and had been so frank concerning his own affairs —his devastating love affairs—that Emmanuel had been forced to push his own misery into the background. Louis had been good for him, he had rescued him from falling into a bottomless pit of misery and loneliness; Emmanuel knew and was grateful.

He didn't fancy that in reality Louis suffered much from the deflection of Olympia's affections; he felt that his attitude was a careful pose, and that in reality his wounds were superficial. He had seen numerous photographs of the dancer, and felt—though he did not say so—that Louis was more fortunate than Alfred P. Slater in the matter.

Louis had accepted Emmanuel's explanations about leaving home, but, Emmanuel fancied, with reservations. He never hinted that he had other beliefs, and Emmanuel never offered further confidences; but they understood each other; Louis accepted the story, and Emmanuel left it at that.

Their arrangements were carried through quickly. Louis found a man whom he could trust who would forward Emmanuel's letters for him. Louis decided that his car should be transformed into something which might be used to transport goods and smaller pieces of furniture. Without a shudder, he saw his luxurious touring car changed into a regular commercial traveller's vehicle, and applauded the change.

They set out one bright morning in July to travel south and find a suitable place for the centre of their activities. As they were leaving Paris, Louis decided that he must stop for a last cocktail at the 'only possible bar in Paris'. It was there that Emmanuel found an English paper, and scanning it idly, while Louis talked to a crowd of friends as immaculate and unbelievable as himself, saw that the election was over. Hating himself for caring, he looked down the lists, and found what he sought for.

Harroby. Conservative gain.
Gollantz, J. E............ 45,762
Herbert, W. F............ 45,031

Louis came back smiling and declaring that his friends all believed that his 'affliction had turned his brain', then stopped suddenly and said:

'Are you ill, Cousin Emmanuel? Please, what is wrong? You're not yourself, you're upset, unheppy.'

'No,' Emmanuel said, rising and throwing the paper down, 'none of those things; only rather angry, and for no reason at all, which makes it all the more annoying. Let's get on, shall we?'

For the remainder of the morning he sat back in the corner of the car, without speaking, allowing his mind to go back over the events which had led to his banishment. Julian was in. The first success had come to him, everyone at Ordingly would be delighted. Max would tell everyone, Angela would pretend to make light of it, and in her heart realize that she was the proudest woman in England, even Bill would have to admit that 'old Julian had done it pretty well'.

He let Louis drive, he saw nothing of the country through which they passed, he had forgotten that he was a young man starting off on an adventure, in a strange land. He was only young Emmanuel Gollantz, who was very lonely, and who wanted desperately to find himself back in London, with a telephone before him, so that he might ask Viva Heriot to dine and dance with him.

Louis let him alone, perhaps he knew something of what was going on in Emmanuel's mind, and judged that it was wiser to let him fight his battles alone. Not until they stopped outside a long, low, old-fashioned inn about two in the afternoon did he break the silence.

'Here, if you are willing,' he said, 'we might eat. It is too hot to eat very much—an omelette, salad and some fruit—and wine, eh?'

Emmanuel's face lost some of its misery, his eyes lighted:

'Louis, I'm a dull devil, and a sulky one. You're a damned nice fellow not to tell me so.'

'Even if I thought so, I should never say so, it would be neither polite nor wise.' He laughed. 'You are bigger than I am!'

They pushed on, always going south, at night they sat outside old inns and discussed plans and finance. Louis was astute, and declared that they were going, if not to make fortunes, at least to earn a good return for their invested capital.

'Milan,' he said, 'is the place. There are rich people in Milan; newly rich people who want to buy from the old poor people. They don't know how to set about it. We shall show them. You will bring your knowledge, and I shall be ready in the shop—oh, yes, it must be a shop—to sell what you have found.'

Emmanuel grumbled that he hated Milan, that Milan was freezing in winter and insupportable in summer. Louis said:

'We don't go for our healths, we go to make money. After all, there are 'eroic people who live in Man-ches-ter.'

In a fortnight they had found a shop. Emmanuel reflected that it was strange that Louis, who was exquisite in everything, had apparently no dislike of the shop. Emmanuel, used as he was to the dignified offices, galleries and showrooms of Gollantz and Son, hated the idea of a stuffy little shop, with a counter and a bell that clanged when anyone entered. Louis watched and smiled and said nothing. The commercial side of his French nature was uppermost, and it amused him that anyone should differentiate between showrooms, galleries, offices and—shops. What did it matter? They were all means by which one earned money. If one earned money at all it was a matter of indifference what one called the place where one intended to make it!

He had grown to have a great affection for Emmanuel. He knew that somewhere there lurked a tragedy, but what form it had originally taken he did not greatly care. Sometimes he wondered if it had been a woman—or horses—or dogs or cards? What did it matter? Emmanuel had left his home suddenly. Emmanuel didn't want to talk, therefore the matter must be left a mystery.

At the end of August he sent Emmanuel away on his first 'voyage of discovery'.

Louis had bought maps, had planned out the tour, and sat in the little sitting-room over the shop one sweltering night, and handed the lists and time-tables over to Emmanuel.

'There, Kris-to-pher Kolombus! Take these and the car. It is ready for you. See—here is the route—Brescia, Verona, then North to the Dolomites—Trento—Bolzano—we used to call it Bozen, Merano, then come back by Riva and a queer place called Satlo—back to Bergamo and here to Milan. That will be a great journey, and you will bring back all that is possible in the car, and what is too large, hev it sent.'

Emmanuel set off, and as he drove away from Milan, he thought how six months ago the idea of such a trip would have thrilled him. How he would have planned, how he would have hoped and sought, how he would have tried to track down this bit of furniture and that old half-forgotten picture. Now—it didn't matter. He would do his job, because it was his job, and he owed a duty to his partner, but the zest was gone, the joy had vanished and he was doing it all as a matter of business routine. His training had been too good, and his own taste was too critical to allow him to do his work in any other way than the best of which he was capable. He loved beauty in whatever form he found it, and his eyes were sufficiently keen to miss nothing. He found more than he had dared to hope for, and returned to Milan with a load of antiques which delighted Louis, and even gave Emmanuel some satisfaction.

He showed his cargo with a certain amount of pleasure, and when Louis praised him, lauded his ability and his taste, Emmanuel felt some of his old joy in his work returning to him. Louis was generous, he gave unstinted praise, and yet gave it so kindly and with such sincerity that it was impossible to believe that he lacked honesty.

'These chairs—how beautiful; the painting how charming. No, not great art, but how delightful! That brocade, I believe that you stole it from a priest—no? Well, I must take your word for that. The old jars—from a chemist in Riva? So! And what is this? I have never seen one before. Cousin Emmanuel, how do you *know* these t'ings? It is wonderful. I congratulate you, and congratulate myself because you are my partner.'

The work started, and the news of the little shop, where

such charming things might be obtained, began to be known in Milan. Money began to filter into their cash-box. People came and liked the two men, the one so tall and grave, with his slightly old-fashioned air, the other with his queer accent, his over-elaborate clothes and his charming manners.

Letters came for Louis, even orders, but for Emmanuel, who had resolutely kept his name from the firm's paper and billheads, nothing came except long letters from Angela. They were forwarded from Paris, by the man Louis Lara had found. She wrote affectionately and yet a little regretfully; she seemed to feel that Emmanuel was treating her unkindly, keeping something from her. She seldom mentioned the subject of their last interview, but Emmanuel knew that she missed him, and that she still felt that he and his father had conspired to keep the whole truth from her. No one else wrote to him—he had not expected them to.

He threw himself into his work, he forced himself to find occupation from morning until night. He knew no one; Louis might make friends if he wished, might be asked to dine here and sup there, but Emmanuel refused to know any of the people who Louis assured him were both kind and cultured.

'I don't want to make friends,' Emmanuel said; 'it's not that I don't think these people mightn't be awfully nice, I'm sure that they are. I want to work, and just—be let alone. I'm an ill-tempered devil, and I don't think that any company would be the brighter for my presence.'

Louis would sigh, and protest that he was certainly not ill-tempered, and that his presence would brighten the most select assembly. 'If only you might fall in love, Cousin Emmanuel! That's what I wish for you!'

Emmanuel said, 'God forbid!'

'You are afraid?'

'No—not afraid. Just it's not my line. I don't want people.'

'But—a person; the—person.'

'No, Louis, no! Leave me alone, I'm all right.'

The hot summer ended, and the days shortened as the year slid into autumn. Emmanuel saw the country change from green to the softer colours of the dying year. He was beginning to get some happiness from his long drives into the country, he was growing to know and understand the people, and their kindness and friendliness touched him. He was amazed at the interest which they took in him and his work. Time and time again some old peasant would walk a mile out of his way to meet him and tell him of a chest which was worthy of his attention; or some old woman would hobble out at the sound of his car, and give him information concerning an old chair which might be found in a cottage further down the road. To them he was Signor Emmanuele, and he wanted no other name from them.

As the autumn passed, he watched the mountains becoming covered with snow, and those heights, purple topped with unbelievable whiteness, gave him a sense of comfort and stability. Day after day, as he drove north in search of things for his shop, he would find that he turned his eyes towards those silent, immovable hills with a sense of relief. Once he found himself saying, softly: 'I will lift up mine eyes unto the hills whence cometh my help.'

There were days when he needed help very badly, days when all his old hatred of his brother returned and almost shattered him. There were days when he longed for Ordingly and all that Ordingly stood for. At such times he would sit, his face cupped in his hands, and stare blankly before him, seeing pictures which were painted for him alone. Angela, and the big crackling wood fire, the tea tray with its silver and gleaming china; the dinner table, with Angela at its foot, and Max in his severe black and white; the long drawing-room cleared for dancing—Henry, Bill, Viva, Betty and the rest dancing there, with Angela watching them, smiling a little and turning her eyes very often towards the door—waiting for Julian.

Sometimes he saw nothing, but heard their voices so clearly that he could have believed that they stood at his elbow. Angela's, so clear and so musical, Viva's, sharper and more decisive, saying amusing, impertinent things, laughing at everything that was serious, Max, low and deep, Bill's lighter and often bubbling into laughter—and Julian's—arrogant, charming and—hateful!

Then he would rise suddenly, and catching up his hat would walk out and pace the streets, trying to shake off the misery which mastered him. Louis watched and kept silent, and tried in a hundred ways to help his cousin. Sometimes he would succeed, and if he could make Emmanuel smile, if he could make his dark eyes light up with amusement, Louis counted himself well paid.

That winter he persuaded Emmanuel to come with him to the Scala; the fact that he despised any music written before 1900, did not prevent him from enjoying the fare which the Scala offered.

Together they listened to *La Bohême*, to *Aïda*, to *Butterfly* and to *Carmen*. Louis, exquisitely dressed, with a white carnation in his buttonhole, his hands encased in immaculate white kid gloves, and his shirt unbelievably tucked and pleated; Emmanuel, straight and impossible to mistake for anything but an Englishman, even with his small affectation of eccentricity in his dress. He had never believed that he cared for music very much, and he could remember wondering how his grandfather and Angela could have been so passionate over some dead and gone composer and his works. Now, he would sit there, in a foreign country, and let the music break over him, listen to voices which tore at his heartstrings and know that his eyes were wet.

'It's old-fashioned, I suppose,' he said to Louis one evening as they walked home, 'probably out of date, and obviously no consumptive could sing as she does in the last act, but it gets you.'

Louis nodded. 'Old-fashioned and yet never old-fashioned,' he said. 'When will love, and hate, and self-sacrifice become old-fashioned? Not in your lifetime or in mine, and so these things—have got you, as you say.'

'No,' Emmanuel agreed, 'I suppose you're right. Love and hate and self-sacrifice must have been pretty much the same for Greeks and Romans, as they are for us, eh?'

'And yet, each time, new for everyone. A miracle, I believe.'

'Miracle!' Emmanuel repeated. 'Love may be; there's not much miracle about hate, my son, believe me.'

Louis shrugged his shoulders. 'I have never hated anyone, except the son of Isidore Lara—Lucien—I hate him because he smells and his nails are bitten so that they bleed!'

'It's quite easy to hate a man who doesn't smell, and whose nails are perfect,' Emmanuel told him.

'Oh, I can believe it.'

It was a week later that Louis came to him pale and excited.

He held a French newspaper, and a letter in a huge envelope of violet in his hand.

'Emmanuel,' he said, 'we talked of miracles, and one has happened! Olympia has returned to Paris, she is tired of Broadwalk and of that dreadful old man—Slatter—and she—I cannot read you the letter, for obvious reasons—but it is most enheartening.'

Emmanuel said: 'Heartening—not en-heartening. She wants to see you?'

Louis flushed. 'She asks that I will hev supper with her, after the performance at the Casino any evening next week. I shall go, of course.'

'You're a fool,' his cousin said shortly, 'she chucked you once before, how do you know that she won't do it again? She's not good enough for you, and you ought to know it. Don't be a damned ass!'

Louis's face expressed astonishment. 'But—my dear Emmanuel,' he said, 'what is this violence? I know thet she—chucked me, once. I know that she is not—good enough!' He lifted his hands in protest. 'I return simply to prove to myself that Olympia cannot hurt me again, never in this world. It is over, but I wish to make insurance doubly insecure.'

'You cold-blooded little devil!' Emmanuel grinned. 'And you've got it all wrong anyway, you and your insurances!'

'Olympia is a—bacilli—a germ in my blood,' Louis said, with great seriousness; 'she has been mastered. Now I go to lay myself open to infection, and I shall not become infected! That is all! Then, assured—or is it insured?—I shall return—as the English poet says—commanding my soul and covered with blood.'

'Whose blood? Olympia's or yours?'

Louis laid down his paper and the huge violet envelope, and came over to where Emmanuel stood. His face had lost its look of excitement, and his eyes were serious, and affectionate.

'Emmanuel, I shan't be away very long. Will you be content alone? Only one thing would prevent me from going to Paris to see this superb, but no longer dangerous, creature—and that would be if you said that you did not wish to be alone in Milan.'

Emmanuel was touched, he liked his queer cousin, and had

grown to understand him. Under all his affectations, his pose, he was a good friend, and a decent fellow. He laid his hand on his shoulder.

'I shall be as right as rain,' he said. 'Off you go to Paris, and sup with your Olympia. She sounds larger than life-size to me with that name. You don't call her that when you're talking to her, do you?'

Louis hesitated for a moment, then said: 'No, Emmanuel —I used to call her—Tu-Tu.'

The silly pet name ought to have made Emmanuel smile, but he caught sight of Louis's face, and something in its expression made him feel that he had never wanted to smile less than he did at that moment. He felt that Louis really had loved this woman with the preposterous name, and that even if he were cured, a scar remained. For the first time, Louis Lara seemed to him an entirely real person.

'Get along,' he said, 'and get your beautiful bags packed with your most ravishing clothes. Come back as soon as you want to.'

But he did miss Louis, and he missed Louis's ability to cope successfully with the Italian servant, and the heating arrangements. When Louis was in the place the radiators functioned properly, left alone Emmanuel found that he was continually being forced to expostulate, in fluent but inaccurate Italian, that he disliked being frozen alive. He caught a cold, and sniffed through a week of intense misery. He hated everything and detested everybody. He even loathed the suave Italians who came in to buy his goods, he hated the even more pleasant ones who came in to sell their goods to him. He wore his thickest overcoat in the shop, and when his servant hailed it with comments of '*Che bravo! Che bravo!*' Emmanuel snapped back: 'I don't wear it for pleasure, but only to save myself from being frozen to death! For God's sake heat up that furnace!'

Louis wrote short notes every two days; they said nothing except that he was still 'most satisfactory immune' and that he would return very soon. Angela wrote that England was very cold, and that she hated the winter more every year. She thought that she was getting old and stuffy. She told him of fogs, and hail, of snow that turned to slush in a few hours, of rain and the difficulty of not getting the cold into one's bones. Yet when Antonia reported to Emmanuel that the

Giornale stated that England was covered with snow, that there were dense fogs everywhere, and that it was raining now perpetually for a month, he snapped:

'Just a pack of lies—damned silly rubbish. Better than Milan any day! Oh, can't you get these blasted radiators—*hot*?'

Then, suddenly, the cold ceased, the sun shone and his cold disappeared. He hung up his overcoat, smiled at Antonia and told her that the spring had come in earnest. He was very busy in the shop, and occupied himself with taking stock and correcting prices. He was busy in a corner one morning, sorting out a tray full of old rings, bracelets and seals, when he heard the shop door open. The place was rather dark, and Emmanuel, knowing that he was possibly, and probably, dusty and dishevelled from his work, did not switch on the electric light. He rose and went to the counter, and waited for the woman who had entered to speak. He had a vague impression that she was tall, and that her fur coat must be very hot for such a day.

'Your shop's rather dark,' she said, speaking in Italian.

'I will switch on the light. One moment, please.'

He came back to find her standing over the tray which he had laid on the counter. Her coat collar was turned up and covered the lower part of her face, and the little hat which she wore, Emmanuel decided, was an effectual protection for her eyes. He stood, his hands on the counter, watching her and deciding that her coat was the best he had seen since he left London.

'This is—the shop that is kept by a Frenchman?' she asked, without looking up from the tray.

'He's away in Paris,' Emmanuel said, 'but I am his partner.'

For the first time she looked at him, and Emmanuel felt a conviction that he had seen her before. He wondered if she felt it too, for she looked at him curiously, her eyes, which he could just see, puzzled.

'But you are English?'

He smiled and said, speaking in English: 'Half-English, half-Austrian.'

'I see. The Contessa Bolghese advised me to come to you. She said that you had some tapestry, and some brocade that might be useful for panels. Might I look at them?'

For the next half-hour he showed old brocade and tapestry

which he had collected, he measured and made notes on one of his bills, he held pieces up to the light, and gave her information concerning them.

'I have a villa above Menaggio,' she said, 'it's hideous, at present. Would it be possible for you to keep these until I see how the measurements fit? That's charming of you. The day after tomorrow then, about this time.'

He held open the door and she went out without even glancing at him. Emmanuel went back to his old rings and bracelets.

Somewhere he had seen her before. She was lovely; he had thought so before when he saw her at—where the devil was the place?

CHAPTER FIFTEEN

THE next day Louis returned. A Louis who had cast off his dark clothes and appeared in a suit of light grey, with shirt, tie and hat to match, so splendid and so obviously new that Emmanuel stared at him.

'You like it?'

'My dear fellow, you look like some wonderful advertisement for an expensive dry-cleaners!'

'That, I take it,' Louis said, settling his shoulders more exactly into his coat, 'is a compliment. I have hurried back, my dear cousin, to tell you the news. Can you guess what it is?'

'You're going back to Broadway with Olympia?'

Louis laughed. 'How ridiculous you are! Olympia was charming, as superb as ever. We are very good friends, and Paul Morovio has bought her a beautiful house in Paris, with a garden. Olympia among the flowers! No, I am in love, ideally and successfully!'

'With Olympia?'

Louis raised his eyebrows as if offering a silent but obvious rebuke. 'Have I not said that my friend Paul Morovio has bought her a house?' he asked. 'No, no, with the daughter of a Senator—I think that is what he is—though I am not clear as to the duties of a Senator. He makes prohibition laws I believe, and puts gunmen on spots. It is all Greek to me. More than Greek, for I have studied that language. But he is an American gentleman, his family went to America on the *Mayflower,* he tells me. His name is Richard Hendred Watson. His daughter—words fail me, Emmanuel. She is so young, so lovely, and so—so—untouched! We are very much in love, and at times I have moments of shame that I should know so much of the world—one side of it at least—and that she should know so little.'

Emmanuel grinned, and said: 'Teach her!'

'Please,' Louis expostulated, 'please, this is not a time or a subject when, and on which, I welcome cynicism or flippancy. On the contrary, I shall try to forget a great deal that I know.'

'I shouldn't, she'll like you much better for having had a past.'

'Not Eleanore! Her father calls her—Babs! You don't know her, I only wish that you did. I return to Paris almost at once, so that the father may meet my relations, and know just what type of family his daughter is marrying into.'

'Good Lord! It's got as far as that, has it? I must say, Louis, that you're a quick worker!'

Louis pulled up a chair and sat down nearer to his cousin. Emmanuel looked at him, smiled, then held out his hand.

'Congratulations. I hope that you're a lucky fellow, and I'm certain that she's a lucky woman. But, it's the end of our partnership, Louis, isn't it! You won't want to live in Milan, eh?'

'It would be impossible. Her father wishes me to go with them to New York. He says that he can find work, work with a great deal of money attached to it for me. I refuse to put people in spots or bump men off something or other. I read a book on New York life in the train. It was called *The Recollections of a Gunman.* Life in New York must be very dangerous—and Chicago—quite impossible—everyone must be dead in that city by this time. But you will stay here. We can still be partners in name, Emmanuel. You can use what money of mine there is still in the bank, the car is of no use to me, and from time to time you will send me balanced sheets to say how much money we have made. Then you will take seventy-five per cent. and "mail me"—you see that I am learning American already—the rest. It will be quite simple.'

'And damned lonely without you,' Emmanuel said. 'Confound you and your wretched love affairs! You're a bore, Louis, a damned bore.'

'Which means that you will miss me a little, perhaps?' He took out a huge gold cigarette case, which Emmanuel felt instinctively was a present from the young woman, and lit a cigarette with great care. 'After all, there is many a slip between the cup and the mouth,' he said, 'one never knows—but at the moment, I am in love, and I must go to America to see if the affection will bear exporting, Emmanuel. There are kinds which will bear transportation, and others which will not. We shall see. I keep an open mind.'

He returned to Paris the following day, having first discovered a young man who might act as assistant in the shop. Emmanuel was ready to believe that the fellow was clever, that he was the son of an impoverished but noble family; but he hated his scent, hated his long finger-nails, and detested the rings which decorated his long, slim fingers. He felt that once again Fate had not been too kind to him in removing Louis. He had grown very fond of Louis, and had come to rely upon his judgment and his taste. Now, Louis had gone, he was left without a single friend in Milan, and the old sense of unutterable loneliness descended on him more heavily than ever.

For six months he had seen no one that he knew, his only letters had been from Angela, who, though she wrote long and amusing letters, always seemed to him to be 'walking warily' lest she might awaken something which was better left sleeping. In her letters he felt there was a faint hint of unreality. He knew that she loved him, and knew that she was writing letters which she felt were wise, rather than the letters she would have wished to write to him. But the rest—his father—Bill—and Viva—the three people who mattered most to him after his mother—might have been living in another world for all he knew of them. Their names cropped up in Angela's letters, but only in brief allusions, only in sentences which really told him nothing that mattered in the least.

In his heart his hatred of Julian still smouldered, and at such times as these, when his loneliness was brought home to him, it flared and flamed again, leaving him almost weak from the intensity of his passion.

On the morning after Louis had left, Emmanuel stood in the shop, doing nothing in particular, except wonder vaguely why his new assistant wanted two hours in which to eat his lunch. In the old days at Bond Street, everyone had taken an hour—a rule which included Emmanuel and even Reuben Davis. Here, young men wanted two hours to eat a plateful of macaroni and drink a half-litre of cheap wine! It was ridiculous, a waste of time. The business side of Emmanuel's nature rebelled against it; the personal side congratulated himself that he was shot of the exquisite, long-nailed Guido Something-or-other for a couple of hours.

It was during Guido's two hours that the Englishwoman came back with the measurements for the tapestry and brocade. She was less muffled to the eyes, and Emmanuel could see her face clearly. Again he had the conviction that he had seen her before; and once or twice he felt that she believed that she knew him.

She brought out her measurements, and together they went through his stock of materials. The pile mounted; she would be able, she said, to use a great many of them with a little adapting. The selection over, she sat down in a big chair which he had brought three weeks before in Satlo, and asked if she might smoke a cigarette.

Emmanuel bowed, produced his own case, and when she said that she preferred her own, lit it for her, thinking as he did so: 'I've seen her somewhere. Where the devil was it?'

'The villa that I have taken,' she said, 'is, at the moment, my despair. The rooms are hideous, like band-boxes enlarged. The walls are covered with the most abominable colours, and no one seems to want to produce any others. Yet, I must have it, because it has a garden, and looks over the lake, and has windows which really open and let in the sun and air. It's a problem——'

'We might be able to advise you,' Emmanuel said, tentatively. 'We did some rooms for Signora Ridolfi a few weeks ago, and she was very satisfied, I believe.'

'Oh, you do decorating as well as antiques! But how wonderful! Would you really come and give me some advice?'

He bowed, just a little stiffly, he was playing the complete shopman, and rather enjoying it. If she puzzled him, he knew that he certainly puzzled her. 'With pleasure, madam.'

She glanced up and met his eyes, then said abruptly: 'You know, I am quite certain that I've met you before. I can't think where.'

'I was with a large firm in London until six months ago,' he said, and knew that his mouth twisted as he said it. How he hated to remember six months ago, and yet how he enjoyed torturing himself!

The woman leant back in her big chair and watched him, curiously and attentively. Emmanuel decided that she was very beautiful, past her first youth, just a little—not overblown, but more generously built than the modern woman. He thought that she must be well over thirty. She was obviously rich, for her clothes were perfect, and the two rings which she wore were, he knew, very valuable and very old. Mentally he classed them as 'collector's pieces'.

She was drumming with her fingers on the arm of the chair, her eyes still on his face, then the drumming ceased and she leant forward and smiled:

'I have it!' she said. 'I saw you at Ordingly.' Then the smile faded, and her voice softened. 'You were at the funeral of a very dear friend of mine—Emmanuel Gollantz. How curious, I was staying there a fortnight ago.' Then the puzzled look returned as Emmanuel did not reply, and she sat silent again, then continued: 'I know now, and I hope that I haven't hurt you, or been intrusive. Of course, you're Emmanuel Gollantz, Angela's eldest son, aren't you?'

'Yes—but——' he hesitated.

'But——?' she prompted him.

'But I'm out of the firm. No one knows that I am here. My father and I don't—see eye to eye. Please don't mention me if you write.'

'I won't, of course.'

Emmanuel went on: 'I thought that I knew you the first time you came here. You're Miss Forbes—I mean, Mrs. Vernon Seyre. I once stayed at your place in the country, somewhere near Reading, years ago——' He stopped suddenly and remembered what had happened at the end of that visit, how he had driven her up the Great North Road to where her lover, Leon Hast, lay—they all believed—dying in a hospital after a motor accident, when he had been driving with Emmanuel's aunt, Lady Stansfield.

She rose, and held out the end of her cigarette to him.

'Will you put that out for me? Thank you. Yes, I remember. I won't mention this meeting to any of them, of course. They—they are all very well. Angela looked beautiful. Good-bye, Mr. Gollantz. Will you send the tapestry?' She opened her bag and gave him a card. 'That's the address. I'll send a cheque when I get home.'

He held open the door, and she passed out. He wondered if he had hurt her, by stumbling on the past as he had done. She hadn't said anything more about the rooms. Well, that was her business, if she wanted help she knew where to find him. He turned back to the counter and began to fold up the materials. He hoped that he hadn't hurt her. The old story came back to him now. Eight years ago—it was a long time. He was sixteen then.

Emmanuel left the work that he was doing, sat down, his elbows on the counter, and went back over those eight years. Sixteen. He remembered how much he had disliked Seyre, and—a smile touched his lips—how he had imagined that he was in love with Juliet Forbes. Now, he had met her and not even remembered who she was! She had changed, she was older, more mature—still beautiful, but it was the end of her beauty, not the beginning. Eight years ago, she had been young, he had felt that they were almost the same age. Now, she seemed to be just a friend of his mother's, then she had seemed to be the only woman he could ever love!

Compared with Viva—— He turned back to his work—what did he want to think of Viva for? Thinking only made things a damn sight worse. Why couldn't he let things alone and not go digging and probing and remembering!

Her cheque came by the second post the next day. He turned the letter over and decided that even her writing was a little old-fashioned. Long loops and slanting letters, and the cheque signed in a big, rather attractive hand—Juliet Forbes. She had written a note saying that she had forgotten about the decorating, and that if he cared to do it she would be grateful for his help. That was all. No reference to their having met before, nothing. She was writing to him as she might have written to any decorator who was not quite a tradesman.

'Know anything about decorating rooms?' Emmanuel asked Guido. Guido shrugged his shoulders. 'Very little, I regret to say. My own rooms are decorated by myself and my artistic friends, but they are to please ourselves.'

Emmanuel thought: 'I bet that they wouldn't please me, either! I can see 'em—all bits and pieces, sham junk. Slightly decadent, and more than slightly dirty.'

Aloud, he said: 'A client of mine has a villa above Menaggio, she wants some decorating done. I thought that you might have had a look at it. I'm very busy and have to go over to see a chap at Brescia next week.'

Guido smiled, said that he would, of course, do his best, but that his knowledge of English taste—if the client was English—was small.

'Your taste of most styles would be all in your mouth,' Emmanuel thought again. 'You're no damn use to us, my lad. You're not even decorative—to my taste, anyway.' He said: 'All right, I'd better go. You'll have to cut down that luncheon hour of yours a bit while I'm away, you know.'

Guido shrugged. 'All shops—of standing—close for siesta in Milan.'

'Well, mine isn't a shop of standing then,' Emmanuel retorted, 'and get rid of the idea that it's one for sitting either. That's all you do most of your time, that and clean your nails with a pocket knife.'

'You would prefer them to remain dirty, perhaps?'

'If you want to know,' Emmanuel said, 'I should prefer them clean and short. Both those operations can be performed in your own bedroom. And while I am on this subject, the next time you use that fifteenth century stiletto to pick your teeth—there'll be trouble and you'll be in it!'

But Guido bore no malice, and the next morning arrived with a small bunch of beautiful violets, which he arranged in an old glass vase and set carefully on Emmanuel's desk. Emmanuel sniffed the flowers, and said:

'Where did they come from? They're pretty, aren't they?'

Guido said, showing his perfect teeth, and with his beautiful eyes shining with pleasure:

'I bought them for you. I—inadvertently—annoyed you. I regret it. In future I shall use my bedroom more for my toilet.'

It was on the end of Emmanuel's tongue to thank him

briefly and tell him not to bring him flowers again, when he caught sight of the fellow's smile, and something stopped him. It was a very nice smile, very frank and very friendly. The chap would no more understand why he shouldn't bring flowers, than he would understand why he shouldn't clean his nails in the shop!

Emmanuel lifted the vase and smelt the flowers.

'Thanks very much,' he said, 'it was awfully kind.'

The old dreadful homesickness had swept over him. At Ordingly there was a big violet bed, and in a few weeks, Angela would be picking them, carrying them back to the house, and making everyone smell them, saying that they were the loveliest things in the world. God, how he ached to be back there!

When he left two days later for Brescia, and told Guido that he should come back by Como, and see to the decorating job, Guido smiled and nodded.

'You shall have a great surprise,' he said, 'when you return and find out how much I have sold! The shop will be empty and the kesh-box overflowing! And look!' He extended two hands, the nails of which were cut so short that Emmanuel felt certain that they must hurt like the devil. '*All' Inglese,*' he said with pride.

He interviewed his man at Brescia, and in a shop not far from the hotel where he lunched, the waiter told him that he would find something that might interest him. The waiter was an old friend of Emmanuel's, he spoke English, and had once been waiter at the Hyde Park Hotel. 'Head waiter,' he said, but Emmanuel discovered that Italy was full of 'head waiters' from the Ritz, the Berkeley, the Savoy and the Hyde Park hotels.

'I don't want fancy stuff, or fancy prices,' he said.

'No, cheap,' the man assured him. 'And while you are here, at the cinema there is Carlo—in *London Lights*. Do not miss it! It is wonderful—Carlo is the hero of my life! Carlo and Mussolini.'

Later he bought more brocades, lovely pale colours which seemed to have caught some of the sunshine, beautiful rich scarlets and purples which might have been steeped in the juice of the grapes from the hillsides. There was an old piece of embroidery, too small to be of much real use, but worked in silver thread, and decorated with bursting pomegranates—

he hesitated, then bought it. He would take it as a peace offering to Mrs. Seyre, in case he had hurt her.

Bergamo, which he took on his way back to Como, proved uninteresting. The dealers had nothing new, and only annoyed him by trying to sell him what he had refused on his last visit. He went back to the car and set off for Menaggio. His head ached, and his whole body felt terribly weary. Not the contented weariness which comes at the end of a long day, and is almost pleasurable, but an awful sense of exhaustion, which made him nervous as he drove, and made him long to be going home, really going home. He wanted an English bath, he wanted to find his clothes laid out ready for him, to dress slowly smoking a Virginian cigarette as he did so; he wanted to go down and drink a good cocktail, and follow it by an English dinner, eaten at a table round which English people sat and talked of English things and English concerns.

Once or twice he glanced at the olives and cypress trees as if he hated them; he stared at the lake in the distance and said that it was too blue, and that Windermere was infinitely more beautiful.

It was after five when he got to the villa, and decided that he hated it, and wondered how any woman of taste could care to live in such a place. It was painted a bright, warm pink, with shutters of brilliant green. True it had a huge garden, but Emmanuel was in the mood to add: 'And what a garden! Like Kew palm house run to seed!'

He wished that he hadn't come, wished that he had driven straight back to Milan, and sent a letter to say that Menaggio was too far, and that she must find a local decorator.

His sense of humour reasserted itself faintly. 'Hang it, I'm too good a business man to turn down work,' he said, as he climbed out of the car and went up the long, wide flight of steps which led to the front door.

'What the deuce do I call her?' he thought, all his old irritation returning, 'Miss Forbes—Mrs. Seyre—the Signorina or the Signora? What a bore this all is! And what I'd give for some decent tea!'

The door was opened by a tall Italian woman, who stood and waited for him to speak.

Emmanuel decided that the 'signora' would be safe enough. The woman took his card, and said in unexpected English:

'Very goot—vill you pleese vait.'

He looked at the hall while he waited, and decided that something might be done with it. The black and white tiles weren't so bad, and the size was good. That long window which looked over the lake was excellent. How hideous the electric wiring was—all indecently uncovered!

'Pleese come this way . . .'

Juliet came to meet him. He thought that she looked younger without a hat. He liked the feeling of her hand, cool and smooth, he liked her voice when she said:

'This is kind of you, Mr. Gollantz.' Then to the servant: 'Tea, at once, Ottavia, please.'

Then turning back to him: 'Or would you like a cocktail? Or a whisky and soda?'

For a moment Emmanuel looked like a boy, he smiled, and he forgot how tired he was, forgot how badly he was hating pink villas, and olive trees and everything.

'Might I have a whisky and soda first, and tea afterwards?'

'If it won't make you feel terribly ill, certainly. Ottavia, whisky and soda first—quickly. Sit down, you're tired.'

'I believe I am,' he said, 'it's a long way—Brescia, Bergamo and on here. I started early and—oh, I'm just tired and very bad-tempered. There are days when I loathe blue skies and cypress trees, and lakes and smiling people more than words can say. Days when I think that an overdone steak at Lyons Corner House would be better than anything that Savini can produce.'

She laughed. 'I know—I have felt like that about every town in Europe that boasts a concert hall—and in England too. I nearly died of homesickness for Italy when I was in New York last year.'

'Did you?' He remembered that she was a famous singer, and that, he imagined, must be a fairly lonely existence.

As he sipped his whisky and soda, he twisted the glass in his fingers, and noted that it was old—really old, not a Venetian imitation. He was too tired to talk very much, but lay back in his chair, and enjoyed the sensation of sitting in what he called 'a real chair' again. Italians couldn't make modern chairs fit to sit in, either they were so hard that they hurt, or stuffed so full that they were abominably hot. The room wasn't a bad shape, he decided, and there were plenty of good things in it, things that deserved a better background than pale blue distemper of the tint which reminded him of parish halls and Methodist Chapels. The rugs were excellent, there was a lovely old mirror in a faded gilt frame, there were two vases that made him wonder where she could have found them in Italy, and there was a huge Chinese screen that was like something out of a fairy tale.

Juliet Forbes spoke as if she had read his thoughts. 'They are nice, aren't they? It's rather a shame to have transplanted them, for I can only be here for odd months in the year. But I couldn't live without them, they're part of me.'

He set down his glass with care. 'That's the first nice glass I've met for six months,' he said. 'Now, what about the walls. They're impossible as they are, an insult to your own things. I have some brocade for you to see, in the car, and a little bit of—what in "the trade" we should call—nice junk, that I bought for you. Let me get them.'

He ran down to the car, his tiredness had gone, his headache had vanished. He came back with his arms full of shimmering brocade and let it fall in a long shining trail over the polished floor.

'Apple blossom,' she said, 'and young green leaves. I must have it. In a room with white walls—dead white, opaque, not a bit of gloss except the brocade.'

She gave him tea, and he nibbled small hot cakes, which might have come out of their own kitchen at Ordingly, and for the first time these things did not awaken in him a sense of homesickness, for the first time he accepted them gratefully, without allowing his bitterness to be roused by them. The china was old Worcester, the tea was perfect, and the teaspoons were old Dutch silver, very thin and smooth.

'And this,' he said, as he picked up the bit of embroidery, 'Is only a little bit of useless beauty. Look at the pomegranates, and the silver thread. It's rather fun, isn't it?'

She looked at it, smoothing the silk flowers with the tip of her finger. 'It's fifteenth century, isn't it?'

'I think earlier—late fourteenth, I fancy.'

She laughed. 'I don't agree, but it's perfect. I want it, please, to hang behind a little statue of the Madonna.'

'It's for you——' he said, and felt suddenly shy.

'For me! How kind of you. Really?'

'I got it in Brescia. I'd like you to have it, because I felt that I'd not been very—well, gracious—the other day. It's a peace offering.'

Without looking at him, with her finger still tracing the outline of the silken fruit, she said: 'I know—you remembered too much. I didn't mind, you were very kind to me years ago, I *can* remember that. Now, shall we go and look at the other rooms?'

CHAPTER SIXTEEN

'STAY to dinner,' Juliet had said, 'and then we can go on settling about these rooms.'

He had stayed, and had enjoyed the dinner that she gave him. He had liked the polished table, the lace, the old silver and the china that bore the monogram of an Emperor who had died a hundred years before. There were the things that he knew, understood and loved.

Then later she had glanced at a clock and said:

'You can't possibly go tonight. It's far too late, and you're tired to death. Stay here and leave as early as you like in the morning.'

'I must be back in Milan before ten.' He hesitated. He didn't want to go, he was finding it so pleasant to hear an English voice again. She wasn't particularly brilliant, except when she began to talk about the old things which she had gathered round her. Then, he thought, she talked like a connoisseur; but the whole atmosphere was soothing, and his nerves were badly jangled by weeks of loneliness.

'You can be called at six,' she said. 'I'll tell Ottavia to get your room ready.'

He did not see her in the morning. His breakfast was brought to him as the little clock on his table struck six. His bath was hot, and the car had been cleaned by someone. Ottavia opened the front door for him, and when he asked that she would convey his thanks to her mistress, she answered:

'The moment that she wakes, she shall have your message.'

He drove back to Milan, and arriving there was met by Guido, who, if he had not sold the entire contents of the shop, had at least apparently turned everything upside down in his attempts to make customers buy.

'You are back too soon,' he said, smiling; 'not too soon for my wish, but for customers. Today I have Conte di Carodori arriving to inspect that big chair, and his wife to look at some old lace and a fan. There are others who will come, for I have not been idle. At a dinner last night, I told everyone that you were an English duke who prefers work, to living in idleness in his great palace in London! They are all coming to buy from the English duke who is incognito!'

'You idiot!' Emmanuel said, half-amused, half-annoyed. 'They'll know when they come that I'm nothing of the sort.'

'Not at all,' Guido replied, unmoved. 'None of them know in the least what an English duke looks like or how he behaves.'

'Do you?'

'Not with any certainty. I think that there are very few left, because the fog kills them. It is always fog in London, I know that, and rain and snow. No wonder that you came to Milan.'

'I shouldn't call Milan exactly a health resort,' Emmanuel said, 'it's been hell this winter, I know that.'

Guido wagged his shining head. 'You have forgotten, no doubt,' he said, 'what London is like. Now, we will tidy the shop ready for the Conte and his wife, shall we?'

In his spare time Emmanuel hunted for the shades of paint which he had decided were the right tints for the villa on Lake Como. He went here and there, buying a few tins here and a few there, even bringing tins home and mixing them in the little back yard, where Guido had planted some weary looking flowers and small shrubs, because, he said: 'The English cannot live without gardens.'

Emmanuel had looked at them and wondered how long they could survive Guido's overwatering, and said:

'The trouble with you, young Guido, is that you're too kind.'

'All my life,' Guido returned with smug satisfaction, 'I have had a peculiar devotion to Saint Francis.'

But it was Guido who found what Emmanuel hailed as a really satisfactory treasure trove. Some young man, one of his numerous artistic friends, had had a 'disaster', which meant that the art shop which he had financed had failed and the stock was sold.

Guido was inclined to be scornful, and told Emmanuel of it with many shrugs and head waggings.

'He would not be guided,' he said, 'we all tried to advise him. He bought rubbish. He bought—in other words—from his friends! For example—he had a friend, an artist who designed papers for walls. And another friend who printed it by hand. There it is, rolls and rolls of rubbish, only fit for the servants to cover shelves!'

Only after many arguments would he allow Emmanuel to go round and inspect the paper and the rest of the stock. Emmanuel went through everything carefully, disregarding Guido's efforts to make him buy seven complete tea sets exported from Japan, in large imitation leather cases. The paper was beautiful. Old patterns had been copied and printed with care. There were patterns of Chinese origin, patterns taken from old brocades and other materials, and all printed in lovely subdued colours.

Emmanuel heaped the lot together and said: 'I'll take that.'

Guido whispered: 'Are you mad, please! There are dozens of rolls.'

'Shut up, my infant, and leave me alone.'

Guido wandered off to return with a carved ivory replica of the Taj Mahal, which he stated to be a thousand years old and of a value which was incalculable.

That night Emmanuel looked again at the papers and smiled. He had everything now. Paint, and now this find of exquisite paper. There were even seven rolls of real old gold paper, stuff which must be at least a hundred and fifty years old.

He closed the shop on Saturdays at twelve, a habit of which Guido approved wholeheartedly, and went off to Menaggio with his precious load of papers and paint. As he drove there, he knew that he was looking forward to meeting Juliet Forbes again, that he was longing to hear her speak his own language, and that the whole atmosphere of the house was attracting him enormously.

She was delighted with the results of his search, and praised the papers unstintedly. Together they decided which rooms would be most suitable, which walls were crying out for paper, and which for paint.

'Now,' Juliet said, as they sat together and drank tea, 'only one thing remains, that is to find a man who can carry out the work. That's going to be difficult, because I shall be away after next Tuesday for a month. I wonder if there is anyone in the village——'

Emmanuel said: 'Oh, I didn't know that you were going away so soon.' His voice had lost some of its colour, it sounded flat, even in his own ears.

'Berlin, Hamburg, London, Edinburgh, Leeds—think of Leeds after this!—back to Paris and home—that's here—by way of Vienna. A month's racing about, staying in uncomfortable hotels, and knowing that this blueness is increasing every day, and that the sun is getting stronger, and the flowers—oh, I really don't want to go.'

That evening he went down to the village and found a man who declared that he was not an ordinary workman, but an artist among house decorators. He had a friend, who proved to have the appearance of a stage brigand, and whose manners were those of the mildest of English curates, who agreed to work with him. Emmanuel brought them back with him, lectured them, and gave minute instructions; but some of the joy had gone, he felt that once again he was going to be left dreadfully and devastatingly alone. Juliet listened, and thought how horrible life must be for this young man, how he must hate living in two rooms in Milan, after living all his life at Ordingly.

'While I'm away,' she said, 'why don't you spend your week-ends here? Ottavia will look after you, and you can keep an eye on these men. It's a good idea, I think.'

Emmanuel nodded. 'It sounds like heaven to me,' he said. 'It's far too kind of you.'

'And,' she hesitated, 'remember that this is all—on a business basis. You won't try to get out of the—bill part of it, will you?'

The next week-end found him back at the villa, a villa which he found very lonely for all the beauty of its surroundings. He missed Juliet, he missed her voice, her arguments, and her knowledge. She had written to him once, a short letter only, telling him that she could bring back anything that he wanted. She gave the address of her agent in London, and asked him to write there. He spent the week-end examining the work which had been done, and arranging for what was still to be done the following week. He went back to Milan very early on the Monday morning, feeling dispirited and tired.

The Sunday following, Emmanuel made his tour of inspection. The place was finished, and all that remained was to arrange the furniture. It was a hot spring morning, and some of the sunshine reached his heart. He went about his work whistling contentedly. He planned and arranged, he pushed furniture here and there with the help of the 'artist decorator' and his brigand friend, and after luncheon, took a long chair into the garden, and sat there smoking, staring over the blue lake which lay below him. Gradually sleep stole over him, his eyes closed and he felt the warmth on his lids; his whole body relaxed, the paper, which he had pretended to read, dropped from his hand, and he slept there in the bright sunshine, under the high vault of blue sky.

He was half-awakened by the sound of voices; they reached him through the mists of sleep, and dimly he knew that one was an English voice, speaking English words. He did not open his eyes, he was certain that the voices were part of his half-waking, half-sleeping dreams. He often dreamt that he was back in England, often awoke with English phrases ringing in his ears. Then, through his half-consciousness he felt that someone was watching him, and the realization made him shake off sleep and sit upright—wide awake. Over there, behind that thick green hedge which separated one garden from another, someone had looked at him, someone had parted the branches and stared through.

He frowned, picked up his paper—an English *Times*, three days old—and tried to force his attention back to the parliamentary reports. Once he saw Julian's name, read a speech which Julian had made, and in another part of the paper, saw that he was hailed as a young man with a future. Emmanuel stirred restlessly—how he hated to remember that this man was his brother, to remember that for his sake he was an exile.

Ottavia was coming towards him from the house, carrying a tray and tea. With his black mood still triumphant, Emmanuel decided that he hated drinking tea alone.

As she set down the tray on the little stone table, she said:

'And there is one who wishes to speak to you.'

'Me? Who is it? The painter fellow?'

She shrugged her shoulders. Emmanuel knew that half the time she didn't understand what one said to her. She pretended that her English was much better than it really was.

'Ask him to come here,' he said. 'Here, in the garden.'

He poured out his tea, and turned to see who wanted to see him. Over the short grass, still brilliant green because the sun was not yet sufficiently strong to have shrivelled it, he saw a tall man coming towards him. He stared, and felt suddenly weak. The man was his father.

Max said stiffly: 'I hope this isn't an intrusion, Emmanuel. I was calling on your next door neighbour. I heard of him from my cousins in Vienna. An impoverished nobleman. I'm on my way to Milan and Florence. I looked through the hedge, your neighbour praised this garden. I saw you. I felt that I must come in and speak to you.'

'Yes,' Emmanuel said, 'won't you sit down? Have tea?'

Max sat down as if he, too, were overcome by the meeting. His face was grave, Emmanuel remembered that he had not offered his hand. So it was still—war! He turned back to the house and called to Ottavia to bring another cup, then went back to his father.

'You live here?' Max asked.

'I'm only here at week-ends.'

'Do you work?'

'Certainly.'

'Not here?'

'No,' quickly, 'in Stresa.'

Max turned round and looked at the house. 'This isn't your own place, is it? It's very pretty.'

Emmanuel felt a sudden desperate fear come over him. He had nothing to fear, he had done nothing wrong, and yet the knowledge that his father was watching him with cold critical eyes, frightened him. He wanted to get up and run away, to refuse to speak—anything to get out of range of those cold eyes. Ottavia came out with the cup for which he had asked, she set it on the table, and folded her hands.

Emmanuel glanced up. 'Yes?'

'Will the gentleman be here for dinner?'

Max said quickly: 'No—no. I'm going on to Milan immediately.'

Ottavia turned back to Emmanuel: 'What time will you

have dinner? Manuello is here with some fresh fish, will you have it?'

'Yes—dinner? The same time as usual. Get the fish, Ottavia.'

She went back to the house, Max said again, 'This isn't your own place, is it?'

'No, of course not. I only stay here sometimes.'

His father's face seemed to sneer at him. 'You give orders pretty freely, don't you?'

'I'm alone at the moment——' then he went a step nearer to his father. 'What do you mean?' he asked, 'what are you driving at?'

Max rose and faced him; they were almost of a height, their eyes met and stared at each other very coldly.

'Only that your neighbour told me that the villa belongs to a woman—a singer—who lived alone but who had a friend. I presume that you are the friend?'

Emmanuel knew that he lost his head, knew that his fear overmastered him. He flushed, he felt that his eyes wavered a little, and when he spoke the words came very quickly.

'It's r-ridiculous,' he said, 'it's abominable. The owner of this villa is——' he checked himself, 'a fr-riend of mine. I have been doing some work for her, decorating and so on. I'm here on business—— Why must you always believe the worst of me? It's not fair—it's not r-right. Let me explain——'

'Thank you,' Max said. 'I think explanations are unnecessary. I happen to know to whom this villa belongs, you see. I apologize for intruding. It's entirely your business and hers.'

'Then you ought to know her sufficiently well to know what's the tr-ruth! She met me by accident. She offered me work. I think—that she was sor-rry for me.'

The moment after he had spoken he could have cut his tongue off for the suggestion that he was asking for sympathy. He wondered how much longer he would have to meet those cold eyes, and see that hard mouth. This wasn't the Max Gollantz that he had known at all!

'I have not the slightest doubt that you made your own case good,' Max said, 'and, I remember that she always had a large heart.'

Emmanuel recovered himself. As he watched him Max felt

that it might have been the old Emmanuel speaking, sixty years ago.

'You are taking advantage of the fact that you are my father. Even that gives you no right to insult this lady. May I ask you to go, at once.'

Max wanted terribly to sit down again, wanted to beg this handsome son of his to talk to him frankly, to explain and make it possible for them to come to some understanding. What had happened six months ago was past. He had thought so often of Emmanuel, had listened to scraps from his letters which Angela had read, and gradually had come to believe that somewhere, someone had made a ghastly mistake. He had come on one of his business tours through Europe, and in every town had looked and wondered if he might not come upon his son. The idea had grown, and he had felt that he was setting out, in reality, not to find antiques, but to find Emmanuel.

Then that doddering old fool in the next villa, a horrible old creature, had whispered scandal about a beautiful Englishwoman, a singer, and had tried to get his foul tongue round her name. He had told Max that her garden was beautiful, and that there was a statue there which was undeniably good. He had drawn back the little branches of the hedge, and Max had peered through and seen Emmanuel.

Even in the old days he had never liked Juliet Forbes very much, he had judged her and felt that both Angela and his father were weak where she was concerned. Though he had never liked Vernon Seyre, he had liked Leon Hast even less; and when Juliet had left her husband for a crippled and bedridden Hast, Max had felt that there was something almost revolting in the idea.

She had been beautiful then, but when he had seen her last at Ordingly, it had struck him that she looked more mature than Angela. He had said so, and Angela had laughed and said:

'Max dear, you and your prejudices! She's lovely still. She looks what she is, a singer. They don't run to flat chests, you ought to know that. Anyway, Mr. Cochran says that we've all got to have a real shape again! I don't envy Juliet all her money and her success, she's a lonely person, poor darling.'

Now he had come here to find his son installed in her villa, his son giving orders about the time he wanted dinner and about some fish which had been caught. The master of the house! Emmanuel—at twenty-six, and Juliet Forbes, Seyre, or Hast, whatever she called herself—was thirty-five or thirty-six.

Emmanuel's eyes did not waver this time, his voice was perfectly steady as he said again:

'May I ask you to go, at once?'

Max made a violent effort; he loved this son of his, he wanted to get back to their old footing. The last six months had been one long-continued regret. They had aged him. Angela wasn't happy, Bill pestered him to know where Emmanuel had gone, Viva Heriot looked at him sometimes, under her painted eyelashes, as if she hated him.

'Emmanuel,' he said, 'can't you see that I want to protect you?'

'I have managed without your protection, thank you, for the past six months.'

'This woman—Miss Forbes—is too old for——'

'I don't think that we'll discuss her, please.'

'But it's impossible that——'

Again Emmanuel's cold voice: 'Six months ago you were quite ready to believe that I was a pervert; now you are equally ready to believe that I'm a gigolo. Shall we leave it at that? Good-bye.'

'I'm asking you to explain everything,' Max said desperately. 'I don't care what it is, offer me explanations about what happened six months ago—about this; only, for God's sake, don't stand there talking as if your voice had just come off the ice!'

'What happened six months ago is over, whatever there remains to find out concerning it rests with you. There is no explanation of this last insinuation of yours. Even to discuss the matter is unfair to Miss Forbes.'

Max frowned, it was impossible to go on begging this boy to give reasons and to explain. Damn it, he had some pride left, he couldn't go on begging for ever.

'Very well, you prefer that I should think the worst of you?'

Emmanuel smiled, a dangerously pleasant smile. 'Oh, you decided to do that on the suggestion of your old friend in the next villa. Again—Good-bye.'

'Only one thing——' Max said and hesitated. Emmanuel

looked at him with his eyebrows a little raised as if he was surprised at his bad taste in continuing the interview, his whole expression was patiently and unwillingly tolerant. 'Only one thing,' he repeated, 'you're not married to Juliet, are you?'

'No.'

'Are you going to marry her?'

'I couldn't say. I shall ask her to marry me, after this.' Then his man-of-the-world air dropped from him, and to Max his sudden lapse into what was almost schoolboy English was heartbreaking: 'I should have to tell her about the affair in England. I'm not everybody's money, am I? Oh, for God's sake, go and leave me alone! Can't you see that you're only torturing me, father?'

Max turned and walked back to the big gates where his car was waiting. He did not turn, or he would have seen Emmanuel drop into his chair and bury his face in his hands.

'Milan,' he said to the chauffeur. 'I don't want to stop anywhere.'

That evening as Emmanuel sat at dinner, a telegram was brought to him. It was from Juliet.

> 'Staying Ordingly week-end stop Angela very well stop has talked about you so much and so kindly stop Juliet.'

He read the words twice, then folded the paper and put it away in his pocket-book. She must have learnt that habit of telegraphing 'stop' when she was in America. Very few English people did it.

How strange that while his father had been speaking to him in Juliet's garden, she should have been, in all probability, sitting talking to Angela at Ordingly. He had said to his father that he should ask her to marry him. He didn't love her, he didn't think for a moment that she loved him. He liked her, he admired her, and she had made life more bearable for him. The fact that she had been Hast's mistress didn't affect him; whatever feeling he had for Juliet Forbes was removed from any sense of possession and sexual passion. It was a warm friendship, nothing more. Until his father had put that question he had never considered the idea of marriage. It had come as a shock, and he had felt that—if this old scoundrel next door was talking scandal--he ought to tell Juliet and give her the opportunity of refusing him.

It was all very ridiculous, very tiresome, because it might make his visits difficult, and he had enjoyed coming here. He believed that she had liked it too. But marriage—the whole idea was foolish. He sat back, sipping his coffee and smoking, and remembered how years ago he had felt that he wanted to die for her. He remembered how he had hated her husband, with his tousled yellow hair, and his hearty manner. He remembered the scene at their house outside Reading, when Juliet had sung, and Seyre had interrupted and knocked things over while she was singing. An ash-tray or something had gone tumbling on to the floor, and she had stopped and said:

'My God! How can I sing with this awful noise going on!'

How lovely she had been then, and how unhappy! He had driven her up the North Road, with Seyre sitting in the dicky asking dreadful personal questions all the time. 'If Hast gets better will you go back to him?' and 'If he dies will you come back to me?' The fellow had lost his head, he was crazy for love of her. Hast had got better and she had gone back to him, to look after him and nurse him. That couldn't have been easy for her. Then Hast had died—had he heard that he committed suicide?—and she'd been left all his money. Poor Juliet, life hadn't been too easy for her. He didn't know if Seyre had ever divorced her or not. Didn't know if she ever called herself Mrs. Seyre now.

He thought a great deal about her during that week. Never with any sense of loving her as he loved Viva, but with a feeling that they had both had a bad time, and that had drawn them close to each other. He would ask her to marry him, because of what his father had said. She'd probably laugh at him, for all he knew she might be in love with some fellow somewhere; but it was the right thing to do, even though it was only a formality. Then his thoughts would turn back to Viva, and he would wonder if he would ever see Viva again, if she ever thought of him, and what was going to be the end of it all?

Viva—laughing at everything, making fun of everything, and yet so clever, and so intolerably dear.

CHAPTER SEVENTEEN

JULIET was at home again; she had written to ask him to come over for the week-end; she had said that she wanted to congratulate him upon his work; then she had telephoned to ask if he had got the letter, and to say that she would be in Milan on the Saturday morning and would call for him.

Guido who answered the telephone first, said:

'The voice of an angel with a bad Italian accent! I am certain that she is very beautiful.' He sighed, his dark eyes full of sentimental curiosity.

Emmanuel said, 'She is very beautiful indeed.'

Again Guido sighed gustily. 'Some are indeed fortunate——'

'And some are not,' Emmanuel returned sharply.

'She loves you!'

'Certainly not!'

'You love her and are sad because your love is not returned?' he suggested with the air of one who discovers the key to a situation.

'For Heaven's sake,' Emmanuel said, 'stop gassing about love. You'd think that the world was one huge love affair!'

Guido nodded. 'It is, to people of sensibility.'

For the first time Emmanuel felt that he did not want to spend the week-end at the villa. He knew that Juliet would be certain to talk about Ordingly and his mother; and though he was hungry for news, he knew that it must inevitably hurt him to hear it. Then he must tell her of his father's visit, and of her unpleasant old neighbour's insinuation. If he asked her to marry him first, and told her afterwards it looked as if he said:

'Please marry me, and then I will tell you what makes me ask you.'

If he told her of the scandal first, she certainly would realize what made him ask her to be his wife. He decided not to mention his father's visit, or to retail the remarks of her neighbour. That part of the story might be allowed to remain untold.

Before, it had been so good to slip away from Milan, to know that quiet and pleasant companionship waited for him.

He had believed that it might have lasted, and that he might have come to be tremendous friends with Juliet Forbes. But nothing ever lasted, he thought, all his old bitterness flaming again. Everything he wanted or prized must, apparently, be automatically snatched from him.

He went out to join Juliet in her car, his face sullen and overcast, his whole temper frayed; he was ready to find fault with everything.

'The house is beautiful,' she said. 'I came back to find a real home waiting for me. Thank you, Emmanuel.'

'I'm glad you like it,' he said. 'It wasn't difficult.'

'Would you like to drive, or shall I?'

'You, please.'

He watched her as she drove out of the town, thought how well she looked, how cleverly she managed to slide through the traffic; no fuss, no continual hooting, or cursing everyone else who happened to be on the road. Capable and certain of herself. Her face looked very soft, yet firm, under the tight-fitting hat that she wore, her hair caught the light and shone in the sun, her eyes were steady and never restless. She was beautiful, too, with her lovely face, her fine neck and shoulders which looked so strong. Her voice, whenever she spoke to him, was so musical, and yet so controlled. It seemed that it was an instrument upon which she played, making it yield whatever beautiful tones she wished. There was a certain lack of excitement about her; she neither chattered nor asked continual questions. To be with her was very restful, and as they left the town behind them, Emmanuel felt that his nerves were losing their awful sense of being strung too tightly; he felt that his ill-temper was being left behind in the outskirts of Milan.

'Was the tour a success?'

She nodded, without looking at him. 'Yes, a great success. The day is over when I was afraid of my audiences; they can't hurt me any more.'

'Can nothing hurt you unless you are afraid?' he asked.

'Very few things, I think. Certainly nothing can hurt you so badly, once you have thrown fear overboard.'

'I wonder——' Then abruptly, because he wanted to hear and yet wanted to get it over, 'How was Angela?'

'As wonderful as ever,' this time she turned and smiled at him. 'Talking a great deal about you, wondering about you. I felt something of a traitor that I couldn't say that I had seen you. She was alone for the week-end, your father was away.'

'And Bill?'

'Bill is apparently doing great things at Oxford. He's going to be brilliant, evidently. And Julian—pictures in the papers, making speeches in the House, and generally being hailed as the Prime Minister of the future. He came down on Sunday afternoon. Looking very handsome and being very amusing. Viva Heriot was there. She doesn't like him very much, does she? There was no pandering to the successful young politician there, I can tell you! Angela thinks that he wants to marry her, you know.'

There it was! He had wanted to hear, and now that she had told him the pain was unbearable. All the old homesickness had come back, and he hated the long white road before him, hated the dark trees, the silver olives, and the whole country round him. Julian with his success, his charm, his ability and his anxiety to marry Viva! Again, he felt as he had felt so often: 'I must go back. Even if it means breaking my word, I must go back!'

Then his wiser, saner side whispered that it was too late, that it would be very difficult to prove. It would be Julian's word against his—and the man who had written the letter was dead! He sank back, his chin sunk on his breast, staring out at the long white road which lay before them.

'Lunch at Como?' Juliet said, and her voice, breaking in on his own miserable thoughts, startled him.

'If you wish.'

They sat in the garden of a little hotel, Emmanuel still with his mind going back to England, his hatred of Julian and his longing to go back. Juliet struggled bravely to make him either talk or show some interest in what she said. His answers were monosyllabic, his interest perfunctory and half-hearted.

'You're tired, Emmanuel?'

He lifted his sombre eyes and met hers. 'You mean that I'm bad-tempered.'

'Perhaps one accounts for the other. You ought to take a holiday. You grilled in Milan all through the heat, spent the winter there, and now you're tired out.'

'I don't think so. I like work.'

'How is your wonderful Guido?'

'All right, thanks.'

She stirred her coffee in silence, watching him, and wondering what was wrong. She had thought that he might have been glad to have news of Ordingly, of his mother, and yet his interest had been very lukewarm. Now, he sat staring straight before him, and she had to drag every word out of him. Either he was wretchedly miserable, unutterably tired—or bored. She realized how long ago it was when he had sat and never taken his eyes off her, those years ago, when she was married to Vernon. He had been almost pathetic with his romantic adoration and his amusing little affectations. Now, she felt so much older than he was, it seemed as if the years had widened the gulf. He was still so young, and she had realized when she was in England, that Viva Heriot, Julian and the rest had regarded her as a contemporary of Angela's. She wished that she could have had a son like Emmanuel Gollantz. Her son and Leon Hast's. He would have given her some real reason for her work. Now she only worked because she felt it part of her duty to Leon to prove to the world that he had been right; Leon had said that she was a great artist, and she wanted to show that Leon had known.

She gathered up her things. 'Ready?'

'Quite ready.'

She waited for him while he paid the bill, and decided that if this deadly silence was to continue, the week-end would be unbearable. She couldn't allow him to behave like a bad-tempered child, even if he was tired and wanted a rest. It was ridiculous!

Tomorrow little Gilbert was coming, and Bill Masters was bringing two people from Pallanza; she must shake Emmanuel out of his bad temper by then.

'If it wasn't for his mother, and the real nice part of him that I know,' Juliet reflected, 'I'd send him back to Milan now!'

As they turned into the gate he leant forward. His voice had lost some of its heaviness, the atmosphere of the place had begun to reach him again. The villa—beautiful things—Juliet's voice—and peace from that everlastingly jangling shop-bell—he must make himself forget the things which had hurt him. He must not ask questions about home and Angela and Viva again.

'I'll run her into the garage,' he said, 'if you'll get out here.' Then with that smile of his which was so pleasant: 'I've been behaving very badly, but I've thrown the "black dog" into the lake, I won't bring him into your villa—ever.'

Back in the villa he was himself again. Together they admired his work and the things which Juliet had brought back with her. They sat in the garden and had tea, and Emmanuel was content once more.

Something of Juliet's charm was reaching him, even disturbing him a little. He knew that when she said that Gilbert, Bill Masters and two friends were coming on Sunday, he experienced a quick sense of impatience. He felt that he wanted them to be alone, he didn't want to share her with anyone.

'Bill won't say that he's met you here,' she said, 'neither will Gilly. They're terribly sensible.'

'I remember Gilbert,' Emmanuel said. 'Little chap, fair——'

'The best accompanist in the world, and one of the best friends.'

'Masters, of course, I've known all my life.'

'Yes, Bill and your mother are the two people who really know everything about me,' Juliet said. 'They have never let it make the slightest difference. Oh, one more—your grandfather.'

He said, trying to make his voice sound indifferent:

'I don't see that anything ought to make a difference.'

'Don't you? I wonder? It does, you know, with most people. I don't blame them either. It would make a difference to me, I think—if I wasn't—me. It always made a difference to Max.'

'Juliet,' Emmanuel said suddenly, then stopped and realized that he had never called her by her Christian name before, realized that he had never called her anything; when he had written he had said 'Dear Miss Forbes'—'I don't know if you hate being called "Juliet",' he said, 'it slipped out. I've always heard you called Juliet at home, you see.'

'What else should you call me? I call you—Emmanuel.'

'Yes, I know, but——'

'Don't remind me that I'm much older than you are,' she said, 'after all, you call your mother, Angela.'

'One of our small Gollantz eccentricities,' he said. 'You know, we rather specialize in them. Angela likes it, encourages it. As a family we understand the value of judicious advertising, even quite privately.'

She said, 'Somehow, that doesn't sound like you speaking.'

'Doesn't it? Or is it that you don't like me when I talk naturally?'

'I don't believe that half-sneering is natural.'

He laughed shortly. 'No, possibly. It's an art that I am learning to acquire, a sort of chain mail that I am weaving link by link.'

'Why should you wear chain mail?'

'Protection! Perhaps, as an article of clothing it's a little out of date, but it's eminently satisfactory.'

Juliet moved her chair so that she faced him directly, and looked him up and down, her eyes curious and appraising.

'I think that you're all rather out of date,' she said, 'at least the three of you that I have known well. Your grandfather was in everything, but he had the best fundamental characteristics of the past. Mentally he preferred horses and well-sprung victorias to motor-cars; but he also preferred the Christianity of Christ to the philosophy of nineteen hundred. Max—and don't think that I don't admire your father, I do, immensely, but he didn't go back as far as old Emmanuel. Some of the narrowness of the early Victorians got tangled up with his heritage, and it's stuck. He makes rules, and he is as intolerant of anyone who breaks them as he is of a faked old master. Emmanuel had only rules for himself, in other people he looked for motives.'

'And the third Gollantz,' Emmanuel asked, 'what about him?'

'The third Gollantz,' she said, 'oh, he has his grandfather's spectacular impulses, and just a little of his father's rigidity, and a great deal of that amazingly nice person, his mother, in his make-up. I think,' slowly, 'that you over-rate your strength, Emmanuel. You pick up weights, hoist them on to your shoulder, and believe that you can carry them. Then that awful devastating pride of your people—I don't mean only your family, I mean the Jews—won't let you put them down and admit that they were too heavy. You're trying to carry something now that is too heavy for you, and chain mail won't make it any lighter, you'll only have added another burden.'

'I don't know——' he hesitated. 'Juliet, you don't know all about me, do you?'

'I know that your father came here last week,' she said.

'How?' He rapped out the word in a way that reminded her of his grandfather.

'Ottavia told me. At least, she described the man who came here, and my objectionable neighbour told me that he had sold most of the last of his furniture to a great London dealer. I put two and two together. Naturally, I don't believe that you left London simply because you didn't get on with Max. Anyone who behaved decently, who was decent, could get on with him. I'm not asking questions. I don't want you to confide in me, unless it might help you.'

Emmanuel shivered. 'I couldn't confide in anyone, I think. If I *could* talk to anyone, I think that I could talk to you, Juliet.'

'That's nice of you.' She paused. 'I gathered, too, that Max was not very pleased to find you here. I wonder if I know why?'

Taken off his guard for a moment, Emmanuel said impulsively, 'I hope to God you don't!'

To his surprise she laughed. 'Oh, how lacking in originality Max Gollantz is! My dear, don't look so angry. What did you expect him to think, being Max? It's not being unkind or uncharitable, it's being what he believes is logical. He says: "This and this has happened before, therefore it's logical to believe that this and that will happen again". He wants to protect you, obviously, from a person whom he adores as an artist—his musical taste like his artistic taste is unimpeachable—but whom he suspects as a woman. When Max finds himself in New York, or Paris or Berlin, and sees that I am singing there, he never fails to come and hear me, never fails to come and see me, he is charming. But when I go to Ordingly, he is just a little too polite, just a little too formal.' She leant forward and smiled at Emmanuel's angry face. 'Emmanuel, if I can keep a sense of humour about it all, can't you? It's very natural.'

'It's astonishingly foolish,' he said. 'To me, at least, it was damned painful.'

She saw that it was wiser to let the subject drop, and not to continue speaking of either his father or himself. He was in a mood when such a conversation, continued an instant too long, might drive him back into his fit of depression, or force him to make some confidence that he would regret later. But though she said no more about herself or Max, Emmanuel felt that they had come closer by reason of his father's inability to understand either of them; he felt that a new link had been forged between them.

The next day he had apparently thrown off his weariness and his black mood with it. He took the car down to Como to meet Gilbert, and they came back the best of friends. Juliet listened to Gilbert, with his funny half-nervous manner, addressing Emmanuel as 'My dear young man', and remembered that was how he had spoken to him eight years ago. Bill Masters arrived with two Americans, a smooth-haired young man and a slightly tousled young woman, and though he was obviously surprised to find Emmanuel there, said nothing until they were walking in the garden after luncheon.

'What's Angela's boy doing here, Juliet?' he asked.

'What are you doing here, Bill?' she responded. 'He's doing the same; staying here for the week-end.'

'Has he heard you sing yet?'

She stopped short and looked into his pleasant, plain face.

'Bill, you're trying to be subtle, and it doesn't suit you.'

'Not a bit of it, my dear. He only wants a little music, your voice and a few stars to push him over the edge. I know the romantic strain in that family, they all have it. What's he doing in Italy, anyway? Oh, I heard things—Max told me one story, manifestly untrue, Max is so simple. He never tells lies except under compulsion, and when he does, he never thinks that you won't believe him. Don't get mixed up with a wrong 'un, Juliet.'

'What nonsense!' she said, half-annoyed. 'You've only to look at that boy to know that he hasn't a bad streak in him. Whatever it is, whatever people say or think, it's quite evident to me that at the worst he's only been a fool, and I suspect a romantic fool!'

That evening after dinner they sat in the long room which between them Juliet and Emmanuel had made so beautiful. The big windows were open, the night air was very soft, and felt very young, as if the year had not yet realized that its life had begun. The stars hung low in the sky, and glimmered and twinkled like lamps. The soft light of thick yellow candles threw lovely shadows round the room, and their rays touched the old pale brocades with tender shafts of radiance. Gilbert sat half-crouching in his chair, his thin hands round his knees, his pale, short-sighted eyes on Juliet; Bill Masters with one leg propped on a stool before him, watched Emmanuel with a half-tender, half-amused smile on his face. He reflected that the fellow was the image of his grandfather, and yet there was something in his expression from time to time that recalled Angela. Emmanuel stood by Juliet's side, and listened as she talked to the two Americans. Whenever the girl answered, he knew that he compared her voice with Juliet's.

He scarcely listened to the words, only the tones of their voices came to him; the one very clear and sharp, the other softer and infinitely more soothing.

'And tomorrow,' Juliet said, 'you go on to Milan?'

'And Venice,' young Drewett said. 'That's where our schedule takes us tomorrow.'

Juliet laughed. 'I resent the way you people "do" Italy,' she said. 'What can you see of Milan and Venice in one day? Nothing at all!'

Mrs. Drewett said: 'Oh, but, Miss Forbes, we're staying two days in Venice. I believe there's quite a bit to see there.'

'Miss Forbes won't think that enough, Miranda,' her husband said. 'What you don't realize, Miss Forbes, is that we've only got a limited time. We've got a schedule and we've got to work to it.'

'You'll never see Italy so long as you set a time limit on it, or have a schedule in your pocket,' Juliet said. 'It's against all the mentality of the country. Besides, time——!' She made a little expressive movement as if she swept it away.

Drewett smiled, and shook his smooth head so that the candlelight caught the sheen of it and made it look as if it was polished.

'Time exists just the same,' he said. 'I've got a lot to see, and so has Miranda, before we get too old to enjoy it.'

Gilbert said, from his big chair: 'Miss Forbes will give you two reasons against that argument. Don't get too old to enjoy anything, or else—don't get old at all.'

Drewett said, with a little formal bow: 'Miss Forbes must give me her prescription for both those things. I take it that she has one.'

'Certainly she has,' Gilbert said, 'but she won't give them away. You wouldn't come and sing, Juliet, would you? That piano has been watching you with silent reproach for the last hour.'

She turned and made a little grimace. 'Gilly, didn't we have enough during the tour to last us?'

Emmanuel, scarcely knowing what he did, put out his hand and laid it on her shoulder:

'Will you?' he said. 'Please, will you?'

As she walked past Bill Masters, she heard him chuckle softly, and stooped down and whispered:

'I don't think that I'm liking you very much tonight, Bill. I shan't ask you again!'

'I don't wait for invitation, Juliet. Go and sing!'

Emmanuel stood by the open window, his tall figure outlined against the long pale curtains, his hands sunk deep in his pockets, his head thrown back. Juliet, from where she stood at the piano, could see him—slim and straight, his pale face catching the light, and the dead white of his shirt front showing hard and cold. She knew that he was going back to the last time that he had stood and listened to her singing. She remembered it all so clearly; remembered too what she had sung, and how, when it was over, he had said that it was almost too beautiful, that it was so beautiful that it hurt.

'Yes, Gilly—that will do——'

The notes trickled towards him, Emmanuel felt that they came like little waves and broke over his feet, cool and soothing. He saw Juliet, and once, before she began to sing, their eyes met and she smiled at him. Then she sang, and he was conscious of nothing except the wonder of her voice. He wondered if it had been as beautiful eight years ago? He couldn't remember; he only knew that he was realizing, feeling, experiencing real beauty and that it was almost breaking his heart. The song ended, and Drewett said:

'Very many thanks, that was charming.'

His wife repeated, 'Perfectly charming.'

Gilbert peered round the corner of the piano at Bill Masters:

'Have you heard the new one that Seelig wrote? No? Will you sing it?'

It seemed to Emmanuel that she hesitated, before she said: 'It's German—I don't know if Mr. and Mrs. Drewett understand German. I know that Bill doesn't.'

Gilbert clicked his tongue impatiently. 'Tut, tut! Let them listen. You're not reciting to them!'

'Tyrant you are, Gilly. Very well then.'

Emmanuel thought: 'She doesn't want to sing it. I wonder why?' He waited, and listened and wondered if he half-understood.

'. . . Lerne nur das Gluck ergreifen:
Denn das Gluck ist immer da.'

Bill Masters said, 'Clever chap that Seelig, isn't he?'

Very lightly, almost too lightly, Emmanuel thought, Juliet answered:

'Oh, give me a little credit for the way I sing it! No, that's enough for one night, Gilly.'

Drewett leant forward and said softly to Emmanuel: 'I don't speak German. What exactly were the words, Mr. Gollantz?'

'Roughly,' Emmanuel said, conscious that his voice carried in the suddenly quiet room, ' "Only learn to grasp happiness, because happiness is always there".'

'Indeed,' Drewett said, 'it's a very nice sentiment, isn't it?'

CHAPTER EIGHTEEN

'YOU won't sing again?' Bill asked.

'Not tonight,' Juliet said. 'That's quite enough boredom for you for one night.'

'All right,' he agreed. 'I know you too well to make protestations, you realize that. What about bridge?'

Juliet's eyes were turned towards the long windows. Emmanuel had disappeared. She forced herself to attend to her guests.

'Bridge?' she said. 'Why, yes. You and Gilly and Mr. and Mrs. Drewett. No, Bill, you know my bridge of old. It's just highway robbery. There's a table in the next room, and cards and drinks. Come along and let me see you all settled down.'

'Charming room,' Drewett said, and his wife dutifully echoed:

'Oh, too lovely.'

Masters said, 'Emmanuel again?'

'Partly; partly—me. There, have you all you want? If you want to play late, don't worry. Just the last person switch off the lights. I go to bed early.'

'Where's that nice young man?' Gilbert asked. 'Won't he play?'

'Probably he's gone to bed, like me he works hard and likes lots of sleep. Good night, all of you.'

She turned back and walked into the long room, closed the piano and went to the long windows. She looked out into the star-lit garden and wondered where Emmanuel was. She wished that Gilly hadn't chosen that song of all songs to-night. She had caught sight of Emmanuel's face as he had given the translation to Drewett; had seen it, paler than usual, with tight lips, and eyes that looked full of pain. He had gone out into the garden, where he could be alone. She hated to think of him out there, under that purple sky, under the stars, fighting out some battle.

Like some wounded animal who creeps away into a dark corner to suffer its pain alone. She hesitated for a moment, then went out into the garden. Her feet made no sound on the short turf, and she came upon him, sitting on the long stone bench at the end of the lawn, his face buried in his hands. She stood and watched him, and once heard a strangled sob break from him. She couldn't bear it. She had always hated pain, always hated to watch people suffer; even in the old days when she had learnt to hate Vernon Seyre, she had hated to see him hurt. That had added to her problems always.

She went forward and laid her hand on his shoulder.

'Emmanuel——'

His voice came muffled and angry. 'Oh, for Christ's sake, leave me alone.'

'My dear, I can't leave you out here, lonely and unhappy.'

This time his voice came more clearly. 'I'm usually both. It doesn't matter where I am, does it?'

'Can't you talk to me about it all? Can't you trust me?'

He lifted his face, she saw that his eyes were still wet. The rather exquisite young man had vanished, in his place was a man, scarcely more than a boy, miserable, longing for sympathy and understanding.

'Can I?' he said. 'Can I? I wonder? It's not a pretty story.'

'Very few human stories are pretty.'

He began to speak, at first stumbling and halting, then with greater certainty as if he gathered courage. Gradually the whole story was told. He spoke plainly, he did not attempt to soften anything, to conceal anything. As she listened, she heard his hatred of Julian flare up and make his voice shake with passion again and again. He made no mention of Viva, the story was told only about himself, and his brother. It ended and they sat silent. At last Juliet spoke.

'You ought to go back, and tell them the truth.'

'My mother—I told you what Nathan said—it's impossible, she adores Julian. She's so proud of her wonderful son! It would mean the end of everything. I couldn't.'

'Then you'll remain an exile all your life?'

'Unless some day he either gives himself away, or tells them.'

'And if he does neither?'

'Then I stay here.'

For a long time neither of them spoke, but Juliet felt his hand close over hers as it lay on the cool stone. The pressure was nothing but that of a lonely child seeking someone to mitigate its solitude.

'It's the loneliness,' he said at last, with a catch in his voice, 'it's the everlasting day in day out in Milan—no one except Guido. That's what kills me——'

'I know,' she said, softly. 'It's horrible.'

'Do you get terribly lonely, Juliet?'

'Yes, despite my work, and my friends, and they're very good, wonderful, but I've been lonely for six years.'

'Poor Juliet—it's awful not to—belong to anyone or to have anyone belong to you, isn't it?'

He began to speak again, almost as if he spoke to himself.

'Your singing tonight. It brought it all back again. Angela—I miss Angela more than anything—Angela and tea-time at Ordingly! She's so alive, she vitalizes one. She's got everything. Tolerance, wisdom and understanding. Then that song, at first I was afraid that you might sing that Irish Famine song as you did that night eight years ago. But this one, about grasping happiness, happiness that is always there! It was so desperately painful, so impossible for me. There's nothing ahead of me. A little shop in Milan, making just enough to keep me alive. I shall never be able to build anything big out of it. It's just going on, day after day. Grasp happiness!'

'Life is always going on day after day, my dear.'

'I can't——'

'You must——' she closed her fingers more tightly on his.

He shook his head. 'I can't. You see, I'm a coward. My grandfather used to say that there were two kinds of courage, one hot, one cold. He said that almost anyone had the first, said that almost anyone could dash into tight places, lead forlorn hopes, rescue people from death. That was hot courage. But he said that cold courage was the going on, day after day, never allowing yourself to get soured, or embittered, never looking back and regretting anything. He said that acting without thinking was easy, but that it was difficult to sit and think and still keep your courage. I haven't got cold courage. I regret what I've done even though I did it for Angela.'

'But you don't regret it sufficiently to go back and explain?'

With a return of his old cynical tone, he said:

'Perhaps it strikes me that it might be very difficult to make them believe. That may influence me a good deal.'

'It might be a chance——'

'That I daren't take, because I should be afraid that Angela would rather have her dream son than me. Let's leave it—there isn't anything to be done.' He lifted her hand and carried it to his lips. Then said softly, 'You're very good to me, Juliet.'

'My dear, I wish that I could do something to help you.'

He sat, still holding her hand to his lips, his eyes on hers, then after a silence which seemed endless, he said:

'Juliet, will you marry me?'

She drew her hand away from his clasp, and sat leaning back a little, the palms of her hands flat on the stone bench, her lips parted, without speaking.

'Juliet, will you marry me?'

'Because we're both lonely?' she asked gently.

'Not quite. Because I loved you a long time ago, and tonight I knew that I—I hadn't forgotten. Oh, I know that I was only a boy then, but it was real enough and it's real now. Will you?'

'Is this partly because your father thought—as he did? Is it because you're chivalrous, and romantic, Emmanuel? Don't think that I'm belittling either. I love them both. But think, my dear, think.'

'At first it was because of my father. I said that I'd ask you because of what he believed. Then tonight—oh, Juliet, can't you see, can't you realize that you're all I've got?'

'I'm ten years older than you are, Emmanuel. I've been married, I've lived with Leon Hast as his mistress and all the world knew. My husband divorced me. How should I fit into Ordingly?'

'I'm never going back——'

'If you ever could, if you ever wanted to. What then?'

'Juliet, you're saying everything except either "Yes" or "No". Don't try to find excuses, answer me. Give me your hands—both of them—now tell me. Will you marry me?'

'I don't know,' she said, hesitating as she spoke, 'I don't know. I'm a little afraid. I don't know if I love you, or if you really love me. I think that perhaps we are both trying to grasp happiness too hard. We're tempted. Wait—give me a little time. Let me think. Next week, Emmanuel, when these people have gone.'

'You'll tell me then?'

'If I can't answer you before, yes, I promise.'

He sighed. 'Very well.' Then with his old impulsiveness: 'Oh, I'd make you so happy. I'd work because of you. I wish that you were poor, Juliet, so that I could work for you, quite literally.'

'We must go in,' she said abruptly. 'It's late. It's beginning to get cold. I daren't stay here—my voice——'

He sprang up and held out his hands. 'You shan't. I forgot, your wonderful voice.' He took her hands and drew her up so that she faced him. 'Good night, Juliet——' then he drew her closer and bent his head so that his lips touched hers. 'Good night—lovely Juliet.'

She twisted herself from his grasp and turned her head away.

'My God! Don't ever say that to me again, Emmanuel! My dear, I'm sorry—— Good night.'

She left him, and he stood, half-puzzled, watching her cross the grass and go back into the house. She did not turn, and Emmanuel stood wondering what he had said to hurt her. Then he, in his turn, walked back to the house, closed the long windows and walked slowly up the wide marble stairs.

He did not see her again. At breakfast he found the Drewetts, and Gilbert. The Americans were driving to Milan, and Bill Masters was staying on at the villa. Juliet did not appear but she sent a note down by Ottavia for Emmanuel.

'Please drive back in the car. Gilly wants to go into Milan. Send the car back with Gilly by one of the men from the garage in the Via 22 Settembre. You know which one I mean. Until next Saturday. Juliet.'

The Drewetts drove away. Emmanuel said: 'Let them get clear away. We don't want their dust, do we?' Gilbert agreed, and they stood smoking a last cigarette until the cloud of dust which marked the progress of the Drewetts had faded into nothingness.

'Now,' Emmanuel said, and climbed into his seat, giving one last backward glance at the villa. He felt puzzled this morning; last night he had gone up to his room, and felt that if only Juliet would agree to marry him, he might have found the solution to his problems.

She was lovely, they were wonderful friends, their tastes were the same, and she knew his whole history and still believed in him. Ten years were nothing, she didn't look ten years older, he decided as he looked at himself in the mirror. Already there were grey hairs on his temples, and the lines round his mouth were deeper than they had any right to be at his age. Dear, dear Juliet—he would try to make up to her for all the miserable years which were past. Together they would make a wonderful life here in Italy, and London should slide away and be forgotten. He had lain down in bed feeling comforted and less lonely. He had felt soothed and re-established—the future must be all right. But in the morning, he had felt less certain. He had hoped that he might have seen her for a moment, that he might have carried away a last impression of her, standing by the big gates as he drove away. She hadn't come down. He had heard Ottavia ask Mrs. Drewett to excuse her mistress, then escort her upstairs to say 'Good-bye'—— That was all. There had been no figure at the gates and in his mind the recollection of another figure was already forcing its way forward. Viva Heriot. As he drove, he thought that he had never remembered her so clearly, that he had never been able to listen, mentally, to the tones of her voice with such distinctness. It was as if she was actually with him, talking to him, telling him that he might go away, but that she would bring him back again.

Juliet had said that Angela hoped that she would marry Julian. The thought made him suddenly force the car to leap forward, so that little Gilbert gave a smothered exclamation of surprise.

Emmanuel said: 'Sorry,' and drove on trying to leave the picture of Viva behind him. It was over, his life in England was over, and his dream of marrying Viva Heriot must go with all his other dreams. 'Learn to grasp happiness.' He would, he would grasp what offered, and the rest must go the way of all dreams. Juliet knew his story, Viva could never know it. Juliet, if she married him, would do so, realizing that she was marrying a man who had lost everything. There could be no question of Viva, he'd lost her when he lost everything else. Out of what was left, he must make some sort of a life, and find happiness where he could. He was lonely, Juliet admitted that she too had suffered as he had done. They could help each other, and make a life together. As if he tried to convince himself, he added that it would be a wonderful life, complete and secure on a foundation of real understanding, and genuine love.

Gilbert, who had been trying vainly for the past five minutes to light a cigarette, suddenly caught his attention.

'Wait a minute,' he said, 'I'll slow up. There, that's it. I'm afraid that I'm very dull. I'm planning my work for the week.'

Gilbert said: 'Yes—she, Juliet, told me about it. She—er—asked me not to mention that you were in Milan, if I saw—er—anyone.'

'Thanks, that was good of her.'

'She is good,' Gilbert said with intense earnestness. 'That's just what she is, my dear young man, goodness itself. We've travelled over most of the world together—and I ought to know something about her. Eight years, it's a long time. Mind, she has a temper! Oh, dear me, yes. I've seen it once or twice.'

Emmanuel, his eyes on the road, said: 'Yes, so have I.'

Gilbert drew his breath sharply through his teeth. 'Whew! I remember the last time. When Seyre tried to begin divorce proceedings with a dead man as co-respondent. Not pretty, far from pretty. He'd had long enough before, Heaven knows! He hadn't wanted to get married himself then though. Nasty feller. He's married now. I saw him when we were in New York with his wife. Met him in the entrance of some hotel. He's got very fat and very red. He came to her concert. One of 'em. I saw him again. He waited for me afterwards, spoke to me.'

'Seyre did?'

'Seyre did. I never told her. He puffed out his lips—always a trick of his—asked how I was? As if he cared! Then, how was she—Juliet? I said she was very well. He said, as if you were twisting the words out of him with a corkscrew: "Lovely as ever?" I said: "More lovely, by God," I said, and I don't often swear, my dear young man, but I said: "By God, it took Leon Hast to discover how lovely she was, didn't it?" Seyre blinked at me, I fancy that he drinks more than he ought, his wife's very rich, he probably has his own bootlegger or whatever they are, he said: "He used to call her—Lovely Juliet, didn't he?" I could have killed him! I said, then—oh, it was abominable of me, but I don't regret it, I said: "There was one thing he wanted to call her and you wouldn't let him—that was Mrs. Leon Hast. I wish you a very good morning," and I left him.'

Emmanuel said: 'Good for you,' and thought: 'So that was why she said "My God, don't ever say that to me again!" ' Hast had said it. Hast still mattered, the thought of Hast could still hurt her. Poor Juliet!

Gilbert was burbling on again. 'I ought not to have told you that, perhaps, but you and your dear mother have known her for so long. Your mother—dear Mrs. Gollantz—knows just how wonderful she was. A very grand woman, your dear mother, very courageous.'

'Yes, she's all that and a great deal more,' Emmanuel said.

He let Gilbert chatter on, only half-listening to him, except when he mentioned Juliet's name and then Emmanuel realized that his senses were wide awake, and that he only relapsed into that state of half-attention when Gilbert talked of other matters. Juliet—the sound of her name had suddenly assumed tremendous importance to him. He was conscious that he waited for it, and that when it came he experienced a sense of longing, satisfied.

Guido met him, smiling and pleased. He had obviously dressed with care, and waited for Emmanuel's approval. His tightly-buttoned blue coat, with brass buttons, his grey trousers, and his blue and white spotted tie, reminded Emmanuel vaguely of a cheap tailor's window somewhere along the Strand.

'Very dossy this morning, Guido,' he said. 'Going to a wedding?'

Guido assumed an expression, as one who should say: 'This is nothing! Imagine your noticing it!' He smiled with an air of deprecation.

'This?' he said. 'This is only *all' Inglese*. The trousers have for ever turn oops. Naturally in England they must have them so, to save them from the perpetual mud, eh? They have style, I think.'

'I should change the brass buttons, I think. Have black ones.'

'Yes? I thought that the brass were more suitable for sportivities and so on.'

'They may be, but we shan't be indulging in sportivities in the shop.'

Guido smiled and nodded, showing all his teeth. 'How true! They shall be changed during the siesta hour, on my word of honour!'

The week dragged through. A dozen times Emmanuel wondered if he should write to Juliet, and a dozen times decided that he mustn't worry her. A hundred times his mind went back to Viva Heriot, and each time he pushed the thought of her from him, and repeated that she belonged—as so many things must—to the past. The future could never include Viva. He looked round the shop, at the stock which he had collected and which was beginning to move so quickly that he was always having to buy more, and smiled. Less than a year ago he had walked through the galleries of Gollantz and Son, with their magnificent pictures, bronzes, china, and furniture; he had worked in offices which were, old Lane declared, far too good for their job, he had been one of the great firm whose name was known all over the world, he had been someone. Now, he was part owner of this little shop tucked away in a small street by the Scala. His stock was small, and it was collected from the little villages which were within sixty miles of Milan. Only twice had he been able to spare the time to extend his activities and go into the Dolomites to find materials. The shop was stocked with things that neither Max nor his grandfather would have bothered to carry home; small things—nothing that would have interested a real connoisseur. He was doing well enough. He could live, have sufficient to eat, he was even adding to the balance at his bank. Louis Lara's request for twenty-five per cent. was ridiculously small, and the profits were not crippled by it. The shop was a success—but a small success, and Emmanuel, who had been brought up in an atmosphere of old masters, museum pieces and china which made collectors' mouths water, felt that it was all rather cheap and second-rate.

He flung himself into his work, not because he found it particularly interesting, but because he had found that work was the best and cheapest drug in the world. Even Guido with his smiles, his impossible clothes and his kindness was a drug. He wondered what Bill would say to Guido.

'Bill—this is Guido Moroni, my friend who helps me with the shop.'

Bill would say: 'How are you?' but his eyes would exclaim: 'Good God, where did you find it?'

Still, Guido was a good fellow, despite his eccentricities, and his ambition to wear English clothes, to model his manners upon those of Emmanuel, was touching.

'Thank Heaven,' Emmanuel said on Saturday morning, 'that this damned week's over at last.'

Guido sighed, then smiled. 'Ah,' he said, 'I understand Time goes the slowest when one wishes it to fly! You have all my good wishes.'

Emmanuel grinned back at him. 'You're a clever little

beast, aren't you, Guido—but you don't know everything, my lad.'

'I do not wish to do so—to know everything would be to lose every illusion. Illusions are charming things, Mr. Gollantz.'

'Very breakable——'

'Not if you handle them with care,' Guido returned. 'And if they break—make new ones. New illusions are just as good as antique ones.'

He drove over to Lake Como, in his queer old car with its box at the back for goods, and forgot that he must look like a commercial traveller. At first, he had hated that box at the back, had hated to draw up at an hotel and know that the porters knew that he was a tradesman. Now he didn't care, he never remembered it.

He would take Guido's advice, he would have none of his old broken illusions, for ever reminding him that they were cracked and broken. He would scrap the lot, and if he wanted new ones then they should all centre around a new pivot. England—Ordingly—his mother—his brother Bill—and Viva had been his old world; Juliet should be his new one.

Gilbert met him at the gate. 'I'm just going back to my hotel,' he said, 'we've been hard at it this morning. Voice perfect. This climate suits her. I shall be back this evening. She's asked me to dinner. She asks me every night. She's in the garden, my dear young man.'

He walked towards her, he knew that his heart was beating faster than usual. Juliet Forbes—famous, lovely, sought after—and he, Emmanuel Gollantz, who had left his country for his—he paused and corrected the phrase—his brother's good, was going to ask her again if she would marry him. For the first time he thought of Julian without that terrible rush of concentrated hate seizing him.

She held out her hand to him. 'Emmanuel, you must have had a horribly dusty drive. Tell Ottavia to bring you something cool—lemonade and ice—even a whisky and soda, though I don't advise it.'

'No,' he said. 'I don't want anything yet. They're not important—cool drinks. Something else is. Juliet, will you marry me?'

She laughed, he thought that she was as nervous as he was. 'At least sit down and smoke.' Then: 'Emmanuel, I have thought this all over—not once but a hundred times. I haven't very much left to give you—or anyone. I've tried to find content and happiness alone, and it's evaded me. Like you—I'm lonely and rather afraid. That isn't love, Emmanuel, is it? It's friendship, and sympathy and understanding—that I have left to give. Is that enough, I wonder?'

'The rest—might come—afterwards.'

'To you,' she asked, 'to me—or to both of us?'

'I love you, Juliet.'

'I know, I know,' quickly, 'as I love you, my dear. It's not an urgent thing, it's not something stronger than you are—admit it.'

'It's very real——'

He came nearer and took her hand in his. 'Juliet, don't let us probe and dig and put things under microscopes. Let's—grasp happiness.'

She smiled. 'Emmanuel, my dear, I'm ten years older than you are. You know all about me, I've been honest, but if you'll be patient, if you give me time and help me, I'll marry you. Oh, let's both find happiness somewhere, shall we?'

He said, with his eyes on her face: 'I think that I've found it.'

CHAPTER NINETEEN

JULIAN walked down Piccadilly, on the sunny side, and felt that life was a good business. His progress had been steady, each time he had come before the public gaze he had kept up a marked improvement. The newspapers wanted him to write for them, and he read his articles with satisfaction. They struck him as being both sound and readable. He never worried his readers with indigestible masses of figures, but when he did allow himself to indulge in them, they were used with effect. He neither wrote down to his public, nor required them to enter upon a course of mental gymnastics to reach what he was driving at. When he spoke, his methods were the same. He never attempted anything that he could not perform and perform well. Only last night the Great Man himself had stopped and spoken to him, given him a delicious bit of praise for some information which he had given to a very bored and tired House. He had stirred them into life, men had sat upright, tilted their hats off their foreheads and listened with attention.

Twenty-three. In a year he had simply rushed forward; given another two years he might reach pinnacles of which he now only dreamed. Success—success—success—golden goals—prizes—honours. All those should be his, could be his, for the taking. He had brains, looks, and youth all on his side; and what was more, he knew how to use them all.

There had been one horrible moment when the whole of his career had been threatened, when he had shivered and felt sick with apprehension; but it had passed. Emmanuel had stepped in and saved him. Julian looked back on the last scene which he had with his brother. Emmanuel had lost his head a little, had allowed himself to grow just a little melodramatic, and had given himself away by his sentimentality. Julian smiled. If only he hadn't been so palpably worried about Angela! That had shown the weak place in his armour, that had given Julian his cue. He had taken it, and he wasn't ashamed to remember it, either. When men were in tight corners, they must take whatever escape offered, and the weakest must suffer. His future meant more than Emmanuel's, his career was something worth safeguarding, and Emmanuel's—well, the world hadn't lost much because Gollantz and Son had lost its future owner. Pictures, china, furniture—these things didn't materially affect the future of the nation.

Anyway, that fright had brought him to his senses. Whatever proclivities he had once had, they were conquered now. The game wasn't worth the candle. The gods had all fought on his side, they had helped him through. The man had died. After a year, Julian could scarcely remember him. Emmanuel had come forward, and again he smiled, he was very grateful to the gods for their interest in him.

He turned down Bond Street. He had half an hour to spare and he might drop in and see his father. Max liked him to drop in for a chat, and his old sherry was excellent, his dry biscuits really crisp and fresh. As he turned he ran into Walter Heriot.

'Hello, Walter! How are you?'

He didn't want to hear, he had finished with Walter. The fellow was growing too obvious, getting himself too much talked about. One day he'd find himself in Queer Street, and serve him right. Julian made no attempt to stop, but Walter shoved his great bulk before him.

'Julian, just a minute—shan't keep you long. I want to talk to you about something.'

'Talk to me?' Julian stopped and felt a very faint qualm. 'What's the trouble? You look frightfully glum, Walter.'

'Come into the Mayfair,' Walter said. 'We can't stand in Bond Street and talk.'

'I don't know that I have time——'

'Then you might make time, for once,' Walter's fat face looked ominously bad-tempered. 'Come on.'

They sat down, Walter ordered the drinks, and Julian, crossing one immaculately trousered leg over the other, waited. They could not have presented a greater contrast—Julian, slim, and eminently good looking, his eyes clear, his skin fresh and tingling with health, his whole appearance that of a very successful young man; Walter, fat, heavy and slovenly, his face heavy and white, his eyes dull and stupid, his hands—with their bitten nails—shaking a little. Julian looked at him with distaste and impatience.

'Well, Walter—what's the trouble?'

Walter stared at him. 'Money's the trouble. I want five hundred quid, and God knows where it's coming from.'

'I'm afraid that I have less knowledge than the Almighty!'

'Don't be clever,' his cousin retorted. 'I don't want that smart stuff. Can't you find it for me?'

Julian smiled. 'My dear Walter! Be reasonable. The cost of living's tremendous.'

'I know that—damn it, the Guv'nor's always rubbing that in.' His tone changed, there was the hint of a whine in it. Julian thought that he sounded like some old beggar asking for a night's lodging.

'Blast it, Julian—you might help a fellow. It's not much to ask. I've stood being shoved on one side pretty decently. I never resented it, never tried to queer things for you, did I?'

'My dear Walter, what *are* you talking about!'

Walter stuck his unpleasant puffy face nearer to Julian's, his eyes narrowed suddenly.

'That doesn't cut any ice, Julian,' he said. 'A year ago,

if I'd gone to your father, what about that? I might even go now, you know, and talk to him. You wouldn't look so damned self-satisfied then, would you?'

'That would depend upon what you said. In all probability I should look exactly as I look now. If you think my father is likely to come over with five hundred after a conversation with you—upon whatever subject—I think you're backing a loser.'

'If I told him about—Wilfred——'

Julian's face did not change. 'Wilfred—who?'

'You know—Wilfred—who,' Walter said. 'The chap who died.'

'I don't know who you're talking about, Walter, I think you're going mental. Honestly, there's something radically wrong with you. Pull yourself together!' His voice was suddenly sharp as if his patience was exhausted.

Once again Walter came a little nearer, once again he pushed his face closer to Julian's.

'I've got three letters of Wilfred's,' he said. 'He mentions you in them.'

'Really! What was he—a cheap journalist? My dear chap, without undue conceit a good many people mention me in their letters. That's nothing. What does he say about me?'

'He says—"E. J." said so and so, and "E. J." said something else. He used to write very—chatty letters, y'know.'

'I don't know,' Julian's easy smile had returned, 'and what is this—E. J.? I don't understand. You're making a mistake, Walter. You're confusing me with my brother—he's—E. J. I'm J. E.'

'But——' Walter's heavy face looked not only angry but distressed, as if he was beginning to doubt his own sanity, the heavy rolls of fat quivered as he spoke with great intensity, 'but, Julian, *he* always called you E. J. Don't you remember? After that show at the old Bluebottle, you gave your name as E. J.'

'My dear Walter, I don't know *what* you're talking about. I think you've gone out of your mind. What is this rubbish about E. J.? It's by me—entirely.' He leant forward and laid his hand on the table. 'Now look here, Walter. I don't know what you're driving at. I fancy that it's something pretty ugly. If you've got something up against my brother,

Emmanuel, I'll tell you frankly that—I don't believe it. Emmanuel had some row with my father, what it was I don't know. But whatever you've got to say, say it and say it to my father or to Emmanuel. But this silly story about one of your nasty little pals—even if he is dead—and a lot of talk about E. J. and J. E.—leaves me cold. It's true that I went to a couple of night clubs with you, and very nasty they were. They gave me all the information that I wanted, and I had no further use for them or for you. I must go. Good morning, Walter.'

He paid for the drinks, and walked out into the street. He longed to take off his hat and wipe his forehead, but he decided that it might look bad. Walter—great, fat fool!—might have followed him, might be watching. He crossed the road, turned up Hay Hill and made his way to Bond Street.

Max smiled and nodded as he entered the little office.

'Hello, Julian. I saw that you'd made them wake up last night. Angela read it to me this morning while I was shaving. She's delighted. Says that you have a sense of humour. Have you, I wonder? I don't think that my family have much. Hers have, perhaps.'

Julian sat down, and smiled. 'If the sample I have just listened to is the Heriot humour, it makes very little appeal to me. Walter Heriot, getting offensive because I won't lend him money.'

Max pursed his lips. 'Nasty fellow. I should leave him alone, Julian. His father was never a favourite of mine, and this lad's worse than his father ever was. The girl's worth fifty of him.'

'Oh, I agree.'

'Have a drink, Julian. Sherry and a biscuit?'

Julian considered for a moment, then said: 'I wonder if I might have a brandy and soda? I've felt cheap all this morning. Late night last night. I didn't leave the House until after three. Thanks awfully, father.'

Walter Heriot sat and stared at the empty glasses on the table before him. For a few moments he wondered if he really was a little mad, wondered if the old fool of a doctor had been right, when he said:

'Now, Walter, I've known you since you were a boy, and it's got to stop! I warn you. Your father's distressed and your poor mother is almost heartbroken. That's my last word—this must stop unless you want to end your days in a lunatic asylum.'

Then he ordered another drink, felt it pull him together, and his face cleared. There was nothing wrong with him, he'd been talking by the book all right; that smooth, smiling stuff was Julian's blasted bluff. Bluff! He hadn't a damned thing in his hand really. Swank! He hated the lot of them anyway. The old man had looked like something out of Clarkson's back shop; Max was so full of straightness and clean living that he was like a Methodist preacher; Bill was just oozing with heartiness and disappoval and cold baths; Emmanuel had been the best of the lot. He, at least, never said anything—but he used to—look, damn him! And this last one—Julian, with his fair hair, and bright skin, his wonderful clothes, and his confounded certainty and bluff! Member of Parliament. Going to be a bloody Prime Minister! That was funny, when you knew what Julian had been once; when you remembered the old days at the cottage with poor Wilf and Tommy and Claude. Not so much of the Prime Minister about Julian then!

Walter heaved himself out of his chair, shook one leg gravely to get rid of the numb feeling that he had felt so often lately, and nodding to the waiter he walked out and turned towards Grosvenor Square. He might as well lunch at home and save money! As he walked he went over all that Julian had said, and what was left of his soul writhed as he remembered Julian's light, contemptuous voice. He must have that five hundred quid. His mother must find it. She could sell some of that old-fashioned stuff that she wore on high days and holidays. She'd damn well have to!

'My mother in to luncheon?'

'No, sir. Her ladyship is lunching out; Sir Walter has gone up to Gloucestershire this morning. Miss Viva is lunching.'

'That's jolly! So am I.'

'Very good, sir.'

Viva looked up, then laid down her spoon, and said:

'What have you come back for?'

'Food. D'you mind?'

'Rather, but it can't be helped. You're looking cheap, Walter.'

He sat down and hunched his shoulders. 'That's what I

feel. Damned cheap.' Then to the servant: 'Get me a brandy and soda.'

He looked at the glass when it was brought to him, sniffed it, then set it down with a bang.

'I don't call that a brandy and soda. For God's sake, make it stronger than that.'

'Very sorry, sir. That's all there is. Her ladyship has the keys with her.'

Walter glared at Viva. 'That's pretty. I can see through that easily.'

'I think she expected you to. No—cheese, not sweets.'

They spoke very little, Walter turned over the food which was put before him, tasted it and pushed it away. He hadn't any appetite these days. With a good brandy and soda he might have managed to eat, but his mother had taken the keys. That was pretty, showing him up before the servants. Viva sat there, eating, saying nothing. She looked fit enough. He wondered if she was going to marry Julian. She shouldn't if he could put a spoke in Julian's wheel! That might be a way to get back at the brute!

Viva said: 'Take the coffee to my room, Collins. Walter, I can give you a drink if you want one badly. I've some brandy in my flask.'

His heavy white face had looked so wretched that she wanted to do something for him, even if it was only to give him a brandy and soda that was bad for him. Oh, well, she didn't care!

'Can you? That's decent of you. All right, I'll come.'

In her room he walked about, picking things up and putting them down again until she could have screamed. Her nerves were all to bits these days. Emmanuel had been away a year, he had never written and she had found out nothing. She wouldn't write until she had. Even then she didn't know where to write to, probably Angela knew. Angela was the only person who heard from him. Looking at a small photograph, Walter said: 'That's Emmanuel, isn't it?'

'Yes . . . taken with the dogs when he stayed with us, d'you remember?'

'No. I don't like him. Don't like any of them.'

'That will blight their young lives, Walter.'

'Lot of prigs, and bluffers—swankers—hypocrites!'

'Lot of words, you know. They could probably use far

worse ones about you, and with truth, my dear.'

Walter sat down heavily, and rubbed his leg. 'Damn my leg, it's gone to sleep again. That's better!' Then with tremendous gravity, for he had already disposed of two brandies, he said: 'And whatever—one of them at least—could say about me, I could say the same about him. Now, sort that out!'

He was too tired and too full of his own worries to notice that Viva's eyes narrowed suddenly, or to notice that she glanced at his glass before she said:

'Really? Another brandy? Good thing I have a full-sized flask. What's all that about? Whatever they could say of you—you can say of them. You know what all London's saying about you, don't you?'

'Let 'em say what they like. I know what I'm talking about.'

'I should like to hear what Bill Gollantz would say if you suggested that he rowed in your boat, Walter.'

'I didn't say—Bill, did I?'

'You didn't say anyone. It's obvious that it can't be Julian. He couldn't be where he is, if that were true.'

Walter sipped his brandy, and wondered where Viva got such good stuff from, just like Viva to get hold of the best!

'I don't make statements,' he said slowly, 'that I can't prove!'

'I bet you anything you like that you can't prove that,' she said. 'You're tight, Walter. The Gollantz boys are, all of them, as straight as dies. It's only jealousy makes you talk like that.'

'What will you bet me?' She shrugged her shoulders. 'Will you bet me five hundred quid!'

What a chance if he could put a spoke in Julian's wheel and get his five hundred at the same time! He was glad that he'd come home to luncheon. Damned glad!

'Five hundred!' she laughed, and the slight nervousness in it did not reach Walter's fuddled brain. 'That's a devil of a lot! I'd say yes if I thought that you'd stick to your bargain. You're bound to lose and I can do with five hundred very well. You're a frightful bluffer, Walter, aren't you? It's so clear that you've only got hold of some silly bit of cheap scandal.'

'Le'rrers,' he said. 'I mean—let-ters.'

'To whom?' She was still laughing.

He closed one eye, and tapped the side of his nose with his finger.

'You'd like to know, wouldn't you? What about the bet? Are you ser-rr'os? You are, you mean it? Let's see the colour of your money, first. What se-urrity—what se-currity have you gotter offer?'

'Does one usually ask for security on a bet? Oh, you do? Well, I've got Aunt May's fender that she left me. That's worth more than five hundred. It's mine. I can do what I like with it.' She laughed again. 'I might take it to Max and see what he'd give me for it.'

'That 'ul do. That's a bargain.' He fumbled in his coat pocket, took out his letter-case and produced three letters, all written in the same small, affected hand. 'If I show you these, when will you let me have the money?'

'Tomorrow.' She knew that her fingers twitched, as she heard that gamblers' fingers twitched when they played high. 'Tomorrow. But I want the letters for good—not just to look at.'

He blinked at her, shook his head as if to clear his brain of some cobweb that trailed over it. 'Was tha' the bargain? All ri'—all ri; whatever I am, I'm a sporr'sman. You can have them. Take the damn things, I'm glad to be rid of them.'

'Have another brandy while I read them—that empties the flask I think.' Her fingers shook, she pulled out the first letter and glanced at the first page, she read it and flicked over to the next with an expression of intense disgust on her face; suddenly it changed. Had Walter not been engaged in extracting the last drop of brandy from the flask, he might have noticed. She sat down and laid the letter on the little table near her, because her hands shook so that she could not see the words if she held it. 'God, it's—Emmanuel!'

Walter turned and grinned. 'That's the joke,' he said, 'it's not!'

'It says—"E. J. told me last night that you said——" Damn it, Walter, what beastly friends you have!' she burst out.

'Steady, steady,' Walter said. '*Non mortuis nil*—and w'arrever it is, the chap's dead. "E. J." isn't Emmanuel—it's Ju'rrienn.'

'I don't understand——'

'I'll tell you. Gosh, it's really damned funny! Listen—it

was this way——' and slowly, slurring his words, bursting into idiotic giggles at intervals, Walter told Viva the story of Julian Gollantz. 'Back to the first ni' when we went to the old Blueborrle,' he said, 'tha' was where he met this chap—poor Wilf! He gave his name as E. J. Go'rrantz. Damn smart, but I was just as smart, warren't I?'

'Smarter, perhaps.'

She gathered up the three miserable letters in their violet envelopes, with their mean, affected writing, and stood up. For one moment she thought:

'I'm going to faint. I wish I'd not given Walter the last of the brandy!' Then she steadied herself, and walked over to her brother. 'Stay here,' she said. 'I'm going to sell that fender and bring you back the money. Go to sleep, Walter—wait until I come back.'

As Viva walked to Bond Street, she tried to rehearse what she would say to Max, tried to make plans, but her mind refused to work. Her thoughts were too disordered to lend themselves to arrangement, she only knew that she might have stumbled on something which would bring Emmanuel home. She cared nothing for Julian's feelings, for his career, it mattered nothing to her that she was going to inflict pain upon Max Gollantz—nothing mattered except that she might be able to bring Emmanuel home again.

Max was walking through the big outer office as she entered, he was talking to an elderly man with a large nose and an over-large tie-pin. He turned as he saw her and smiled.

'Just a minute, Viva. I won't keep you. Go into my office.'

A moment later he returned. 'Nice of you to come and see me,' he said. 'To what am I indebted——?'

'I want to sell Aunt May's fender, Max, please.'

He raised his eyebrows a little. 'My dear, can you? I mean, won't your father and mother be very angry?'

'It's my very own,' she said, 'and I want five hundred.'

Max frowned. 'It's worth more than that, if I remember it rightly. Look here, I'll tell you what I'll do. I'll take it, lock it in the safe and you can have it back when you want it. You can have the five hundred now.' He smiled. 'Dressmakers or gambling, Viva?'

'A bet,' she said. 'I lost it to Walter. I bet him that he couldn't prove something—and he did.'

'It sounds very mysterious, my dear.'

'No,' she leant back in her chair because it was a relief to feel its hard solidity against her back, 'not really. He bet me that whatever people said about him—you know what they're saying about my brother, Max, don't you?—that he could prove that they had a right to say it about—one of your sons. I lost. He can prove it.'

Max Gollantz stared at her, his face was deathly white, his lips had lost their colour, they were set in a hard line. She saw that he had clenched his hands, that his knuckles stood out white. His voice had lost its kindness, it had lost everything except the mere sound of the words which he spoke.

'Thank you, Viva,' he said. 'I don't discuss these things with women. I know this already. You're too late, if you've come to try to make trouble for any of us.'

'I've come to put something right,' she said, 'and it's going to be put right now. It's gone on for a year. I've suffered, and he's suffered, and now he's coming back. I don't care who pays, but he shan't! Emmanuel's got to be cleared, Max—now!'

He moistened his pale lips. 'Emmanuel—I don't understand. Viva, you don't know what you're trying to do. Let things rest as they are.'

'That's what you've all done,' she retorted, 'that's the way you've let Emmanuel pay for something that he never did. He wouldn't speak, and you all believed, what you wanted to believe. I promised to marry him. The morning he—went away, he came and backed out. I wanted to know why, and he told me some half-hearted, garbled story about letters and money and imputations. I'm a little tired of waiting for him to come home, and today these letters,' she opened her bag and held them out to Max, 'came into my hands.'

'How?'

'They belonged to Walter. I made Walter tight and got them— Oh, it's no use looking disgusted, I don't care, I don't care what I do, so long as I get what I want. Now, Max, sit down and listen to me. It's going to hurt you, well; I've been hurt for a year, and so has Emmanuel. I'm going back to that first time when there was that row at the "Bluebottle".'

She talked, keeping her voice very even, telling him the whole story, making out her case against Julian carefully and calmly. Max sat, his eyes staring at the great inkstand on his desk, his face drawn and twisted with pain. The even voice went on, until the story was told.

'There,' she said, 'now, for the first time you've heard the truth that Emmanuel wouldn't tell you. He must come back, Max—at once.'

'I think that it will kill Angela.'

Viva stood up. 'May I have the letters back? No, it won't kill her. I know the Heriots and the Drews. What will hurt her most is the knowledge of the horrible injustice that's been done to Emmanuel. May I write and tell him to come home?'

Max faced her. 'Viva, will you be generous and give me twenty-four hours?'

She nodded. 'Yes, Max, twenty-four hours. Will you give me five hundred pounds? I want to pay it to Walter at once.'

CHAPTER TWENTY

HIS father had sent for him, and Julian, once again, felt that unpleasant sinking in the pit of his stomach, as he heard the message over the telephone. He disliked Hannah Rosenfelt, and the sound of her rather thick voice did not tend to make him feel better tempered. He wondered, for the thousandth time, why his father surrounded himself with a mob of Jews!

'What is it, Miss Rosenfelt, what does my father want?'

'I couldn't say, Mr. Julian. He only said that he wanted you to come down at once.'

'But, didn't he say what it——'

'No, Mr. Julian.'

'Haven't you any idea what——'

'Not the slightest, Mr. Julian.'

'Very well. I'll be down at half-past ten.'

He went back to his room and dressed, realizing that his impatience and his apprehension were increasing every moment. Not that he intended allowing anything to hamper him. He would admit nothing, and if admission were forced upon him—well, Walter wasn't a very creditable source of information, and the initials were wrong anyway! Emmanuel had shouldered things once before, Emmanuel must shoulder them again. He entered his father's room, smiling and very much at his ease. Whatever qualms he felt, he showed nothing. His voice was as pleasant as ever, his whole air breathed success.

'Yes, father. What did you want?'

Max lifted his heavy eyes, Julian was almost shocked at his grey, tired face, and the listlessness in his voice.

'Sit down, Julian. You know that Emmanuel left home a year ago, do you know why?'

'I heard a good many things. Naturally I should never believe anything that anyone told me against my brother.'

'You heard many things, did you? Now you're going to hear the truth, or what I believe to be the truth.' Very slowly, very carefully, Max told the story of the letters and of Emmanuel's expulsion. When it was finished, he said: 'And yesterday, I saw more letters, I was told that "E. J." was not Emmanuel, but you. Wait! Don't say anything yet. You remember a young man called Gregson, who was here? Hannah Rosenfelt knew where he lived, and I've seen him. He tells me that letters addressed to "E. J. Gollantz" used to come here marked "Private and Confidential", and that he—acting under your orders—forwarded them to you at Ebury Street. What have you to say, Julian?'

Julian hoped that his face would not betray anything, he was certain that his voice wouldn't, he had it well under control.

'I have nothing to say,' he said. 'Nothing.'

'Then you admit the truth of what I have said?'

'I neither admit nor deny it. What do you propose to do?'

'Bring Emmanuel home again—and——'

'And expel me? What good will that do anyone?'

Max stared at him. He was so much at his ease, so certain of himself, so handsome—his voice did not falter, his face showed no sign of distress or guilt. It remained beautiful and impassive.

'Julian,' he said, his voice shaking a little, 'can't you see that if this thing is true, if Gregson's statements are true, if these letters are not forged, that it's impossible for your brother to go on suffering for a crime that he never committed?'

For the first time Julian's eyes hardened, his mouth lost its curve, he stiffened in his chair and leant forward towards his father.

'Suffer!' he cried. 'Tell me what right you have to make anyone suffer for anything? Tell me that! Crimes are dealt with by the State, not the private individual, and you know it. Who made you judge and jury? Who gave you the right to exile a man, to call him back? My dear father, the whole thing is ridiculous. If Emmanuel hadn't been so constituted that he never faced facts, that he continually went about with his head in the air, he'd have called your bluff and refused to go.'

'Julian, how dare you speak to me in that way?' Max rose and faced his son across the big desk. 'Listen to me—were those letters written to you, were these other letters written of you? I want an answer at once.'

Julian smiled, he had given his little exhibition, and now he could return to his nonchalant manner again. It was a relief, he hated exhibitions.

'Of course they were neither written to me nor of me,' he said.

'You're lying!'

'I have answered your question.'

'Untruthfully——'

Julian shrugged his shoulders. 'Oh, of course, if you only ask questions in order to deny the truth of my answers, there is nothing more to be said.'

For perhaps the first time in his life, Max Gollantz was entirely at a loss. He did not know how to deal with this handsome young man, who remained so coolly insolent, and who never allowed his insolence to degenerate into rudeness. It was inhuman, unnatural.

'Just suppose,' he said, 'for a moment that I follow one of the two courses open to me. One is to give the knowledge that I have to Scotland Yard—the other is to hand it over to your Party organization.'

'Of course, you'll do neither. The Yard wouldn't thank you, and it would make things terribly difficult for the Party.' He rose and opened the big silver cigarette-box that stood on his father's desk.

'Do you mind if I smoke? I left my case at home.' He lit his cigarette and walked over to the mantelpiece, where he stood watching his father, detached and impersonal. 'If you'll allow me, I think that I can help you. This business all comes from people bungling. That's by the way. We will suppose, for the sake of argument, that I was guilty of a ridiculous piece of folly over a year ago. We will suppose that the other person concerned is dead, that they have emigrated, married —anything you like. There is, at all events, no further danger from them. For the past twelve months my life has been what is called an open book. I have worked hard, I am making my way a good deal faster than is usual for a man of my age. As a Member of Parliament, as a public character my life has been immaculate. I don't drink, I don't gamble, I don't run after women. I am useful, even valuable to my Party. Supposing that these things were true of me—this is all supposition, of course—isn't it wiser to allow dogs which have not only slept, but been very comfortably buried for twelve months, to remain in their graves? A disinterment isn't, I imagine, a very agreeable sight.'

'But, my God, can't you see the injustice of it! Can't you see that for a year, your brother has suffered for you and through you.'

Julian smiled again. 'Suffered, we will suppose, for me, but suffered through you. The injustice was yours. You took upon yourself to pass sentence, might I remind you? Will it have made the past twelve months any more pleasant for Emmanuel when he hears that you have thrown me out of your house? I doubt it. What is over—is over. If Emmanuel committed this folly, he has paid; if I did then I have rather obviously repented, and my present life is proof. Surely the matter might very well, and very wisely, be closed.'

'I think,' Max said, slowly, the words coming painfully, 'that you are probably the most perfect egoist I ever met. You've no thought for anyone except yourself. It's hard to believe that you are your mother's son and mine! For the first time—I wish to God that you weren't. I have it in me to hate you, Julian, hate you.'

'I'm sorry. You would prefer me to make a confession, to beg you to send for Emmanuel to come home, and to cast myself forth on the world with, if not "The Brand of Cain" on my forehead, at least another and very unpleasant word written there. And how much good would it do anyone? Not a ha'porth. The only thing would be that Angela would have to listen to another story of one of your sons not being able to "hit it off" with you. I wonder how much she believed the first time? She's a clever woman, you know.'

'Then you advise me to do nothing, say nothing, to have you at my house, receive you as my son, and eventually watch you marry some decent girl. It's impossible, impossible! I loathe trickery, as much as I loathe degeneracy! Once a degenerate—always a degenerate!'

'What you do in your own house, is your own business. I don't trouble Ordingly very much, I shall probably trouble it less in the future. I certainly advise you to do nothing. Except with regard to your private relationship with me. That, of course, is your own business. As regards my marrying some decent girl—why not? I should probably make a very decent husband. Once a degenerate, always a degenerate is nonsense, and if you'll think for a moment, you'll realize it. I defend nothing, I have admitted nothing, but children grow out of bad habits, so do boys at school, so do young men who are born with insatiable curiosity. Given enough work, and enough ambition, they become, to use a word that appeals to you, decent members of society. I am one—I know what I'm talking about.'

'My God!' Max stared at him with haggard eyes, stared as if he was seeing his son for the first time, as if he was seeing a stranger in the place of the son he had loved. 'My God! You're hard—hard and cold and utterly self-centred, Julian.'

Julian nodded, his face had lost its smile; for the moment he looked very young, very beautiful and almost appealing.

'Father, I've made myself those things. I'm hard, because I know that softness leads nowhere; I'm cold, because I distrust feverish minds, and feverish impulses; and I'm self-centred because I am more interested in myself than in anything else in the world. I've learnt to do without people. The only people I want are the people who mean something in the world; in the life that I've chosen. I can do without games, and dancing and young people. I'm willing to sit with the old men, and learn and listen. I'm the one person in the family who has reverted to the type of Jew who makes a success of life. The rest of you are sentimentalists; you believe in uprightness, truth and integrity, because you think that by those things you will make men confess that your race is altogether admirable. You believe that the world's opinion of the Jew rests in the hands of the House of Gollantz. I know that the world will find more to admire in me—by the time that I am thirty—than it will ever find in your truth and dignified uprightness. We've had one Jew who was Prime Minister of England, and, by God, we shall have another!'

He flung his cigarette into the fireplace and walked over to the desk and took another. 'It won't be easy, it won't be very warm, I shall be lonely.' He laughed. 'So, I fancy, was Benjamin Disraeli, First Earl of Beaconsfield. I don't care; I've done with sentimentality, and gatherings of the tribes at Ordingly, I've done with this terrible integrity that makes you, the kindest of men, turn his son out of his house and become a wanderer on the face of the earth. You live for the House that your father built, and you expect your sons to do the same. My dear father, this one of them is going to live for himself, his ambitions and his ultimate success.' He laughed again, and his voice went back to its old, light, insolent tone. 'I don't give a damn for Ordingly, and the tradition of—always the best in everything. This is the day of small things, and I'll take them and use them so that I can handle the big things when they come my way. Oh, don't be afraid, I shan't indulge in any follies—always supposing that I ever did. Too many people will watch and wait and try to trip me! The honour of the House of Gollantz is quite safe in my hands.'

Max said, 'Your confession of faith, eh?'

'My confession of faith—in myself. I can't stop, father, indeed there isn't anything to stop for, is there? This matter can drop, can't it? If, as I suspect, this came through Walter Heriot—or,' he paused and his smile broke out again, 'or his sister—I fancy that's where it came from, she's a hard young woman if you like!—they won't chatter any more. Walter will be dead in a year, and Viva will marry Emmanuel, once you bring him home. Of course, you will bring him home?'

'Yes, I shall send for him. But, Julian, what about you? It's not reasonable to suppose that I can ever feel as I did about you.'

Julian felt that the man who sat at the big desk, the man who was known all over the world for his taste, his knowledge and his ability was actually pleading with him. He didn't want things to change, he wanted his son back, that he might admire him, feel pride in him, and love him.

For a moment he felt that he was older than his father.

'No, you can't,' he agreed, 'and perhaps it's as well. It frees me from the responsibility of Ordingly and its demands. I'm busy in these days. Don't think about me at all, father, and when you meet me try to see me as someone you never knew before. You might actually get to like me in time. I must go. Good-bye.'

'Good-bye, Julian.'

The door closed behind him, he hadn't hesitated, he hadn't waited to see what his father would say. He had gone, and Max could imagine him hurrying out into Bond Street, glancing at his watch, and saying:

'Good Lord, I'm damned late. Taxi!'

Max touched the bell on his desk, and waited. He felt shaken, old and very tired.

'Oh, Hannah, send a telegram for me, will you. Take it yourself. It's private.'

'In code?'

'No.' Max covered his eyes with his hand, as if the light hurt him. 'No, it's not in code, I don't mind your reading it. Take it down—it goes to Paris—no, wait—I'll risk the other address. Send it to Miss Forbes, the Villa Dante, Menaggio. "Please communicate with Emmanuel. Ask him to come home at once. I have been a fool. We want him very much. Max." There, send that off at once.'

He looked at her, then frowned, 'What's the matter, my dear?'

She sniffed. 'Nothing, Mr. Gollantz. I'm silly, that's all. It's nice that it's got straightened out, isn't it? I am glad.'

He sat alone in his office, making no attempt to either open his letters or transact business. It was—straightened out and Emmanuel was coming home. Julian had said: 'Viva will marry Emmanuel, once you bring him home.' Viva had said that she had promised to marry Emmanuel twelve months ago. Then he went back to the garden of the villa, he imagined that he could see Emmanuel, standing before him, tall and straight and very angry. Emmanuel, listening to what he said, and answering very coldly Max's question:

'Are you going to marry her?'

'I couldn't say. I shall ask her to marry me after this.'

Emmanuel to come home—either married to, or intending

to marry Juliet Forbes, Vernon Seyre's divorced wife, Leon Hast's 'Lovely Juliet'! Max pressed his fingers to his aching eyes, he was past caring for anything. Julian—Emmanuel—Viva—even Juliet Forbes—they must go their own way and leave him to go his. He was too tired to battle any longer. The last twelve months had tried him, he had seen Angela's half-reproachful glances, had known that she wanted her son home again, and that not even Julian's successes could atone for the absence of Emmanuel.

That evening as they sat together after dinner, Angela watched him closely. He was very tired, his eyes were sunken and heavy, and his whole appearance was that of a man who is carrying burdens which are too heavy for him. She had known for months that he was unhappy, she had heard that his voice was losing its old content, noticed that his laugh was less frequent. She had said nothing because she believed that in the end, if only she could be patient, Max would confide in her. She loved Max Gollantz very deeply; her affection for him was tinged with maternal love, and yet it had remained through all the years they had spent together, a very real, living thing, filled with every emotion which went to make their marriage one which was—in Angela's mind at least—ideal.

Now she decided that if Max was going to continue to shut up his worries in his own heart, the time had come when she must speak. She had been very patient, she had tried to believe that Max would do nothing without having good reasons, reasons which were founded on kindness and tolerance. But it was obvious that something had miscarried, and that his plans had not worked out as he had wished; else, why his look of utter weariness which went to her heart.

'Max, dear,' she said, 'don't you think that I deserve better treatment at your hands?'

He started. 'What do you mean?'

'I mean that for twelve months I have been very patient. I have asked no questions. In my letters to Emmanuel, I have not asked them of him, either. Now, I think that I might ask for my reward. Come, Max, out with it! Let me hear everything. It's quite evident that somewhere you've made a mess of something, or you wouldn't sit with a grey face and eyes that look like two holes burnt in a blanket.'

'I've had a heavy week, I'm getting old.'

'So have I—so am I. We're quits—go on from there!'

He sat silent, his hands closed on the arms of his chair, his face almost stubborn in its determination. She sighed, rose, and came over to him, laid her hand on his shoulder and said, very gently:

'Now—tell me. Do you remember once before you were frightened and tried to keep me in the dark? Do you remember how Emmanuel, with his wisdom, turned on the lights and flooded the dark places and let in the air and the sunlight? He isn't here to do it this time; but I learnt my lesson then. Come, Max.'

He caught her hand and lifted it to his lips. 'Darling, I won't have you worried. It's bad for you, and anyway there is nothing to worry you with.'

Angela laughed, as if she had suddenly seen light, then sat down on the arm of her husband's chair.

'Ah, that little beast Nathan Bernstein!' she exclaimed. 'I knew it. After I had 'flu—heart—and all the rest of it. That's a year ago, and anyhow, he's a frightful alarmist. Max——' she laid her hand on his cheek and turned his face to hers, 'now that I have got on the track, you're going to do me far more harm by not telling me, than by making a clean breast of whatever this mystery is. Now—come into the library, no one will disturb us there, you can sit at your own desk and feel like Jove spending an evening at home, and tell me.'

'It's not amusing, Angela.'

'No, darling,' she held out her hand, 'but I am. Come along.'

In the big, dignified room, where everything reminded them both of old Emmanuel, where the polished wood gleamed as the light caught it, where the old pictures hung on the walls as lasting mementoes of Emmanuel's taste and discrimination, Max began to tell her the whole story. She sat very still, once or twice interjecting a question, once exclaiming suddenly, but with great intensity:

'Max, Max, why didn't you tell me then!'

'Wait,' he said, 'listen, let me tell you what happened yesterday.' His low, even voice went on, telling his story clearly, and without passion. Giving her the bare facts, and the result of his interview with Julian that morning. When it was ended he sighed, and leaning back closed his eyes.

'That's all, Max?'

'That's all—— My God, it's enough, isn't it?'

'It's over,' she said, 'it's over, like a horrible, unbelievable nightmare. We have that comfort, Max.' He opened his eyes and the pain in them hurt her unbearably. Poor Max, who had been so proud of his son—as proud as she had been. At the moment, Angela Gollantz forgot everything except that the man she loved and had loved for twenty-five years, was suffering. Her sons receded into the background, all she wanted was to comfort Max.

'Comfort—it's cold comfort!'

'It's comfort, all the same. Max, did you never do anything that was beastly, I mean really low and—well, just beastly?'

He did not answer for a moment, then said: 'Yes—when I was very young. I fell in love, no, not that; I felt a desire for a woman, who had been my brother's wife. And,' as if he determined to speak the whole truth, however painful, 'and I gratified that desire—in a dirty little street off Tottenham Court Road. I was twenty.'

'You couldn't do it now, Max?'

'Angela, dear!'

'A year ago, something very like that happened to Julian. He couldn't do it again, I know that he never will. I can forgive that—oh, yes, my dear, I can. I know and you know what awful pitfalls youth makes for us. How we love to peer into dark corners, how we love to—know. You did—you've just said so—well, so did I! Oh, not so completely, but that might have been due to lack of courage on my part—I may have had a greater realization of the danger! What I can't forgive—oh, what nonsense to say "can't forgive", for, of course, I shall forgive and forget in time—mothers can't help themselves! What I find it hard to forgive, is that he allowed Emmanuel to bear the blame of something that he'd never done. Julian will suffer, it's inevitable. Perhaps it's just, because you and I shall suffer in knowing that he suffers. We gave him too much. I know that Emmanuel had the same material things, we were just enough there, over the things that didn't matter; but we both gave Julian some of those "unbuyable" things that we never gave to his brother. Just that little extra bit of admiration, of love, of the things that Emmanuel wanted so much and deserved so well.' For the first time Max heard her voice shake for a moment as she went on: 'I don't want to see Julian—not yet—and Julian won't want to see me. Be patient, Max, and one day we shall find that we're saying again, scarcely noticing that we do say it, because the pride in our voices will hide everything else and we shan't hear—"My son, Julian". Once we have said it, we shall know that Julian's paid his debt to us, and that we have paid ours to Emmanuel. Max, it's over—it's past. Julian's safe, utterly and absolutely safe. We've all paid, and now we must forget what's over and look forward.' She came to him, laid her cheek against his, and whispered: 'Max, dear, smile again. I can't bear to see you looking so wretched. My dearest, it's over—over—over.'

'I've sent for Emmanuel.'

'Naturally, and naturally, I shan't wait for him to come, I'm going to bring him back. Do you know where he is, Max? I don't—I've sent letters to Paris, and I've had letters back with a Parisian postmark—but he isn't there. He could never have stayed away from me for a year if he'd been as near as Paris. Where is he, Max?'

Again Max told his story, of the visit to Como, of the thick hedge between the gardens of two villas, and of his finding Emmanuel. 'The villa belongs to Juliet Forbes, Angela. I—I admit that I said foolish things, unwarrantable things——'

'All right, Max. I know that you never really liked her. What did Emmanuel say?'

'He said that he was going to ask her to marry him——'

'Marry Juliet—I wonder!' Then quickly: 'You'd hate that, wouldn't you? I thought so. One half of me would hate it. I know that ten years are nothing. I know that what's over is nothing any longer; but—oh, I don't know. And yet, it might be wonderful for them both.'

Max said: 'But yesterday, Viva told me that she had promised to marry Emmanuel a year ago——'

Angela nodded. 'Did she? Well, I start for Como tomorrow, Max. Oh, of course, I can manage it. No, you're not to come with me. I'll take Eleanor, and—oh, I'll manage quite well.' She rose and held out her hand. 'Poor, tired, puzzled Max. What an illogical lot we are. We'd rather that he married Viva Heriot—who has a decadent brother, a drunken father, and whose mother was a chorus girl—and a very nice woman she is too, far too good for Walter Heriot—than have him marry Juliet Forbes. Juliet, who is lovely, brilliant in her art, wonderfully tender and—good, really good; but we don't like it because she's ten years older than he is, and because she was Leon Hast's—"Lovely Juliet", and all the world knows it! Oh, God, what snobs we all are, no wonder we get into these ghastly muddles.'

CHAPTER TWENTY-ONE

LOUIS LARA had returned. He had arrived in Milan, and had come to the shop and greeted his partner as if he had only been away for a week-end.

Emmanuel said, 'I don't like your padded shoulders, Louis.'

Louis raised his hands to heaven and said piously: 'They're the least objectionable thing about America. Oh, my dear Emmanuel, life has been terrible! Devastating! And Senator Watson! Emmanuel, he believed that I was ready to sit in a room with a machine vomiting tape for the whole day. It was impossible, and I told him so. He said that I lacked ambition.'

'And what did you say?'

'I said: "On the contrary, I am filled with it, but it does not lie in the direction of a machine which spews paper all day long." Eleanore—I still maintain that she is charming—but——" he paused, 'my dear cousin, after basking in the—tropical suns of Olympia's affections—I was frozen. Snow, ice, winter in Milan, American sundaes are overheated compared with Eleanore! So I have returned.'

'And I'm very glad to see you!'

Louis caught his arm and pressed it affectionately. 'I reciprocate everything that your English reserve forbids you to say. You have seen the papers, of course?'

Emmanuel shook his head. 'Seen them, yes—but with regard to what?'

'That in a week, Milan will see the last and greatest wonder of the world. Olympia is visiting Milan—professionally—in her capacity of dancer!' He sighed, and his pale face flushed with happiness. 'You see me in a new rôle—the envied of Paris, of Vienna, of Berlin.' His voice dropped. 'Emmanuel, I am the recipient of the love of Olympia, that superb creature!'

Guido, who had edged gradually nearer and nearer, gave a loud and gusty sigh. Louis spun round and grasped his hand.

'Guido, now my happiness is complete! How well you look!'

Guido smiled. 'Everyone tells me that I have become the complete English gentleman. May I, too, offer my felicitations, and then—we have news!'

Emmanuel said hastily, 'Now, Guido, shut up!'

Louis said, 'Guido is to be married—how charming!'

Guido shook his shining head. 'Alas, no, all the world except me. All the world—except me.'

'Emmanuel!'

'Yes, indeed!'

Then the telephone rang and Emmanuel, thankful to escape, turned to answer it. When he finished his conversation, Louis and Guido were talking happily, with many shrugs, smiles and gestures. Emmanuel went into the little office at the back of the shop and began to open his letters.

It was a month since Juliet had promised to marry him, and during that time he had passed from his old state of loneliness into a new world which was warm, sunny and filled with companionship. There were moments when he was seized with his old uncertainties, when he wondered if he could ever erase the picture of Viva, which returned again and again so insistently. At such times, he would long for Juliet, her voice and her intense kindness, for all the things which she gave him so freely, and which soothed and established him again.

He had lost the old rapture, he had never been able again to say consciously and with conviction—'I am perfectly happy' as he had said one night at Ordingly. That was over, but in its place was a steady and very deep love, a great admiration and a profound sense of gratitude. He knew that he looked forward to the future with equanimity, with the conviction that he had left the darkest days behind him. Even when Juliet went away, and she had told him that it was inevitable that she must be away very often, and for long periods, Emmanuel felt that never again could he feel the same old desolation. Always, there would be the knowledge that Juliet was in the world, coming back to him, thinking of him, loving him. Never again could he be so utterly alone.

His week-ends at the villa seemed to colour his whole week's work in Milan. Everything which happened was something which he stored up to tell Juliet, knowing that everything interested her, and that he was amply repaid if he could make her laugh. He saved up 'laughs' for Juliet as a miser might hoard gold, and offered her the results of his week's accumulation so that he might have the pleasure of seeing that adorable smile of hers.

Little Gilbert watched them and rubbed his hands, sometimes he would talk to Emmanuel of Juliet and her work, and never failed to end with:

'. . . and the great thing for her, and for her work, is that she should be happy. It's a great privilege to make her happy, my dear young man, a privilege which many men would be glad to possess.'

'All Gilbert cares about,' Emmanuel said once to Juliet, 'all that he cares for in the whole world, is that I should make you happy. Your happiness is the most important thing in the world to him.'

Juliet had smiled, shaken her head and said:

'You're wrong, the most important thing to Gilly is my voice. People have always put my voice first and my happiness second. Gilbert doesn't think that he does—but he does, all the same.'

'I don't,' Emmanuel told her. 'I don't. I adore your voice, but your voice only exists for you to use, after all.'

'That's why you're such a nice person to have to love,' Juliet said.

'I'm a remarkably contented person, darling.'

Today she was calling for him to drive him back to the villa, and Emmanuel, as he worked, as he listened to the plans and the propositions which Louis Lara had for his consideration, felt that the most important thing in the world was that the hands of the clock should move quickly to twelve o'clock.

Louis said, 'And Guido tells me that she is very lovely—like a wonderful statue of Juno.'

Emmanuel flushed suddenly. 'Juno!' he said. 'What utter rot!'

Juno—a sort of Rubens in stone or marble—opulent and oppressive.

He said again: 'Not a bit like Juno. How like Guido!'

Louis held up his hands. 'My dear Emmanuel, I didn't mean to offend you, neither did Guido. On the contrary, Guido envies you from the bottom of his heart. Only the most immature, the least critical of men prefer—young girls! To fall in love with children of twenty is to argue oneself either a fool or a bored roué.'

Emmanuel scowled. 'I don't want to discuss it,' he said. 'Guido can talk of nothing but love and love affairs. Let's get some business done, Louis.'

But his mind kept going back to what Guido had said, and what Louis had agreed. Guido had obviously told Louis that she wasn't a—girl, that she was lovely, but not young. Emmanuel felt that he hated Guido, and almost hated Louis. These fellows talked too much—knew too much. They could fix a woman's age to a year. Anyway, what did a few years matter? Nothing to him anyway. Juliet was herself, wonderful, beautiful, and he loved her.

But when she came, and he watched Louis bowing over her hand, and he saw how Guido hung on her words and followed her with his eyes, he forgave them both. It was obvious that they realized how lovely she was, evident that they listened with delight to her voice, and they were both ready to be her obedient slaves. As he was getting into the car, Louis touched his arm and said:

'Emmanuel—one moment, if you please.' Then when Emmanuel stood at his side, he bent forward so that his lip touched Emmanuel's ear.

'There is only one word which describes her,' he whispered, 'and that is—superb.'

He got back into the car, smiling contentedly.

'What did he want?' Juliet asked.

Emmanuel's smile widened. 'He wanted to tell me that you were—superb,' he said. 'That word from Louis means everything that is wonderful.'

'Superb,' Juliet repeated the word as if she tried to savour its full meaning. 'I don't like it much—it sounds so very Juno-esque.'

'Nonsense! Juno-esque, indeed!' Emmanuel exclaimed, and wished that the wretched goddess had never been invented. 'Anyway, it's his final hall-mark of approval. I've only heard him apply it to one other woman, and she is his only lasting love.'

'Is he going to marry her?'

'I should doubt that. She is scarcely, I imagine, the sort of woman who married. He appears to be devoted to her. She's a lady with a distinct past; I have heard of various interludes, but she apparently always goes back to Louis in the end.'

Then he realized that he had not chosen his words well, and wondered if she had noticed, and if he had hurt her ever so slightly. He did not look at her, but kept his eyes straight before him, and hoped that she hadn't listened to what he said. Anyway, to compare Juliet and Louis's Olympia was ridiculous.

'A lady with a past, eh?' Juliet said, suddenly. 'Ah, well, her past belongs to herself. Let's hope that her future will belong to that nice Frenchman—although I don't like his adjectives—when he applies them to me.' Then changing the subject, she said: 'I heard from old Drewett of New York, this morning. You remember the man and his wife who stayed for a week-end at the villa—old Drewett is that man's father. He's a terribly big impresario. He wants me to do an American tour, and after that to go to Australia.'

'Australia.' There was dismay in his tone. 'But I thought that you refused to go to Australia?'

'I always have done—but this time—I wondered if we might not go together?'

He turned and glanced at her quickly, her face had flushed a little, and she avoided meeting his eyes. How adorable she was!

'A honeymoon in Australia, eh?' he asked. 'I should think that it's a beastly place, but it would be wonderful to go anywhere with you. Juliet——' he slowed down the car until it came to a final stop under the long narrow shade of a cypress, 'Juliet—don't look away from me. Look at me. A honeymoon—anywhere—I don't care, only let's make it soon. We're wasting time, it's foolish, when we love each other as we do. I've waited a month; it seems like a year.'

She turned her eyes to his. 'I asked you to be patient,

Emmanuel. My dear, it's for life—and life may be such a long time.'

'You love me?' He caught her hands in his.

For a moment she made no reply, only let her hands lie in his, quite still, acquiescent. At last she said:

'Yes, I love you. I do realize that.'

'Then—when can we be married, Juliet? Soon—please.'

She smiled. 'You're very young, very impetuous, Emmanuel.'

'I'll grow old, if it will please you.'

'I wish that I could grow young, to please you!'

'You mustn't change, you mustn't try to change in any way. You are quite perfect. Never, never change.'

'I'm only afraid—— There, drive on, we shall be late for luncheon, and there's fish in aspic for you. No, don't kiss me here, drive on! So you think that I ought to accept Drewett's offer?'

He nodded. 'If it means a honeymoon—emphatically.' Then his face sobered, and his voice, when he spoke, had lost its light tone.

'Juliet, I should have to do something. I mean take stuff over to sell, or work or do something. I've got no money, darling, or only very little.'

'My dear, how foolish. I've got enough for both of us.'

'I can't live on your money.' Then with his voice even sharper: 'I couldn't live on—your money anyway, you know that.'

'It's money that I've earned.'

'All of it?'

'What do you mean?' She was aghast at the new sullen tone in his voice. 'Emmanuel, what do you mean?'

'I mean, that I'd hate to think that I couldn't keep you, and that you lived on Leon Hast's money. I'd hate it, loathe it.'

Without allowing him to hear how desperately he had hurt her, she said:

'Leon's money made it possible for me to earn money as I do. It's only fair to remember that. I don't live on his money. I should never ask you to live on it, either.'

'That's what I say. I want to earn enough for us both. I hate to remember that——'

'We won't talk about it, Emmanuel. Leave it, please.'

But he had fallen into one of his old fits of sullen depression, his face had lost its brightness, his brows were drawn into a scowl such as she had not seen for weeks past.

'But we must talk about it. It's important to me, even if it's not to you. I want your assurance that you'll never——'

'I've given you the assurance that I love you. That should be enough to convince you that I would never hurt you—as you're hurting me now. Shall we leave it at that?'

'Very well.'

They drove in silence for the rest of the journey. Emmanuel with the old sullen look on his face, his lips set tightly; Juliet wondering if she was ever to get away from the pain that people could so easily cause her?

At luncheon Emmanuel was studiously polite to Gilbert, and almost over-attentive to her; but she knew that he never met her eyes unless he could not avoid doing so, and her inquiries about the week's work only produced the briefest possible replies.

He disappeared during the afternoon, and at tea time came in and went off again to bathe. Juliet went to her room, and they met again before dinner. He was standing by the window, staring down at the lake, she came up softly and laid her hand on his arm.

'Emmanuel—please—it's so unnecessary, isn't it?'

'I'm very sorry,' he said, 'but surely facing facts isn't unnecessary, is it?'

'That depends on how you face them.'

'How you face them won't alter the facts.'

'It might make them look different, according to which angle you faced them from.'

Again, he said, 'I'm sorry, Juliet,' then in a voice which told her that the man she loved had returned: 'Forgive me. I didn't mean to be beastly. I didn't really. I just felt suddenly hopeless. If only you weren't so rich, so successful—or if only I was both.'

'You will be,' she said. 'You shall be.'

Later, he said: 'Sing to us, Juliet. Gilly, ask her to sing.'

Gilbert consulted a large gold watch, and smiled. 'Y-ees, I think that she might, if she would. It's sufficiently long after dinner.'

Juliet rose, and as she followed Gilbert to the piano,

stopped and touched Emmanuel's hair with the tips of her fingers.

'What shall I sing—Saul?' she asked.

'I don't care—everything that you sing is beautiful. Sing anything.'

He lay back in his chair and listened; he watched and listened, and her beauty—the beauty of her and of her voice swept over him, and took with it what was left of his sullen fit of despondency and ill-temper. It seemed to him that she had never looked so beautiful, that it was impossible that the whole world could hold anything so lovely as Juliet. It seemed that her beauty was wrapped round him as a cloak, it was something that he could almost feel, touch, hold in his hands. He sat forward, his hands clasped between his knees, his eyes on her face, his heart crying as it had never cried before:

'Oh, lovely, lovely Juliet—you're mine and I am yours.'

What did it matter who had loved her, what did it matter that she had given her love to Hast, she might have given it to twenty other men, and still the best was his. He was her last lover, and he would be her greatest. All the romantic side of his nature rose and came to the surface, all the months during which he had been lonely and when he had starved for companionship asserted themselves and demanded toll of him. He had been starved, he had been lonely, he had longed for companionship, for beauty, for kindness, and he had found them all, here in the woman he loved.

He felt that he understood love for the first time in his life, knew it for what it was—something more powerful than himself. It was carrying him away, it was sweeping him off his feet, making his heart beat faster, and his pulses hammer at his temples.

The song was over; little Gilbert sat with his fair head bent over the keys as if he listened for the last sound of her voice, as if he grudged to lose even the last faint vibration. Emmanuel did not stir, he felt that to move would break the spell which had been laid upon him, the spell of Juliet's beauty and the power of his love for her. He knew that she was watching him, though he would not lift his eyes to meet hers; he wondered how much she could read in them if they met hers.

'One more,' Gilbert said, 'the little one that we tried today —it's wonderful.'

'Very well.'

Emmanuel, still with his eyes lowered, thought: 'If only she could always sing to me! Sing until the earth and the sky melted into one, until the stars were burnt out, and the moon had sunk below the world. Sing—until she came towards me in the darkness, held out her hands to me, and as I took them——'

He wondered if he had been dreaming, his thoughts had carried him away into a world which held only Juliet and himself. He forced himself back, raised his eyes and realized that the song was over. Their eyes met, for a second she looked at him, then turned and said to Gilbert:

'It's not quite right yet, is it? Tomorrow we'll work at it.'

Emmanuel thought, 'She said that because she saw my eyes and knew how much I loved her.'

'Well, Saul—have I played David for you?'

He stood up and laughed back at her. 'I am grateful. The last bit of Saul has gone. He went out of the window while you were singing. Thank you.'

Gilbert rubbed his dry, thin hands. 'I must be off. It's nearly ten. Until tomorrow, Juliet—good night, Emmanuel.'

'Tomorrow, at half-past ten, Gilly. Sleep well, my dear.'

Emmanuel stretched out his hand. 'Come into the garden, let's say "Good night" there.'

She laid her hand in his, and in silence they walked out, and stood by the stone seat, not speaking, but both intensely conscious of the other. It seemed to Emmanuel that they had stood there for years, and that the silence had been filled with the sound of his thoughts and that Juliet must have heard and understood. He looked up at the stars, then turned to her, smiling.

'We came out to say good night, didn't we? It's difficult, here. I don't wonder that Shakespeare chose Italy for his great lovers, do you? I read it again—*Romeo and Juliet*—last week. Read it, and used this garden as my imaginary stage. Shall we make a pilgrimage to Verona one day?'

'No,' she said, very slowly, 'I don't like Verona.' Then softly, 'I first met Bill, and my husband, and Leon Hast in Verona.'

Emmanuel slipped his arm round her. 'Come back to

Verona with me,' he said, 'and I'll make you forget! I'll make you forget everything, except that you and I are together. It's over, darling, and we're both beginning everything new and fresh. Leave the old things behind, that's what I'm going to do. I have you, and that's enough for me.'

She laid her cheek against his. 'You're turning into a philosopher, Emmanuel.'

He laughed. '"Hang philosophy! Unless philosophy can make a Juliet!" Juliet, look at me, hold up your face so that the moon can kiss it. Let me see you! Tell me again that you love me——'

She faced him lifting her face so that it seemed to shine in the moonlight. Emmanuel watched her and held his breath. He was seeing her for the first time, he was realizing her beauty and the depth of his love for her.

'I can quote too,' she said. '"Yet I should kill thee with much cherishing"—isn't that enough?'

'Not quite,' he said, breathlessly, 'no, it's not enough, Juliet, I'm young, we're both young, we're in Italy, and there's a moon. It's dangerous—I don't want to say—good night to you. I can't, my very dear. You're too lovely. Send me away—as the other Juliet sent her lover away—when night's candles were burnt out, not before.'

She lifted her hands and pushed him gently away from her.

'No, Emmanuel, no, my dear.'

'Juliet—I love you—I'm jealous of—the past. I want to wipe it out, to make you forget. From tonight, it's finished like a dream that's over.' He drew her to him, and held her very close. 'Look at me, look at me. Don't hide your eyes. Juliet, I'll make you forget, tonight. Nothing shall ever hurt you again, because you'll have nothing to look back to except a night that held only me and you.'

She spoke so softly that he had to bend his head to catch the words. 'I want, for the first time, Emmanuel, to forget everything except you and me, but I'm afraid.'

'You can't be afraid, if you love me,' he whispered. 'Juliet, why should we wait? I love you, you love me. Marriage can't give us more love. Tonight's ours. Tomorrow, the day after, we'll be married. We've both been lonely, starved, unhappy. We're not those things any longer. Juliet, I want you so.'

'Oh, my dear——' Her voice sounded suddenly regretful, her face was very grave, then she bent forward and kissed him on his lips.

'Very well—tonight shall be—yours.'

They walked back to the house, neither of them spoke. Emmanuel held her hand in his, and they went forward like two children who are entering a new world; just a little afraid, but happy in that they have each other. He closed the long windows, then followed her into the hall. She stood waiting for him by the long table; he came to her and smiled.

'There!' he said, 'the house is closed and everyone is asleep except you and me. Even the lights by the lakeside are going out.'

Juliet leant forward. 'Look,' she said, 'a telegram. Ottavia must have forgotten to bring it in. It must have come while I was singing. Well-trained servants can be almost too well trained. Open it—it's probably from Drewett.'

She handed it to him, and turned to walk up the stairs. Emmanuel tore it open and began to follow her, reading as he did so.

'It says—"Please communicate with . . ."' He stopped, then said, 'Juliet, Juliet—wait—listen——'

Juliet turned, her hand resting on the broad carved rail. 'Yes?'

'"Please communicate with Emmanuel. Ask him to come home at once. I have been a fool. We want him very much. Max." My God! He wants me to go home, Juliet,' he caught her hand, 'do you understand, it's over. He wants me to go home!'

'Yes,' she said. 'I understand. Your exile's over. You're glad?'

'Glad!' She heard the sudden sob in his voice as he answered. 'My God, it's wonderful. Darling, you're glad too, aren't you? Glad for me, glad for both of us. Say so, Juliet, say so.'

'You know it, I don't need to say it, do I?' She smiled.

Emmanuel's voice dropped, he came nearer to her, and took her in his arms. 'Juliet—it's an omen that this should come tonight. Oh, how wonderful. I want you in my arms, dearest, I want to tell you so many things that can only be whispered, very softly, dear, foolish things. Come, dearest, come, Juliet.'

She walked with him to the door of her room, there she paused and turned, laying her hands on his shoulders; he kissed her, and whispered again:

'Dear Juliet—how I love you.'

'Emmanuel,' she said, 'good night. My dear, I didn't realize how utterly tired I was. I've worked too hard perhaps, all day. It's—it's impossible. This must be—good night.'

'Juliet!'

'I'm so tired,' she said again, 'so terribly tired.'

For a second he stared at her, then his face cleared, and he was full of tenderness, solicitude.

'My darling—I'm so sorry.' Then impulsively: 'It's not that you don't love me sufficiently? Just tell me that.'

Juliet took his face between her hands, drew it down and kissed him.

For the first time Emmanuel felt the passion that shook her, knew that her lips clung to his as if she could not bear to let him go.

'I love you so much——' she said, 'that—you must go quickly. Good night.'

CHAPTER TWENTY-TWO

MAX said, 'You'll wire to Juliet that you are coming?'

Angela considered for a moment, then said: 'No, I shan't, Max. I shall leave it. I may telephone when I get to Como. His telegram says that he is writing. That means that he won't be here for some days anyway. I don't want to take too active a part in it all. I mean this—no, don't frown, my dear—I thought this out during the night—if he has married Juliet, then that must stand. If he is going to marry her—that must stand too. I don't want to stop anything.'

Max poured out his second cup of coffee. 'I don't see what you mean. If he has—then that's all there is to it. If he hasn't—well, I hope to heaven that it can be stopped.'

Angela nodded at his coffee cup from the bed where she sat up against masses of pillows. 'That's too strong, Max, put more milk into it. That's better—I don't know, I can't explain, but I don't want to rush in and smash something. Leave it at that. I promise to bring him home, and if Juliet comes as his wife—candidly, I shan't mind. The Heriot half of my make-up may not be very pleased, but I don't like the Heriot side very much, you know. The other side of me, the Gollantz side by adoption, adores Juliet Forbes.'

'Very well.'

'I want to call at Walter's on my way to the station and see Viva. No, don't come with me, darling. Meet me at Victoria with Eleanor and an armful of papers.'

She drove back to London, alone. As she passed down the drive under the big chestnuts, she smiled because Emmanuel would be back in time to see them at their best. The blossom was over, but they would be lovely for another month, with wide leaves and great cool shadows. Angela smiled.

'After all pink blossoms aren't the only lovely things in the world.'

Gradually her face lost some of its content; it was graver, and she looked what she was—a rather tired woman, who had suffered a great deal during the past year. Emmanuel—her old Emmanuel—who had left them and left a gap which could never be filled. She felt that if only he had been alive, this past year might have been so different. Emmanuel would have known, he would have probed and sifted and in the end would have reached the truth. Then Emmanuel's banishment, it hurt her to think of what he must have suffered, of the loneliness through which he must have fought. And now, Julian—her most loved son, the son upon whom she had counted, in whom she had believed! Julian would be all right, he was too wise to make mistakes which might endanger his career. She had almost defended him to Max, but in her heart, she resented that Julian of all people should have hidden behind another man, should have thrown the burden of his own follies on to Emmanuel's shoulders.

'It will be all right again some day,' she thought, 'but it's all so stupid, so disintegrating! It's this wholesale smashing of ideals, and beliefs, it's this disregard for love and kindness that makes the world such an impossible place. We shall grow out of it, and one day it will be apparently just as it once was—but never really. I shall have scars, so will Emmanuel and so will Julian. And Juliet—where is she coming in this procession of people who have wound stripes on their arms? Either Viva Heriot or Juliet is going to be hurt, and Emmanuel will have to suffer because of one of them. All through folly, and self-centredness, and Max's inability to touch dirt and have enough faith to know that his hands will wash and be perfectly clean afterwards. It's the old damned Gollantz pride cropping up again. Dirt—hide it; dishonour—cover it up; disgrace—hide your eyes and don't admit it. Their motto ought to be—"It can never happen to us"—for that's their faith. Max believes it—he paid rather than probe. Emmanuel accepted this dreadful thing that was laid on his shoulders because he wanted to shield me—and his family, and he was the least conspicuous member of it. Julian, with his Gollantz conceit, thought that whoever was suspect, no one could fix on a Gollantz! What's the result? My poor Max is disillusioned, my son has had to spend a year of his life in a foreign country, and Julian will have to make us forget a scandal which might have ruined him. Ah, well,' she leant further back against her cushions, 'in the last generation it was the man with fair hair and blue eyes who almost parted Max and me, who nearly broke Emmanuel's heart—only it was too big and strong to break—and here's the type again. But this time it's not irrevocable. It will pass—Patience, Angela, patience!'

She waited for Viva in the big ugly drawing-room, with the gilt furniture and the satin-covered chairs. How Max hated this room, and how he and Emmanuel had argued over it.

'It is a survival,' Emmanuel had said, 'if only the satin vill lest, it vill be a period room—ven Fifa's children are growing up.'

Viva came in, she had been out riding and her breeches and boots became her very well. Angela held out her hand and smiled, and at the same time wished that the modern girl didn't look quite so like the modern boy—only more masculine.

'I'm going to bring Emmanuel home, Viva.'

She was almost startled at the change in the girl's face. The laughter died from her eyes, her lips parted a little and the whole face looked softer, more gentle. Even her voice altered when she spoke.

'Oh, darling—how wonderful!'

'You've missed him?'

'Dreadfully, and I was so helpless. I knew that there was a catch somewhere, and I couldn't lay my finger on it. Then—the chance came and I took it. It wasn't very prettily done, but I didn't care, and certainly Walter didn't. He's gone off to the South of France.'

'Your mother is very anxious about him, she tells me?'

Viva nodded. 'Yes, poor angel. Sir Mortimer told Daddy that Walter wouldn't last very long unless he pulled up dead short. He won't do that.'

Angela frowned, she hated to hear Viva speak in a hard voice about Walter. Walter might be all that people said, but after all he was the girl's brother.

'Viva, aren't you sorry about it?'

She spoke in no tone of rebuke, only as if her curiosity were aroused. Viva pursed her lips, then said:

'Sorry? Oh, I'm sorry for Mummy and Daddy. It's bad luck for them. But I don't like Walter, I never did. I hate people who have no control and no sense of selectiveness. His friends are unspeakable. I hate men who reek of stale brandy—well—there you are!'

'You're a hard lot,' Angela said, 'you modern young women.'

'We're not really, darling,' Viva protested. 'I should hate to tell you how often I've cried myself to sleep in the last year. We have learnt to protect ourselves though. We won't batter ourselves to bits over things and people that are not worth being battered for. I'd be cut into little bits for Emmanuel, he's worth it—but not for hopeless people like Walter. We conserve our energies for the things that matter.'

'Do you—I wonder?' Angela said, slowly.

'We're just the same as you are, and as you were,' Viva said, 'underneath. We want to marry the man we're fond of, we want to have children—at least the decent ones of us do—and bring them up decently. It's only the top layer that's different. If Emmanuel was ill, I should worry over him exactly as you do over Max. I should probably ring you up in the middle of the night to ask for remedies. We're not different, we only look different. Your great-grandmother called consumption—the sweating sickness; we call it "T.B." We know what things mean, you used to only guess—or pretend to guess. You think that we're crude—oh, yes, you do—perhaps we are, but there's a good deal of strength in those damned crude colours. Like Gauguin and Van Gogh.'

She stood very straight, very slim, with her intelligent, slightly impertinent face, and Angela wondered what she would do if Emmanuel didn't come back alone. She wondered if she would cry her eyes out once again, or if she would shrug her shoulders and—perhaps go the way that Morrie Stansfield had gone—if she would get careless, and hopeless and utterly hard.

'You're looking terribly serious,' Viva said, 'for a woman who is going to bring home a son as nice as Emmanuel. Why, darling?'

Angela patted the shiny satin chair next to her. 'Come and sit down, Viva. You people never sit down, you're always balancing with one foot on fenders or something. That's better. Viva, just suppose that Emmanuel had got tired of crying himself to sleep, and——'

'Found someone to dry his tears—and his pillow?' Viva said, 'Quite frankly, I don't know, darling. It would be the most frightful smack for me.' She laughed, suddenly nervous, and less certain of herself. 'I couldn't bear it, at least, I don't think that I could. You see, Emmanuel means *just* everything to me. I haven't had an awful luck with the men at home here. I mean neither Daddy nor Walter are very top-notch specimens, are they? Emmanuel was just a revelation to me—all your boys were, but Emmanuel most of all. You don't think that he has, Angela, do you? You don't think that he's fallen for some awful Italian wench with black eyes and a lot of chest, do you?' Reflectively she said, as if speaking to herself: 'My God, how I'd hate it!' Then she caught Angela's hand and said again: 'You don't think that he has, do you? If I thought so, I believe that I'd come with you, and bring him home by force.'

'I don't think anything,' Angela said. 'I don't know.'

Viva took out a cigarette case, and lit a cigarette with great care before she spoke again. Then, with her eyes fixed upon it, as if the whole world depended upon its burning properly, she said:

'You see, it's not only that I love him, taking him all

round; it's the idiotic special things that make me go weak when I think about them. His hair grows into a peak at the back of his neck, and his hair grows, naturally, into tiny side-whiskers. Those things make me feel simply terribly tender towards him. Illogical, idiotic, I know, but there it is. I love his affectations, and in anyone else I should hate them. I think that a stock is fatuous on anyone but Emmanuel. On him, it's charming. I like his way of looking at people as if they were pieces of furniture, as if he wondered if they were fakes or not. I'd rather die than have him ever decide that I was a fake. I ought to be able to say that if he has found someone else, there are as good fish in the sea as ever come out of it, only it wouldn't be true—about Emmanuel. Darling, you ought not to frighten me so. You don't know that he's married or engaged or something horrible, do you?'

'I don't know anything,' Angela said. 'There, I must go. I have to meet Max at Victoria.'

Viva nodded. 'Max was so sweet the other day. He sent to tell me that he'd sent for Emmanuel. Poor Max——'

Angela smiled. 'And poor—me, Viva.'

'I don't know. Max looked so Jewish as he sat there. I felt that he stood for his race, and that, poor darlings, they'd suffered such a hell of a lot, it wasn't fair that they should have to stand any more. There, I won't keep you. Darling, swear that you'll bring him back for me.'

'I shall try—you know that. Good-bye, Viva——' She looked at the girl critically. 'You'd be a nice daughter to have.'

Viva said: 'Good-bye, darling, and good luck—and—don't worry about Julian. He'll come out right at the top. Nothing will stop him.'

'I'll give Emmanuel your love—shall I?'

Viva laughed. 'You can't give him any more than he has already.'

During the long journey Angela tried to decide what she should do, and what attitude she should adopt. If they were married, and Emmanuel had said a month ago to Max that he should ask Juliet to marry him, then there was nothing more to be said. If not—she wondered what was the wisest thing to do? She loved Juliet, she cared nothing for what Juliet had been, or what she had done. Life hadn't been easy for her, and Angela had always felt that she had done what was right even though it might have been unwise in the eyes of the world. She knew that ten, twenty years ago she would have said:

'The eyes of the world! They see very little anyway, one can discount them.'

Now, she wondered if one could afford to discount them entirely? Juliet at thirty-six and Emmanuel at twenty-six. It didn't matter now; Juliet was lovely, and would remain lovely for years. But when Emmanuel was thirty-six, and she was ten years older, then the difference would be more marked, they would both be more conscious of it. Children. Thirty-six was old to begin to have children, too old. Then there were the tribes—hers and Max's; on one side, the 'foreign contingent'—the Hirschs, the Bruchs, the Jaffes, with their young wives, or their wives who had grown old with them. Then her people—'the wooden walls of old England'—Heriots, Drews, Wilmots, Wentworths, Bastows and Harrises. She could see them, listening to the news and raising eyebrows and turning down the corners of their mouths. They didn't matter, these people, but their silent air of criticism wouldn't make life any more pleasant for Juliet.

Angela's mother still believed that both playing and singing were 'delightful accomplishments' but felt they should never be cultivated professionally. They had all met Juliet Forbes, and as an artist they had admired her, in their rather lukewarm fashion; but to be asked to receive her as an addition to the family was a very different matter. They would probably have swallowed the 'career', they would have assumed that, naturally, she would give it up when she married; but the old story of Hast, and Seyre's divorce would rankle.

Angela sighed. 'Oh, my poor dear Juliet,' she said softly. 'I hope that even if it hurts him that you've turned him down, for both your sakes—and I love you both.'

The night was over, and the train was tearing through Italy. Angela knew that her apprehension was growing. She wished that the train would go less quickly. She had thought for hours and was still no nearer a conclusion. Como. Her maid came along to gather up her hand luggage. Angela got out and sniffed the warm air.

Eleanor said, 'Feels very warm, madam.'

'Yes, lovely! I want to telephone.'

'Yes, madam.'

'Then I shall want a car to drive to Menaggio.'

Menaggio! The last time she had been here was when they were all children. They hadn't thought themselves children, they had believed that they were very much men and women. Max had loved her then and tried to tell her so, but all her thoughts had been of his brother, Algernon—though she had only known him as Albert Goodman—oh, well, that was over, and she was here to bring her son and Max's home again.

'We'll go over to the hotel, they can get the number that I want there.'

She sat in the cool paved hall and waited. How horrible it was to wait like this! Not to know, not to be certain! Juliet here . . . perhaps Emmanuel was with her . . . and Viva Heriot was waiting in London!

'They have the number, madam.'

'Very well.'

Juliet's voice said, 'Yes, who is it?'

Angela drew a deep breath. 'It's Angela, darling. Can I come over to you? Can you do with me for a night?'

Juliet's voice brought no surprise with it, it was round, even and perfectly unmoved:

'I wondered if you would come. Yes—you have a car? Of course, I can put you up.' Then after a pause, 'Angela, darling, don't worry. I can guess why you've come. It's all right, don't be afraid.'

'Oh, Juliet—my dear——'

'Come along now. Emmanuel will be here soon after nine. He's gone to Milan on business. He's driving back.'

The drive was hot and dusty, and she was very tired. She could never sleep properly in a train however comfortable. Eleanor was getting on her nerves, she always did at the end of a journey. Three times she said that it was very dusty, and four times that the lake was very blue, then Angela closed her eyes and pretended to sleep.

'The driver wants to know the name of the house, I think, madam.'

Angela sat up, opened her eyes. Menaggio—the hotel where they had all stayed, the landing stage was down there, where Max had come to meet them one day when they had been over the lake. It hadn't changed very much—cleaner, perhaps.

'Villa Dante,' she said, and thought again, 'Oh, how I wish that it was all over!'

Juliet came out to the big gates. Angela wondered if she always came to meet Emmanuel, wondered if he came back there every night, wondered if—and hated herself. She smiled and waved, and thought how nice, in spite of everything, it was to see Juliet again.

'My dear, very tired? Then a bath first, and tea.'

Angela realized how desperately tired she was, knew how she longed for warm water, scent and powder, and afterwards, tea.

'You look tired, Juliet.'

Juliet smiled. 'Someone once said that meant one looked plain. I expect I look both. It's been very hot.'

Not a word of Emmanuel, of the reason for her rush over Europe; only Juliet the same as ever, beautiful and very kind. Later, after a bath in water which seemed a little more tinged with blue than the baths at home, Angela went down to the long cool room.

'My dear, how exquisite you've made it all!'

'Emmanuel designed most of it. Found wonderful paints and papers.'

'It's charming.'

Marking time—marking time—and both of them knew it.

'Emmanuel comes back tonight, you said?'

'Yes, he left yesterday morning. I didn't see him, he sent a note up to me, that was all.' Then the guards were off, the buttons taken from the foils, and Juliet spoke.

'Don't be afraid, Angela, my dear, everything's quite all right. We were neither of us in danger except for one moment. Then your telegram came, Max's telegram, and I was sane again. So sane, that I shan't marry him; I shan't tell him why, because his chivalry would be up in arms in a second. He won't suffer very long; it may hurt terribly for a little time, but he's young, and once he's left Italy behind—oh, don't worry, there isn't any need.'

Angela said: 'Tell me about it, explain. You love him. He loves you?' She smiled. 'I don't think that anyone could help loving you, certainly not my son, he's too like me.'

'It will sound so dreadfully out of date, if I say that it's just because I love him that I won't marry him,' Juliet said, 'and it wouldn't be quite true, either. It's partly because I've grown to love myself, my own peace of mind; it's because I've grown terribly afraid of being hurt any more. I couldn't bear to hurt him, and I certainly could never bear it if he hurt me.' She sat with her hands folded, and went on speaking as if she told a story in which she had played no part. Her voice was even, and never once, during the whole story, shaken by a trace of emotion.

'He was dreadfully lonely, you see, and so was I. It just happened. He fell in love, and I loved him. I wasn't—in love. History doesn't really repeat itself, Angela. He thought that he would never go back to England, thought that things could never be straightened out. He told me all about it the evening he asked me to marry him.'

'You didn't believe it?'

'My dear! How could one believe it? I ought never to have said—yes. Because I knew, in my heart of hearts, that things must come right, and I knew that he was ten years younger than I was, that I should never, never be able to live at Ordingly. Everything was against it—age, my work, my whole life—and me, myself. And yet, I said yes. It was terribly wrong. I have no excuse to offer, except that I loved him very much, and that I was lonely.'

'Poor Juliet——'

'That was a month ago, after Max had been here. It's been rather a wonderful month, and he's been happy, almost always. I have, too. I didn't think that I could have been so happy. Then on Sunday—I don't want to hurt you, and if it all sounds brutal to tell you at all, it's only because it's part of the story. It will show you how I came to realize the utter futility of my idea of marrying Emmanuel. On Sunday, Gilly had gone, and we were in the garden alone. He was very much in love. He begged me—not to wait until we were married. He begged me to trust him, and show that I loved him. I think that night I would have done anything to make him happy, anything. I was quite young again, all I wanted was to give and give and not count costs, and think of expediencies. There were only two people in the whole world, Emmanuel and I. We walked back to the house, and I found Max's telegram. I gave it to Emmanuel to open. He read it to me, and I knew then that he would go back and that I mustn't go back with him.'

'How did you know?'

'His voice, Angela, the change. He'd been happy before, but his whole voice altered. Nothing mattered, except that his exile was over and he could go home again. For a moment, he'd forgotten me, I had been pushed back by you and Max and home. I—I—' for the first time her voice faltered a little, 'I said that I was terribly tired, that was all. Because it was Emmanuel, he didn't make any protests, he didn't try to persuade me. He—he does love me, you see. Just then he loved me better than he'd ever loved me. Quite unselfishly. Perhaps,' she smiled, 'perhaps, I had been just a little dimmed by you and Max and home. No, I ought not to say that, that's unfair. I take that back, Angela.'

Angela leant forward and took Juliet's hand in hers.

'You don't need to take anything back,' she said. 'Oh, Juliet, my dear, what a dreadful muddle. You love him and he loves you, and yet you know, as I know, deep down in my heart, that it would only end in worse pain for you. I know it, you know it, every woman in the world would know it. It's damnable, but it's true. What's done ought to be finished with, and it never is! We can talk as we like. I shouldn't care, and Emmanuel wouldn't care, but you'd care like—like hell. That's what it would be—hell, my dearest—pure hell.'

Juliet nodded. 'You're wrong,' she said, 'Emmanuel wouldn't care now—I'm still a very beautiful woman, but in ten years, when I begin to get older, while he was still quite young, he'd care then, and so should I, and so would you. Then there is my work. I can't give it up, it wouldn't be fair to myself to even try. It's part of me. And—there's my money. I'm a very rich woman, Angela. Max is rich, and Emmanuel will be one day, but I'm as rich as Max is now. Only the other day, Bill Masters said that even he didn't quite know how much money I had. No—out here, he might have worked, and I should have been away sometimes and he'd have adored me when I came home again. It might have been possible. We might even have had children—who knows. I should have been—the only person. In England, there'd be other people, he'd make comparisons—oh, without realizing that he did! I should fall short. People would have hinted things, and he'd have got tired of either denying them, or disregarding them. So—it's finished—Angela.'

'I wonder that you don't hate Max for bringing him back!'

Juliet's face flushed suddenly. 'Oh, I could never do that. You see, I love Emmanuel so much, so very much. It's something to have had a dream that lasted for a whole month, Angela.'

CHAPTER TWENTY-THREE

EMMANUEL pushed back the papers which lay before him, and said:

'So you and Guido will carry on—when I go away?' Then very quickly he added, 'I shall come back, of course, that goes without saying, eh?'

Louis smiled, and said in the indulgent tone which one might use to a child:

'But naturally you will come back! Until then, Guido and I shall kerry on. It will be admirable that Olympia should find me installed here as a man of business. She will be filled with admiration. She will probably buy the whole contents of the shop, and pay very highly for them!' He sat down and lit a cigarette. 'Tell me, are you to be married before you leave for England?'

Emmanuel did not answer for a moment, instead he arranged some papers with tremendous care and laid them exactly straight on his desk.

'I don't know,' he said slowly, 'that will depend.' Then with that sudden rapidity which Louis had noticed before, he added, as if he was trying to impress something on his own mind, 'That will depend upon how Juliet feels. It rests with her.'

'Be advised,' Louis said, 'let it rest with you. Women like to have demands made to them, they like pistols held at their heads. They know that the pistols will never be allowed to go off. They dislike to have to decide things for themselves.'

'Frenchwomen perhaps—Juliet is English.'

'Poof! Really, from a psychological point of view, women have no nationality. They are all—women. I once heard an English song—it was so good. It said, "Break me, and take me, and shake me till my wits forsake me." That is what they like.'

Emmanuel laughed. 'Rubbish. You don't know Juliet.'

'I have known that superb creature Olympia for four years, my dear cousin. I have very little to learn, believe me.'

They parted from him with tears. Quite literally—with tears. Louis's eyes swam in pools of them, and Guido's large brown orbs overflowed so that he looked like a weeping cherub by Moretto. Emmanuel wished that they could restrain their feelings, and yet their regret at losing him was touching. They were such funny fellows, both of them. So kind, so obviously insincere half their time; so much men of the world, and yet so simple and childish for the rest. He liked them both, but when Guido held his hand and said in a voice which vibrated with emotion:

'My much more than brother—for I have five and dislike them all! Life will never be the same until you return. . . .'

Emmanuel felt relieved that none of his own people were present. And when Louis kissed him on both cheeks, and declared:

'I believed that I had everything when I regained the love of Olympia, and now I know that my happiness is extinguished—wiped out—emptied on to the desert sand!' He felt that his attitude was scarcely flattering to the superb creature who was to show Milan the eighth wonder of the world.

'I shall come back very soon,' Emmanuel said, 'a month perhaps, and you will have me back finding fault and making myself tedious.'

To which they both replied in chorus:

'In a month—in a month! Wonderful.'

Emmanuel drove out of Milan only conscious that he was going home. That thought was foremost in his mind, no matter how hard he tried to think of other things. Juliet would go with him—they would either be married at once, or immediately they arrived in England. Dear Juliet, wonderful Juliet. He was going back to her, going back as her lover; and as he thought of her, he felt a little thrill of delight and excitement, because she was so beautiful, and because he was going to make life perfect for her. Once, as he thought of England, came the old stab of remembrance. Viva Heriot, and the night under the trees at Ordingly. He pushed the thought from him, that was over. It belonged to the past. Viva would forget, and he, too, would forget in time. Juliet would make him forget.

He ran the car into the garage, told the man who worked on the place, and cleaned everything that might be cleaned exquisitely, to carry his bags up to his room. He washed, and brushed the dust from his clothes, conscious that he was wasting time, delighting in keeping himself waiting before that wonderful moment when he should meet Juliet again. He had telephoned to her both yesterday and today, but that had not really lessened his hatred of being parted from her. There was so much to say, so many plans to make.

He ran down the broad stairs and went into the long room.

'Juliet! I'm back, home!'

'I see that you are! Come and sit down. Dinner?'

'I had all I wanted in Milan. I'm only hungry for you and your voice. Darling, it's a wonderful telephone voice! Kiss me. I've been away for two days.'

'I know.' The smile had faded from her lips, she bent forward and kissed him gravely. 'I know. So many things have happened. First, Angela's here. No, don't go to her. She's travelled all night, she's dead tired and, I hope, asleep. Then, I have a great deal to say, Emmanuel, and, my dear, it isn't going to be easy.'

He stared at her, his face anxious. 'Angela? There's nothing wrong, is there?'

'Nothing. She's come to take you back with her.'

'To take—us—back with her,' he smiled again, his face lost its look of apprehension.

Juliet shook her head. 'No, only you. I'm not going, darling.'

'Not going? But why?'

'Because I'm going to accept Drewett's offer; I cabled this morning. I shall leave in a month. Australia and America. It's too good an offer to lose.'

Emmanuel's face of hurt astonishment dismayed her far more than any outburst could have done. He did not speak, simply stared at her in dumb astonishment, as if she had stunned him.

Juliet hesitated; she wondered if it was possible to go on, if she could face hurting him now, for the sake of the future. 'Dear God,' she thought, 'make it easy for us both.'

'You see, Emmanuel,' she said, 'I must think of my career. It's very precious to me, I can't give it up. I couldn't live without it. If I gave it up, I should have scarcely any reason for living at all.'

'Me——' he said, his voice dull, 'me, Juliet, you'd have me.'

'I wonder how long you would be content to have a wife who ran away and left you for a month, two, six, even a year? My dear——'

It seemed that the full meaning of what she was trying to say dawned upon him suddenly. He looked at her, his face very white.

'Juliet—you don't mean that—you won't marry me?'

'I've been thinking it over, thinking very hard——'

'But, before, you talked of going to Australia. Said that it might be fun, if you didn't go alone.'

Very quickly she retorted: 'But you objected. You talked about money, you said that you'd never live on money that I earned.' She stopped and thought. 'Now, if I hurt him—if I have sufficient courage to make him remember.' She went on slowly, 'You said that you'd never touch any money that Leon had left me.'

'You said that it would never be necessary!' he flashed back.

Juliet shrugged her shoulders. 'I know. One says things—but I like to travel very comfortably, and I shouldn't really enjoy denying myself anything for the sake of a—sentimental objection.'

That had reached him, she heard his sudden whispered exclamation.

'Oh, my God! Then you won't marry me?'

'I don't think that I ought to marry you, for your sake and my own. I don't think it would be a success.'

'I see—success—success—success. Can you only think in concert platform terms, Juliet?'

She laughed. 'Perhaps the habit has grown lately.'

Emmanuel rose, and stood looking down on her. He was

very pale, and his dark eyes looked larger than she had ever seen them. He seemed to have thrown off his youth, and stood before her a man, very hurt and very angry. Again she thought:

'Oh, God, let it soon be over. I can't bear it. He's mine and I'm his! I can't let him go.'

He did not move, only looked down at her as if he was trying to read what was in her mind. When he spoke his voice was very low, and in it she heard a new quality of determination.

'Juliet,' he said, 'I don't believe it. There's something more in it all than you're admitting to me. Has my mother tried to persuade you not to marry me?'

'No—on my word, no!'

'You decided this alone?'

'Yes.'

'When?'

'Yesterday, and this morning.'

'And yet, the night before, you had promised to—to give yourself to me. You can't have forgotten. How can you make that promise and your decision now tally? You can't!'

'That wouldn't have been irrevocable.'

Very slowly, as if such a statement from her was unbelievable, he repeated:

'Wouldn't have been irrevocable——'

Then a moment later, 'You'd have taken me as your lover?'

'In Italy, yes, I think so.'

'And left me at home, as a sort of caretaker, when you went away?'

'That's stupid and crude, Emmanuel.'

'Then, I shall stay here, in Italy. I'll stay under any conditions, and one day you'll love me enough to marry me.' The words rushed from him, he stumbled over them, he stooped down and took her hands in his, holding them so that the tightness of his grip hurt her fingers. 'Listen—Juliet—I don't care for anything except you. I won't go home. I don't care. I thought that I did. I was wr-rong. It's you, you, you all the time. Today, next year, always. You're talking, talking, talking, words, words, words, because you're fr-rightened. I understand, but it won't last. Believe me. I'll make you forget. I'll wipe out ever-rything. There will only be you and me in the world—Juliet, lovely, lovely Juliet!'

She knew that her strength was leaving her, knew that she was shaking, and that she wanted nothing so much as to lay her lips against his and whisper that he was right, and that she had only been afraid. She wanted to see him smile again, hear him answer ridiculous, romantic things, and to know that he was hers, and hers only. Then came the old fear, stronger than ever.

'It's not only for him, it's for me. I couldn't bear to be hurt again. I couldn't bear to be hurt through him. It's no use. I could never, never face it and know that it was certain to come sooner or later.'

'Don't hold my hands,' she said, 'you're hurting me. Emmanuel, it's no use. I've decided. I could never face living in England, and you would never be really happy here. I've made a life of my own, and the world that I've made isn't big enough to hold my work and a husband. I—don't want to be married.'

'Would you take a lover?'

'I don't know. I couldn't say. Emmanuel, it's no use—we might go on and on for ever. Nothing will make me change my mind, nothing.'

As if he had been running, so that his voice came rather breathlessly, he said:

'Then—take me—as a lover. I'll be your lover as long as I live. I only want you. You'll be quite fr-ree—always.'

Juliet moved her head, as if she tried to shake away some pain.

'No—Emmanuel—no.'

He came a little nearer, his voice sank to a whisper:

'Look—you made me a promise two nights ago. You didn't keep it. I hold you to it—now. Even if you r-rob me of everything, you've no r-right to r-rob me of that. It's mine —you pr-romised.'

'Why? One night—it's foolish, it can't mean anything. I promised because I didn't realize. I didn't understand myself.'

'Why?' he echoed. 'Why? I'll tell you, because you don't r-realize how much you love me and how much I love you, and you shall r-realize it.' He caught her in his arms. 'Juliet, my dear, you're lost, you're frightened. I'm here, and I love you. It's Romeo and Juliet all over again. I can say, "I will kill thee with much cher-rishing". My Heart, listen, don't throw away everything for shadows. In the morning they'll be gone. They'll never, never come back again—never. Juliet, trust me.'

She knew that the last vestige of her strength had gone, knew that he was right, and that the whole world held only herself and Emmanuel Gollantz. Nothing else mattered. He might go home, but he would come back, to her. They could make a life of their own. She was successful enough to snap her fingers at the people who might talk! Ten years! Ten years couldn't separate them. She would keep her youth, and if it went slowly, he would never notice. She had other things to give besides her beauty.

'I do trust you,' she said. 'I will trust you.'

In her own room, with the windows opened on to the still garden, and far away the few lights twinkling on the lake side, Juliet undressed quickly. Her heart was beating so that it almost suffocated her. She held out her hands and saw that they were shaking. She couldn't lose him—she would do anything to keep him. Nothing else mattered. She walked to the window and looked out, seeing nothing, only conscious that the cool air was very pleasant; as she turned away she stood at her desk and looked down at the photograph which stood there. Leon had had it taken for her one day when he had come up to London from their house in the country. She remembered the suit that he was wearing, she had always liked it, and he had worn it especially to please her. That tie—she had bought it for him. He had said that she was the only woman who could choose a tie. She had said:

'I can't, really. At least not if I followed my own taste. I try to imagine what would be yours.'

He had smiled, that queer, twisted smile that was almost a sneer. 'You know, lovely Juliet,' he said, 'I don't believe that your own taste is very good. Far better stick to mine.'

And, when things had begun to go wrong, and she had threatened to leave him, he had laughed, that funny, whispering laugh.

'Leave me! You mean go away, don't you? You'll never be able to leave me. I've spoilt you for everyone else, and you know it. No one else will ever make you as happy as I can.'

'Or as unhappy,' she had said.

'Almost the same thing! If I couldn't do one, I could never do the other.'

She turned away from the picture, then turned back, lifted it and opening the drawer of the desk, laid it inside and closed the drawer. And as she closed it, she turned sharply, for she remembered another picture which stood in her room, and she felt that the eyes were watching her.

She crossed the room and lifted down the picture from the broad mantelpiece, on which was spread the green and gold embroidery which had been Emmanuel's first present to her. The picture was of an old man with white hair, and keen dark eyes, an aristocratic beak of a nose, and a mouth which belied the apparent sternness of the face. His chin rose out of a high white collar, surrounded by an elaborate old-fashioned stock. Old Emmanuel Gollantz—and his eyes were watching her, as they had watched her the first time Leon had taken her down to Ordingly. Kindly, questioning eyes, within their depths a hint of pity, because he understood. She could hear his voice, deep, and for all his sixty years spent in England, still retaining its rather over-coloured tones. He had always spoken like a foreigner, always been unable to keep his voice even. Leon had said that old Gollantz played upon his voice as a man might play upon an organ, consciously employing the various stops to get the effect that he wanted. Leon had never liked him very much.

Emmanuel had said once when she went to see him in his big room:

'I hev alvays hatet and distrusted Communism. But I hev alvays beliefed that Lenin vas right ven he said: "Ve don't metter—but there are der cheeldren." I don't know vot he meant, perheps I don't care. To me—cheeldren—are der people who hev not yet hed a chence. Who hev not yet savoured life. Who hev not known loff. Neffer, dear Chuliet, stend in der vay of t'ose people, neffer rob them of chences. Neffer make heavy marks on their minds, marks thet vill not rub out again. The responsibility is too great!'

And once he had said: 'Dear Chuliet, I am very proud to hev known you.'

Juliet turned away, walked over to the door and locked it.

'The responsibility is too great.'

'You shall go on being proud, my dear Emmanuel Gollantz,' she said softly.

As she lay on her bed, her hands pressed over her eyes, because even the soft darkness seemed to hurt them, she heard the handle of her door turn softly. Her hands left her eyes and were laid over her mouth, lest she could not prevent herself speaking. She wanted to explain, wanted most of all to get up, fling the door open and forget everything. Again the handle turned and again the door was tried as if whoever turned it could not believe that it was locked against him. Once she heard a whisper—very low, very gentle:

'Juliet—Juliet——'

There was silence, and she heard steps go very softly, terribly slowly down the long corridor.

It was over. Tomorrow he would go away, back to England, and she might never see him again. Perhaps one day they might meet, and speak conventional words, and clasp conventional hands. He would look at her and wonder—and she would try to believe that the pain was over and that she felt nothing. A month, four weeks, and now she would go on again, as if it had never been. Tours, success, entertainments, dressmakers, new songs, the merits of different pianos, concert halls and railway stations. Those things would go to make up her life. Gilly, with his unfailing kindness, Bill Masters, with his anxiety that no matter how rich she was, she should be richer still. Those men were her friends. Angela must go, because Angela meant Ordingly, and Ordingly meant Emmanuel. They might meet in London, in the artists' rooms at various halls, and Angela would say:

'Why don't you come over and stay with us—Max and me?'

Juliet could imagine herself answering: 'I should love to—one day.'

But that day wouldn't come, because she would be afraid to meet Emmanuel. Afraid to meet him and find that he had forgotten and was content, and still more afraid to meet him and know that he—remembered.

All through the night she lay and let her thoughts drift and carry her where they would. Old half-forgotten things came and went, little pictures, snatches of songs long ago ended, voices came and went, and there was scarcely one of these things that did not hurt her. She wondered if there were any remembrances left that would not hurt her, which would not reopen old wounds and make them bleed afresh. She went back to the first day in Verona, when she had met Bill and Vernon and Leon Hast. From them, there had been snatches of sunlight, but always the clouds had come up and blotted them out again.

Then, five years ago, Hast had died, and all the pain was swamped in the agony of losing him, everything else had been reduced to its proper proportion, and she had known that with Leon—everything had ended.

Slowly, she had begun to live again, to work again, because he had been ambitious for her. Painfully, stone by stone, she had rebuilt the structure of her house, and trained herself to live again. Success, money, fame, then a month ago this brief spell of sunlight, of youth and of love. Emmanuel, with all his beauty, his tenderness, his ridiculous fits of sulkiness from which she could rouse him so easily. She had been young again, she had believed that life might begin again, really begin for her. She had dreamed of work with him to share her success, she had dreamed of children—and it was over. It had to go—as everything else had gone.

Towards morning, when the sky lightened and was shot with pale, young colours, very tender and very soft, she rose and leant her arms on the broad window-sill and looked out on to the quiet garden. The worst agony was over. She felt shaken, and a little weak, but the pain was only a dull ache, not a violent thing that tore and racked her. Her face had lost its look of despair, and as she watched the curtain of night roll away, she sighed as if she knew that her battle was fought and she had won.

'The old faults,' she said softly. 'Perhaps I've been paying for them now. I hurt Vernon—I pushed him on one side, because Leon was so much more important to me. Other mistakes—I suppose I was selfish, but I wanted so terribly to be happy. I always thought that I should find it, with Leon, and I only found it—completely, when I'd lost him, because I never knew until then how much he loved me. Perhaps one day, Emmanuel will understand. Perhaps he'll look back and see that I was the one person who never, never wanted to hurt him. If I've done wrong, God must forgive me, and if I've done right, perhaps He'll help me. I shall need help very badly when he's gone and I shall know that it's over and done with.'

She went into Angela's room, and stood looking down at her, a little smile just touching her lips.

Angela said: 'I've seen him. He wants us to go at once. Juliet, is it over?'

'Yes, darling, all over.'

'I'm so desperately sorry. Sorry for both of you. He looks wretched. He is wretched. He's hurt, he's resentful—and he's so puzzled.'

'Poor Emmanuel! Did he tell you?'

Angela nodded. 'Yes, that you told him last night that you couldn't marry him.'

'Nothing else?'

'No. What else was there?'

'Nothing, darling, nothing. I just wondered. I don't know. I didn't sleep—I'm not at my brightest and best this morning.'

Angela held out her hands. 'Juliet, sit down and listen to me. It's not too late. I wonder if you are—if *we* are—being wise. Isn't it perhaps throwing away a chance of happiness. Think, darling.'

Juliet shook her head. 'No, my dear. It is too late—it would have been too late, for me, years ago. And I don't want chances—and such bare chances—for Emmanuel's happiness. I want certainties. For him, and—even for myself.'

'You think that he'll find happiness?'

'I'm sure that he will. Youth renews itself, thank God.'

'And you?'

Again that little smile. 'My dear, I have my work, and a great deal of money. I must buy things, such things as can be bought. Some of them are very pleasant. They're substitutes, but life's mostly made up of substitutes. There, darling, you must get up and dress, and be away to Como.'

'Wait!' Angela caught her hands. 'Juliet, I've been a snob, and I'm ashamed of myself. I didn't want you to marry him, I let silly conventions override my own heart. Half of me is horribly conventional, the other half snaps its fingers. That half has won this morning. Let me send for him, let me say that it's all a mistake, and that I want you to be married here quickly.'

'But,' Juliet said, 'it isn't a mistake. And really, you don't want us to be married quickly. He's your son, and you mustn't snap your fingers.'

'But,' urgently, 'I do want it. I do snap my fingers.'

'Snapping your fingers quite consciously won't help, darling, Angela, my dear, you've always been so good to me. Go on being good to me. Don't make it harder. Let me go. You must get dressed——'

CHAPTER TWENTY-FOUR

HE OPENED the door, entered and closed it behind him, leaning against it as if he defied her to turn him out.

'Juliet,' he said. 'I'm going in a few minutes.'

He stopped, the whiteness of his face hurt her, his eyes were shadowed and sunken a little. He looked utterly wretched.

'Yes, Emmanuel.'

'I've come to ask you again. Will you marry me?'

'No, my dearest, no.'

'You mean that?'

'Yes, I mean it.'

He came further into the room, and stood before her twisting his hands together; she saw the little beads of sweat on his forehead.

'Do you think that you've treated me decently?' he asked. 'Do you think that last night was—decent? I don't. By God, I think that it was shameful! You tricked me, you made promises and broke them. You've always made promises to me and broken them, haven't you?' He stopped and licked his dry lips. 'And yet, if you'll say "Yes", I'd forget it all—I'd never think of it again. Juliet, marry me!'

'No, for my own sake as well as yours—no.'

'I can't believe it. Don't you love me? You used to love me!'

Juliet felt that her last shred of control snapped, felt that she had stood more than flesh and blood could bear without screaming in its agony. She stood up and faced him, their eyes met and he saw the sudden torment in hers. They were so hurt, her eyes, they looked like the eyes of someone who is slowly tortured to death. Instinctively Emmanuel raised his hand and covered his own eyes to shut out the sight of hers.

'Can't you accept it?' Juliet said; her voice came in a whisper, as if she had no strength left to speak more loudly. 'My God, I've had to accept things that hurt me all my life! I can't bear it. I've fought and tried. I was determined to do nothing that could make me ashamed—and you come here and tell me that I behaved shamefully, that what I did wasn't decent! Can't you see—can't you understand anything? Are you utterly blind? Then go away and carry your blindness with you. You can't understand, then go back to England and think whatever hard thoughts you can. Why should it matter to me? It's over, I tell you, over! Love you! For years I've starved for love, I've starved for everything that love could give me. I was weak, weak with hunger. I made promises—and I broke them and thank God that I had the courage to break them. I tell you that I won't marry you, that not all the pleading in the world could shake that decision. I won't marry you—and I won't marry you because I love you! If my love had only been a wretched cheap physical thing, I should have taken you for my lover days and days ago. It wasn't, it isn't, it's too strong, it's real, Emmanuel; one day you'll understand and know how you torture me. Now, is that enough?' Her voice changed, she held out her hands to him. 'Emmanuel, I can't bear it—go, please go.'

'You love me, and you won't marry me,' he said slowly.

'Because I love you, I won't marry you.'

'But why, Juliet, why? If it's the past, I don't care for it; it's the future that belongs to us. The future——'

'It's—everything—everything—— The past, and the future. They're both against me. Oh, Emmanuel, if you love me, if you really love me, go away. I can't bear it——'

He threw his arms round her, held her to him and kissed her. She was too weary, too exhausted to protest; she lay in his arms, passive and unresisting. He whispered his love for her, he kissed her eyes, her lips, and her hair; he was delirious with his love, and because of his unhappiness.

At last she stirred. 'Emmanuel—go—please. My dear, my dear, you're killing me, I can't bear it.'

'You love me, you said that you loved me,' he insisted.
'Go now——'
He held her less closely, and looked into her face, as if he wanted to read her heart. As he looked, she saw his face change, the feverish light left his eyes, his face lost its expectancy.
'It's over,' he said, as if the words were dragged from him. 'It's all over, Juliet?'
'It's over—Emmanuel.'
'I'll go. Kiss me, once, will you?'
She took his face in her hands, looked at him very tenderly, her eyes filled with tears, then kissed him on the lips.
'Good-bye—my very dear Emmanuel.'
She saw his lips quiver, then with a violent effort he steadied them.
'Good-bye, lovely Juliet.'
When Gilbert came an hour later, she was waiting for him.
'Gilly,' she said, 'can you bear it? We're going to Australia and then back to America.'
'You've heard from Drewett's?' She nodded. 'I see. It ought to be a great success, they advertise wonderfully, not——' with a little ceremonious bow, 'that you need advertising.'
'Thank you, Gilly.'
'And that nice young man,' Gilbert smiled, 'will he come with us?'
Juliet laid her hand on his shoulder. 'Gilly dear, I don't think that we'll talk about him, if you don't mind. I've—treated him very badly. You see, I found out that I couldn't marry him after all. He's gone back to England with Angela Gollantz.'
Gilbert stroked his chin, then glanced at her.
'Perhaps you're right, my dear,' he said. 'I'm quite sure that you think you are. It's always difficult for artists to marry—at least I've always thought so.'
'Perhaps,' almost indifferently. Then: 'We've got a lot of work to do. We sail in three weeks. We shall be away a long time, Gilly. A very long time—— No, I don't think that I want to sing this morning. Let's work out programmes, shall we?'
Later, when he was going back to his hotel, she called him back and said:

'Gilly—if ever I'm tiresome, or irritable—I don't mean it. I'm really very grateful to you, always.'

The train drew out of the station at Como, and as it began to move Angela saw Emmanuel rise, suddenly, saw his hand go towards the door with a movement which was almost convulsive. Then, as if he realized the futility of trying to return, he sank back in his corner and closed his eyes.

Angela watched him, saw his white face, and his attitude of utter weariness, and wondered if there was nothing she could do, no words she could find that might ease the pain which he was suffering? For a long time neither of them spoke. Emmanuel did not move, except once he raised his hand and covered his eyes. The daylight began to fade, the colour was vanishing from the sky, the trees and the fields, the rivers looked grey in the half-light. The whole world seemed melancholy, as if it tried to become in keeping with his mood.

The attendant walked down the corridor, ringing his bell.

Angela said: 'Emmanuel—first or second dinner, darling?'

'Neither, thank you. I couldn't eat.'

'I hate dining alone in a railway train.'

'Then I'll come with you. Only don't try to make me eat. I can't.'

Through dinner he answered in brief sentences, his voice was expressionless—dead. They went back to their carriage in silence. Basel—the sleepers. Emmanuel got out, and Angela could see his tall figure pacing up and down in the gloomy half-light of the station.

'This is yours,' he said, when he took her along to the sleeping car. 'It's not over a wheel. Good night, sleep well.'

'Good night, my darling.' He turned to go, Angela said: 'Emmanuel—my dear, can't you talk to me?'

He shook his head. 'There isn't anything to say, is there? Good night.'

In the morning he came to take her to breakfast. He asked if she had slept well, told her that it was a beautiful morning, that they would have a smooth crossing. All conventional things that didn't mean anything. His face was like a mask, his eyes expressionless.

'Did you sleep, Emmanuel?'

'No, I couldn't sleep.'

Afterwards, she said: 'Come back into my carriage, will you? I want to talk to you.'

His voice was half-defiant, half-pleading, as he answered: 'Oh, darling, *must* you? There isn't anything that I want to hear. I'd rather just be left alone.'

'I can't help it—there are things that must be said before we get to England,' Angela persisted. 'I don't want to hurt you—my dearest, I wouldn't hurt you for all the world.'

'Oh, you can't hurt me,' he said. 'Very well.'

He sat beside her, waiting, showing no sign of interest; she knew that his mind was going back and back over the miles which separated him from Juliet. He didn't want to listen, he didn't care. His joy in returning home had been killed.

She began to speak, very evenly, keeping her voice level so that it might reach him above the noise of the train.

'You're coming home,' she said, 'and everything is going to be fresh and new. The old things must be forgotten. We mustn't keep taking them out and looking at them. They're over.'

He said: 'Over, eh? Yes—and then?'

'About Julian,' Angela went on, taking no notice of his sneer, making herself speak Julian's name firmly, as if it did not hurt her intolerably. 'Julian won't come to Ordingly. He's busy, he has his work; only one day, when you do meet him again, I want you to try and forget what happened.'

'I seem to have a good many things to forget,' he said.

'Don't hate Julian—don't hate anyone—it's so useless.'

'I don't hate him. That's finished. I used to. I don't now.'

She laid her hand on his knee. 'Emmanuel, I can't talk to you while you're so bitter. It's dreadful. All my joy at bringing you home is killed—it's terrible. My dear, don't look back—look forward.'

'I don't want to. What is there to look forward to? Nothing.'

'Everything!'

'Everything I don't want, and not the one thing that I do!'

'My dear, don't I stand for anything? Emmanuel, I used to, and I didn't know it. I put Julian first, oh, I know that I did. I adored him, and now—can't you see that I've been hurt too? Do you think that you are the only person who has come out of this miserable business with scars. I have mine. I have you, I have Bill—you're both precious, more precious than you ever were, but—it wasn't easy to lose Julian. I'm going to have bad hours, I know that. Won't you help me, because you're the only person who can understand? I've been frank with you, at the risk of hurting you.'

'It doesn't hurt,' he said in that awful dull voice. 'I always knew that you loved Julian best.' Then with a sudden break in his tone he said: 'I only want to be let alone. That's all! Can't you see, that losing her is just killing me. It's so final—there isn't any hope for me at all. She—she—oh, Christ, what's the good of going over it all again?'

'Don't—go over anything,' she said. 'You're young——'

'That's the hell of it!'

She said, softly: 'No, my dear, no. "For you the To Come".'

He did not answer and the silence fell between them again. She watched him, but his eyes never met hers, he did not speak, only sat staring at nothing, with his face set and very pale.

On the steamer he found her cabin, laid out rugs and then left her to pace the deck until he came back to tell her that they were almost in.

Angela stood up, and held out her hands. 'Welcome home, my dear.'

'Yes,' Emmanuel said, 'the Channel's put the water between us. That's the end. I can't walk back to her now—I somehow felt that until we had crossed, I might. Oh, well——!'

'The car's meeting us.'

'Father isn't coming, is he?'

'No one is coming.'

As they got into the car the chauffeur handed Emmanuel a note; he opened it and read it, then put it into his pocket.

'Father, saying that he's glad to know that I'm back,' he said.

Angela let him put the rug over her, and not until they had begun to move, did she speak.

'He sent that message by me, when I came. I forgot to give it to you.'

'It didn't matter.'

'Viva sent you a message too—she sent you her love.'

He turned, as if she had suddenly broken down his guard,

and startled him into momentary interest. For the first time she saw the light flicker in his eyes.

'Did she?' he said. 'Did she?'

'Not quite,' Angela corrected. 'I asked if I should give you her love; she said: "You can't give him any more than he has already".'

For a moment she thought that he had not heard, then he said:

'Viva said that, did she? That was kind of her.'